Dance Class

3 in 1

Béka and Crip

New York

Dance Class Graphic Novels available from PAPERCUTZ™

DANCE CLASS graphic novels are also available digitally wherever e-books are sold.

Béka and Crip
Dance Class
So, You Think You Can Hip-Hop?
PAPERCUTZ

#1 "So, You Think You Can Hip-Hop?"

Béka and Crip
Dance Class
Romeos and Juliet
PAPERCUTZ

#2 "Romeos and Juliet"

Béka and Crip
Dance Class
African Folk Dance Fever
PAPERCUTZ

#3 "African Folk Dance Fever"

Dance Class

#4 "A Funny Thing Happened on the Way to Paris..."

Béka and Crip
Dance Class
To Russia, With Love
PAPERCUTZ

#5 "To Russia, With Love"

Béka and Crip
Dance Class
A Merry Olde Christmas
PAPERCUTZ

#6 "A Merry Olde Christmas"

Dance Class
School Night Fever
PAPERCUTZ

#7 "School Night Fever"

Béka and Crip
Dance Class
Snow White and the Seven Dwarves
PAPERCUTZ

#8 "Snow White and the Seven Dwarves"

Béka and Crip
Dance Class
Dancing in the Rain
PAPERCUTZ

#9 "Dancing in the Rain"

Béka and Crip
Dance Class
Letting It Go
PAPERCUTZ

#10 "Letting It Go"

Béka and Crip
Dance Class
Dance with Me
PAPERCUTZ

#11 "Dance With Me"

Dance Class
The New Girl

#12 "The New Girl"

COMING SOON!

Dance Class
3 in 1
PAPERCUTZ

DANCE CLASS 3 IN 1 #1

Dance Class
3 in 1
PAPERCUTZ

DANCE CLASS 3 IN 1 #2

Dance Class
3 in 1
PAPERCUTZ

DANCE CLASS 3 IN 1 #3

Dance Class
3 in 1
PAPERCUTZ

DANCE CLASS 3 IN 1 #4

SEE MORE AT PAPERCUTZ.COM

Also available digitally wherever e-books are sold.

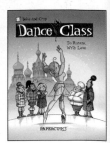

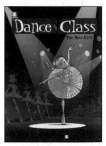

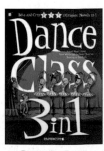

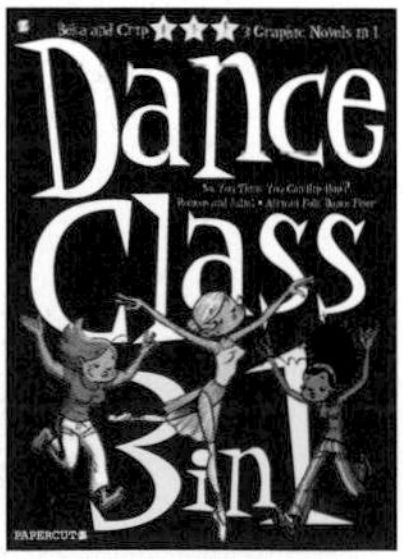

Dance Class 3 in 1

Table of Contents

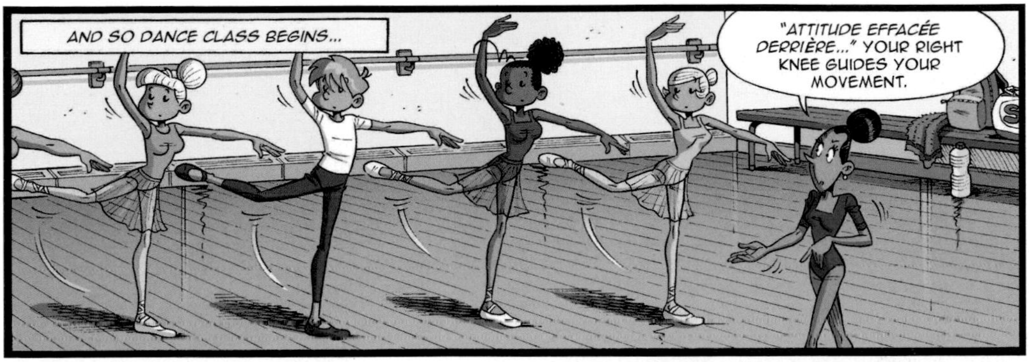
AND SO DANCE CLASS BEGINS...
"ATTITUDE EFFACÉE DERRIÈRE..." YOUR RIGHT KNEE GUIDES YOUR MOVEMENT.

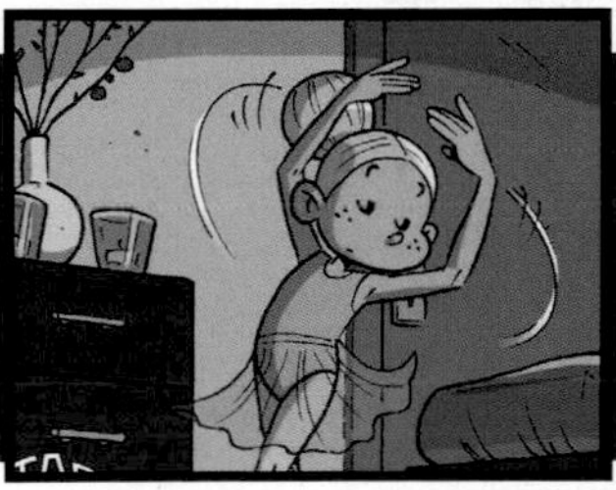

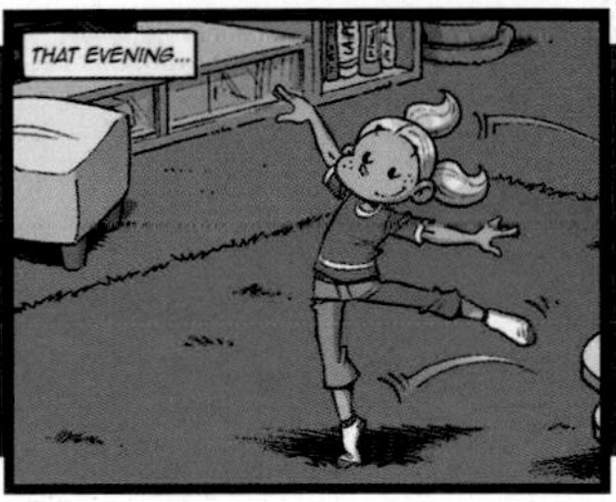
THAT EVENING...

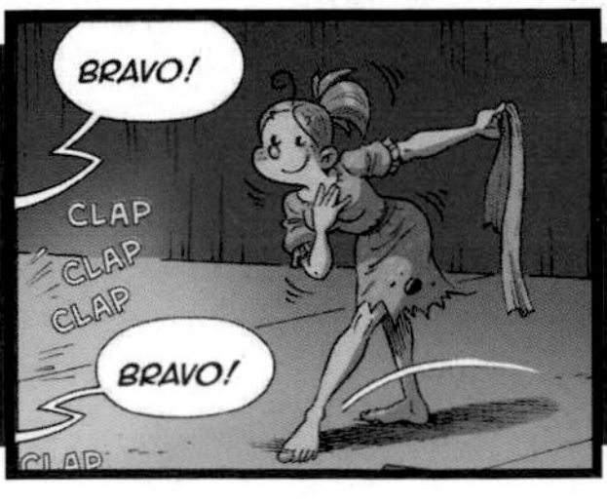
BRAVO!
CLAP
CLAP
CLAP
BRAVO!

DANCE CLASS 3 IN 1

Originally published in France as Studio Danse [Dance Class] Volumes 7, 8, and 9
©2011-2015, 2021 BAMBOO ÉDITION.
www.bamboo.fr
All other editorial material © 2021 by Papercutz
www.papercutz.com

DANCE CLASS 3 IN 1 #3
"School Night Fever"
"Snow White and the Seven Dwarves"
"Dancing in the Rain"

BÉKA — Writer
CRIP — Artist
MAËLA COSSON — Colorist
JOE JOHNSON — Translation
TOM ORZECHOWSKI — Lettering
MARK McNABB — Production
JEFF WHITMAN — Managing Editor
JIM SALICRUP
Editor-in-Chief

Special thanks to CATHERINE LOISELET

ISBN: 978-1-5458-0713-2

Printed in China
September 2021

Papercutz books may be purchased for business or promotional use. For information on bulk purchases
please contact Macmillan Corporate and Premium Sales Department at (800) 221-7945 x5442.

Distributed by Macmillan
First Papercutz Printing

School Night Fever

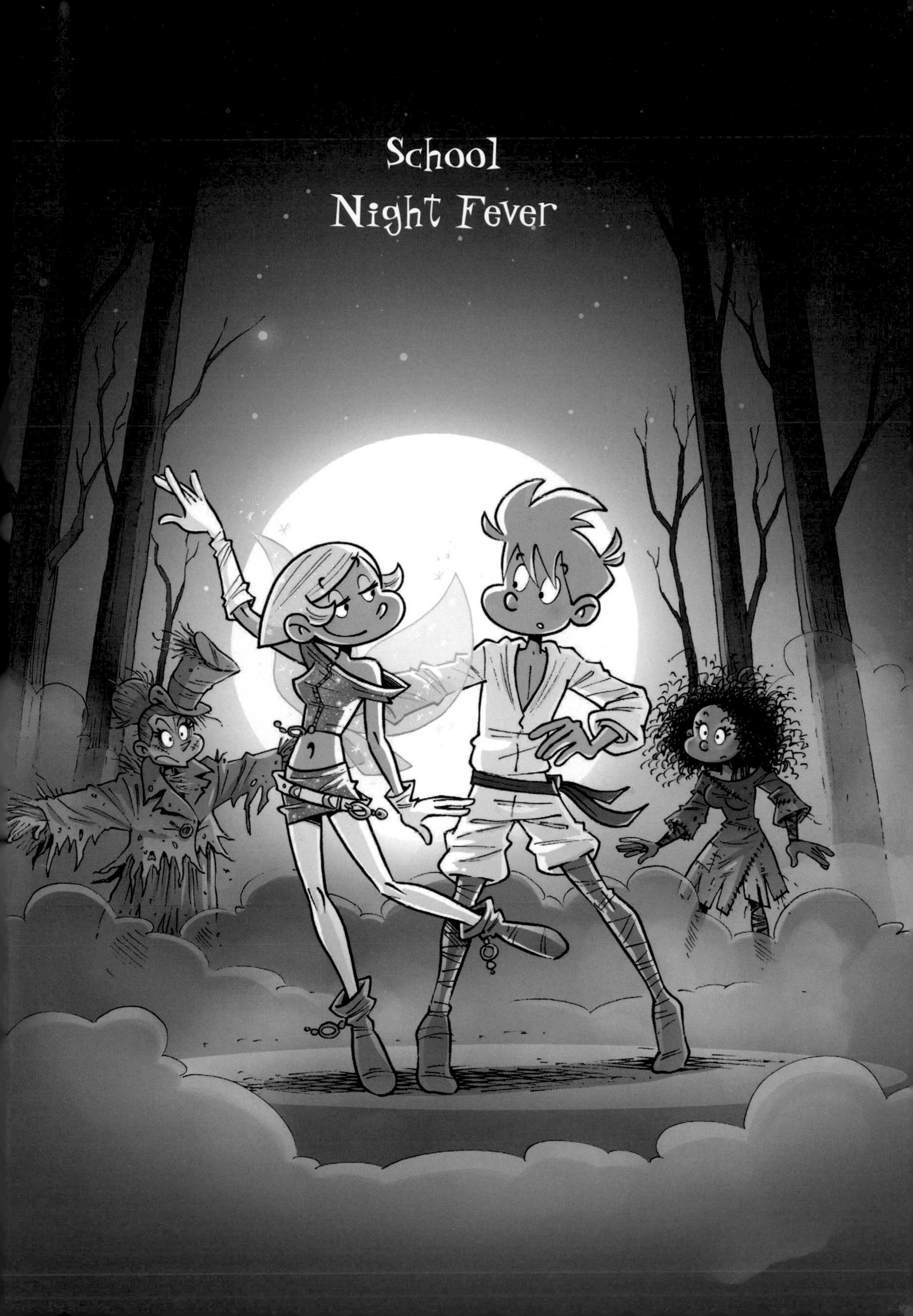

ENTRECHAT 3...

...LANDING WITH A CHANGEMENT DE PIED!

OWW!

CRACK

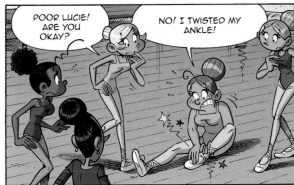

POOR LUCIE! ARE YOU OKAY?

NO! I TWISTED MY ANKLE!

SHE NEEDS SOMETHING COLD FOR THE SWELLING!

I'LL TAKE CARE OF IT, MISS ANNE!

COME ON, LUCIE!

OWW! NOT TOO FAST!

I'LL MEET YOU AFTER CLASS!

LATER...

LUCIE? ALIA? WHERE ARE YOU?

HERE!

I MANAGED TO FIND HER SOMETHING COLD!

IT'S NOT DOING MUCH FOR THE SWELLING YET, BUT IT'S SO GOOD!

!!

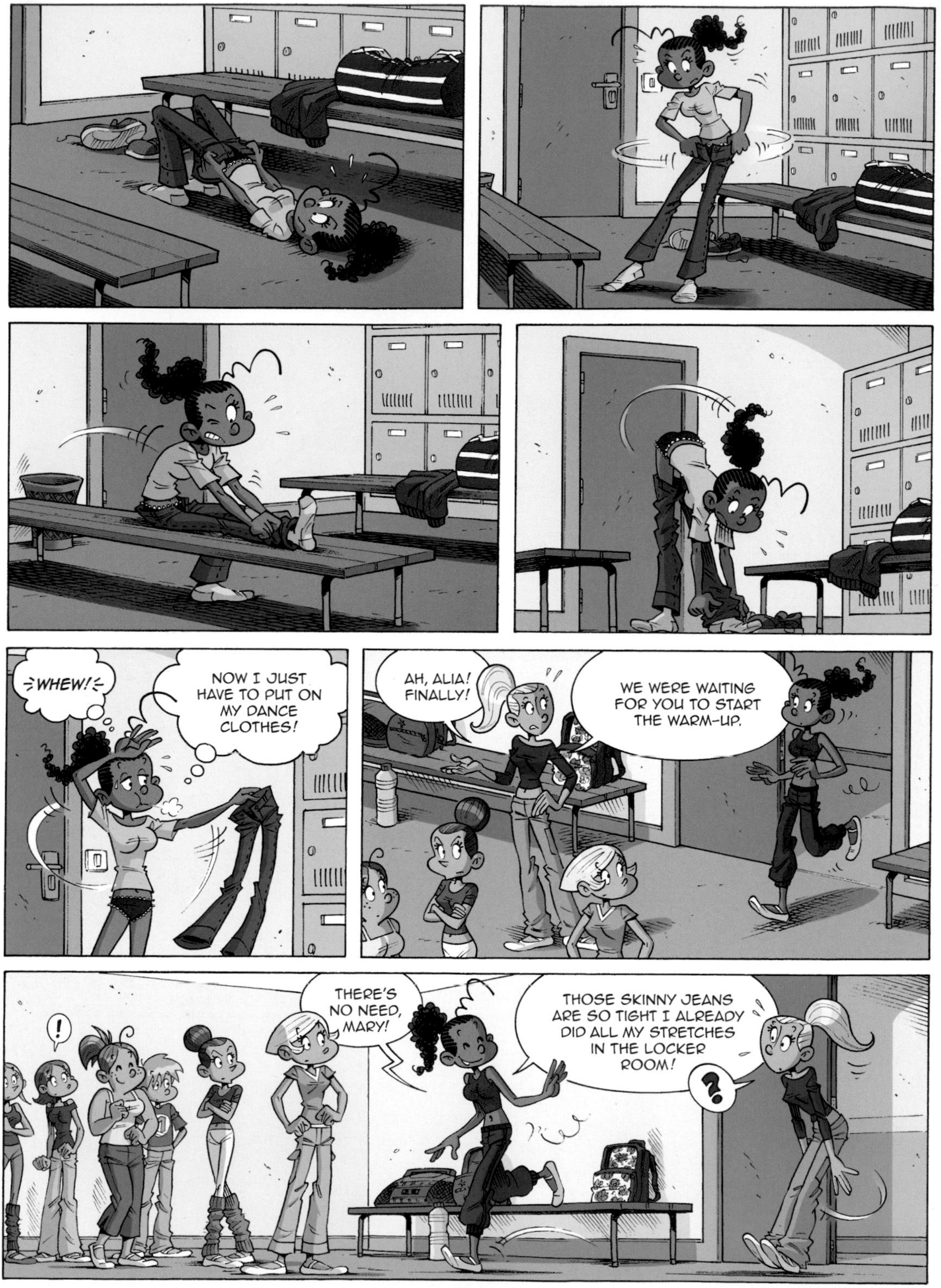

WHEW!
NOW I JUST HAVE TO PUT ON MY DANCE CLOTHES!
AH, ALIA! FINALLY!
WE WERE WAITING FOR YOU TO START THE WARM-UP.
!
THERE'S NO NEED, MARY!
THOSE SKINNY JEANS ARE SO TIGHT I ALREADY DID ALL MY STRETCHES IN THE LOCKER ROOM!
?

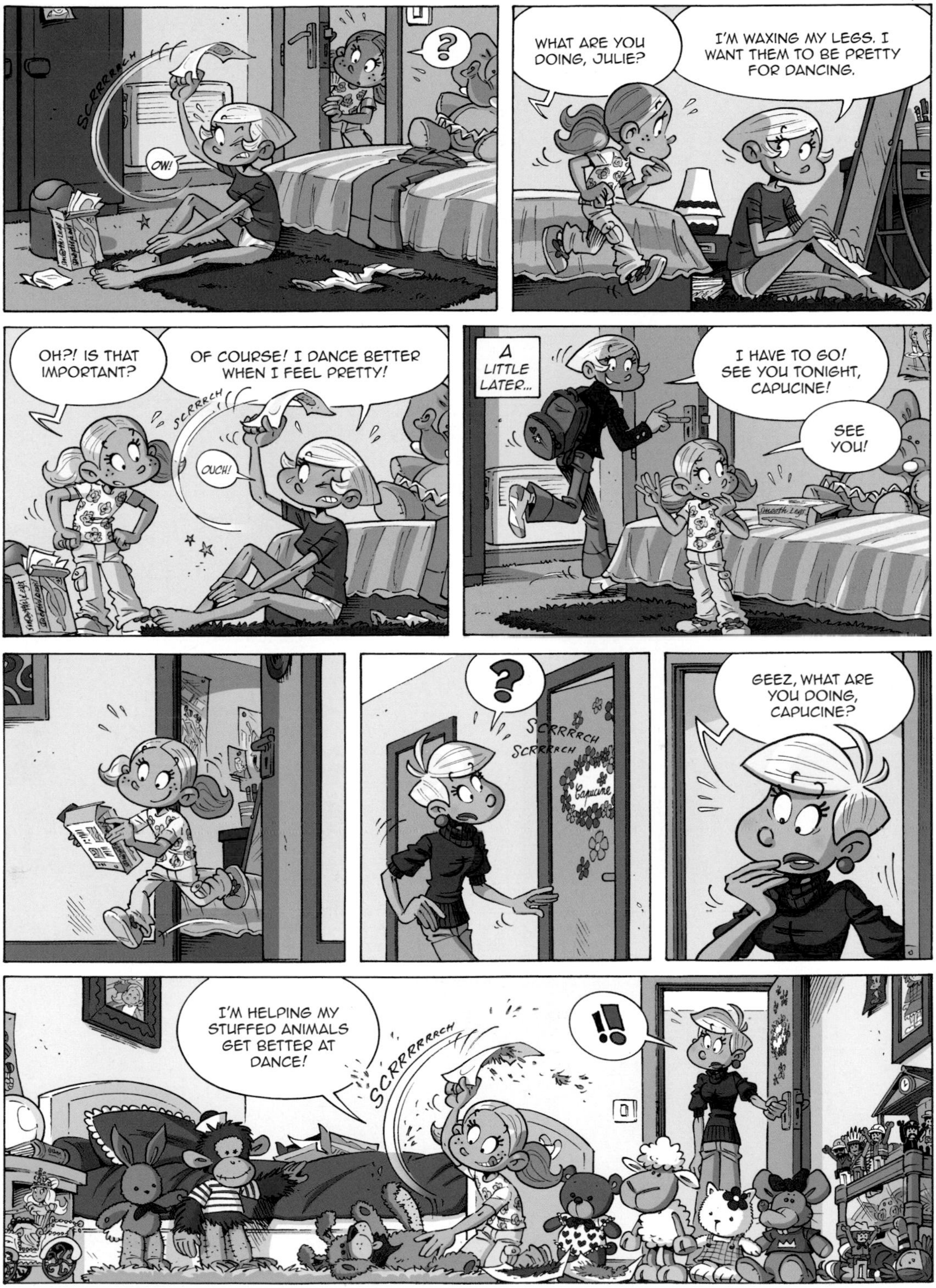
SCRRRRRCH
OW!
?
WHAT ARE YOU DOING, JULIE?
I'M WAXING MY LEGS. I WANT THEM TO BE PRETTY FOR DANCING.
OH?! IS THAT IMPORTANT?
OF COURSE! I DANCE BETTER WHEN I FEEL PRETTY!
SCRRRCH
OUCH!
A LITTLE LATER...
I HAVE TO GO! SEE YOU TONIGHT, CAPUCINE!
SEE YOU!
Smooth Legs
?
SCRRRRRCH
SCRRRRCH
Capucine
GEEZ, WHAT ARE YOU DOING, CAPUCINE?
I'M HELPING MY STUFFED ANIMALS GET BETTER AT DANCE!
SCRRRRRRCH
!!

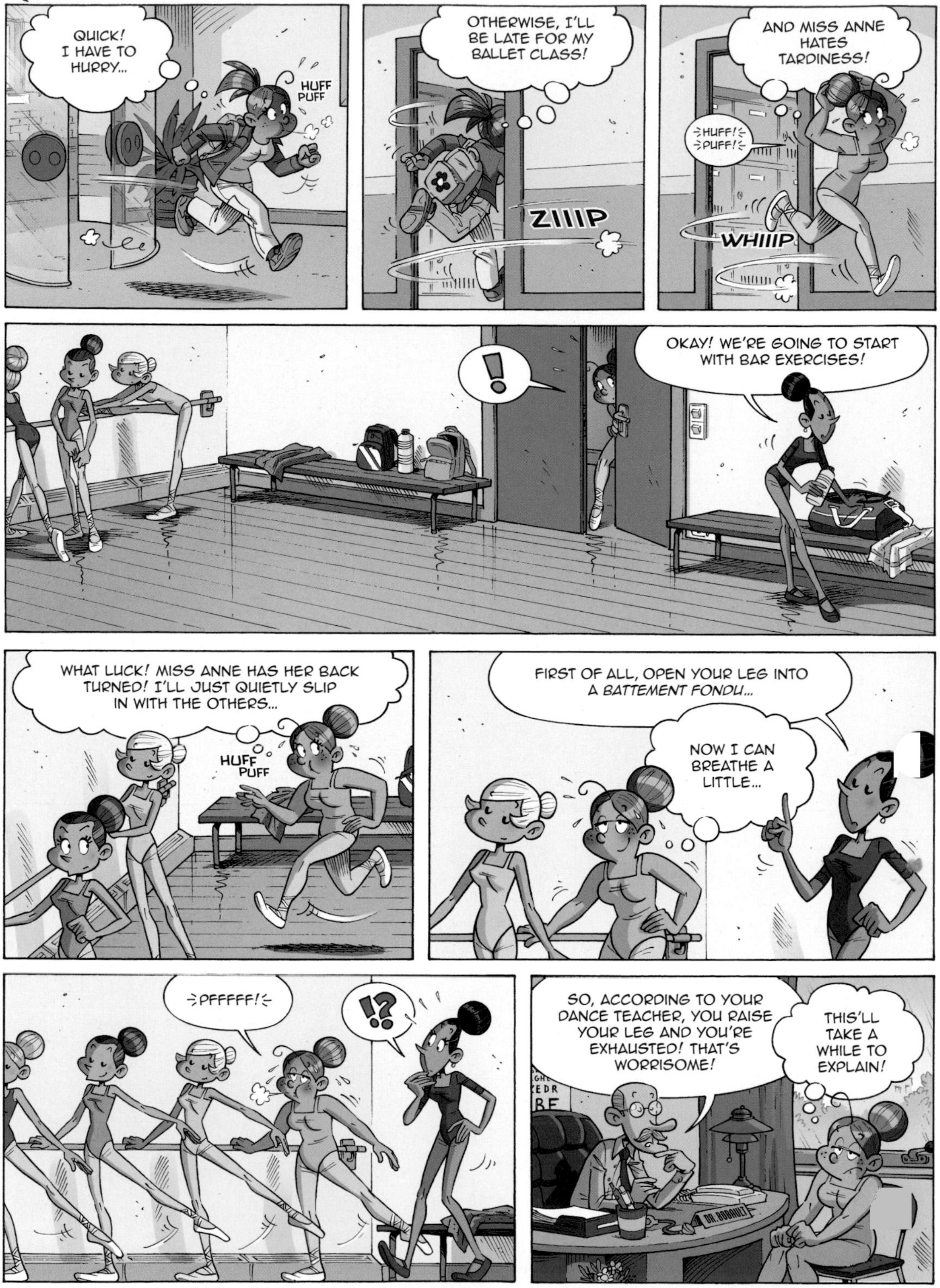
QUICK! I HAVE TO HURRY...
HUFF PUFF
OTHERWISE, I'LL BE LATE FOR MY BALLET CLASS!
ZIIIP
AND MISS ANNE HATES TARDINESS!
HUFF! PUFF!
WHIIIP
!
OKAY! WE'RE GOING TO START WITH BAR EXERCISES!
WHAT LUCK! MISS ANNE HAS HER BACK TURNED! I'LL JUST QUIETLY SLIP IN WITH THE OTHERS...
HUFF PUFF
FIRST OF ALL, OPEN YOUR LEG INTO A *BATTEMENT FONDU*...
NOW I CAN BREATHE A LITTLE...
PFFFFF!
!?
SO, ACCORDING TO YOUR DANCE TEACHER, YOU RAISE YOUR LEG AND YOU'RE EXHAUSTED! THAT'S WORRISOME!
THIS'LL TAKE A WHILE TO EXPLAIN!
DR. BORBULT

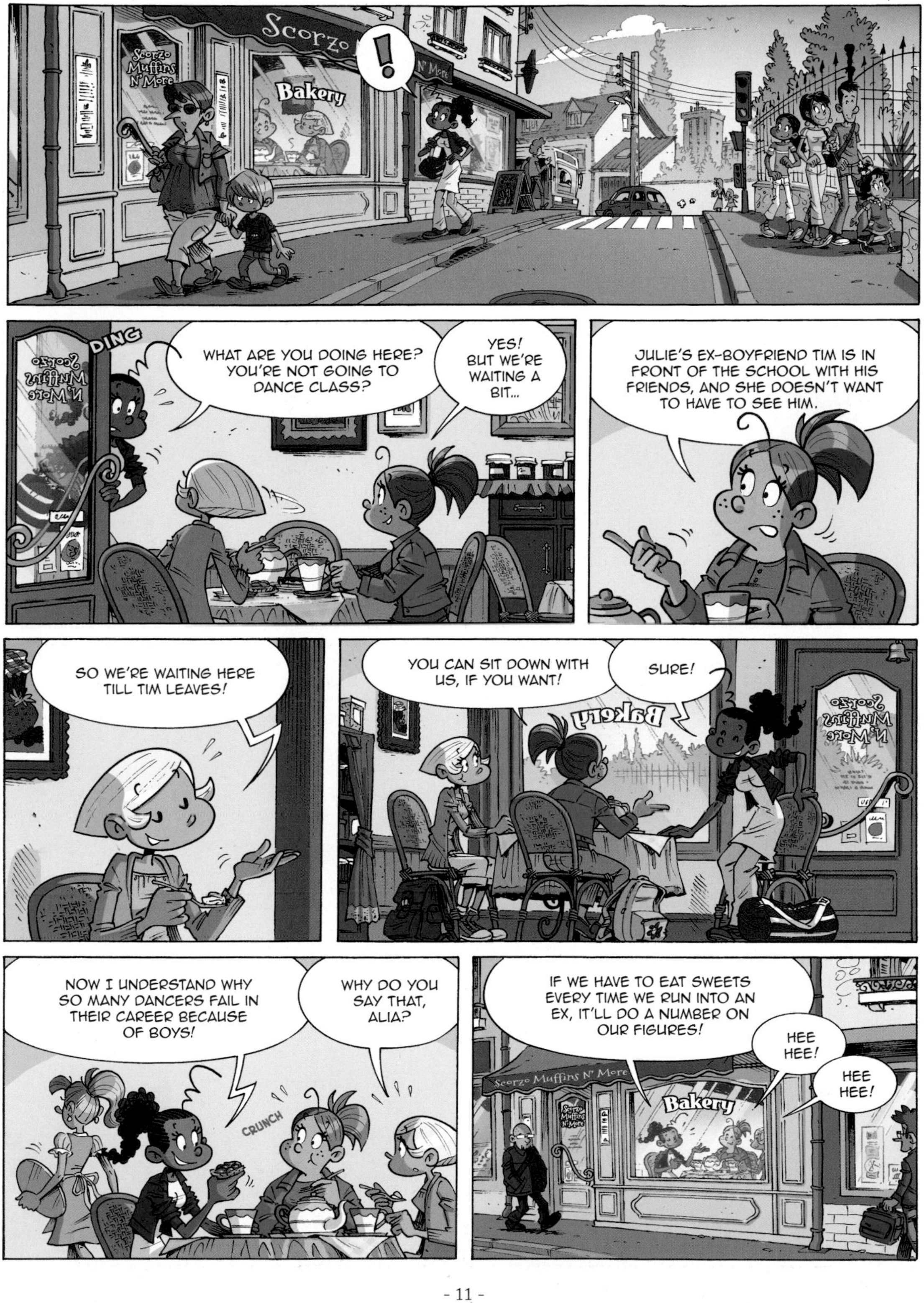
Scorzo
Scorzo Muffins N' More
N' More
Bakery
!
DING
WHAT ARE YOU DOING HERE? YOU'RE NOT GOING TO DANCE CLASS?
YES! BUT WE'RE WAITING A BIT...
JULIE'S EX-BOYFRIEND TIM IS IN FRONT OF THE SCHOOL WITH HIS FRIENDS, AND SHE DOESN'T WANT TO HAVE TO SEE HIM.
SO WE'RE WAITING HERE TILL TIM LEAVES!
YOU CAN SIT DOWN WITH US, IF YOU WANT!
SURE!
NOW I UNDERSTAND WHY SO MANY DANCERS FAIL IN THEIR CAREER BECAUSE OF BOYS!
WHY DO YOU SAY THAT, ALIA?
CRUNCH
IF WE HAVE TO EAT SWEETS EVERY TIME WE RUN INTO AN EX, IT'LL DO A NUMBER ON OUR FIGURES!
HEE HEE!
HEE HEE!
Scorzo Muffins N' More
Bakery

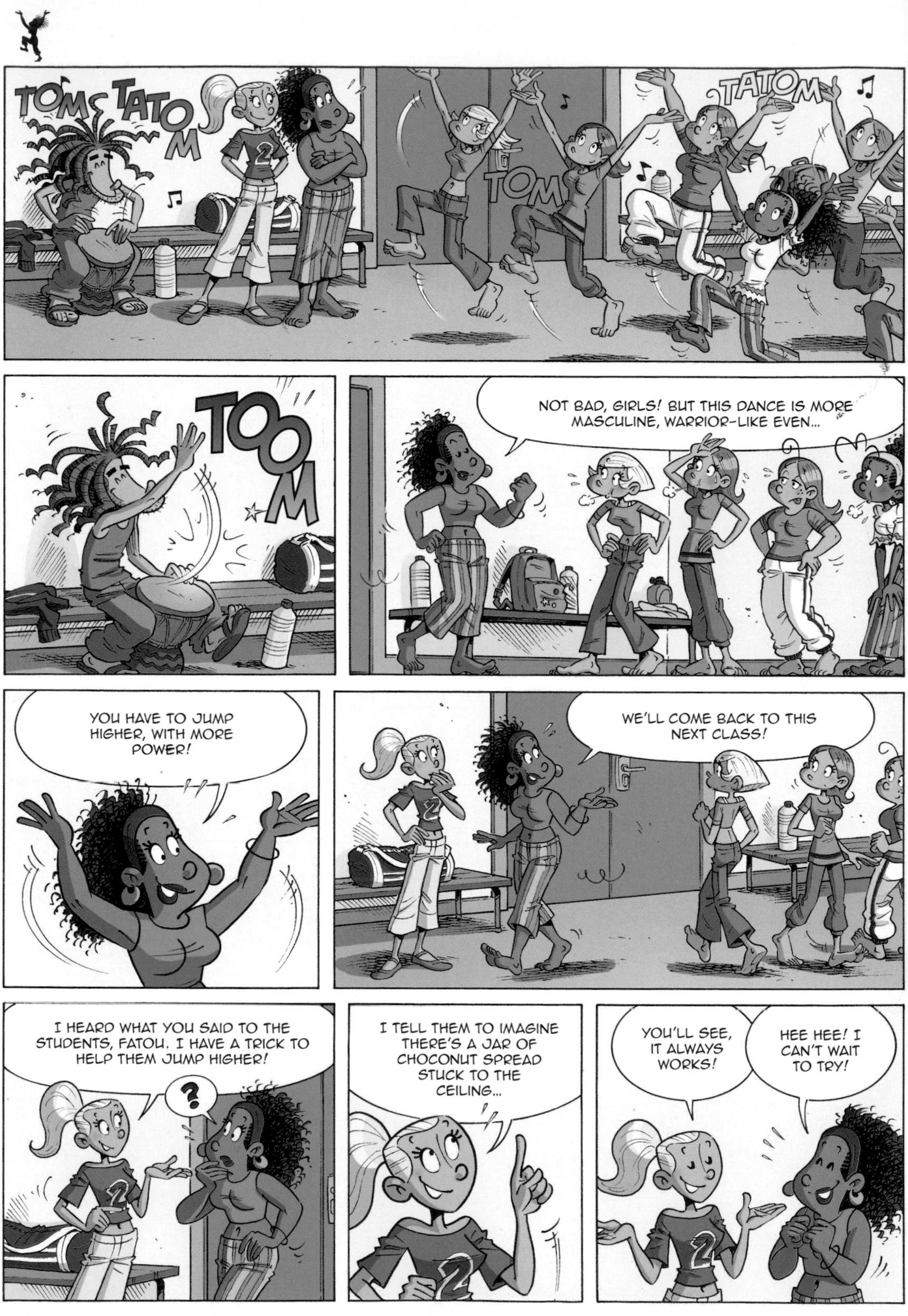
TOM TATOM
TOM
TATOM
TOOM
NOT BAD, GIRLS! BUT THIS DANCE IS MORE MASCULINE, WARRIOR-LIKE EVEN...
YOU HAVE TO JUMP HIGHER, WITH MORE POWER!
WE'LL COME BACK TO THIS NEXT CLASS!
I HEARD WHAT YOU SAID TO THE STUDENTS, FATOU. I HAVE A TRICK TO HELP THEM JUMP HIGHER!
?
I TELL THEM TO IMAGINE THERE'S A JAR OF CHOCONUT SPREAD STUCK TO THE CEILING...
YOU'LL SEE, IT ALWAYS WORKS!
HEE HEE! I CAN'T WAIT TO TRY!

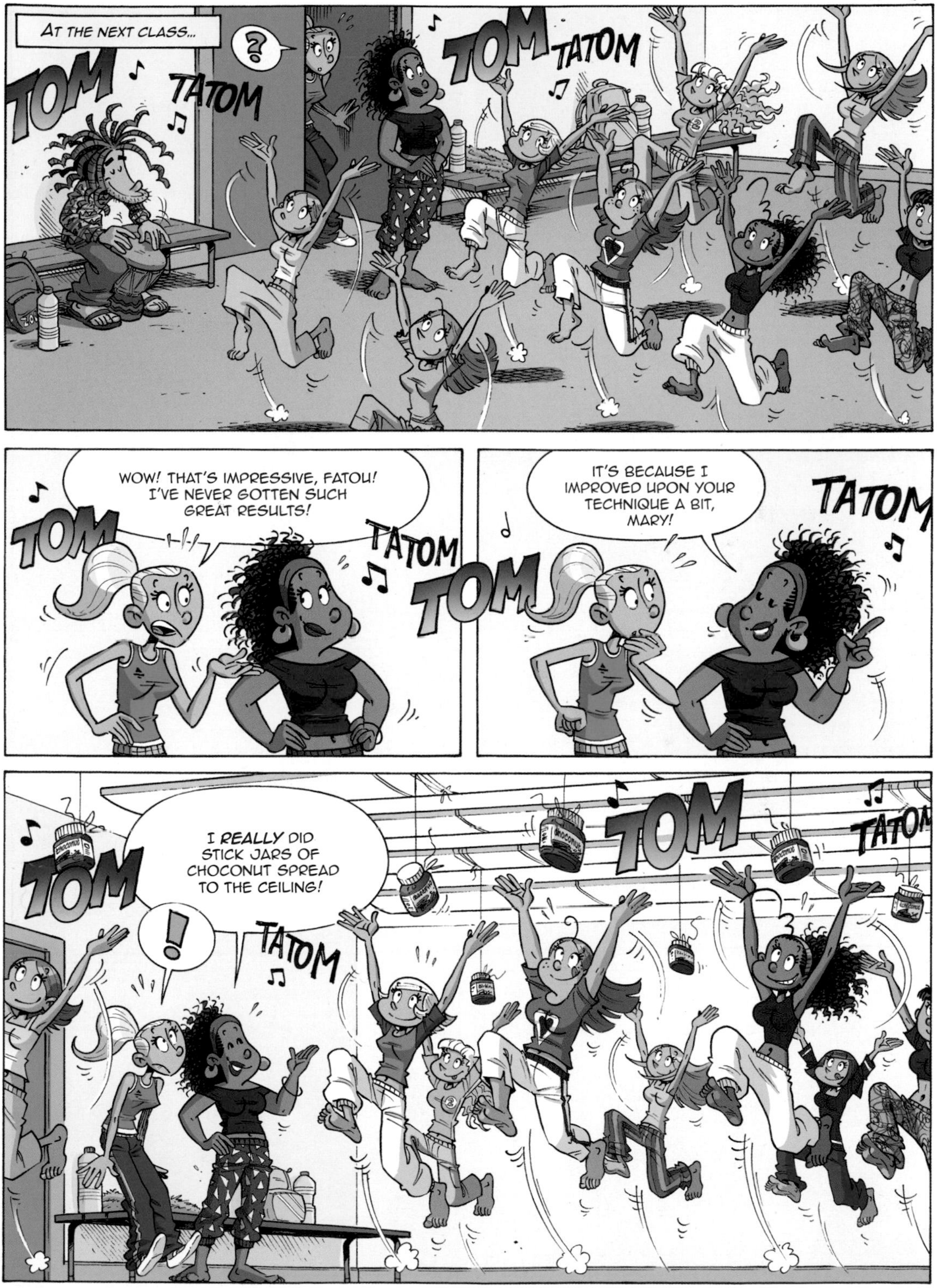

At the next class...
TOM
TATOM
?
TOM
TATOM
WOW! THAT'S IMPRESSIVE, FATOU! I'VE NEVER GOTTEN SUCH GREAT RESULTS!
TOM
TATOM
IT'S BECAUSE I IMPROVED UPON YOUR TECHNIQUE A BIT, MARY!
TOM
TATOM
I *REALLY* DID STICK JARS OF CHOCONUT SPREAD TO THE CEILING!
!
TOM
TATOM
TOM
TATOM

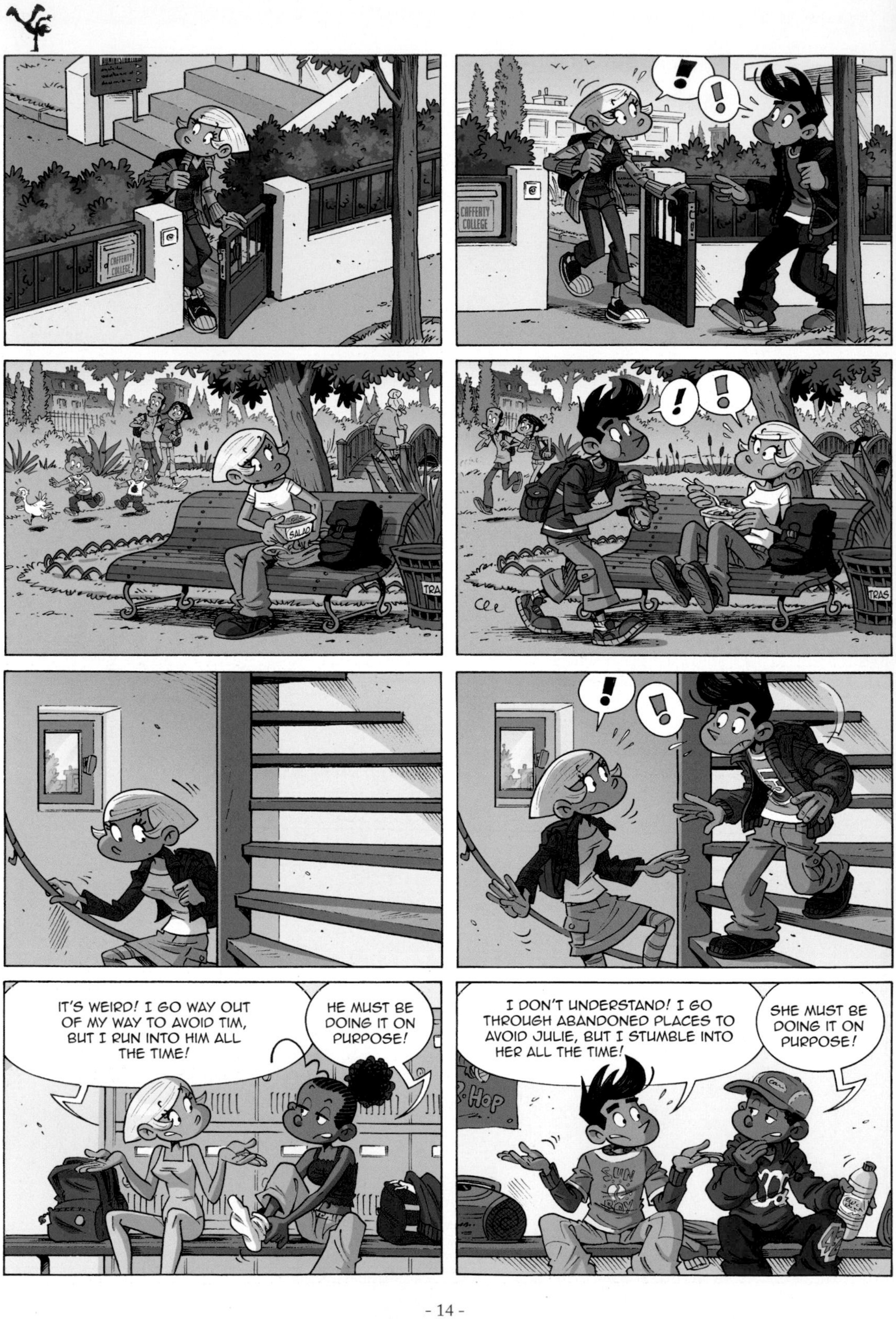
CAFFERTY COLLEGE
CAFFERTY COLLEGE
!
!
SALAD
TRAS
!
!
TRAS
!
!
IT'S WEIRD! I GO WAY OUT OF MY WAY TO AVOID TIM, BUT I RUN INTO HIM ALL THE TIME!
HE MUST BE DOING IT ON PURPOSE!
I DON'T UNDERSTAND! I GO THROUGH ABANDONED PLACES TO AVOID JULIE, BUT I STUMBLE INTO HER ALL THE TIME!
SHE MUST BE DOING IT ON PURPOSE!

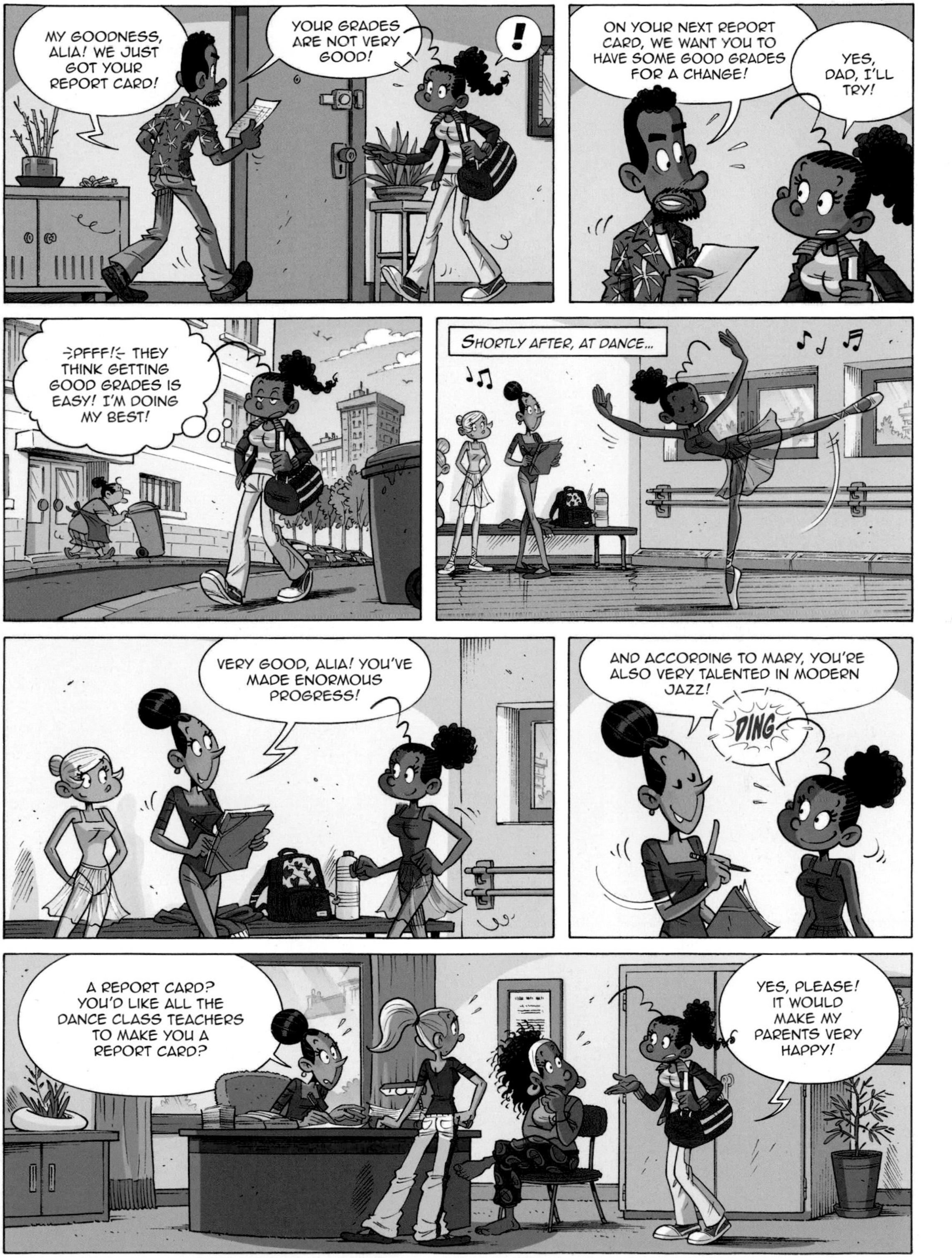
MY GOODNESS, ALIA! WE JUST GOT YOUR REPORT CARD!
YOUR GRADES ARE NOT VERY GOOD!
!
ON YOUR NEXT REPORT CARD, WE WANT YOU TO HAVE SOME GOOD GRADES FOR A CHANGE!
YES, DAD, I'LL TRY!
PFFF! THEY THINK GETTING GOOD GRADES IS EASY! I'M DOING MY BEST!
SHORTLY AFTER, AT DANCE...
VERY GOOD, ALIA! YOU'VE MADE ENORMOUS PROGRESS!
AND ACCORDING TO MARY, YOU'RE ALSO VERY TALENTED IN MODERN JAZZ!
DING
A REPORT CARD? YOU'D LIKE ALL THE DANCE CLASS TEACHERS TO MAKE YOU A REPORT CARD?
YES, PLEASE! IT WOULD MAKE MY PARENTS VERY HAPPY!

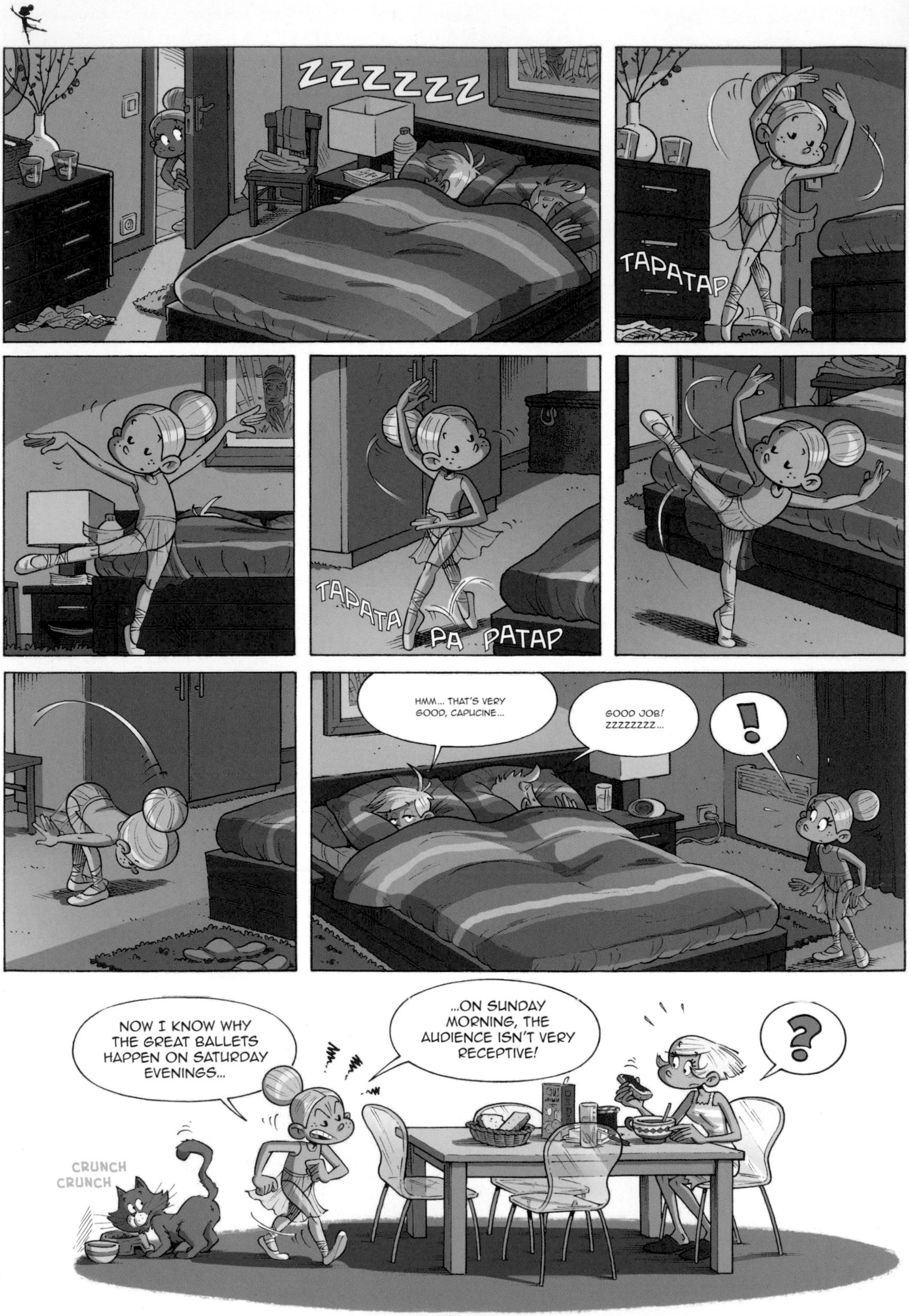

ZZZZZZZ
TAPATAP
TAPATA
PA PATAP
HMM... THAT'S VERY GOOD, CAPUCINE...
GOOD JOB! ZZZZZZZZ...
!
NOW I KNOW WHY THE GREAT BALLETS HAPPEN ON SATURDAY EVENINGS...
...ON SUNDAY MORNING, THE AUDIENCE ISN'T VERY RECEPTIVE!
?
CRUNCH CRUNCH

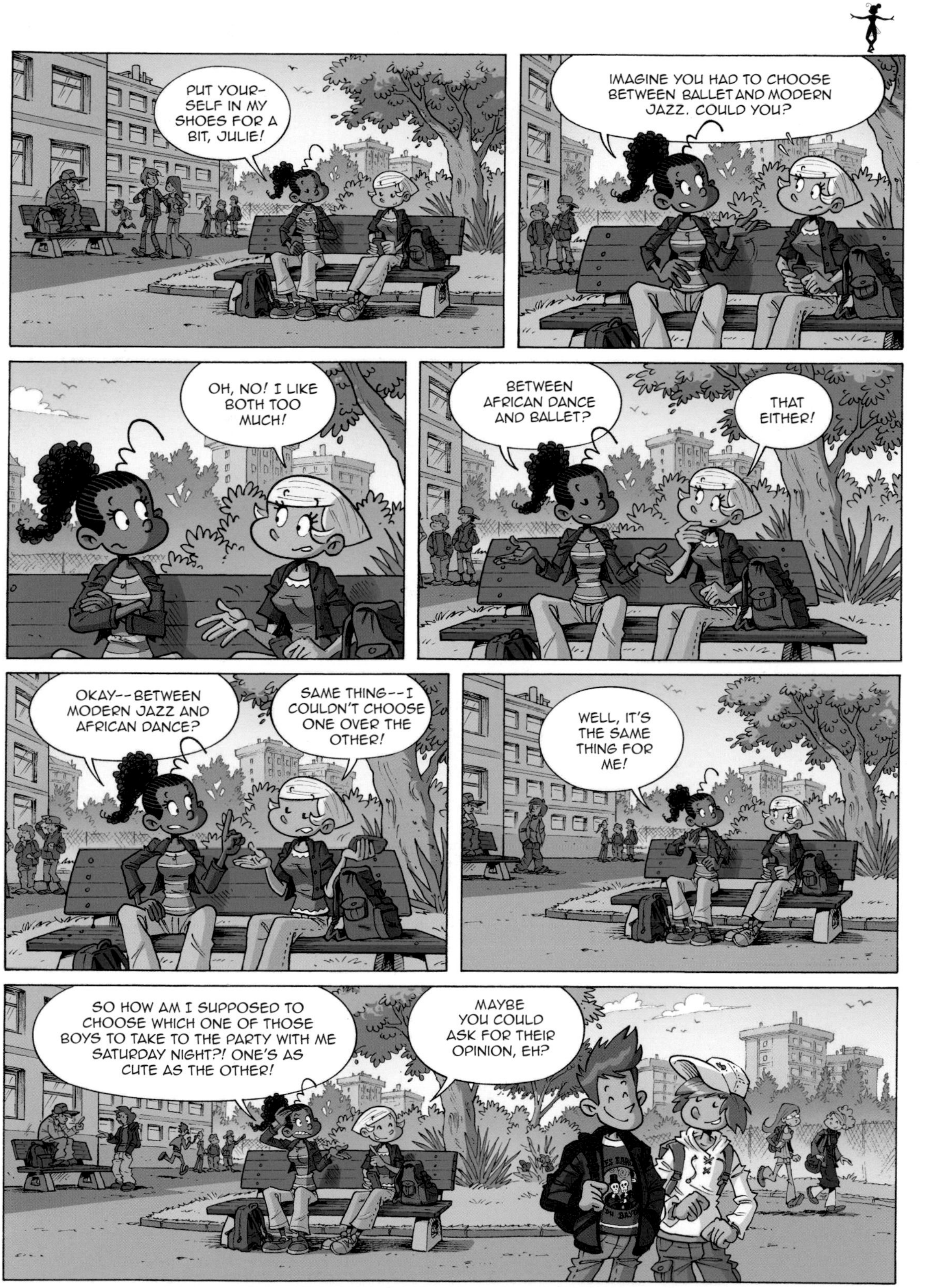

PUT YOURSELF IN MY SHOES FOR A BIT, JULIE!
IMAGINE YOU HAD TO CHOOSE BETWEEN BALLET AND MODERN JAZZ. COULD YOU?
OH, NO! I LIKE BOTH TOO MUCH!
BETWEEN AFRICAN DANCE AND BALLET?
THAT EITHER!
OKAY--BETWEEN MODERN JAZZ AND AFRICAN DANCE?
SAME THING--I COULDN'T CHOOSE ONE OVER THE OTHER!
WELL, IT'S THE SAME THING FOR ME!
SO HOW AM I SUPPOSED TO CHOOSE WHICH ONE OF THOSE BOYS TO TAKE TO THE PARTY WITH ME SATURDAY NIGHT?! ONE'S AS CUTE AS THE OTHER!
MAYBE YOU COULD ASK FOR THEIR OPINION, EH?

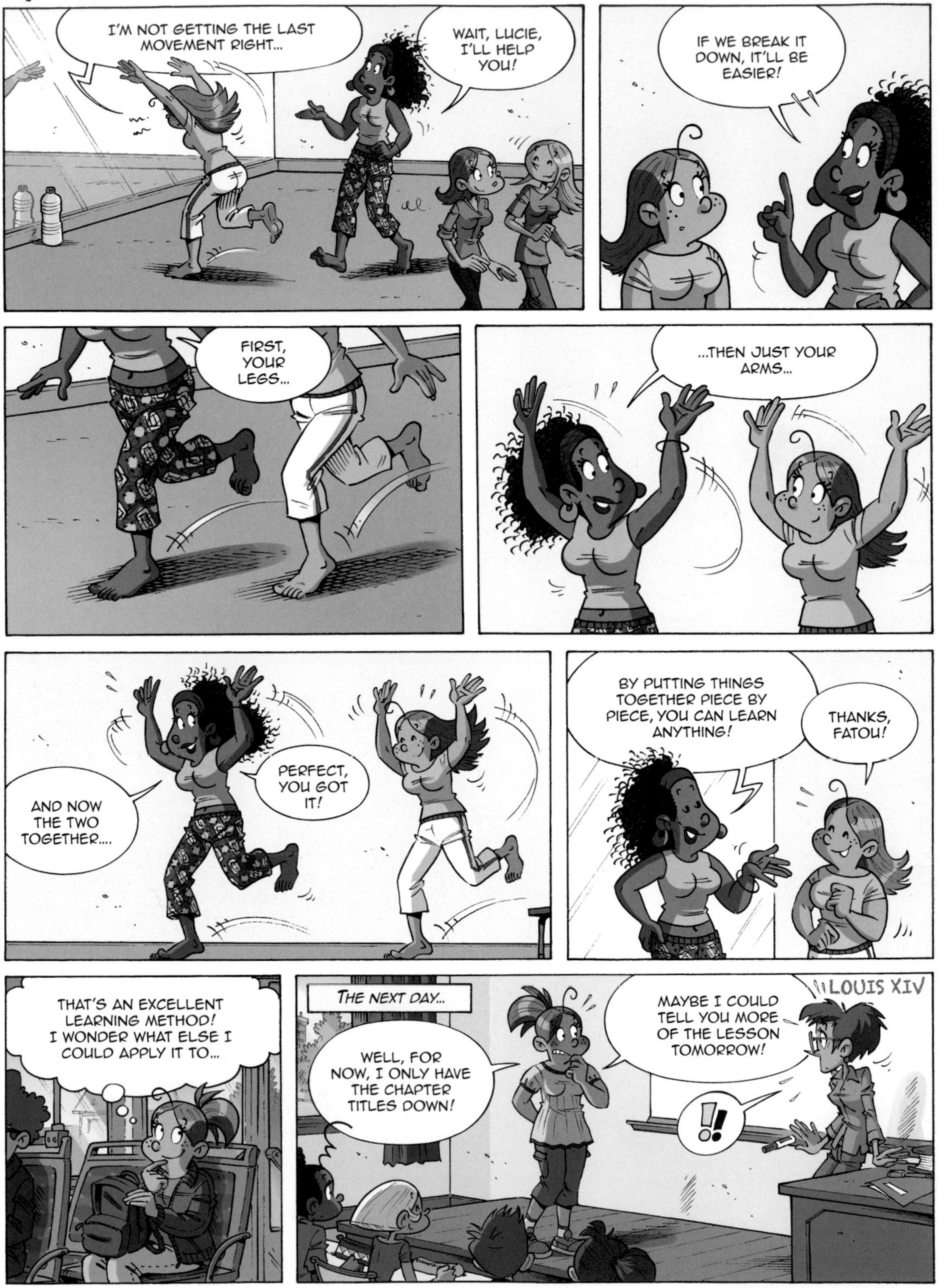
I'M NOT GETTING THE LAST MOVEMENT RIGHT...
WAIT, LUCIE, I'LL HELP YOU!
IF WE BREAK IT DOWN, IT'LL BE EASIER!
FIRST, YOUR LEGS...
...THEN JUST YOUR ARMS...
AND NOW THE TWO TOGETHER....
PERFECT, YOU GOT IT!
BY PUTTING THINGS TOGETHER PIECE BY PIECE, YOU CAN LEARN ANYTHING!
THANKS, FATOU!
THAT'S AN EXCELLENT LEARNING METHOD! I WONDER WHAT ELSE I COULD APPLY IT TO...
THE NEXT DAY...
WELL, FOR NOW, I ONLY HAVE THE CHAPTER TITLES DOWN!
LOUIS XIV
MAYBE I COULD TELL YOU MORE OF THE LESSON TOMORROW!
!!

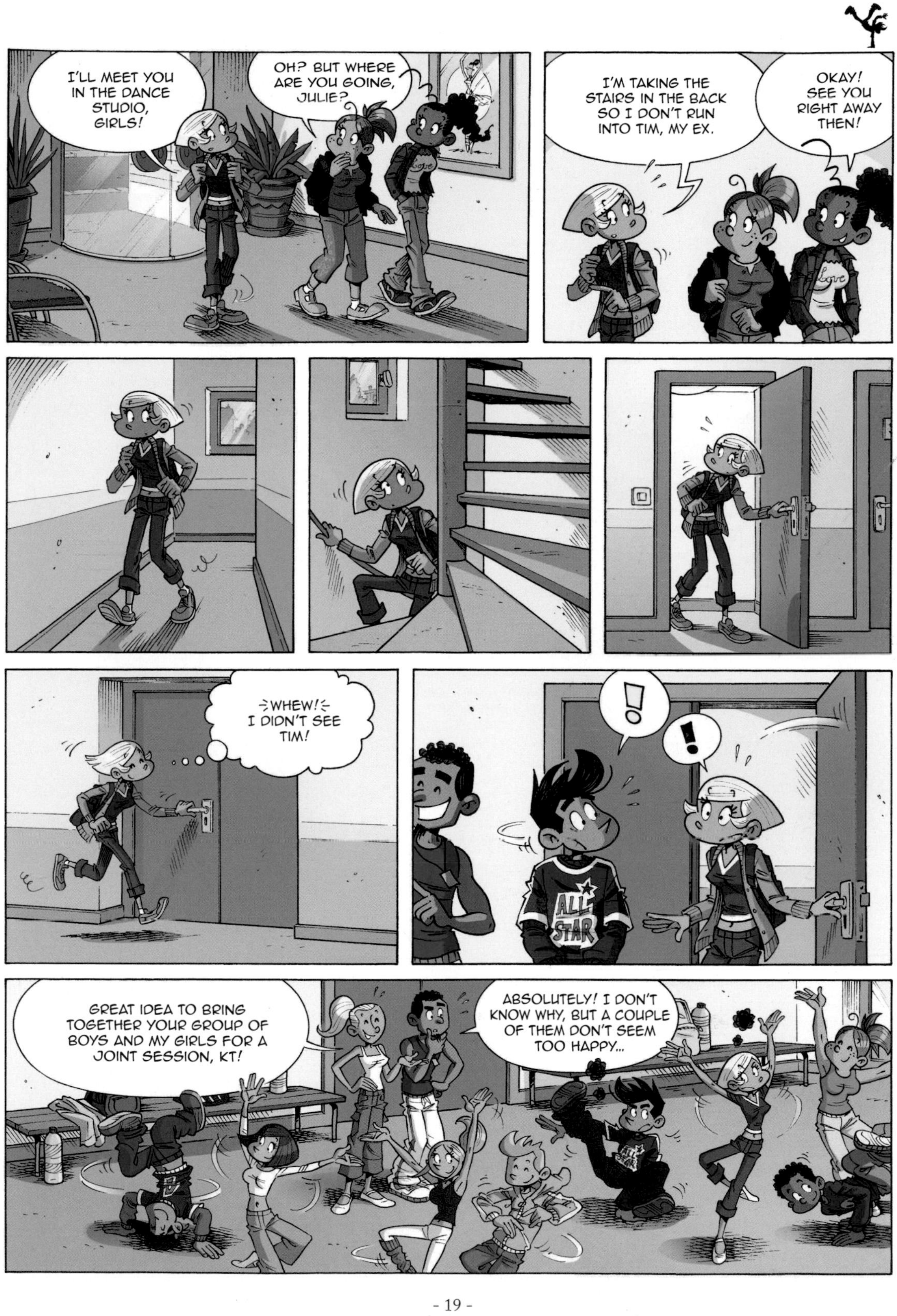
I'LL MEET YOU IN THE DANCE STUDIO, GIRLS!
OH? BUT WHERE ARE YOU GOING, JULIE?
I'M TAKING THE STAIRS IN THE BACK SO I DON'T RUN INTO TIM, MY EX.
OKAY! SEE YOU RIGHT AWAY THEN!
WHEW! I DIDN'T SEE TIM!
!
!
ALL STAR
GREAT IDEA TO BRING TOGETHER YOUR GROUP OF BOYS AND MY GIRLS FOR A JOINT SESSION, KT!
ABSOLUTELY! I DON'T KNOW WHY, BUT A COUPLE OF THEM DON'T SEEM TOO HAPPY...

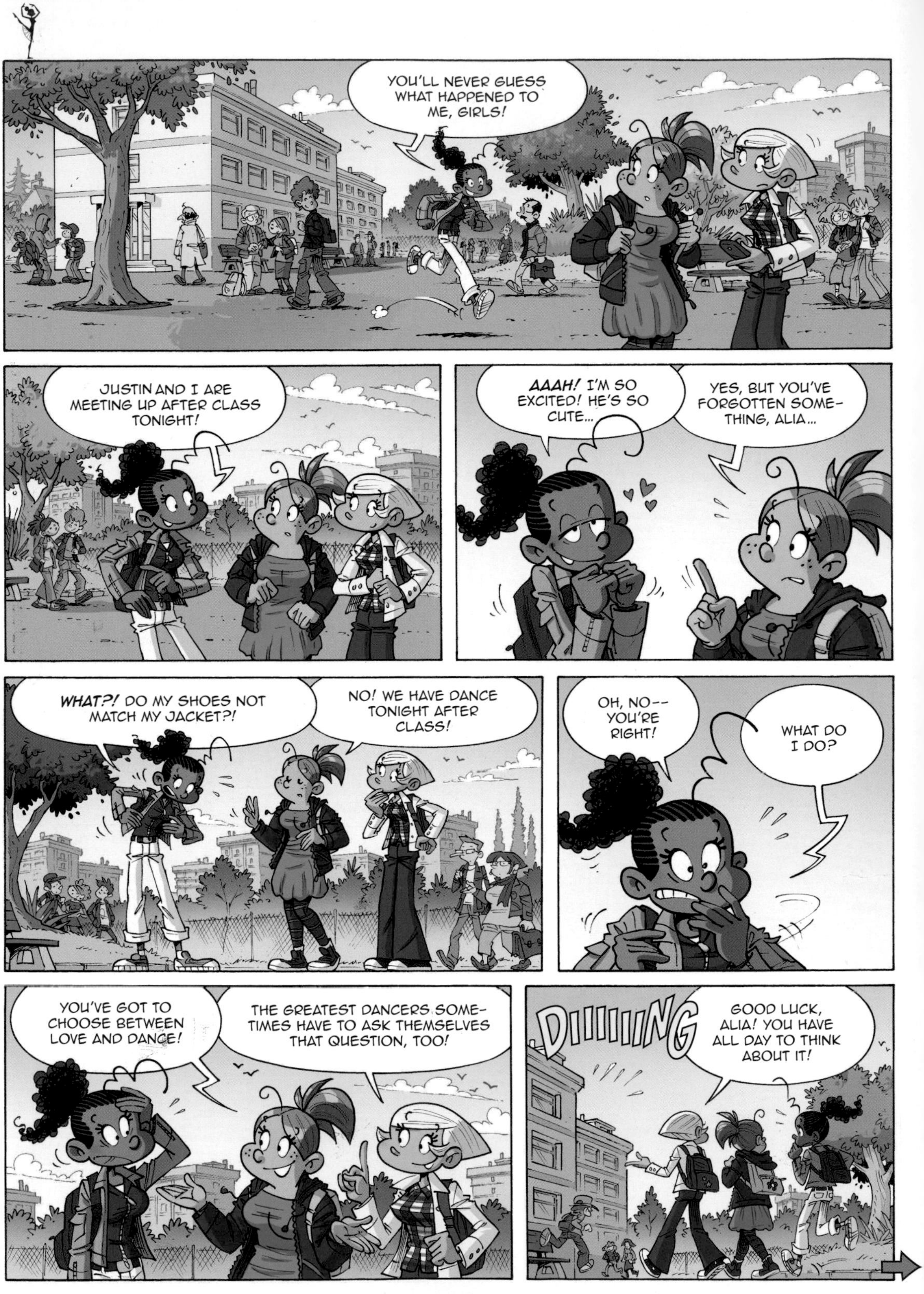

YOU'LL NEVER GUESS WHAT HAPPENED TO ME, GIRLS!
JUSTIN AND I ARE MEETING UP AFTER CLASS TONIGHT!
AAAH! I'M SO EXCITED! HE'S SO CUTE...
YES, BUT YOU'VE FORGOTTEN SOME-THING, ALIA...
WHAT?! DO MY SHOES NOT MATCH MY JACKET?!
NO! WE HAVE DANCE TONIGHT AFTER CLASS!
OH, NO-- YOU'RE RIGHT!
WHAT DO I DO?
YOU'VE GOT TO CHOOSE BETWEEN LOVE AND DANCE!
THE GREATEST DANCERS SOME-TIMES HAVE TO ASK THEMSELVES THAT QUESTION, TOO!
DIIIIIING
GOOD LUCK, ALIA! YOU HAVE ALL DAY TO THINK ABOUT IT!

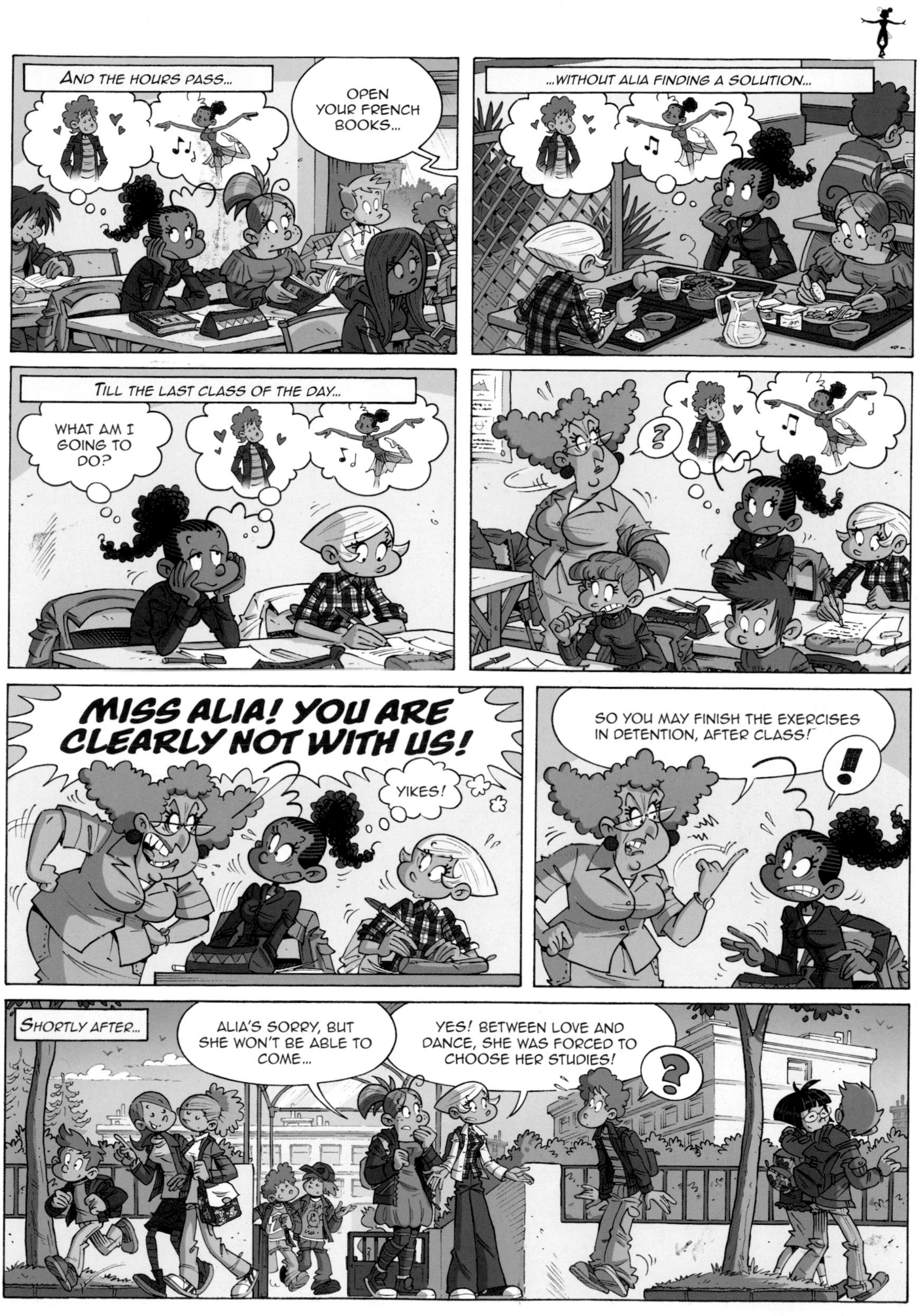
AND THE HOURS PASS...
OPEN YOUR FRENCH BOOKS...
...WITHOUT ALIA FINDING A SOLUTION...
TILL THE LAST CLASS OF THE DAY...
WHAT AM I GOING TO DO?
?
MISS ALIA! YOU ARE CLEARLY NOT WITH US!
YIKES!
SO YOU MAY FINISH THE EXERCISES IN DETENTION, AFTER CLASS!
!
SHORTLY AFTER...
ALIA'S SORRY, BUT SHE WON'T BE ABLE TO COME...
YES! BETWEEN LOVE AND DANCE, SHE WAS FORCED TO CHOOSE HER STUDIES!
?

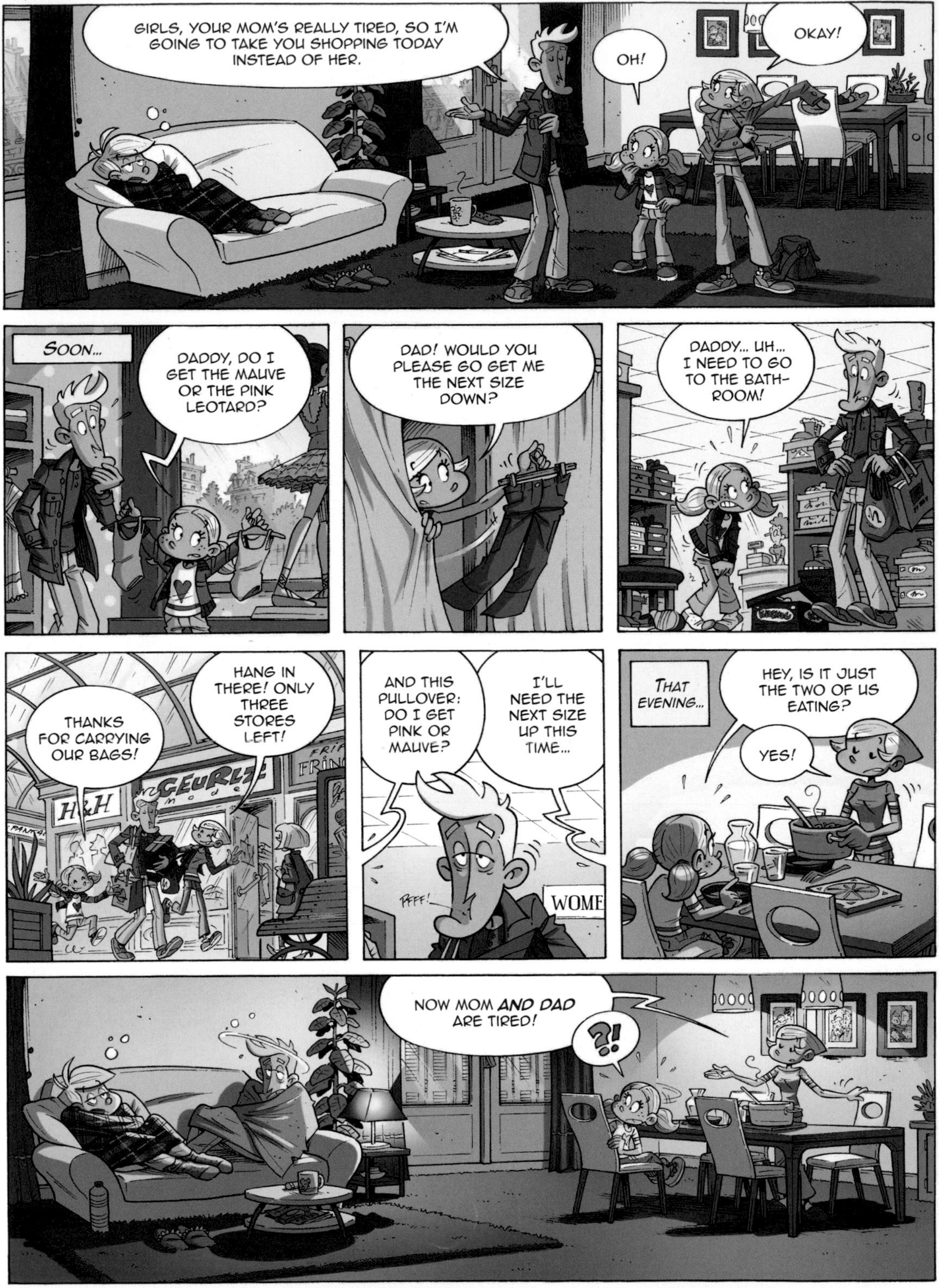

GIRLS, YOUR MOM'S REALLY TIRED, SO I'M GOING TO TAKE YOU SHOPPING TODAY INSTEAD OF HER.
OH!
OKAY!
SOON...
DADDY, DO I GET THE MAUVE OR THE PINK LEOTARD?
DAD! WOULD YOU PLEASE GO GET ME THE NEXT SIZE DOWN?
DADDY... UH... I NEED TO GO TO THE BATH-ROOM!
THANKS FOR CARRYING OUR BAGS!
HANG IN THERE! ONLY THREE STORES LEFT!
H&H
AND THIS PULLOVER: DO I GET PINK OR MAUVE?
I'LL NEED THE NEXT SIZE UP THIS TIME...
PFFF!
WOME
THAT EVENING...
HEY, IS IT JUST THE TWO OF US EATING?
YES!
NOW MOM *AND DAD* ARE TIRED!
?!

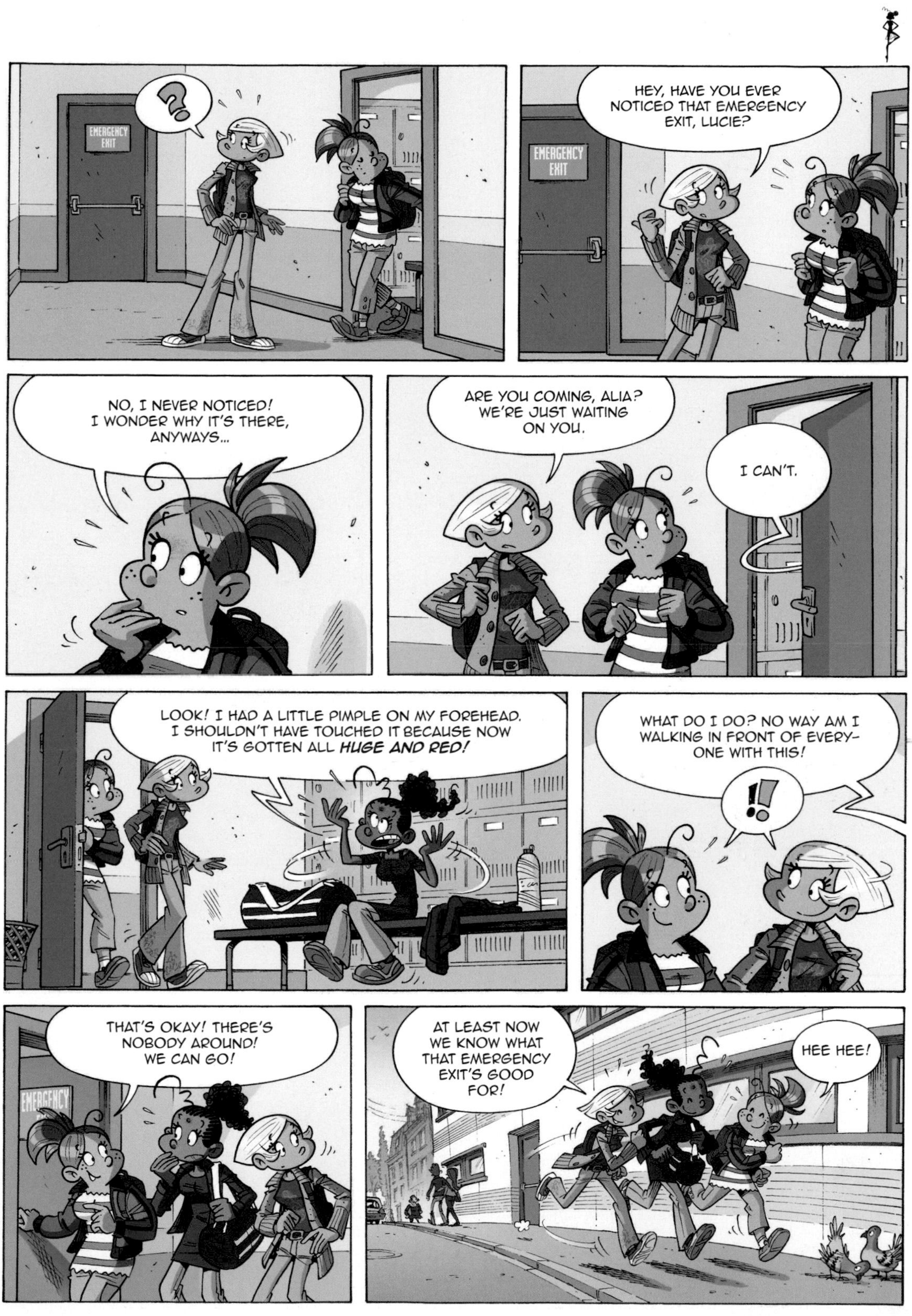
?
EMERGENCY EXIT
HEY, HAVE YOU EVER NOTICED THAT EMERGENCY EXIT, LUCIE?
EMERGENCY EXIT
NO, I NEVER NOTICED! I WONDER WHY IT'S THERE, ANYWAYS...
ARE YOU COMING, ALIA? WE'RE JUST WAITING ON YOU.
I CAN'T.
LOOK! I HAD A LITTLE PIMPLE ON MY FOREHEAD. I SHOULDN'T HAVE TOUCHED IT BECAUSE NOW IT'S GOTTEN ALL HUGE AND RED!
WHAT DO I DO? NO WAY AM I WALKING IN FRONT OF EVERY-ONE WITH THIS!
!!
THAT'S OKAY! THERE'S NOBODY AROUND! WE CAN GO!
EMERGENCY
AT LEAST NOW WE KNOW WHAT THAT EMERGENCY EXIT'S GOOD FOR!
HEE HEE!

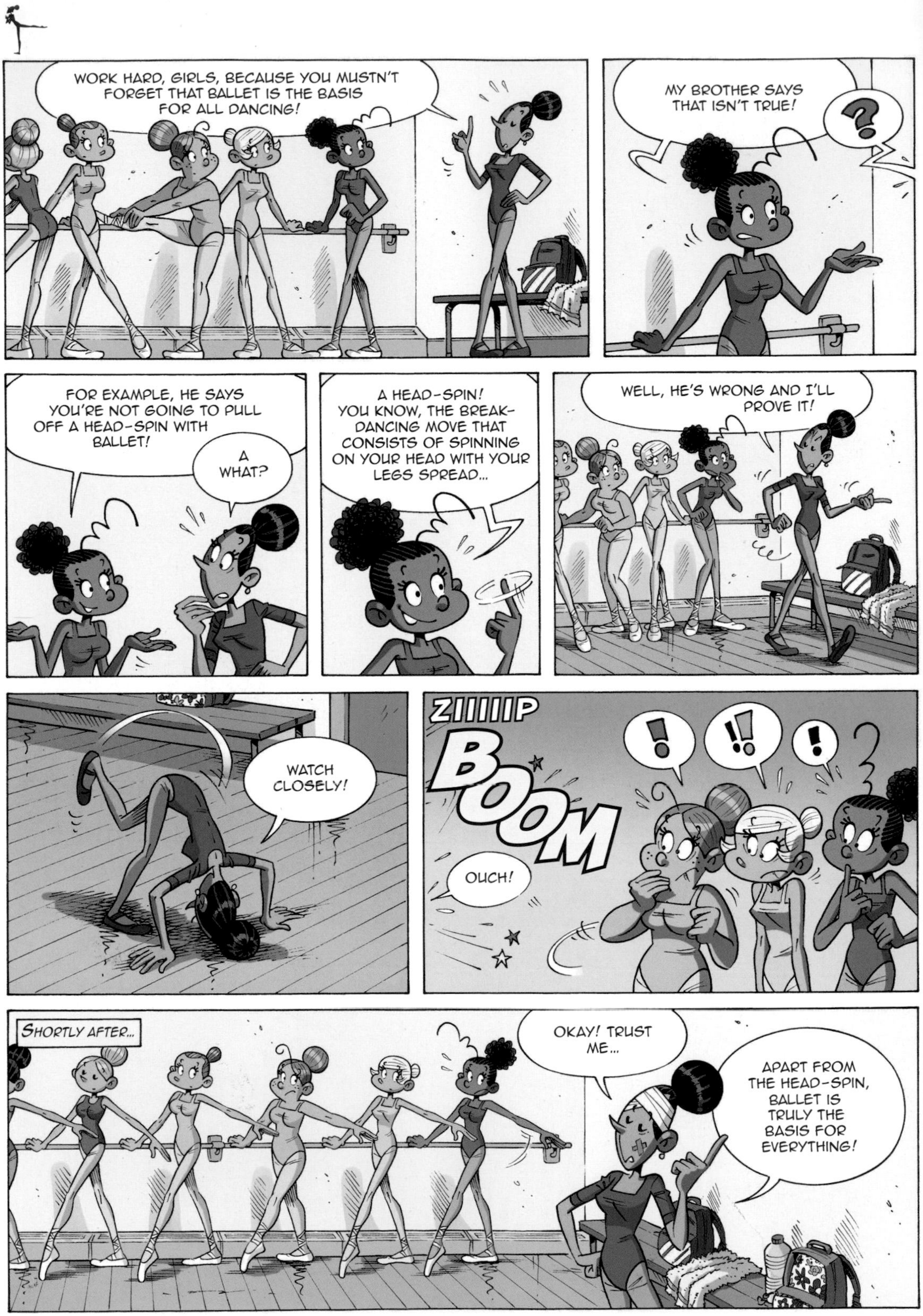
WORK HARD, GIRLS, BECAUSE YOU MUSTN'T FORGET THAT BALLET IS THE BASIS FOR ALL DANCING!
MY BROTHER SAYS THAT ISN'T TRUE!
?
FOR EXAMPLE, HE SAYS YOU'RE NOT GOING TO PULL OFF A HEAD-SPIN WITH BALLET!
A WHAT?
A HEAD-SPIN! YOU KNOW, THE BREAK-DANCING MOVE THAT CONSISTS OF SPINNING ON YOUR HEAD WITH YOUR LEGS SPREAD...
WELL, HE'S WRONG AND I'LL PROVE IT!
WATCH CLOSELY!
ZIIIIIP
BOOM
OUCH!
!
!!
!
SHORTLY AFTER...
OKAY! TRUST ME...
APART FROM THE HEAD-SPIN, BALLET IS TRULY THE BASIS FOR EVERYTHING!

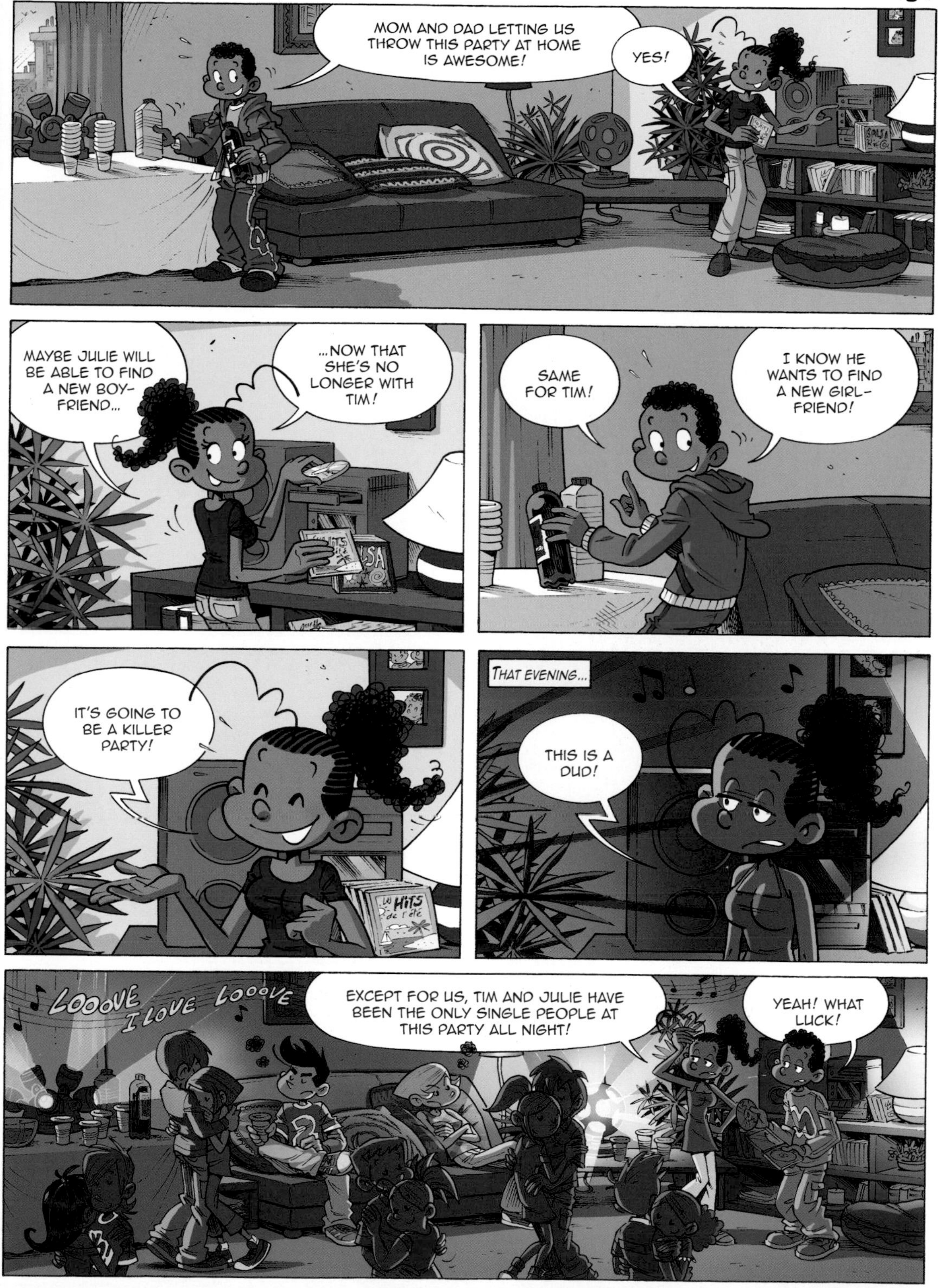
MOM AND DAD LETTING US THROW THIS PARTY AT HOME IS AWESOME!
YES!
MAYBE JULIE WILL BE ABLE TO FIND A NEW BOY-FRIEND...
...NOW THAT SHE'S NO LONGER WITH TIM!
SAME FOR TIM!
I KNOW HE WANTS TO FIND A NEW GIRL-FRIEND!
IT'S GOING TO BE A KILLER PARTY!
THAT EVENING...
THIS IS A DUD!
LOOOVE I LOVE LOOOVE
EXCEPT FOR US, TIM AND JULIE HAVE BEEN THE ONLY SINGLE PEOPLE AT THIS PARTY ALL NIGHT!
YEAH! WHAT LUCK!

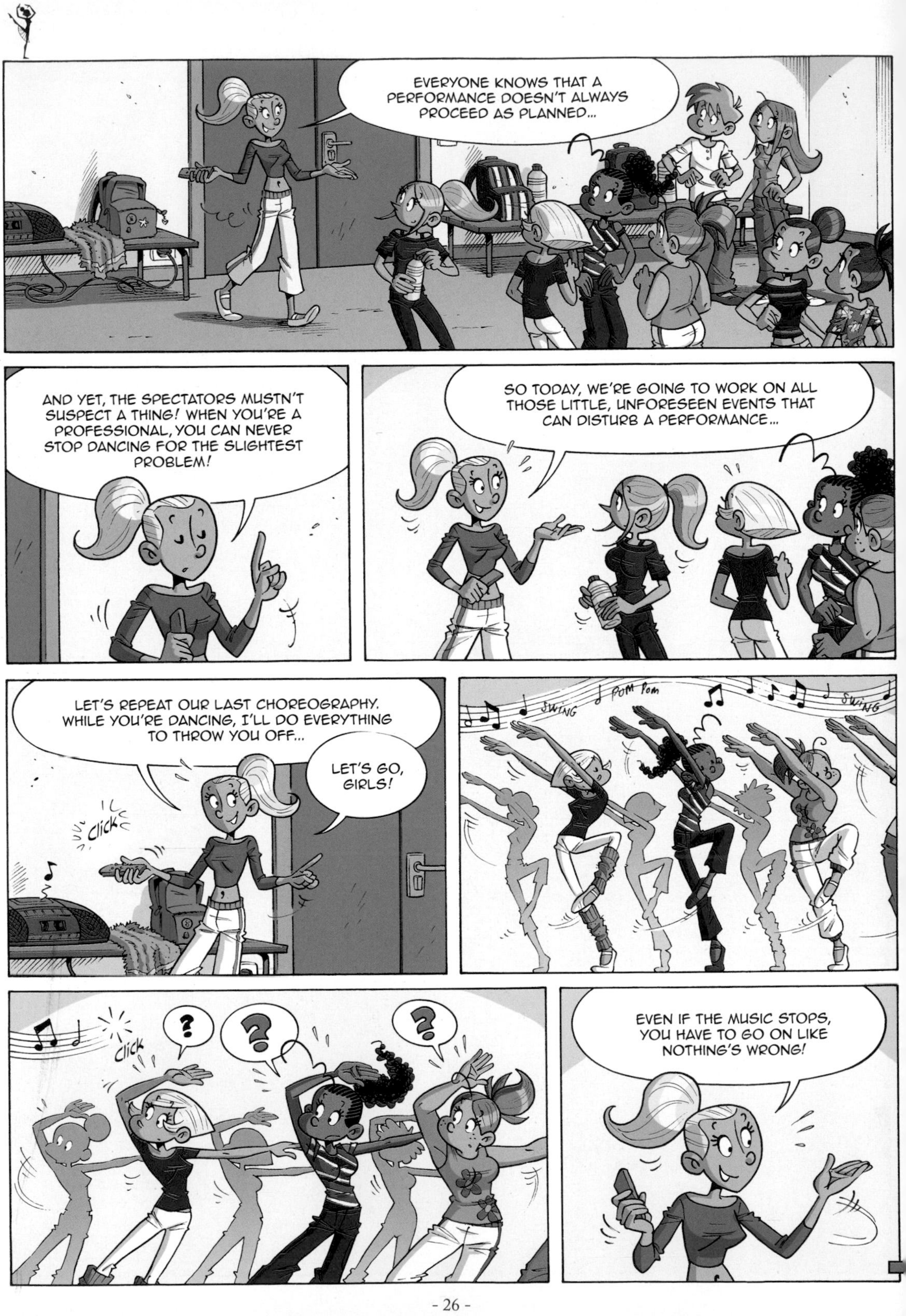
EVERYONE KNOWS THAT A PERFORMANCE DOESN'T ALWAYS PROCEED AS PLANNED...
AND YET, THE SPECTATORS MUSTN'T SUSPECT A THING! WHEN YOU'RE A PROFESSIONAL, YOU CAN NEVER STOP DANCING FOR THE SLIGHTEST PROBLEM!
SO TODAY, WE'RE GOING TO WORK ON ALL THOSE LITTLE, UNFORESEEN EVENTS THAT CAN DISTURB A PERFORMANCE...
LET'S REPEAT OUR LAST CHOREOGRAPHY. WHILE YOU'RE DANCING, I'LL DO EVERYTHING TO THROW YOU OFF...
LET'S GO, GIRLS!
CLICK
SWING
POM POM
SWING
CLICK
?
?
?
EVEN IF THE MUSIC STOPS, YOU HAVE TO GO ON LIKE NOTHING'S WRONG!

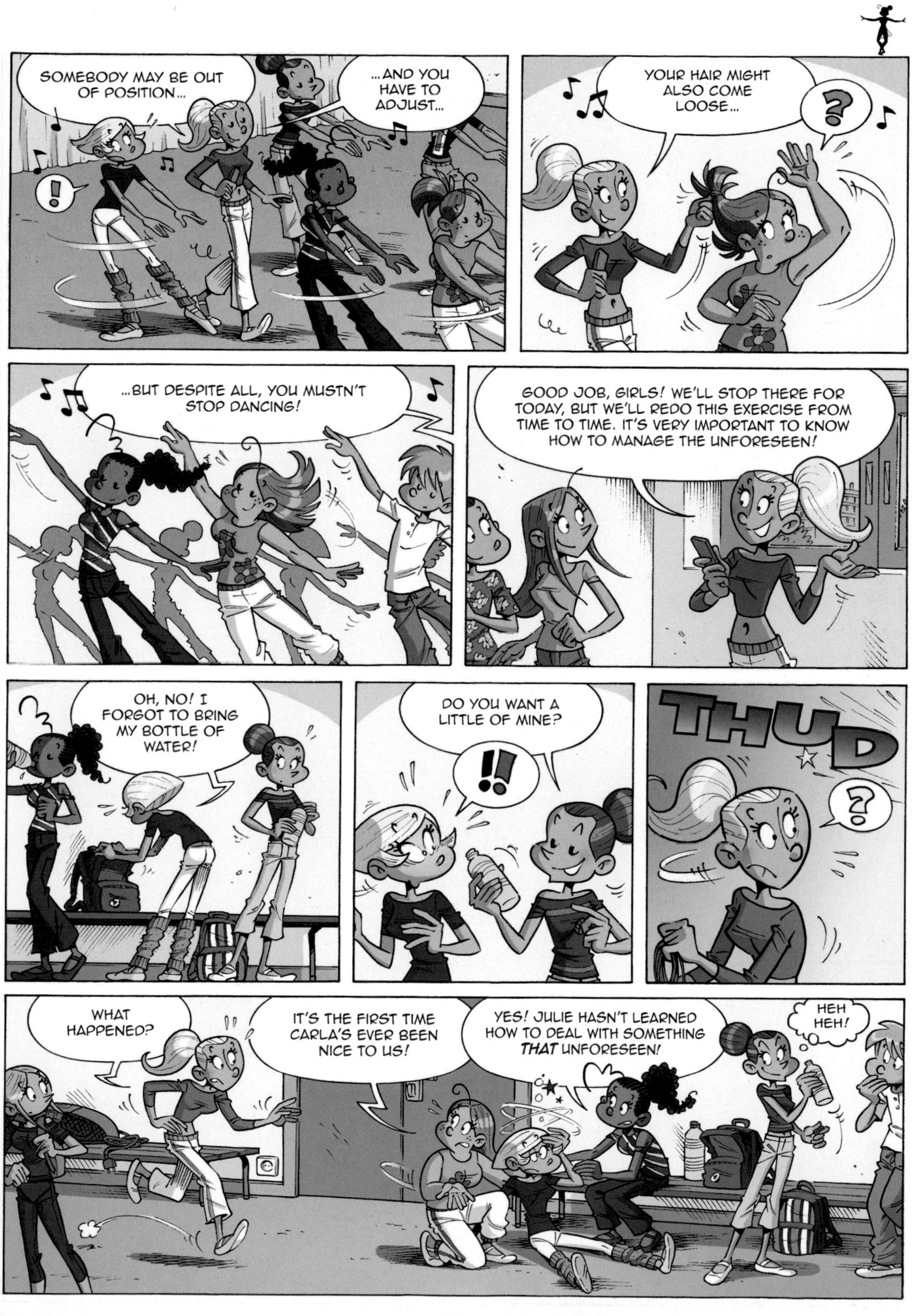
SOMEBODY MAY BE OUT OF POSITION...
!
...AND YOU HAVE TO ADJUST...
YOUR HAIR MIGHT ALSO COME LOOSE...
?
...BUT DESPITE ALL, YOU MUSTN'T STOP DANCING!
GOOD JOB, GIRLS! WE'LL STOP THERE FOR TODAY, BUT WE'LL REDO THIS EXERCISE FROM TIME TO TIME. IT'S VERY IMPORTANT TO KNOW HOW TO MANAGE THE UNFORESEEN!
OH, NO! I FORGOT TO BRING MY BOTTLE OF WATER!
DO YOU WANT A LITTLE OF MINE?
!!
THUD
?
WHAT HAPPENED?
IT'S THE FIRST TIME CARLA'S EVER BEEN NICE TO US!
YES! JULIE HASN'T LEARNED HOW TO DEAL WITH SOMETHING *THAT* UNFORESEEN!
HEH HEH!

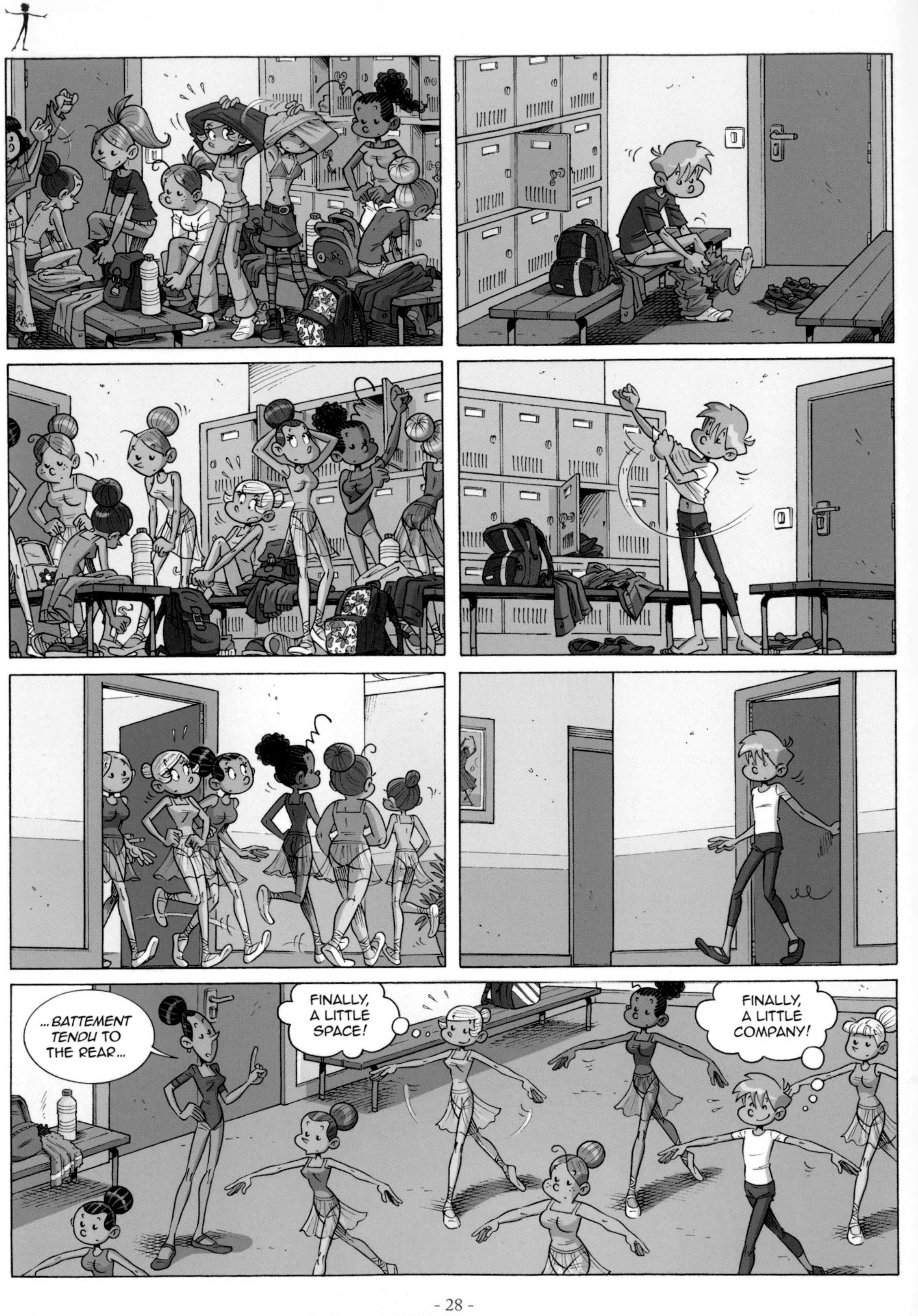
...BATTEMENT TENDU TO THE REAR...
FINALLY, A LITTLE SPACE!
FINALLY, A LITTLE COMPANY!

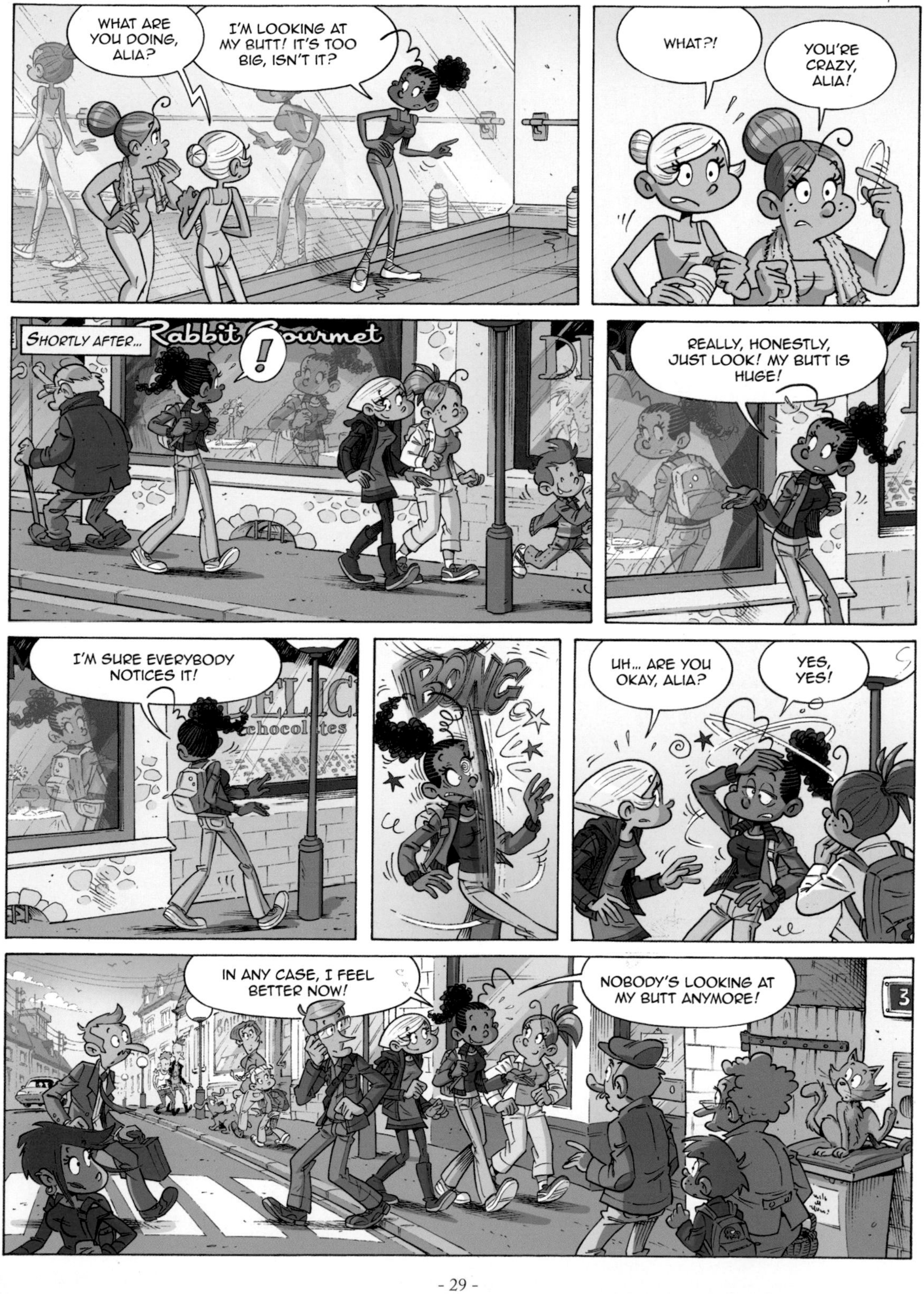
WHAT ARE YOU DOING, ALIA?
I'M LOOKING AT MY BUTT! IT'S TOO BIG, ISN'T IT?
WHAT?!
YOU'RE CRAZY, ALIA!
Rabbit Gourmet
SHORTLY AFTER...
!
REALLY, HONESTLY, JUST LOOK! MY BUTT IS HUGE!
I'M SURE EVERYBODY NOTICES IT!
chocolates
BONG
UH... ARE YOU OKAY, ALIA?
YES, YES!
IN ANY CASE, I FEEL BETTER NOW!
NOBODY'S LOOKING AT MY BUTT ANYMORE!
3

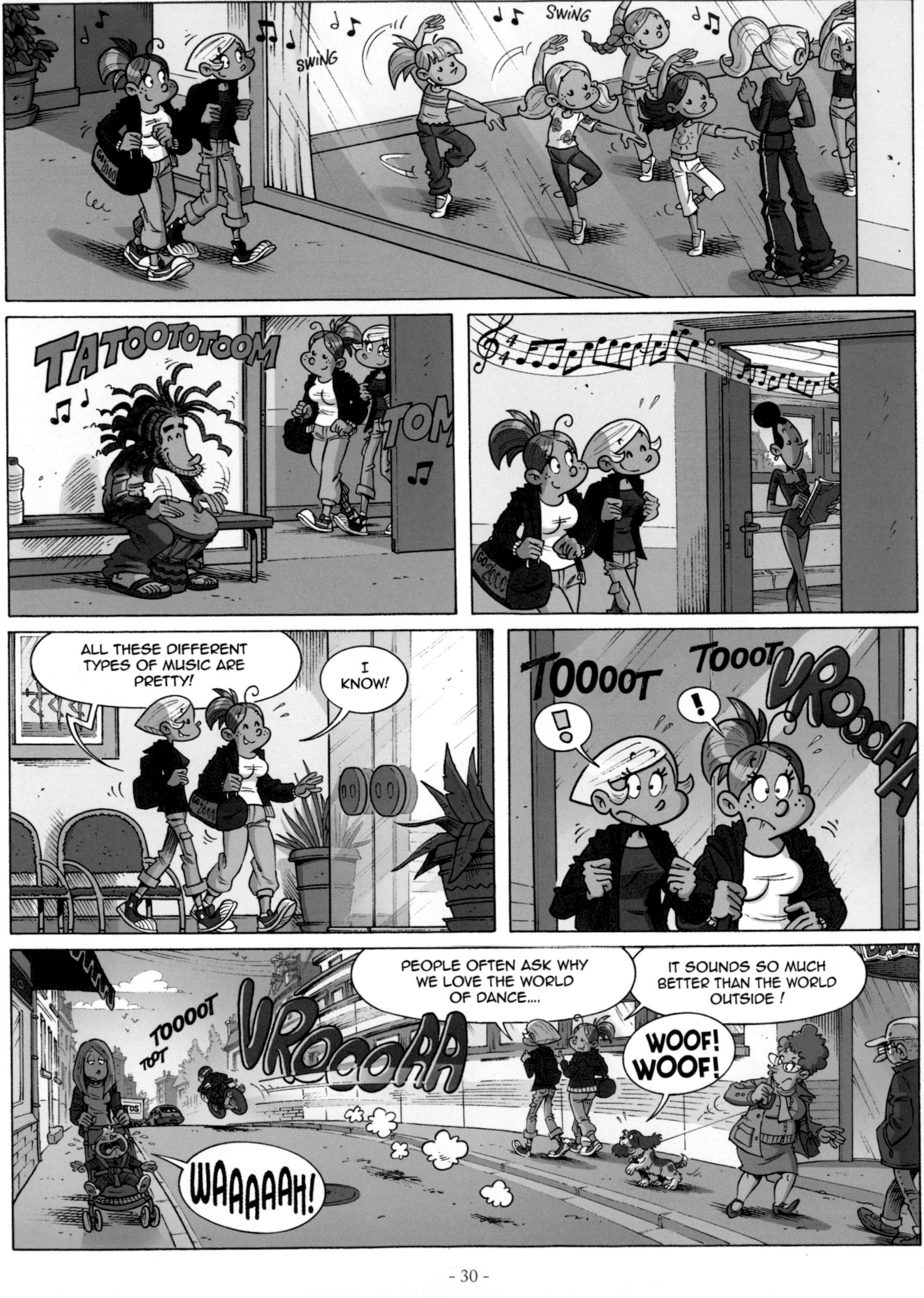
SWING
SWING
TATOOTOTOOM
TOM
ALL THESE DIFFERENT TYPES OF MUSIC ARE PRETTY!
I KNOW!
TOOOOT
TOOOT
VROOOAA
!
!
TOOOOT
TOOT
VROOOAA
PEOPLE OFTEN ASK WHY WE LOVE THE WORLD OF DANCE....
IT SOUNDS SO MUCH BETTER THAN THE WORLD OUTSIDE !
WOOF! WOOF!
WAAAAAH!

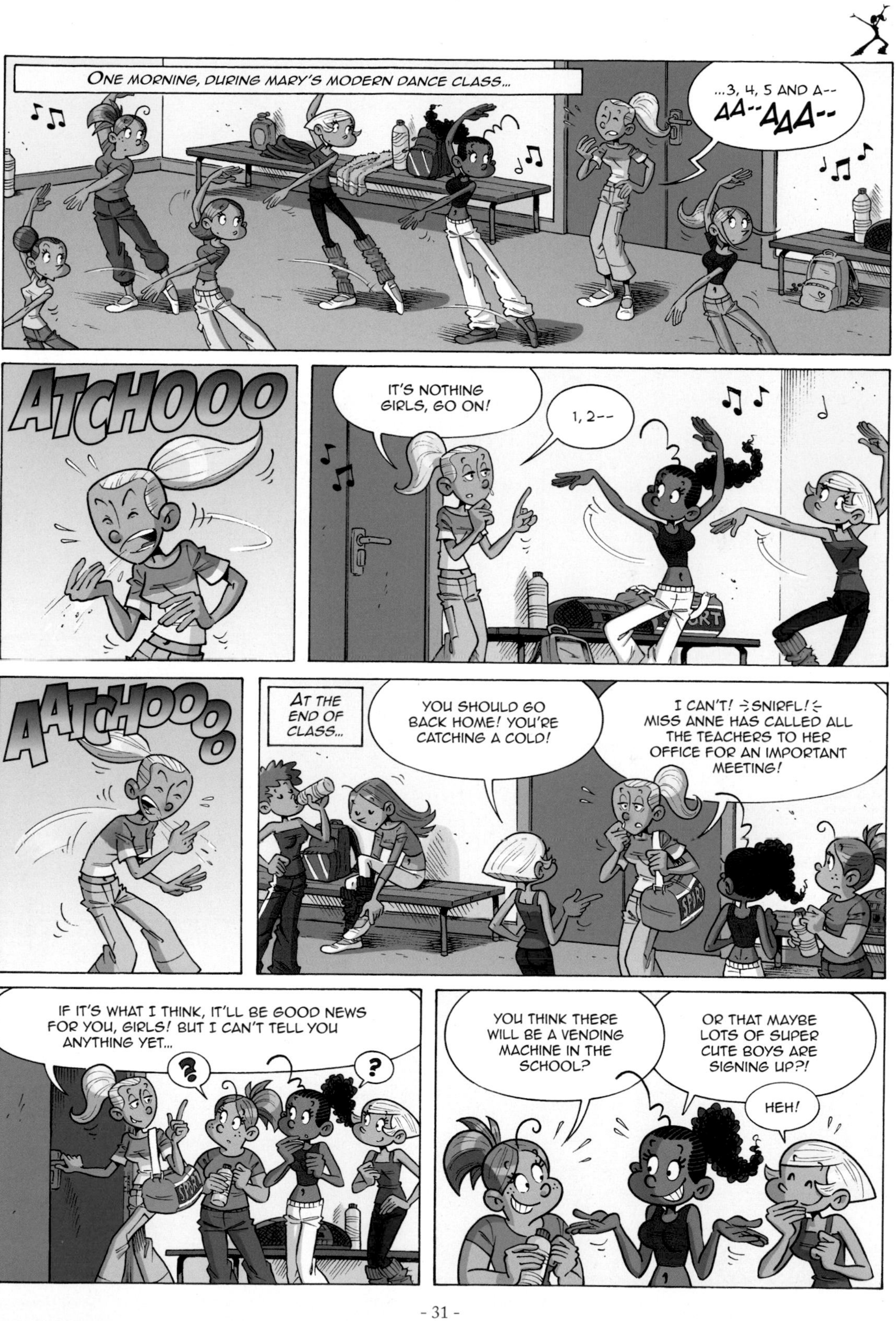
ONE MORNING, DURING MARY'S MODERN DANCE CLASS...
...3, 4, 5 AND A-- AA--AAA--
ATCHOOO
IT'S NOTHING GIRLS, GO ON!
1, 2--
AATCHOOOO
AT THE END OF CLASS...
YOU SHOULD GO BACK HOME! YOU'RE CATCHING A COLD!
I CAN'T! SNIRFL! MISS ANNE HAS CALLED ALL THE TEACHERS TO HER OFFICE FOR AN IMPORTANT MEETING!
IF IT'S WHAT I THINK, IT'LL BE GOOD NEWS FOR YOU, GIRLS! BUT I CAN'T TELL YOU ANYTHING YET...
?
?
YOU THINK THERE WILL BE A VENDING MACHINE IN THE SCHOOL?
OR THAT MAYBE LOTS OF SUPER CUTE BOYS ARE SIGNING UP?!
HEH!

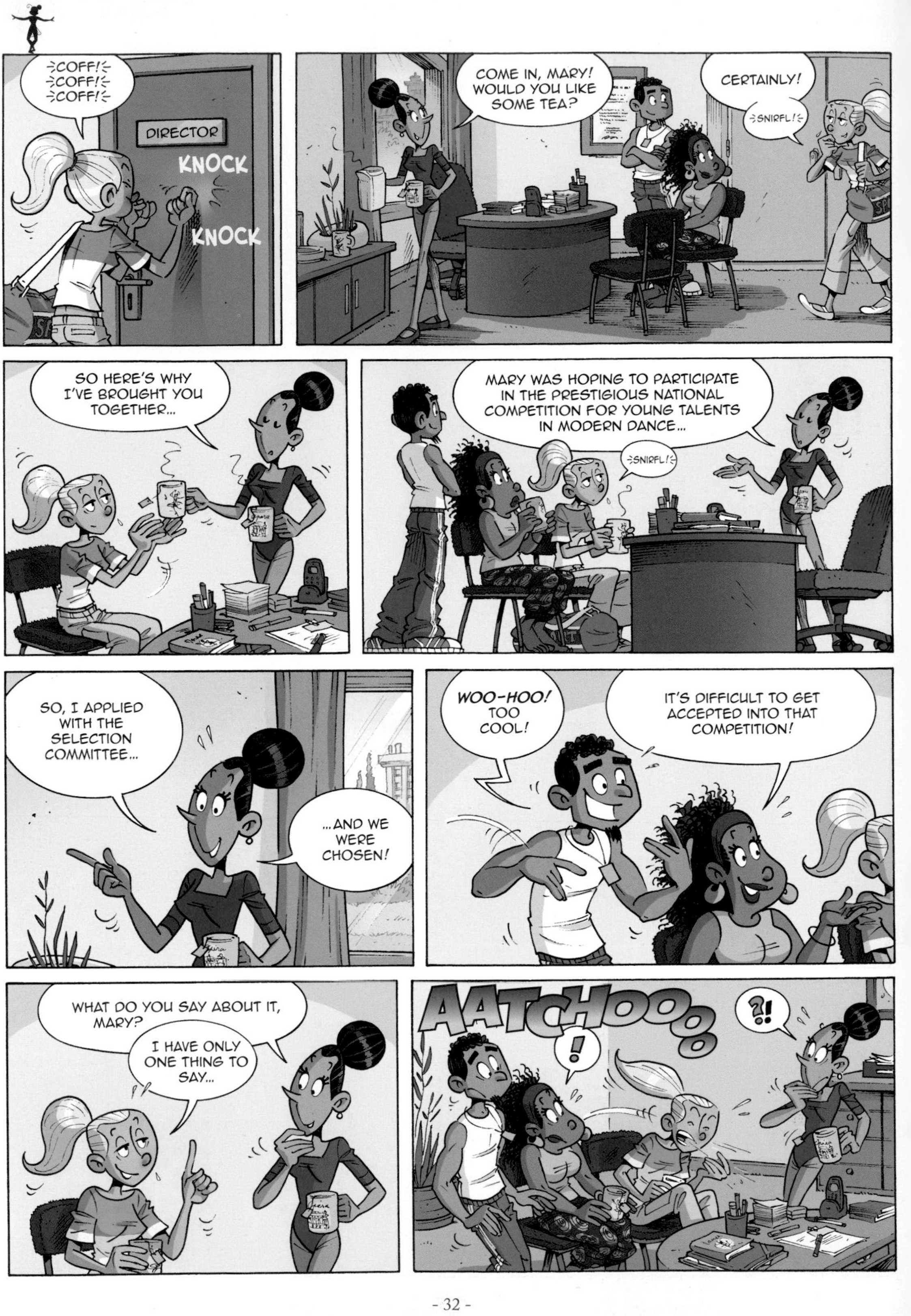

≈COFF!≈ ≈COFF!≈ ≈COFF!≈
DIRECTOR
KNOCK
KNOCK
COME IN, MARY! WOULD YOU LIKE SOME TEA?
CERTAINLY!
≈SNIRFL!≈
SO HERE'S WHY I'VE BROUGHT YOU TOGETHER...
MARY WAS HOPING TO PARTICIPATE IN THE PRESTIGIOUS NATIONAL COMPETITION FOR YOUNG TALENTS IN MODERN DANCE...
≈SNIRFL!≈
SO, I APPLIED WITH THE SELECTION COMMITTEE...
...AND WE WERE CHOSEN!
WOO-HOO! TOO COOL!
IT'S DIFFICULT TO GET ACCEPTED INTO THAT COMPETITION!
WHAT DO YOU SAY ABOUT IT, MARY?
I HAVE ONLY ONE THING TO SAY...
AATCHOOOO
!
?!

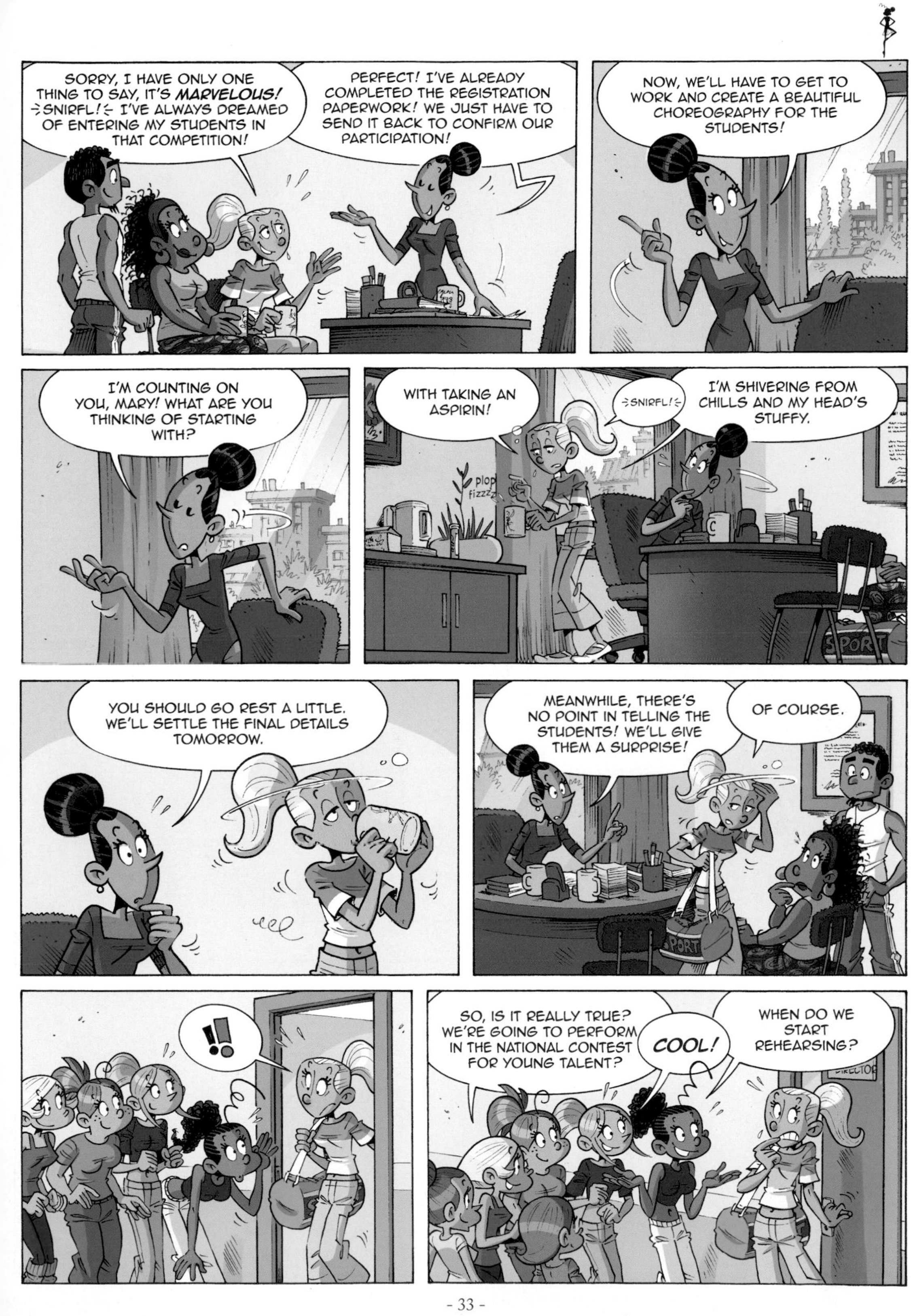
SORRY, I HAVE ONLY ONE THING TO SAY, IT'S *MARVELOUS!* SNIRFL! I'VE ALWAYS DREAMED OF ENTERING MY STUDENTS IN THAT COMPETITION!
PERFECT! I'VE ALREADY COMPLETED THE REGISTRATION PAPERWORK! WE JUST HAVE TO SEND IT BACK TO CONFIRM OUR PARTICIPATION!
NOW, WE'LL HAVE TO GET TO WORK AND CREATE A BEAUTIFUL CHOREOGRAPHY FOR THE STUDENTS!
I'M COUNTING ON YOU, MARY! WHAT ARE YOU THINKING OF STARTING WITH?
I'M SHIVERING FROM CHILLS AND MY HEAD'S STUFFY.
SNIRFL!
WITH TAKING AN ASPIRIN!
plop
fizzz
YOU SHOULD GO REST A LITTLE. WE'LL SETTLE THE FINAL DETAILS TOMORROW.
MEANWHILE, THERE'S NO POINT IN TELLING THE STUDENTS! WE'LL GIVE THEM A SURPRISE!
OF COURSE.
SPORT
!!
SO, IS IT REALLY TRUE? WE'RE GOING TO PERFORM IN THE NATIONAL CONTEST FOR YOUNG TALENT?
COOL!
WHEN DO WE START REHEARSING?

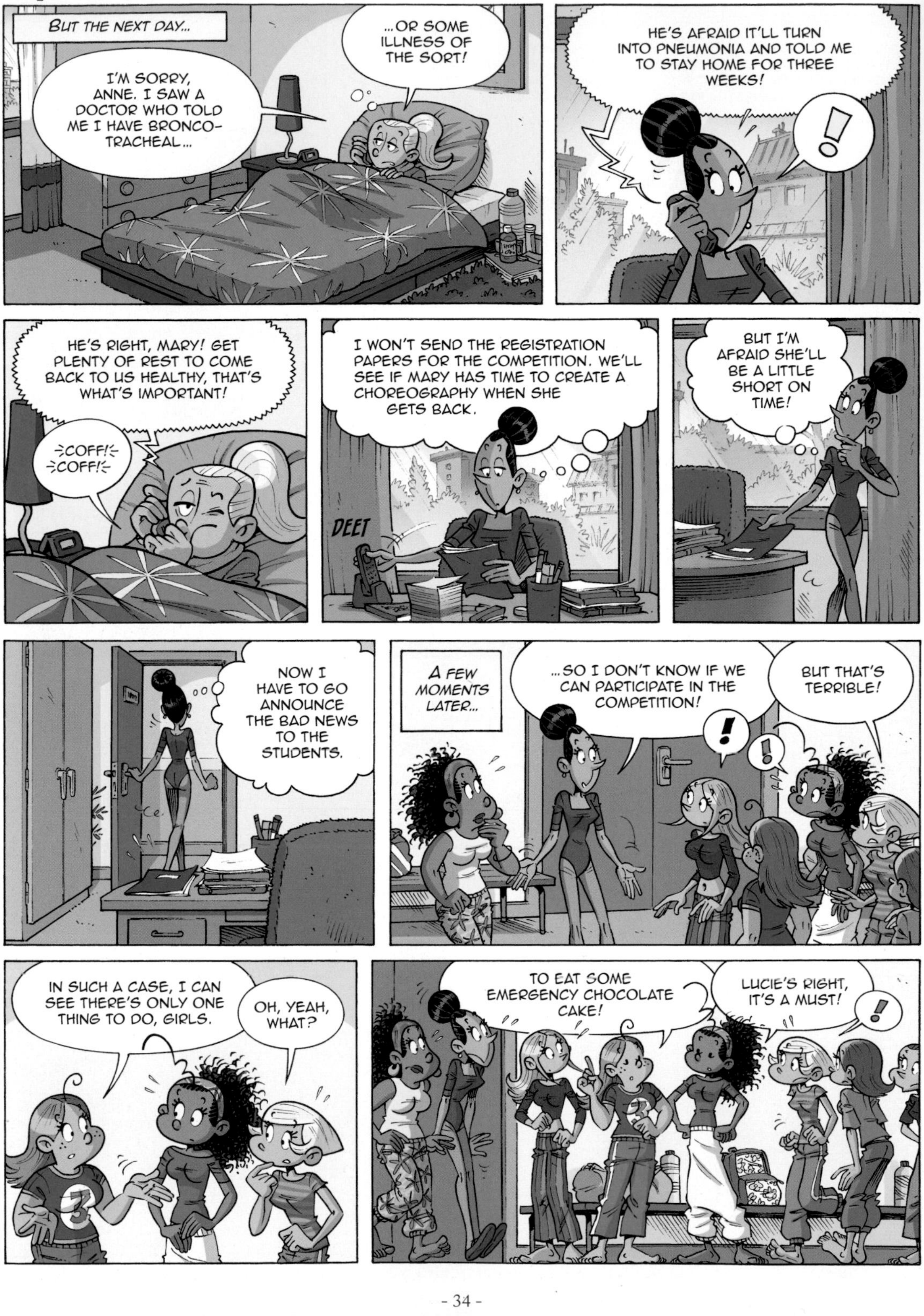
BUT THE NEXT DAY...
I'M SORRY, ANNE. I SAW A DOCTOR WHO TOLD ME I HAVE BRONCO-TRACHEAL...
...OR SOME ILLNESS OF THE SORT!
HE'S AFRAID IT'LL TURN INTO PNEUMONIA AND TOLD ME TO STAY HOME FOR THREE WEEKS!
!
HE'S RIGHT, MARY! GET PLENTY OF REST TO COME BACK TO US HEALTHY, THAT'S WHAT'S IMPORTANT!
COFF! COFF!
I WON'T SEND THE REGISTRATION PAPERS FOR THE COMPETITION. WE'LL SEE IF MARY HAS TIME TO CREATE A CHOREOGRAPHY WHEN SHE GETS BACK.
DEET
BUT I'M AFRAID SHE'LL BE A LITTLE SHORT ON TIME!
NOW I HAVE TO GO ANNOUNCE THE BAD NEWS TO THE STUDENTS.
A FEW MOMENTS LATER...
...SO I DON'T KNOW IF WE CAN PARTICIPATE IN THE COMPETITION!
!
!
BUT THAT'S TERRIBLE!
IN SUCH A CASE, I CAN SEE THERE'S ONLY ONE THING TO DO, GIRLS.
OH, YEAH, WHAT?
TO EAT SOME EMERGENCY CHOCOLATE CAKE!
LUCIE'S RIGHT, IT'S A MUST!
!

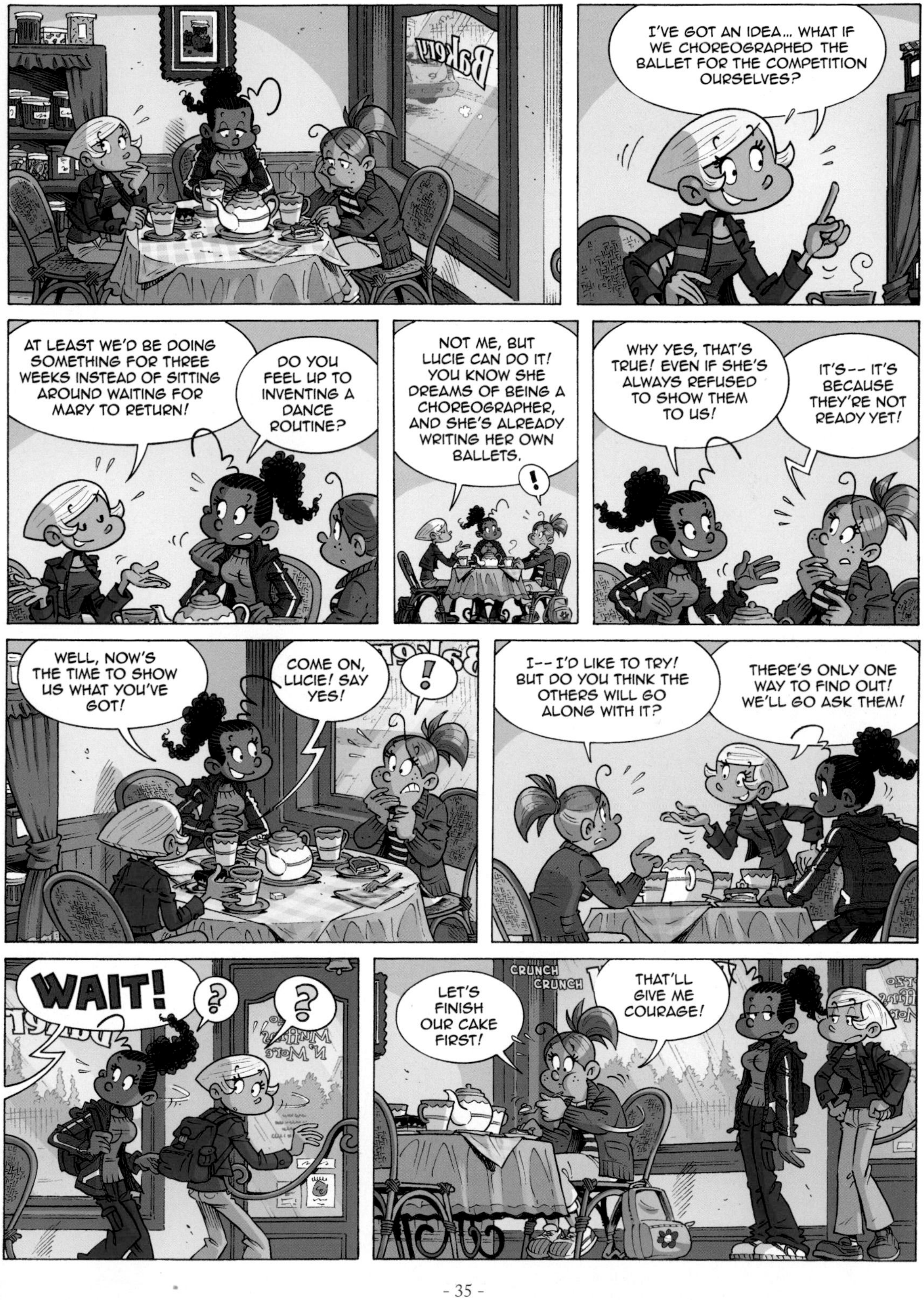

I'VE GOT AN IDEA... WHAT IF WE CHOREOGRAPHED THE BALLET FOR THE COMPETITION OURSELVES?
AT LEAST WE'D BE DOING SOMETHING FOR THREE WEEKS INSTEAD OF SITTING AROUND WAITING FOR MARY TO RETURN!
DO YOU FEEL UP TO INVENTING A DANCE ROUTINE?
NOT ME, BUT LUCIE CAN DO IT! YOU KNOW SHE DREAMS OF BEING A CHOREOGRAPHER, AND SHE'S ALREADY WRITING HER OWN BALLETS.
!
WHY YES, THAT'S TRUE! EVEN IF SHE'S ALWAYS REFUSED TO SHOW THEM TO US!
IT'S-- IT'S BECAUSE THEY'RE NOT READY YET!
WELL, NOW'S THE TIME TO SHOW US WHAT YOU'VE GOT!
COME ON, LUCIE! SAY YES!
!
I-- I'D LIKE TO TRY! BUT DO YOU THINK THE OTHERS WILL GO ALONG WITH IT?
THERE'S ONLY ONE WAY TO FIND OUT! WE'LL GO ASK THEM!
WAIT!
?
?
CRUNCH CRUNCH
LET'S FINISH OUR CAKE FIRST!
THAT'LL GIVE ME COURAGE!

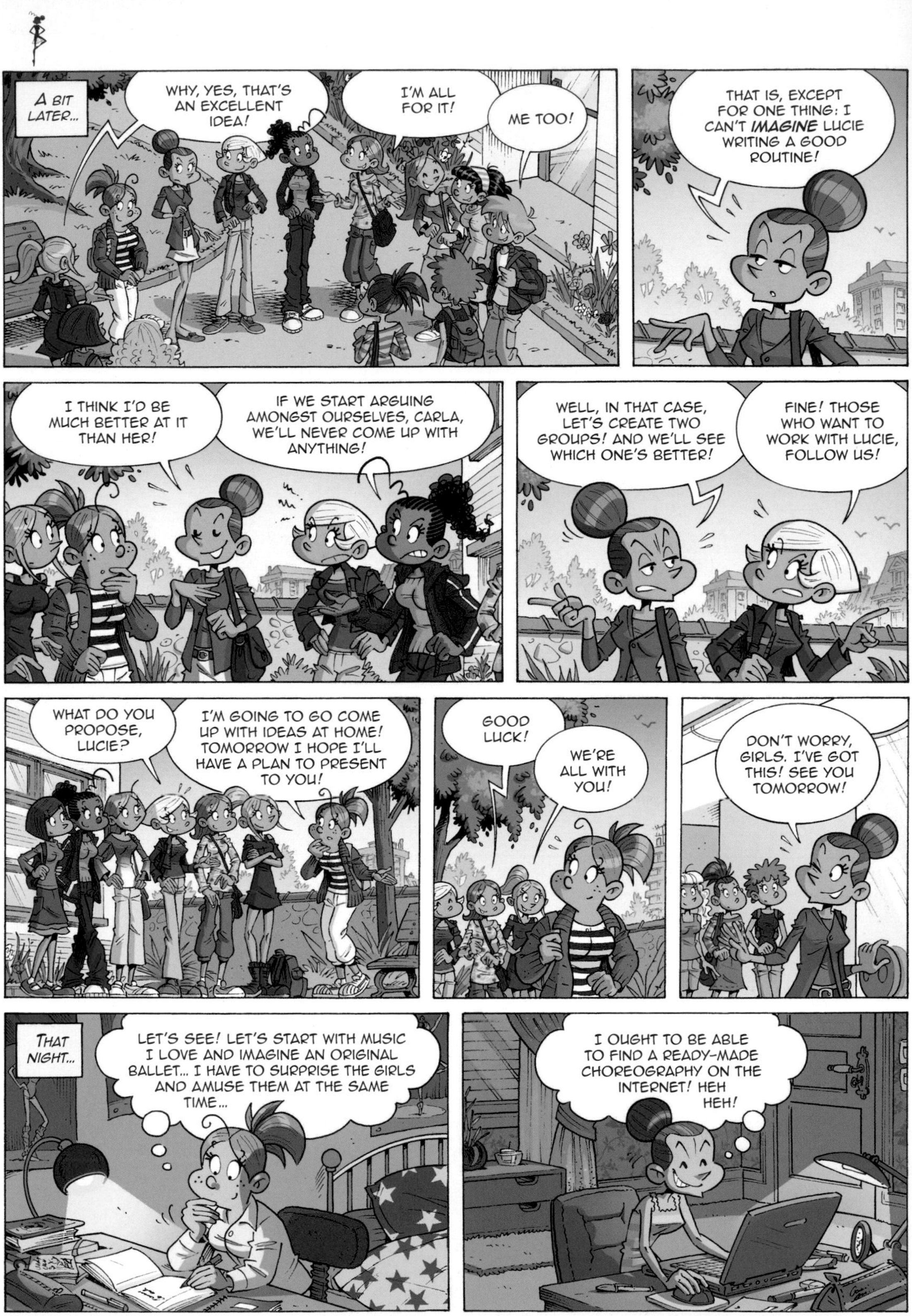
A BIT LATER...
WHY, YES, THAT'S AN EXCELLENT IDEA!
I'M ALL FOR IT!
ME TOO!
THAT IS, EXCEPT FOR ONE THING: I CAN'T *IMAGINE* LUCIE WRITING A GOOD ROUTINE!
I THINK I'D BE MUCH BETTER AT IT THAN HER!
IF WE START ARGUING AMONGST OURSELVES, CARLA, WE'LL NEVER COME UP WITH ANYTHING!
WELL, IN THAT CASE, LET'S CREATE TWO GROUPS! AND WE'LL SEE WHICH ONE'S BETTER!
FINE! THOSE WHO WANT TO WORK WITH LUCIE, FOLLOW US!
WHAT DO YOU PROPOSE, LUCIE?
I'M GOING TO GO COME UP WITH IDEAS AT HOME! TOMORROW I HOPE I'LL HAVE A PLAN TO PRESENT TO YOU!
GOOD LUCK!
WE'RE ALL WITH YOU!
DON'T WORRY, GIRLS. I'VE GOT THIS! SEE YOU TOMORROW!
THAT NIGHT...
LET'S SEE! LET'S START WITH MUSIC I LOVE AND IMAGINE AN ORIGINAL BALLET... I HAVE TO SURPRISE THE GIRLS AND AMUSE THEM AT THE SAME TIME...
I OUGHT TO BE ABLE TO FIND A READY-MADE CHOREOGRAPHY ON THE INTERNET! HEH HEH!

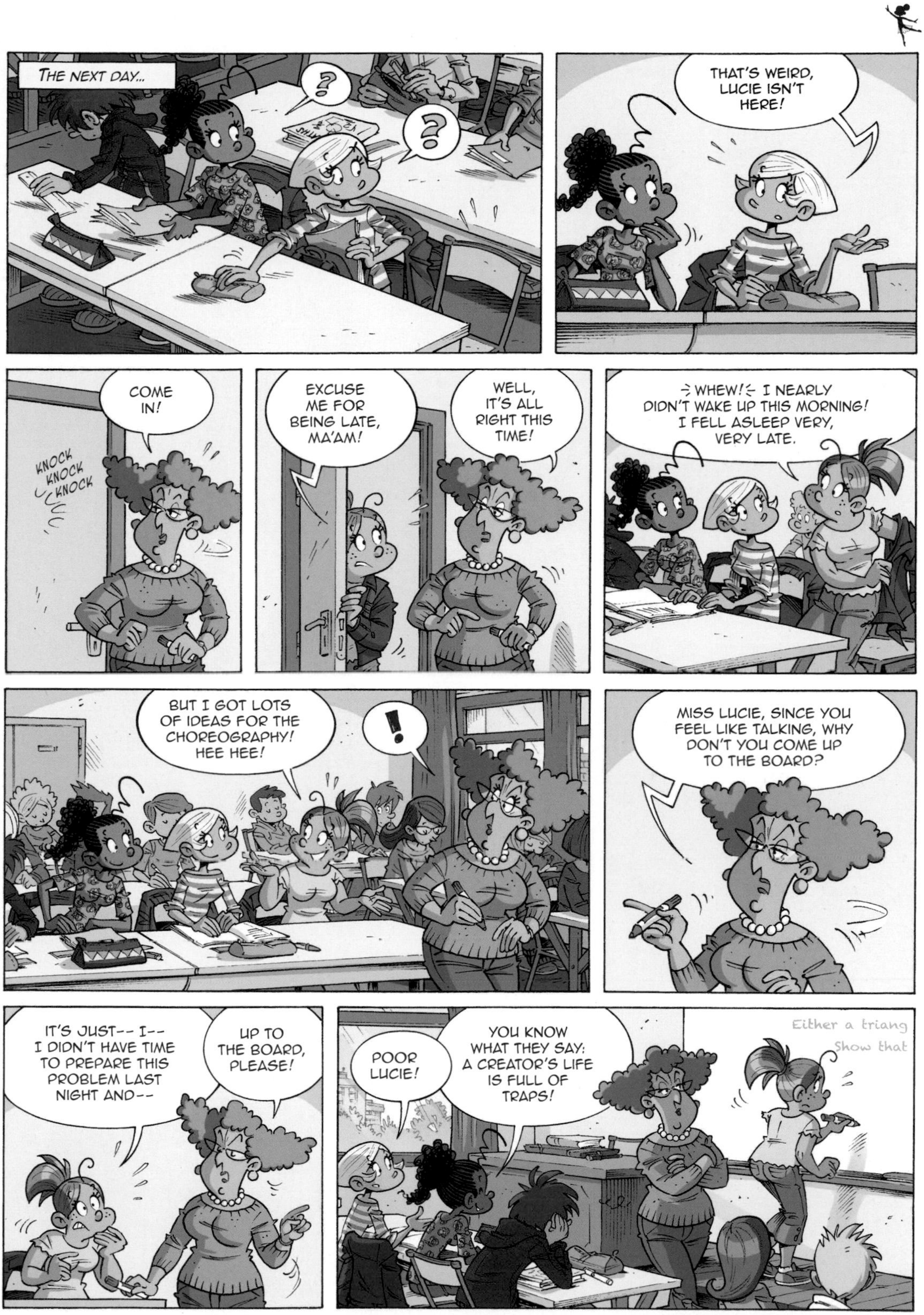
THE NEXT DAY...
?
?
THAT'S WEIRD, LUCIE ISN'T HERE!
KNOCK KNOCK KNOCK
COME IN!
EXCUSE ME FOR BEING LATE, MA'AM!
WELL, IT'S ALL RIGHT THIS TIME!
WHEW! I NEARLY DIDN'T WAKE UP THIS MORNING! I FELL ASLEEP VERY, VERY LATE.
BUT I GOT LOTS OF IDEAS FOR THE CHOREOGRAPHY! HEE HEE!
!
MISS LUCIE, SINCE YOU FEEL LIKE TALKING, WHY DON'T YOU COME UP TO THE BOARD?
IT'S JUST-- I-- I DIDN'T HAVE TIME TO PREPARE THIS PROBLEM LAST NIGHT AND--
UP TO THE BOARD, PLEASE!
Either a triang
Show that
POOR LUCIE!
YOU KNOW WHAT THEY SAY: A CREATOR'S LIFE IS FULL OF TRAPS!

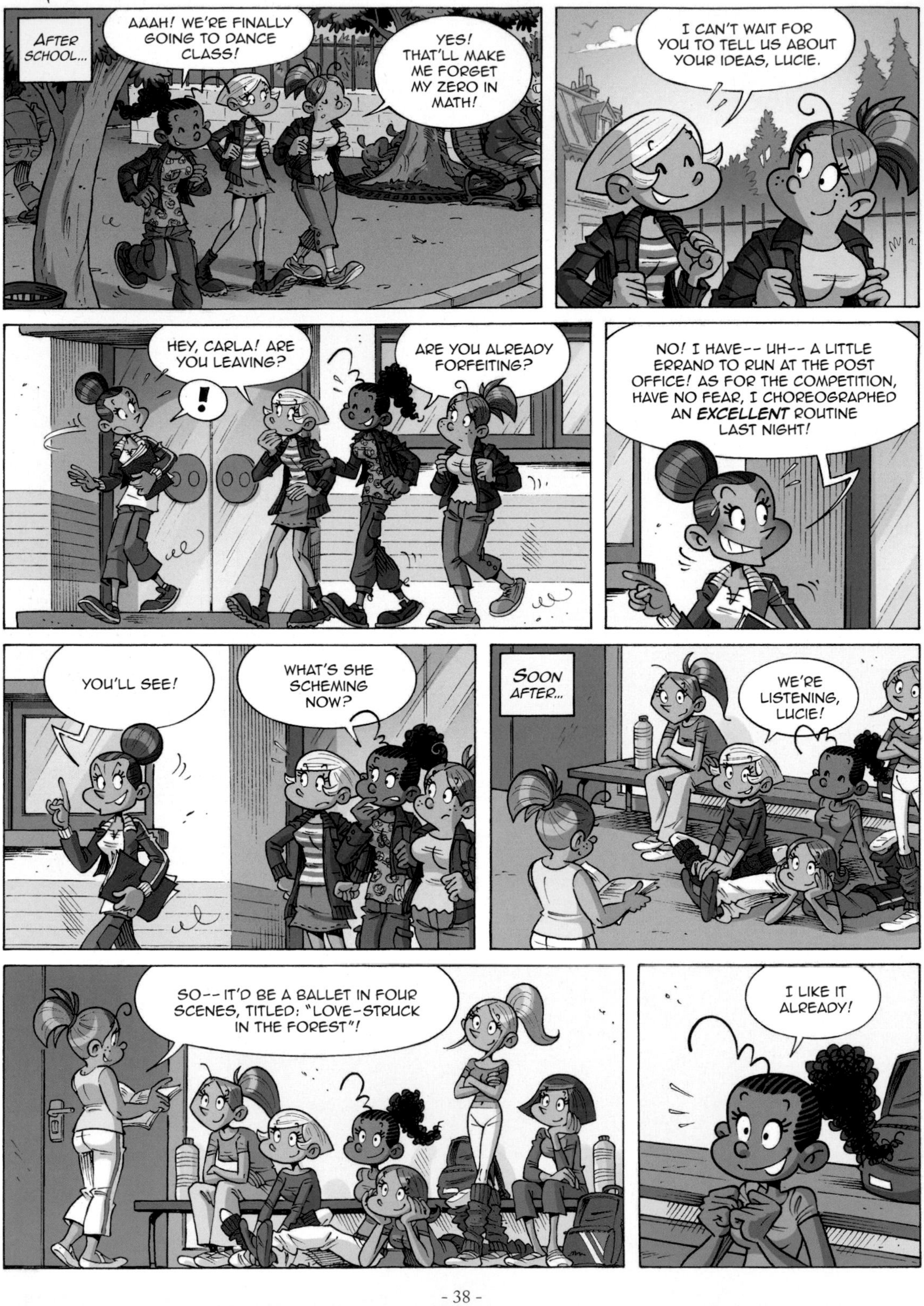
AFTER SCHOOL...
AAAH! WE'RE FINALLY GOING TO DANCE CLASS!
YES! THAT'LL MAKE ME FORGET MY ZERO IN MATH!
I CAN'T WAIT FOR YOU TO TELL US ABOUT YOUR IDEAS, LUCIE.
HEY, CARLA! ARE YOU LEAVING?
!
ARE YOU ALREADY FORFEITING?
NO! I HAVE-- UH-- A LITTLE ERRAND TO RUN AT THE POST OFFICE! AS FOR THE COMPETITION, HAVE NO FEAR, I CHOREOGRAPHED AN EXCELLENT ROUTINE LAST NIGHT!
YOU'LL SEE!
WHAT'S SHE SCHEMING NOW?
SOON AFTER...
WE'RE LISTENING, LUCIE!
SO-- IT'D BE A BALLET IN FOUR SCENES, TITLED: "LOVE-STRUCK IN THE FOREST"!
I LIKE IT ALREADY!

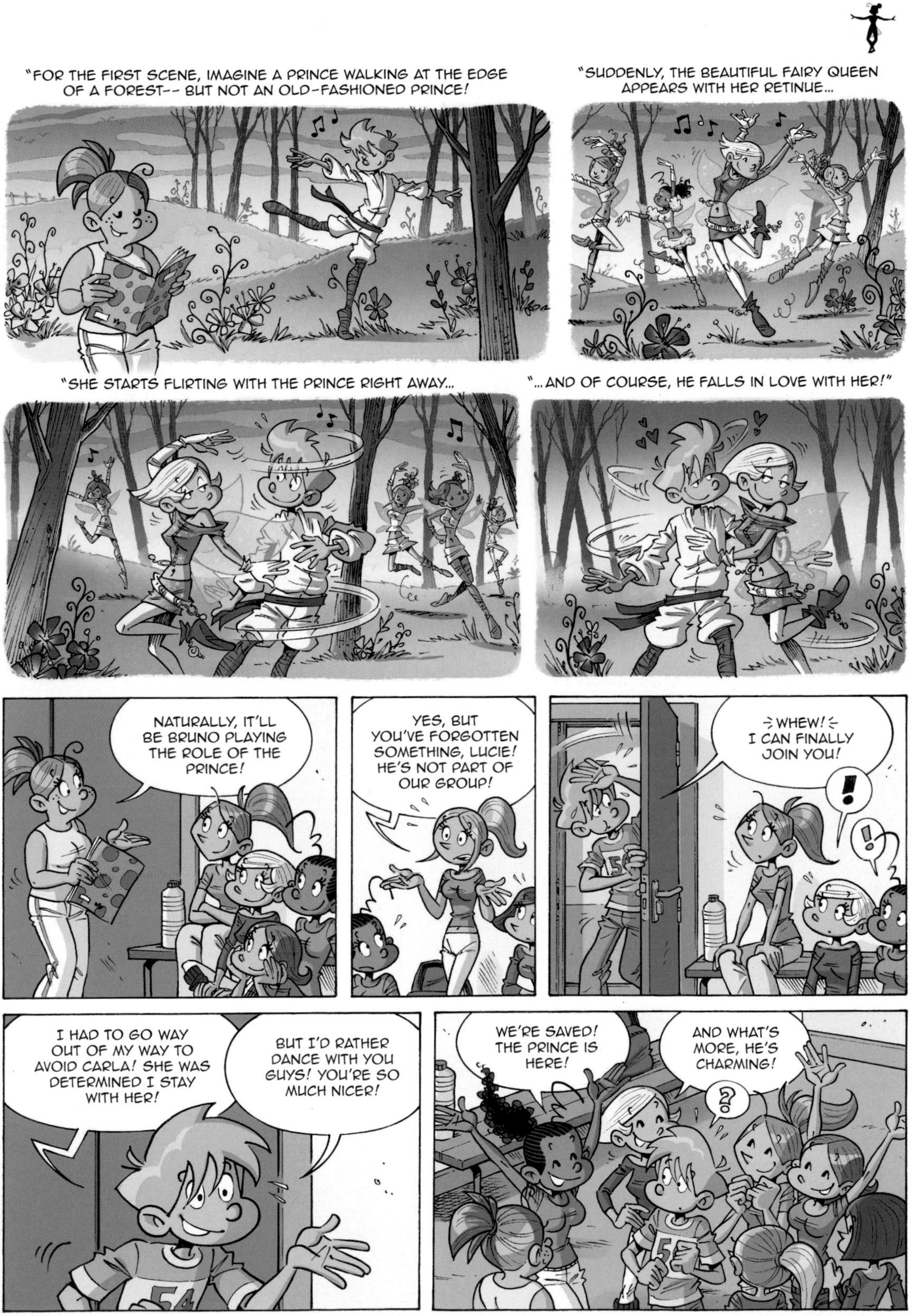

"FOR THE FIRST SCENE, IMAGINE A PRINCE WALKING AT THE EDGE OF A FOREST-- BUT NOT AN OLD-FASHIONED PRINCE!
"SUDDENLY, THE BEAUTIFUL FAIRY QUEEN APPEARS WITH HER RETINUE...
"SHE STARTS FLIRTING WITH THE PRINCE RIGHT AWAY...
"...AND OF COURSE, HE FALLS IN LOVE WITH HER!"
NATURALLY, IT'LL BE BRUNO PLAYING THE ROLE OF THE PRINCE!
YES, BUT YOU'VE FORGOTTEN SOMETHING, LUCIE! HE'S NOT PART OF OUR GROUP!
WHEW! I CAN FINALLY JOIN YOU!
!
!
I HAD TO GO WAY OUT OF MY WAY TO AVOID CARLA! SHE WAS DETERMINED I STAY WITH HER!
BUT I'D RATHER DANCE WITH YOU GUYS! YOU'RE SO MUCH NICER!
WE'RE SAVED! THE PRINCE IS HERE!
AND WHAT'S MORE, HE'S CHARMING!
?

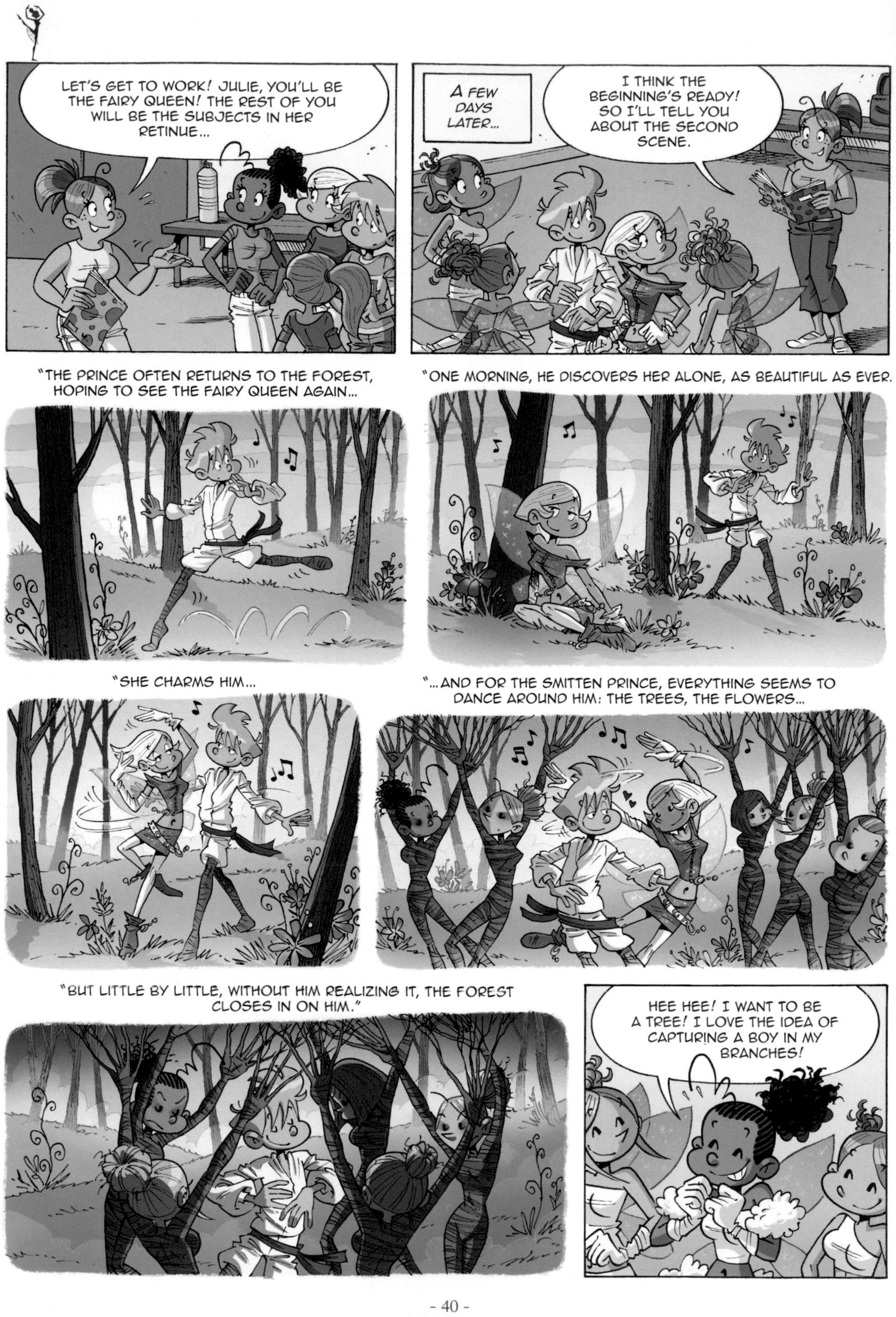
LET'S GET TO WORK! JULIE, YOU'LL BE THE FAIRY QUEEN! THE REST OF YOU WILL BE THE SUBJECTS IN HER RETINUE...
A FEW DAYS LATER...
I THINK THE BEGINNING'S READY! SO I'LL TELL YOU ABOUT THE SECOND SCENE.
"THE PRINCE OFTEN RETURNS TO THE FOREST, HOPING TO SEE THE FAIRY QUEEN AGAIN...
"ONE MORNING, HE DISCOVERS HER ALONE, AS BEAUTIFUL AS EVER.
"SHE CHARMS HIM...
"...AND FOR THE SMITTEN PRINCE, EVERYTHING SEEMS TO DANCE AROUND HIM: THE TREES, THE FLOWERS...
"BUT LITTLE BY LITTLE, WITHOUT HIM REALIZING IT, THE FOREST CLOSES IN ON HIM."
HEE HEE! I WANT TO BE A TREE! I LOVE THE IDEA OF CAPTURING A BOY IN MY BRANCHES!

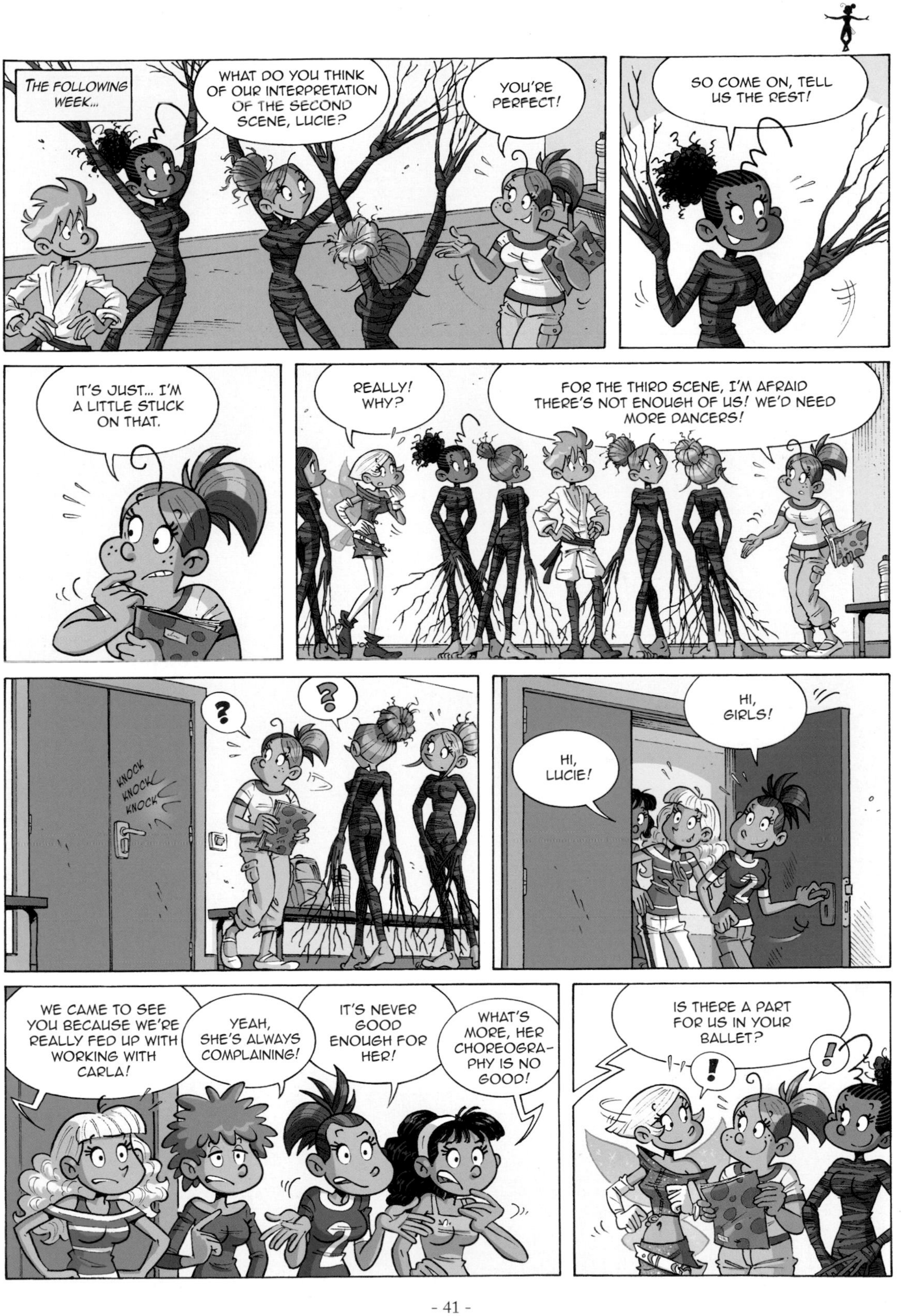
THE FOLLOWING WEEK...
WHAT DO YOU THINK OF OUR INTERPRETATION OF THE SECOND SCENE, LUCIE?
YOU'RE PERFECT!
SO COME ON, TELL US THE REST!
IT'S JUST... I'M A LITTLE STUCK ON THAT.
REALLY! WHY?
FOR THE THIRD SCENE, I'M AFRAID THERE'S NOT ENOUGH OF US! WE'D NEED MORE DANCERS!
?
?
KNOCK KNOCK KNOCK
HI, GIRLS!
HI, LUCIE!
WE CAME TO SEE YOU BECAUSE WE'RE REALLY FED UP WITH WORKING WITH CARLA!
YEAH, SHE'S ALWAYS COMPLAINING!
IT'S NEVER GOOD ENOUGH FOR HER!
WHAT'S MORE, HER CHOREOGRA-PHY IS NO GOOD!
IS THERE A PART FOR US IN YOUR BALLET?
!
!

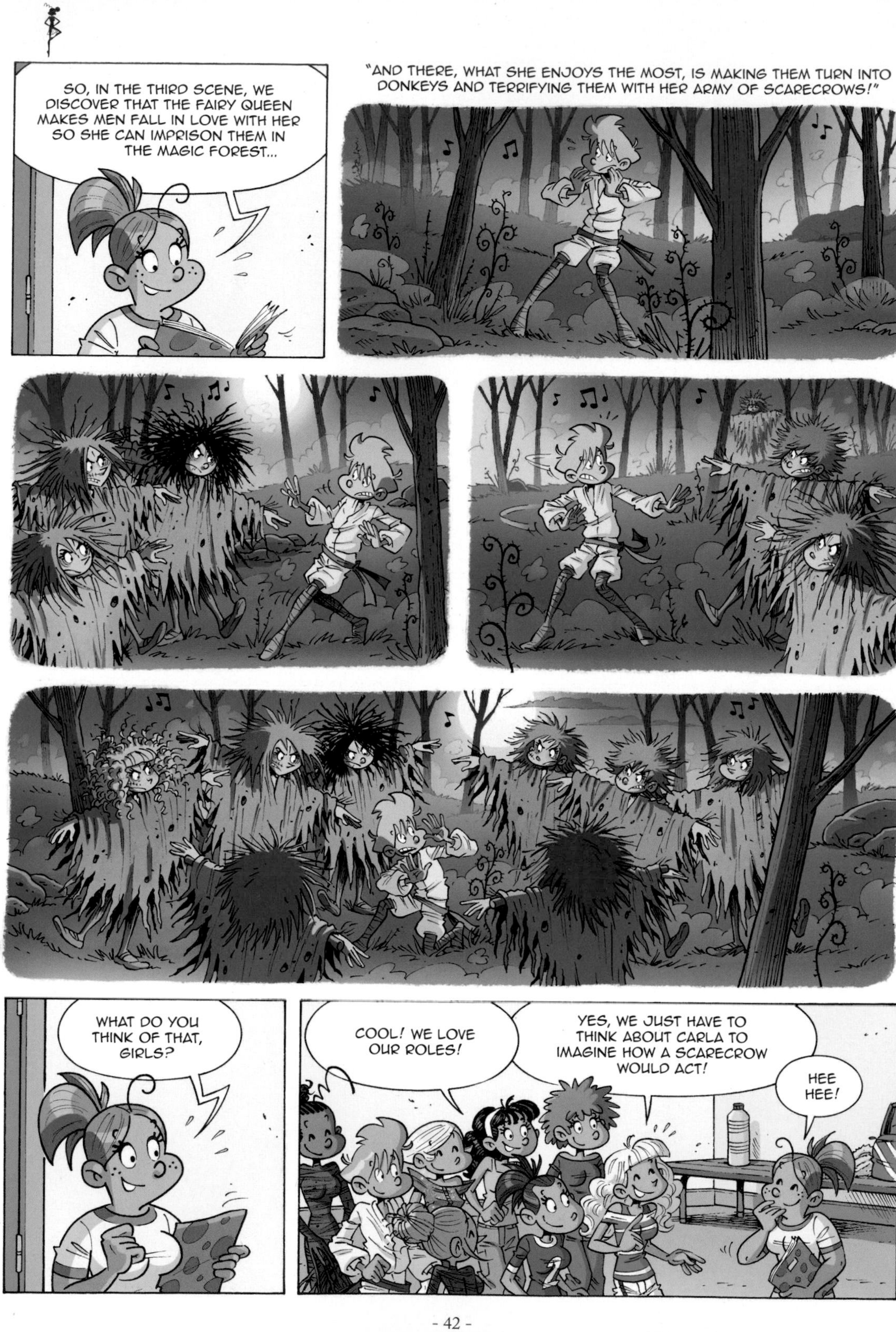
SO, IN THE THIRD SCENE, WE DISCOVER THAT THE FAIRY QUEEN MAKES MEN FALL IN LOVE WITH HER SO SHE CAN IMPRISON THEM IN THE MAGIC FOREST...
"AND THERE, WHAT SHE ENJOYS THE MOST, IS MAKING THEM TURN INTO DONKEYS AND TERRIFYING THEM WITH HER ARMY OF SCARECROWS!"
WHAT DO YOU THINK OF THAT, GIRLS?
COOL! WE LOVE OUR ROLES!
YES, WE JUST HAVE TO THINK ABOUT CARLA TO IMAGINE HOW A SCARECROW WOULD ACT!
HEE HEE!

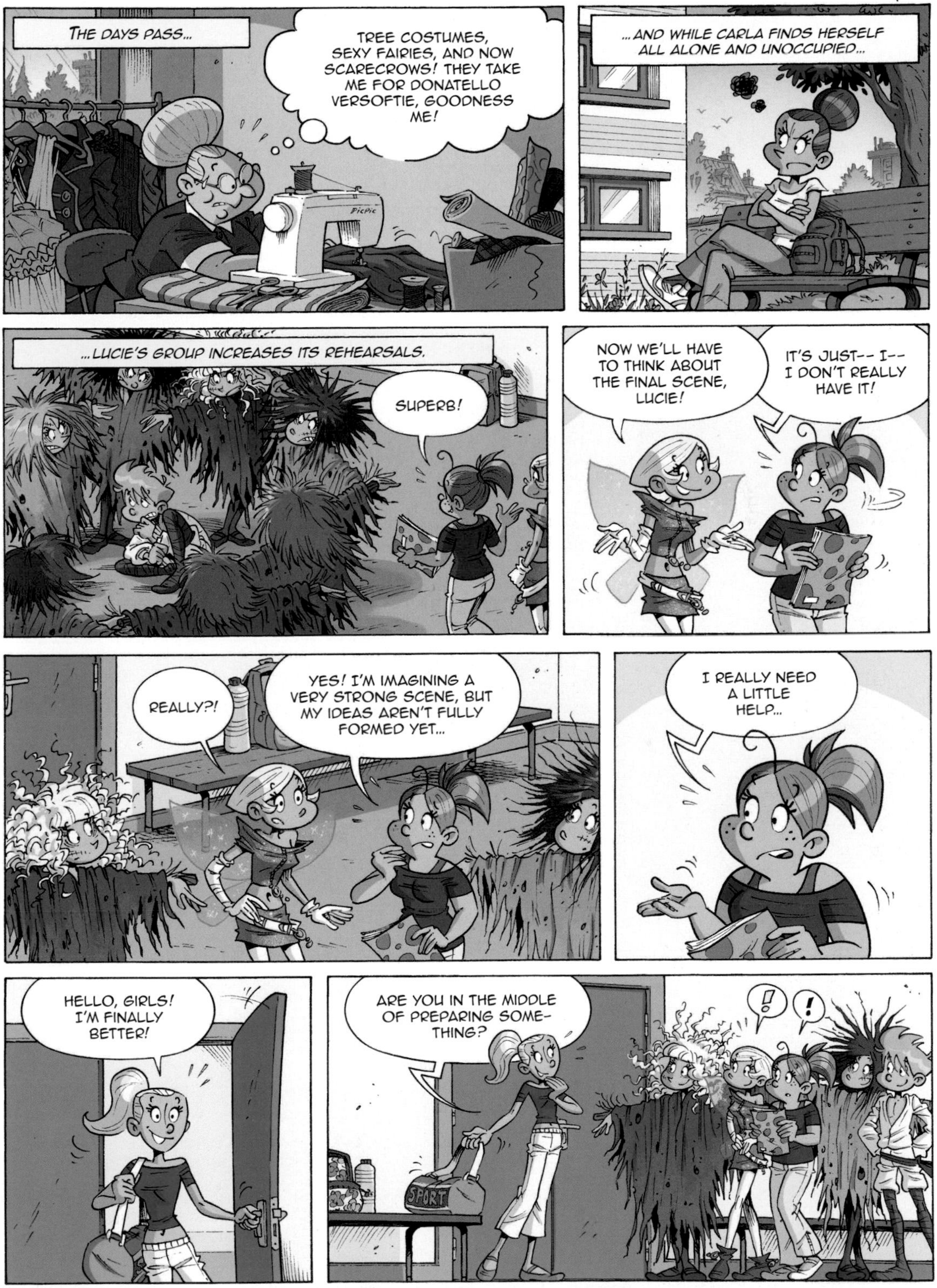
THE DAYS PASS...
TREE COSTUMES, SEXY FAIRIES, AND NOW SCARECROWS! THEY TAKE ME FOR DONATELLO VERSOFTIE, GOODNESS ME!
PicPic
...AND WHILE CARLA FINDS HERSELF ALL ALONE AND UNOCCUPIED...
...LUCIE'S GROUP INCREASES ITS REHEARSALS.
SUPERB!
NOW WE'LL HAVE TO THINK ABOUT THE FINAL SCENE, LUCIE!
IT'S JUST-- I-- I DON'T REALLY HAVE IT!
REALLY?!
YES! I'M IMAGINING A VERY STRONG SCENE, BUT MY IDEAS AREN'T FULLY FORMED YET...
I REALLY NEED A LITTLE HELP...
HELLO, GIRLS! I'M FINALLY BETTER!
ARE YOU IN THE MIDDLE OF PREPARING SOME-THING?
SPORT
!?
!

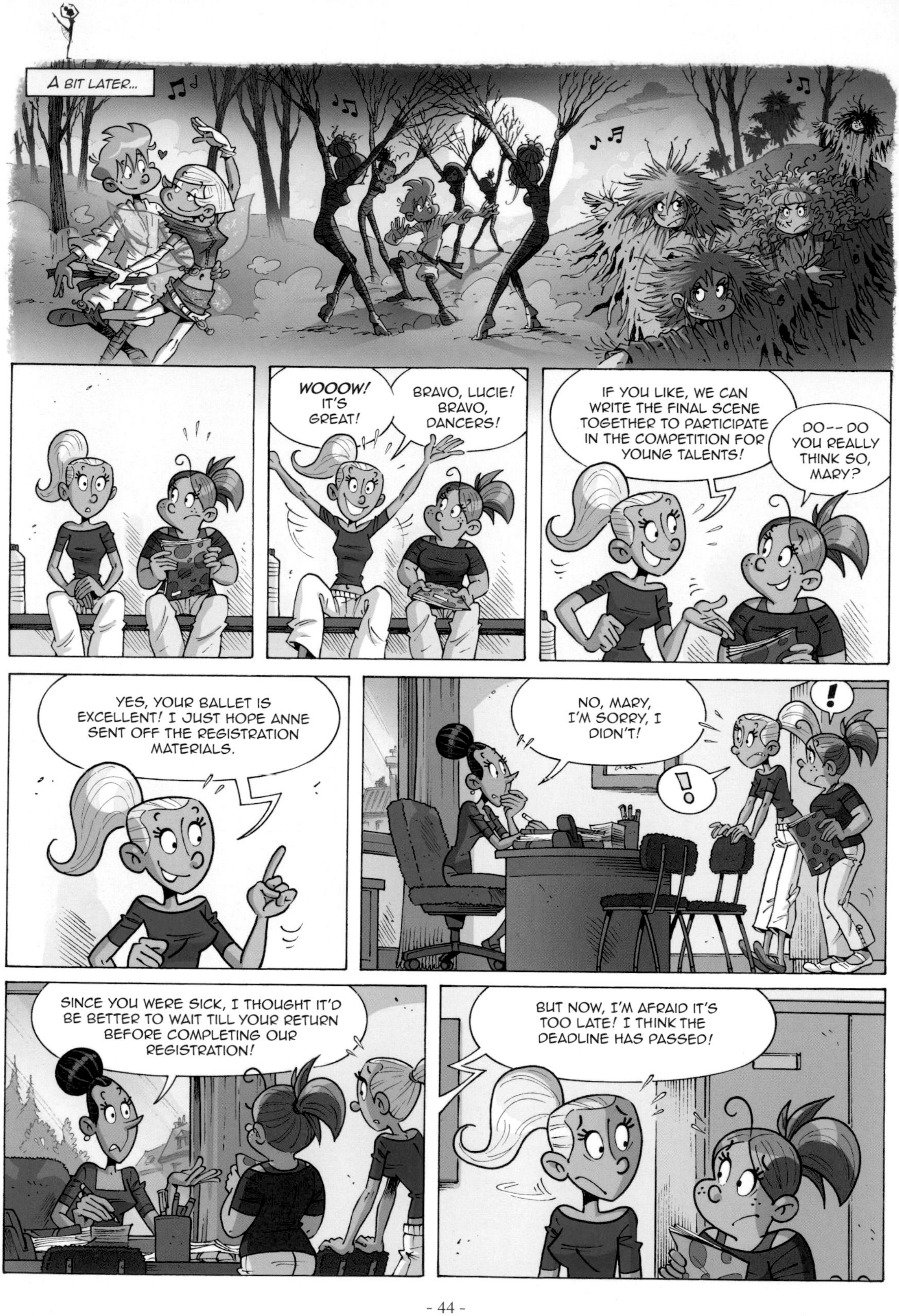
A BIT LATER...
WOOOW! IT'S GREAT!
BRAVO, LUCIE! BRAVO, DANCERS!
IF YOU LIKE, WE CAN WRITE THE FINAL SCENE TOGETHER TO PARTICIPATE IN THE COMPETITION FOR YOUNG TALENTS!
DO-- DO YOU REALLY THINK SO, MARY?
YES, YOUR BALLET IS EXCELLENT! I JUST HOPE ANNE SENT OFF THE REGISTRATION MATERIALS.
NO, MARY, I'M SORRY, I DIDN'T!
!
!
SINCE YOU WERE SICK, I THOUGHT IT'D BE BETTER TO WAIT TILL YOUR RETURN BEFORE COMPLETING OUR REGISTRATION!
BUT NOW, I'M AFRAID IT'S TOO LATE! I THINK THE DEADLINE HAS PASSED!

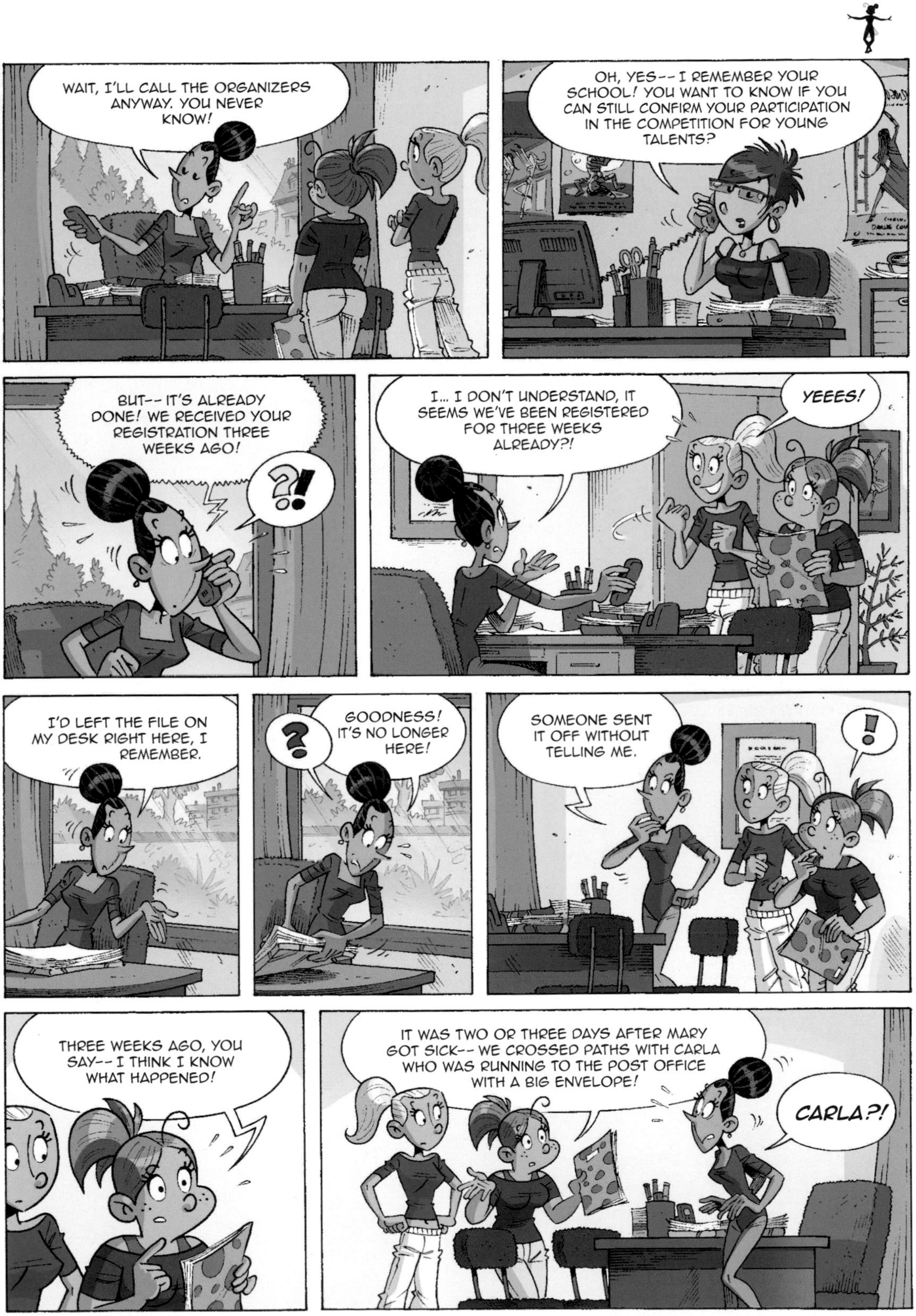
WAIT, I'LL CALL THE ORGANIZERS ANYWAY. YOU NEVER KNOW!
OH, YES-- I REMEMBER YOUR SCHOOL! YOU WANT TO KNOW IF YOU CAN STILL CONFIRM YOUR PARTICIPATION IN THE COMPETITION FOR YOUNG TALENTS?
BUT-- IT'S ALREADY DONE! WE RECEIVED YOUR REGISTRATION THREE WEEKS AGO!
?!
I... I DON'T UNDERSTAND, IT SEEMS WE'VE BEEN REGISTERED FOR THREE WEEKS ALREADY?!
YEEES!
I'D LEFT THE FILE ON MY DESK RIGHT HERE, I REMEMBER.
?
GOODNESS! IT'S NO LONGER HERE!
SOMEONE SENT IT OFF WITHOUT TELLING ME.
!
THREE WEEKS AGO, YOU SAY-- I THINK I KNOW WHAT HAPPENED!
IT WAS TWO OR THREE DAYS AFTER MARY GOT SICK-- WE CROSSED PATHS WITH CARLA WHO WAS RUNNING TO THE POST OFFICE WITH A BIG ENVELOPE!
CARLA?!

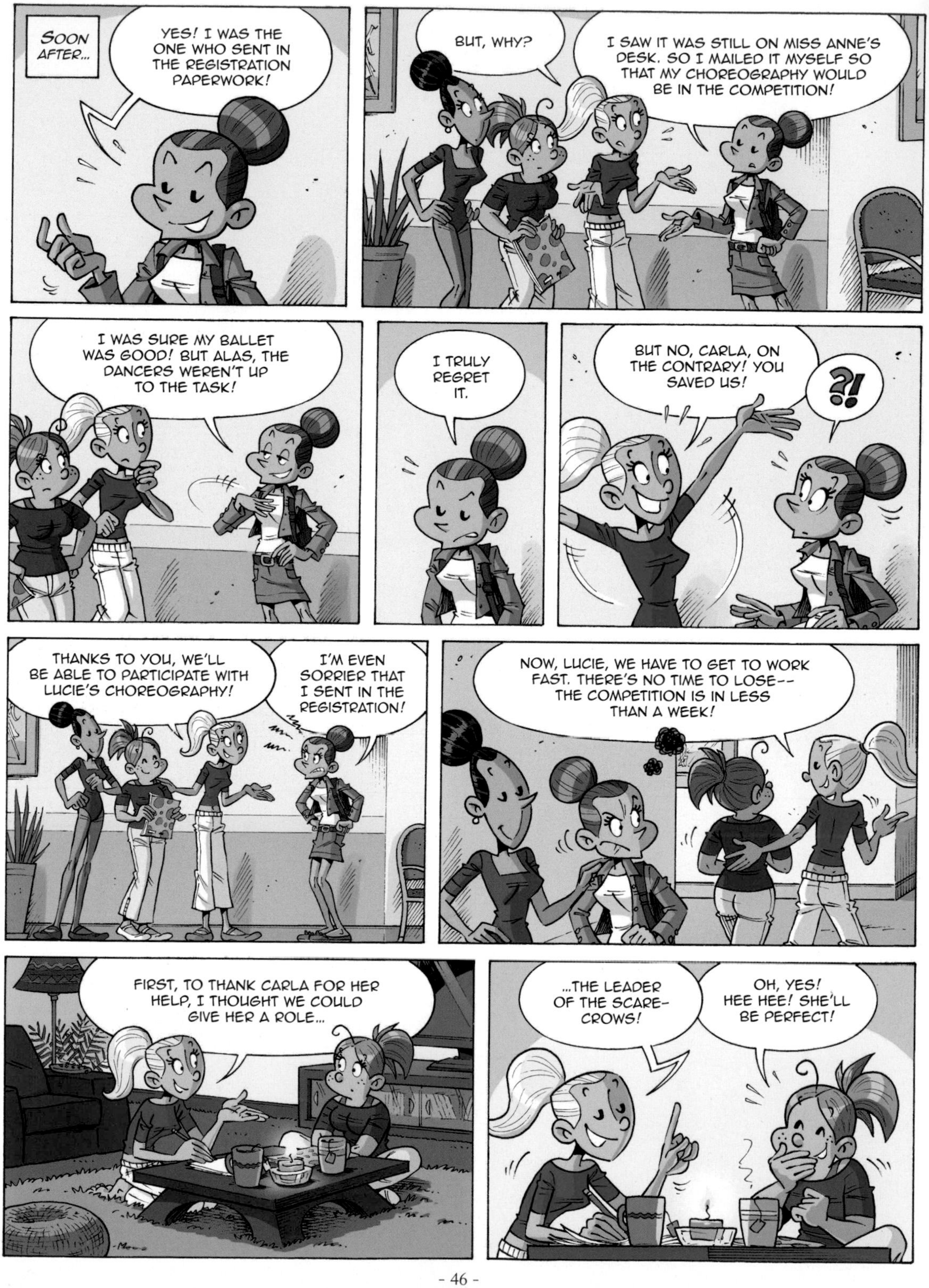
SOON AFTER...
YES! I WAS THE ONE WHO SENT IN THE REGISTRATION PAPERWORK!
BUT, WHY?
I SAW IT WAS STILL ON MISS ANNE'S DESK. SO I MAILED IT MYSELF SO THAT MY CHOREOGRAPHY WOULD BE IN THE COMPETITION!
I WAS SURE MY BALLET WAS GOOD! BUT ALAS, THE DANCERS WEREN'T UP TO THE TASK!
I TRULY REGRET IT.
BUT NO, CARLA, ON THE CONTRARY! YOU SAVED US!
?!
THANKS TO YOU, WE'LL BE ABLE TO PARTICIPATE WITH LUCIE'S CHOREOGRAPHY!
I'M EVEN SORRIER THAT I SENT IN THE REGISTRATION!
NOW, LUCIE, WE HAVE TO GET TO WORK FAST. THERE'S NO TIME TO LOSE-- THE COMPETITION IS IN LESS THAN A WEEK!
FIRST, TO THANK CARLA FOR HER HELP, I THOUGHT WE COULD GIVE HER A ROLE...
...THE LEADER OF THE SCARE-CROWS!
OH, YES! HEE HEE! SHE'LL BE PERFECT!

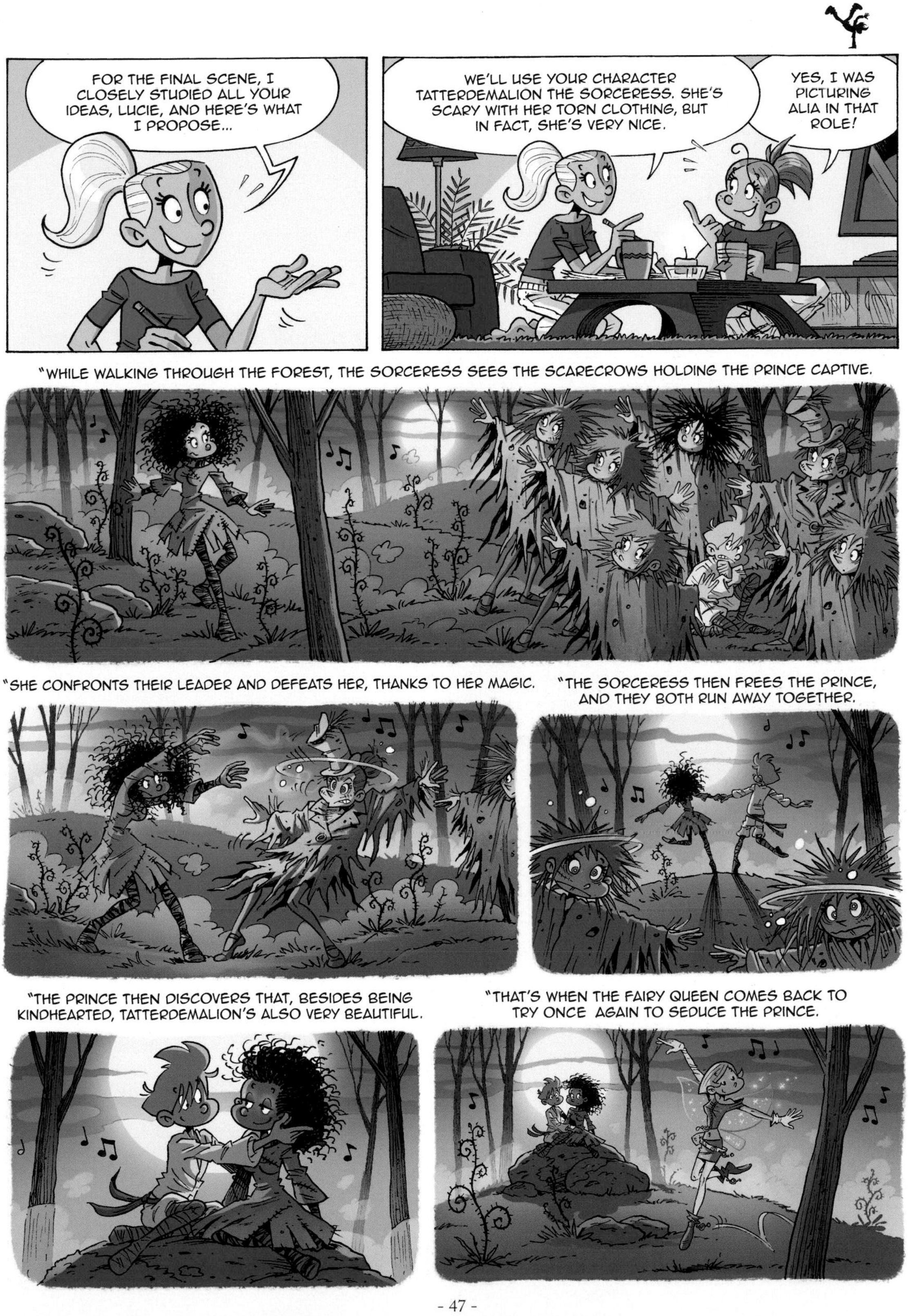
FOR THE FINAL SCENE, I CLOSELY STUDIED ALL YOUR IDEAS, LUCIE, AND HERE'S WHAT I PROPOSE...
WE'LL USE YOUR CHARACTER TATTERDEMALION THE SORCERESS. SHE'S SCARY WITH HER TORN CLOTHING, BUT IN FACT, SHE'S VERY NICE.
YES, I WAS PICTURING ALIA IN THAT ROLE!
"WHILE WALKING THROUGH THE FOREST, THE SORCERESS SEES THE SCARECROWS HOLDING THE PRINCE CAPTIVE.
"SHE CONFRONTS THEIR LEADER AND DEFEATS HER, THANKS TO HER MAGIC.
"THE SORCERESS THEN FREES THE PRINCE, AND THEY BOTH RUN AWAY TOGETHER.
"THE PRINCE THEN DISCOVERS THAT, BESIDES BEING KINDHEARTED, TATTERDEMALION'S ALSO VERY BEAUTIFUL.
"THAT'S WHEN THE FAIRY QUEEN COMES BACK TO TRY ONCE AGAIN TO SEDUCE THE PRINCE.

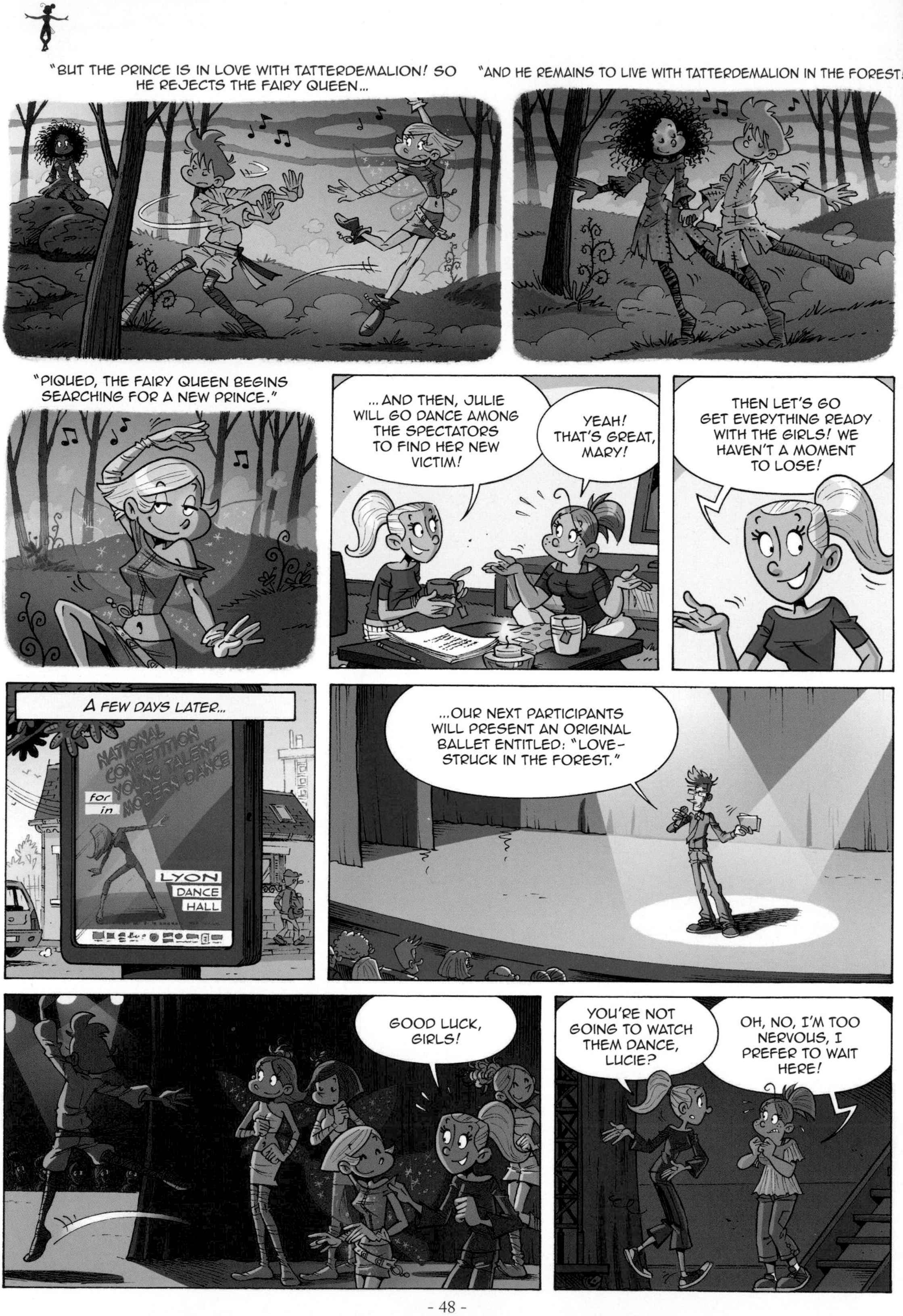
"BUT THE PRINCE IS IN LOVE WITH TATTERDEMALION! SO HE REJECTS THE FAIRY QUEEN...
"AND HE REMAINS TO LIVE WITH TATTERDEMALION IN THE FOREST!
"PIQUED, THE FAIRY QUEEN BEGINS SEARCHING FOR A NEW PRINCE."
...AND THEN, JULIE WILL GO DANCE AMONG THE SPECTATORS TO FIND HER NEW VICTIM!
YEAH! THAT'S GREAT, MARY!
THEN LET'S GO GET EVERYTHING READY WITH THE GIRLS! WE HAVEN'T A MOMENT TO LOSE!
A FEW DAYS LATER...
NATIONAL COMPETITION for YOUNG TALENT in MODERN DANCE
LYON
DANCE
HALL
...OUR NEXT PARTICIPANTS WILL PRESENT AN ORIGINAL BALLET ENTITLED: "LOVE-STRUCK IN THE FOREST."
GOOD LUCK, GIRLS!
YOU'RE NOT GOING TO WATCH THEM DANCE, LUCIE?
OH, NO, I'M TOO NERVOUS, I PREFER TO WAIT HERE!

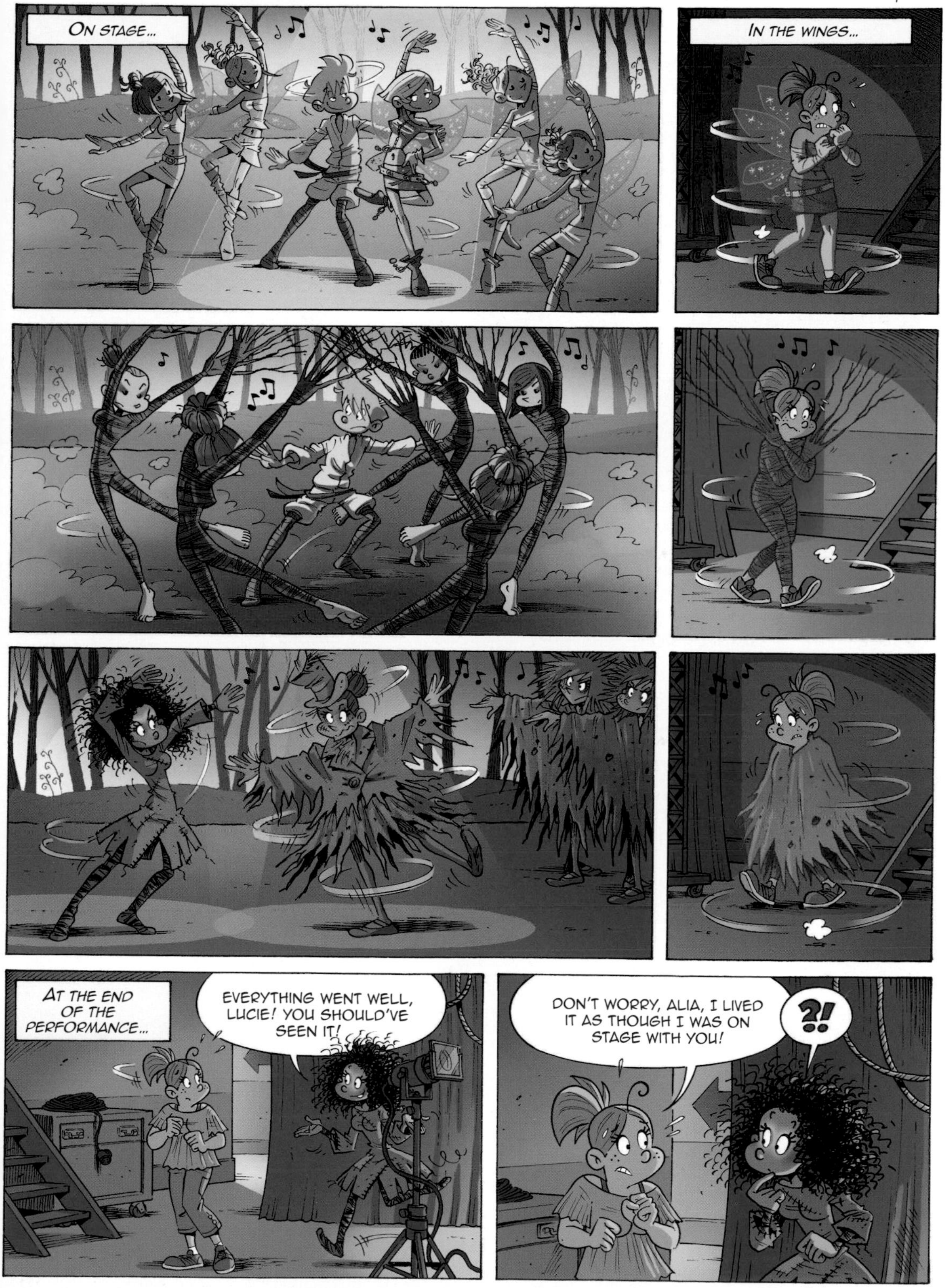

ON STAGE...
IN THE WINGS...
AT THE END OF THE PERFORMANCE...
EVERYTHING WENT WELL, LUCIE! YOU SHOULD'VE SEEN IT!
DON'T WORRY, ALIA, I LIVED IT AS THOUGH I WAS ON STAGE WITH YOU!
?!

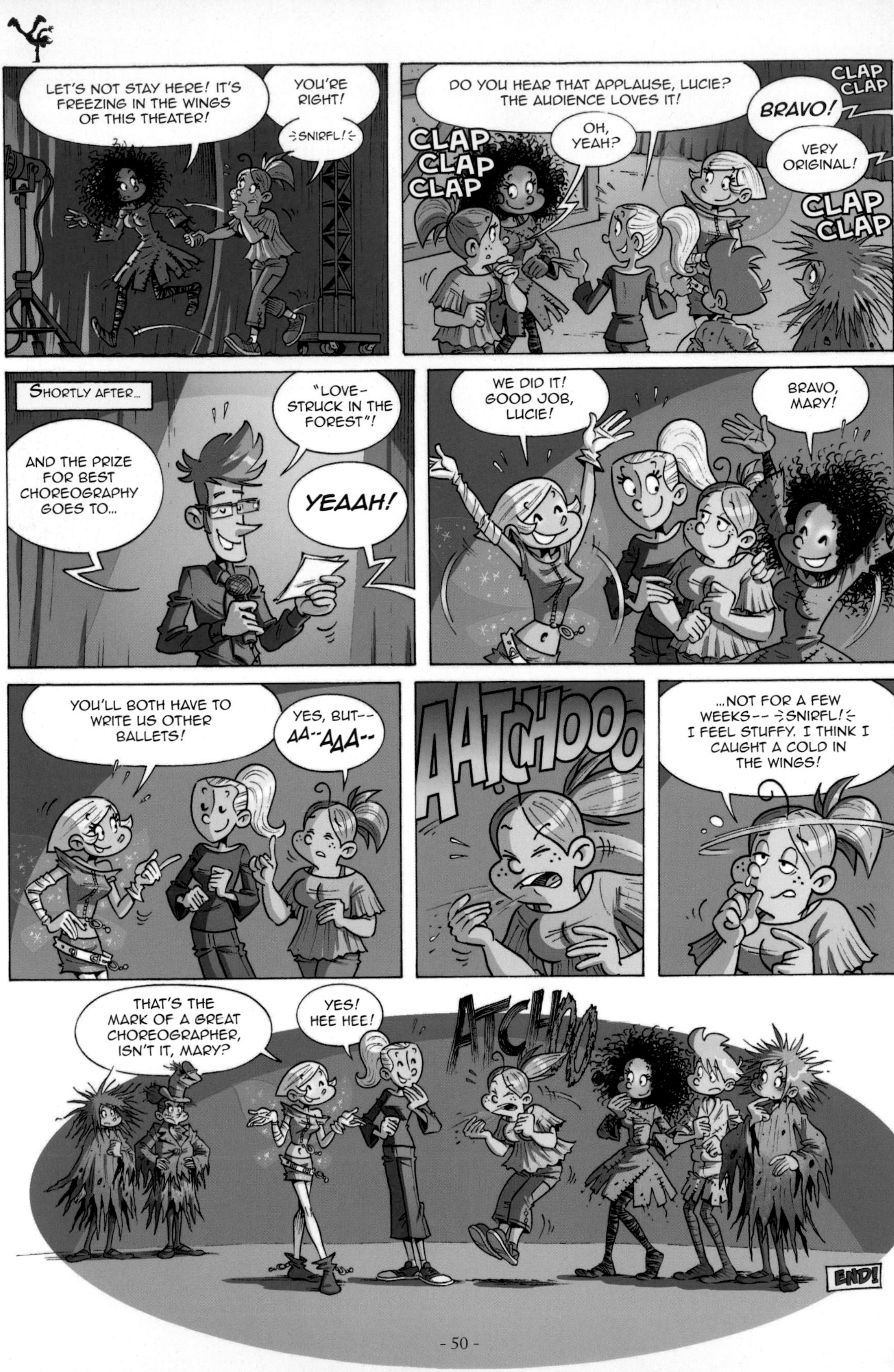
LET'S NOT STAY HERE! IT'S FREEZING IN THE WINGS OF THIS THEATER!
YOU'RE RIGHT!
SNIRFL!
DO YOU HEAR THAT APPLAUSE, LUCIE? THE AUDIENCE LOVES IT!
CLAP CLAP
BRAVO!
CLAP CLAP CLAP
OH, YEAH?
VERY ORIGINAL!
CLAP CLAP
SHORTLY AFTER...
"LOVE-STRUCK IN THE FOREST"!
AND THE PRIZE FOR BEST CHOREOGRAPHY GOES TO...
YEAAH!
WE DID IT! GOOD JOB, LUCIE!
BRAVO, MARY!
YOU'LL BOTH HAVE TO WRITE US OTHER BALLETS!
YES, BUT-- AA--AAA--
AATCHOOOO
...NOT FOR A FEW WEEKS-- SNIRFL! I FEEL STUFFY. I THINK I CAUGHT A COLD IN THE WINGS!
THAT'S THE MARK OF A GREAT CHOREOGRAPHER, ISN'T IT, MARY?
YES! HEE HEE!
ATCHOO
END!

Snow White and the Seven Dwarves

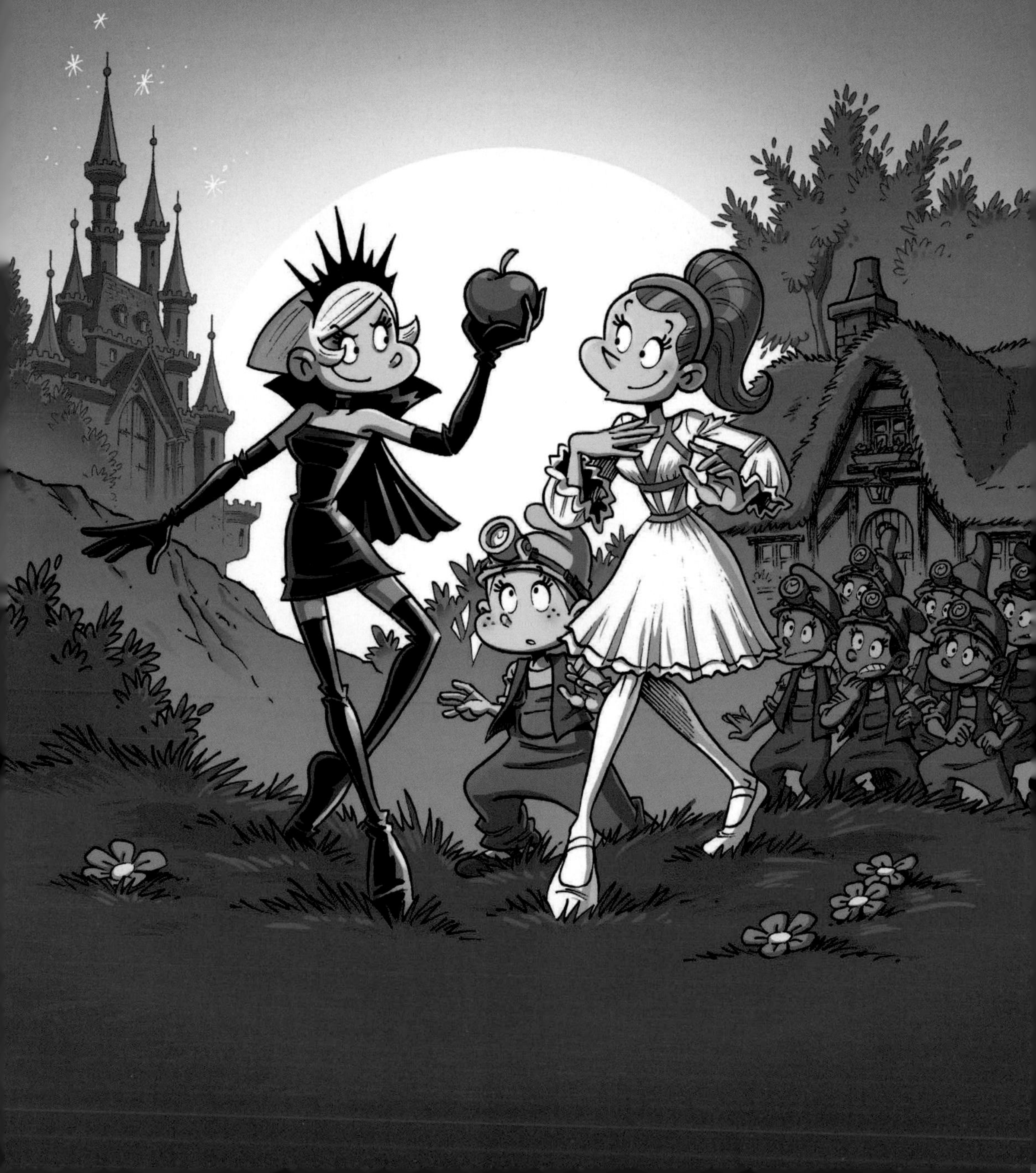

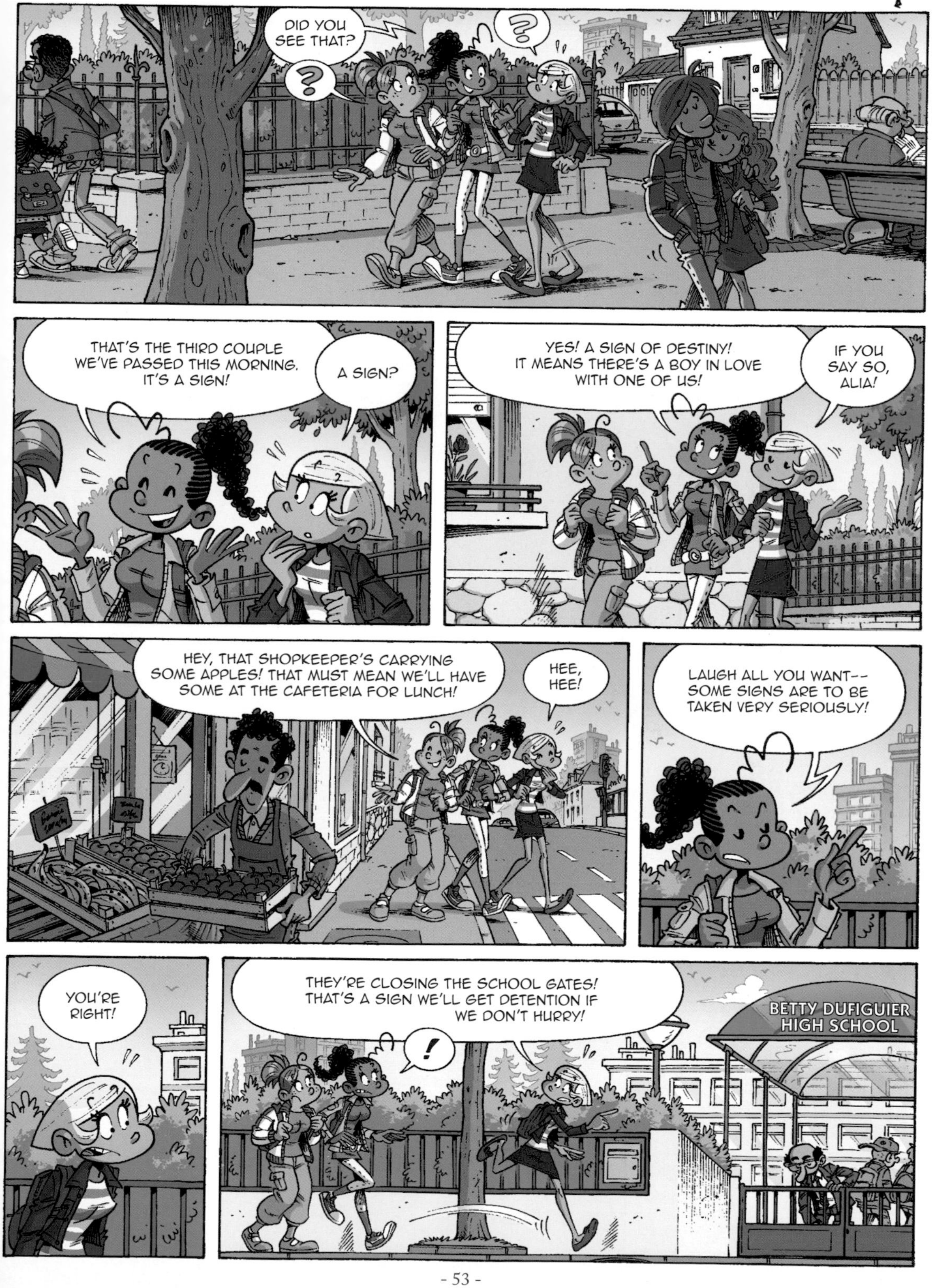
DID YOU SEE THAT?
?
?
THAT'S THE THIRD COUPLE WE'VE PASSED THIS MORNING. IT'S A SIGN!
A SIGN?
YES! A SIGN OF DESTINY! IT MEANS THERE'S A BOY IN LOVE WITH ONE OF US!
IF YOU SAY SO, ALIA!
HEY, THAT SHOPKEEPER'S CARRYING SOME APPLES! THAT MUST MEAN WE'LL HAVE SOME AT THE CAFETERIA FOR LUNCH!
HEE, HEE!
LAUGH ALL YOU WANT-- SOME SIGNS ARE TO BE TAKEN VERY SERIOUSLY!
YOU'RE RIGHT!
THEY'RE CLOSING THE SCHOOL GATES! THAT'S A SIGN WE'LL GET DETENTION IF WE DON'T HURRY!
!
BETTY DUFIGUIER HIGH SCHOOL

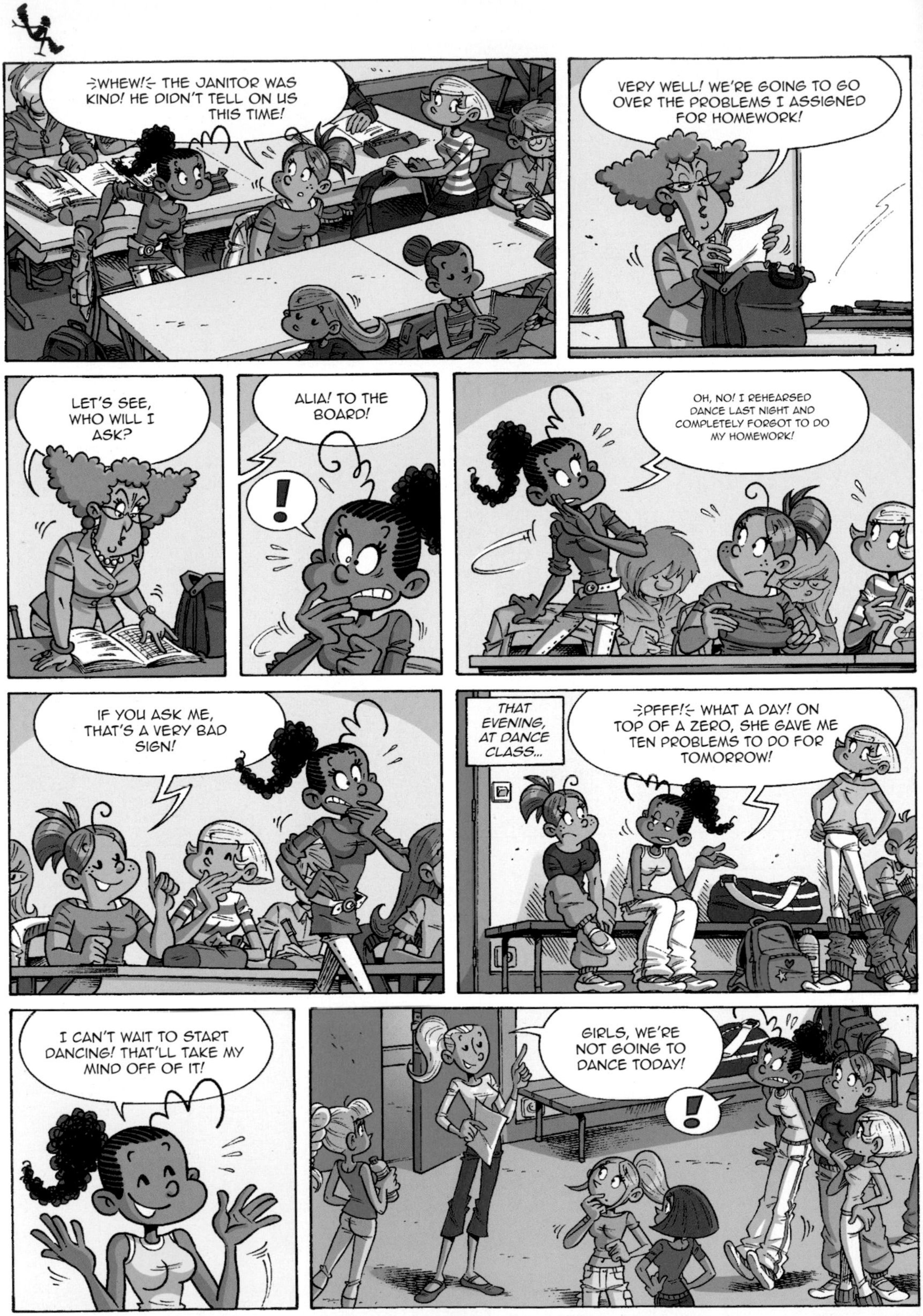

⇉WHEW!⇇ THE JANITOR WAS KIND! HE DIDN'T TELL ON US THIS TIME!
VERY WELL! WE'RE GOING TO GO OVER THE PROBLEMS I ASSIGNED FOR HOMEWORK!
LET'S SEE, WHO WILL I ASK?
ALIA! TO THE BOARD!
!
OH, NO! I REHEARSED DANCE LAST NIGHT AND COMPLETELY FORGOT TO DO MY HOMEWORK!
IF YOU ASK ME, THAT'S A VERY BAD SIGN!
THAT EVENING, AT DANCE CLASS...
⇉PFFF!⇇ WHAT A DAY! ON TOP OF A ZERO, SHE GAVE ME TEN PROBLEMS TO DO FOR TOMORROW!
I CAN'T WAIT TO START DANCING! THAT'LL TAKE MY MIND OFF OF IT!
GIRLS, WE'RE NOT GOING TO DANCE TODAY!
!

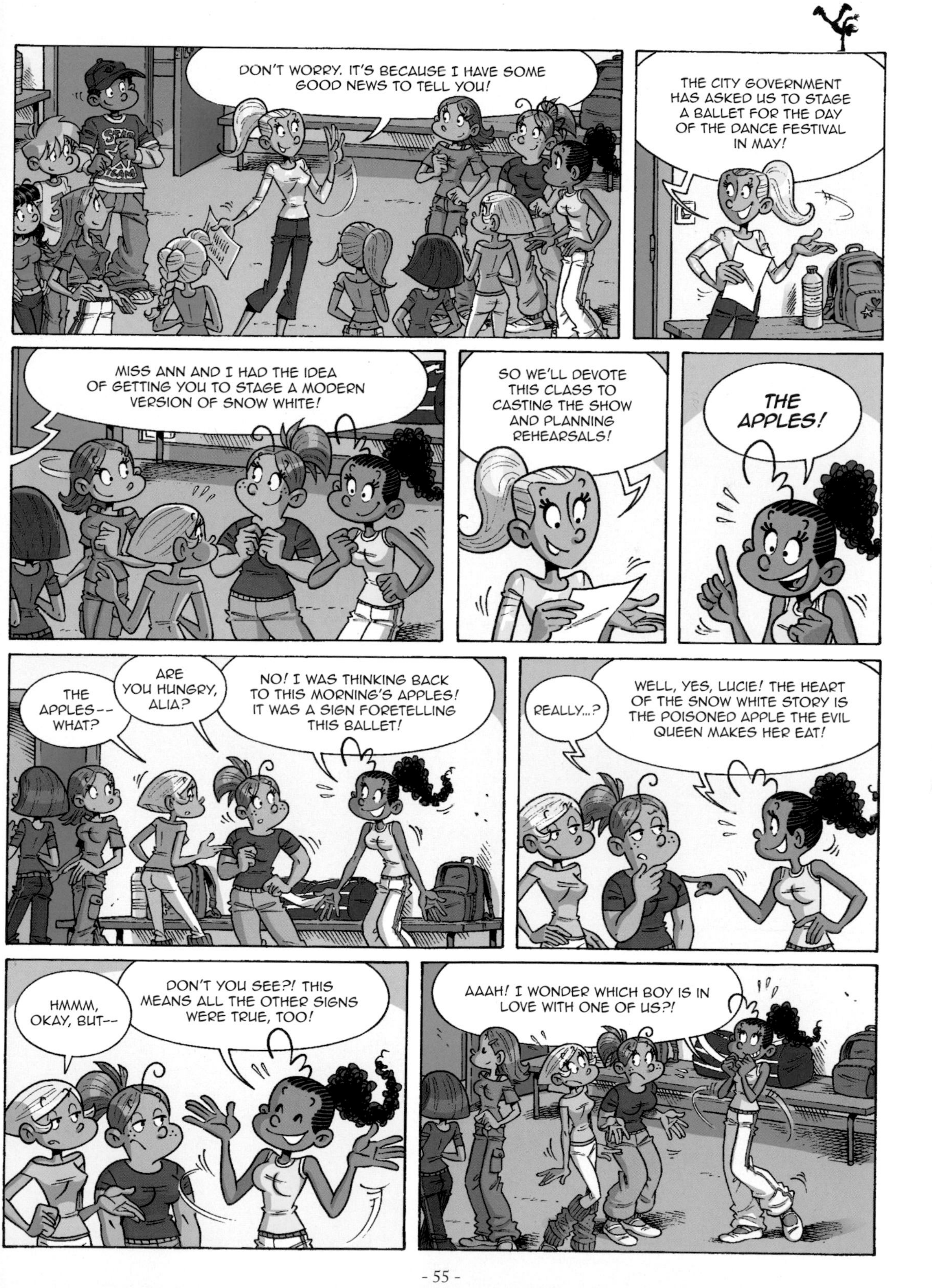
DON'T WORRY. IT'S BECAUSE I HAVE SOME GOOD NEWS TO TELL YOU!
THE CITY GOVERNMENT HAS ASKED US TO STAGE A BALLET FOR THE DAY OF THE DANCE FESTIVAL IN MAY!
MISS ANN AND I HAD THE IDEA OF GETTING YOU TO STAGE A MODERN VERSION OF SNOW WHITE!
SO WE'LL DEVOTE THIS CLASS TO CASTING THE SHOW AND PLANNING REHEARSALS!
THE APPLES!
THE APPLES-- WHAT?
ARE YOU HUNGRY, ALIA?
NO! I WAS THINKING BACK TO THIS MORNING'S APPLES! IT WAS A SIGN FORETELLING THIS BALLET!
REALLY...?
WELL, YES, LUCIE! THE HEART OF THE SNOW WHITE STORY IS THE POISONED APPLE THE EVIL QUEEN MAKES HER EAT!
HMMM, OKAY, BUT--
DON'T YOU SEE?! THIS MEANS ALL THE OTHER SIGNS WERE TRUE, TOO!
AAAH! I WONDER WHICH BOY IS IN LOVE WITH ONE OF US?!

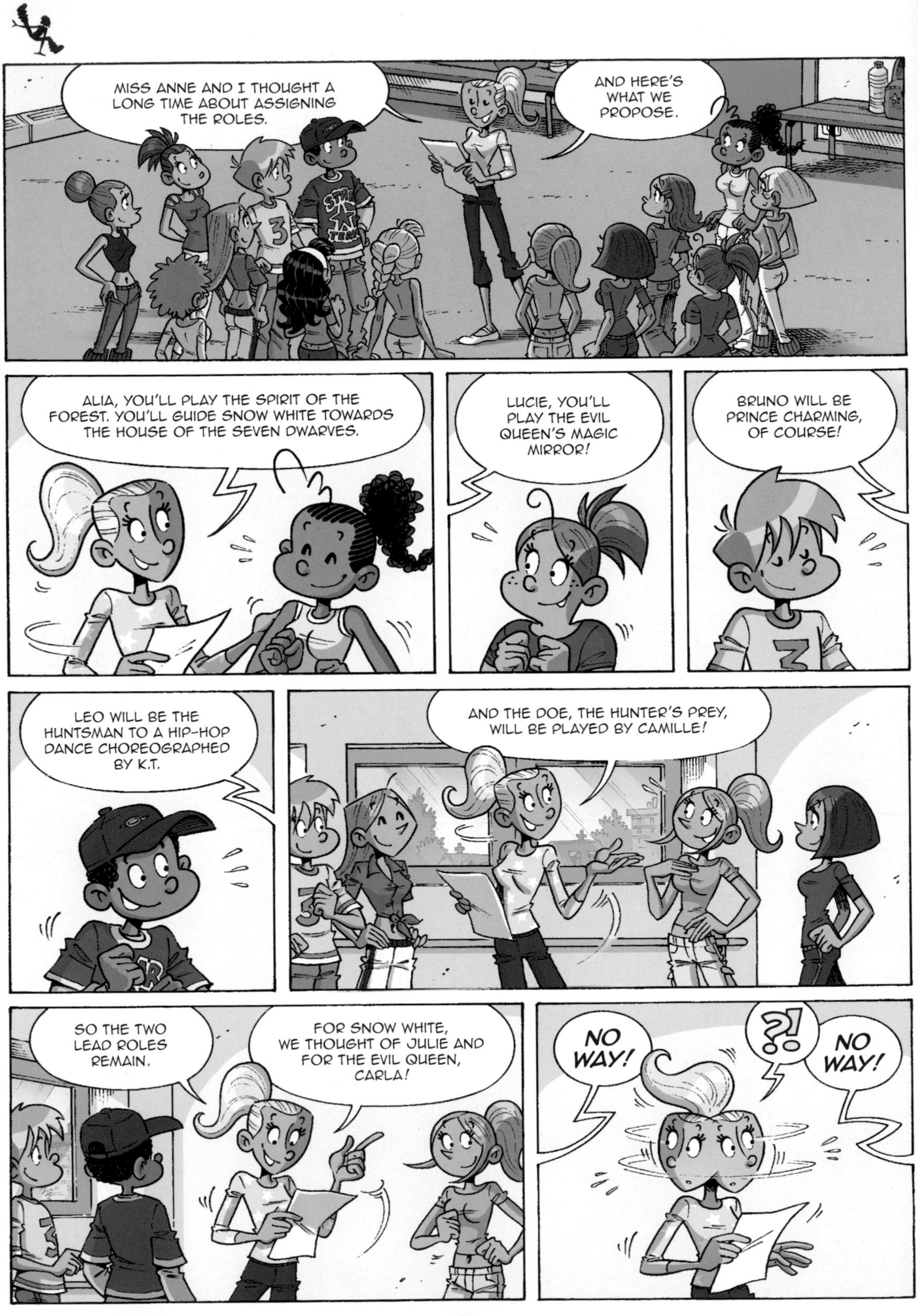

MISS ANNE AND I THOUGHT A LONG TIME ABOUT ASSIGNING THE ROLES.
AND HERE'S WHAT WE PROPOSE.
ALIA, YOU'LL PLAY THE SPIRIT OF THE FOREST. YOU'LL GUIDE SNOW WHITE TOWARDS THE HOUSE OF THE SEVEN DWARVES.
LUCIE, YOU'LL PLAY THE EVIL QUEEN'S MAGIC MIRROR!
BRUNO WILL BE PRINCE CHARMING, OF COURSE!
LEO WILL BE THE HUNTSMAN TO A HIP-HOP DANCE CHOREOGRAPHED BY K.T.
AND THE DOE, THE HUNTER'S PREY, WILL BE PLAYED BY CAMILLE!
SO THE TWO LEAD ROLES REMAIN.
FOR SNOW WHITE, WE THOUGHT OF JULIE AND FOR THE EVIL QUEEN, CARLA!
NO WAY!
?!
NO WAY!

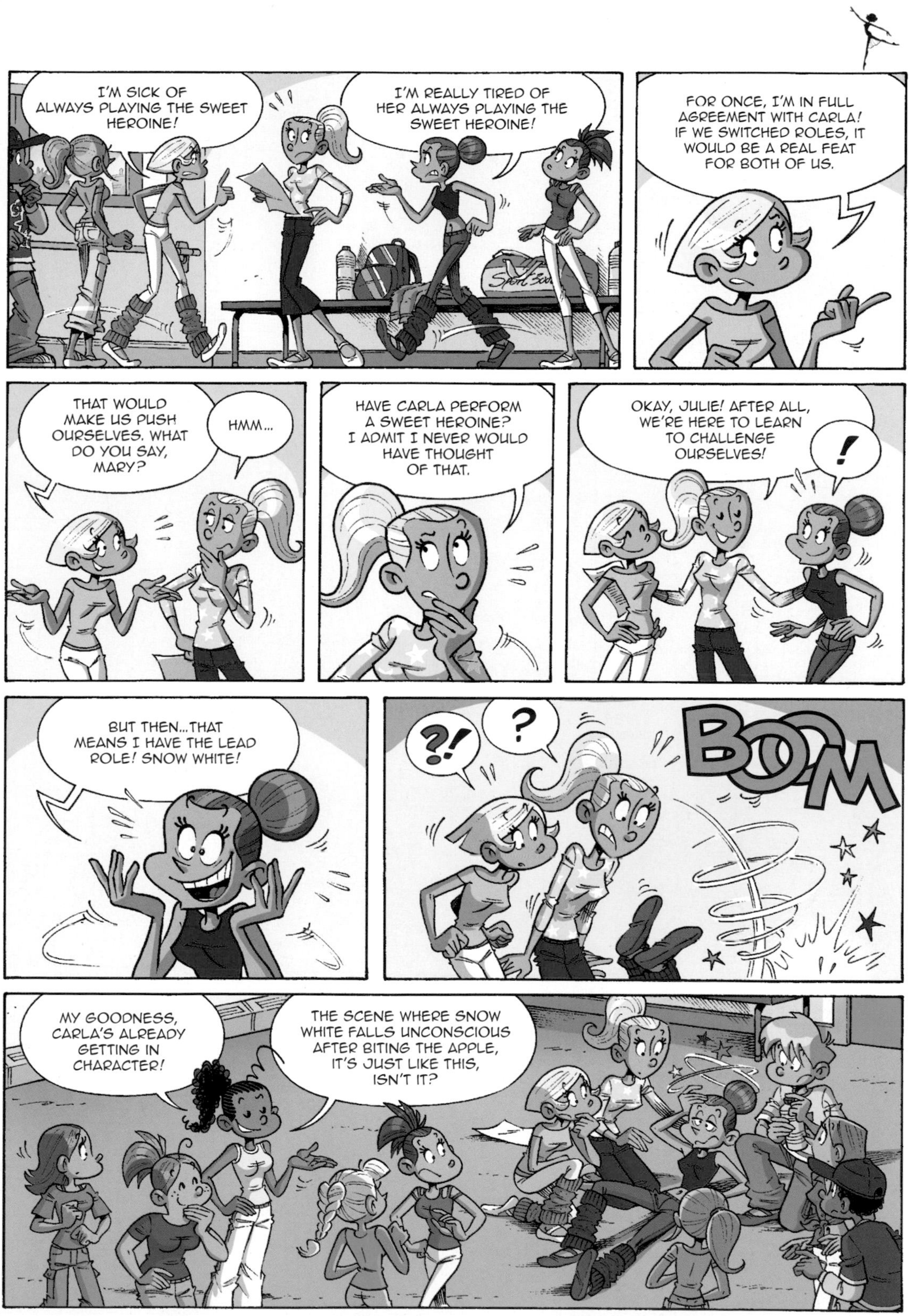
I'M SICK OF ALWAYS PLAYING THE SWEET HEROINE!
I'M REALLY TIRED OF HER ALWAYS PLAYING THE SWEET HEROINE!
FOR ONCE, I'M IN FULL AGREEMENT WITH CARLA! IF WE SWITCHED ROLES, IT WOULD BE A REAL FEAT FOR BOTH OF US.
THAT WOULD MAKE US PUSH OURSELVES. WHAT DO YOU SAY, MARY?
HMM...
HAVE CARLA PERFORM A SWEET HEROINE? I ADMIT I NEVER WOULD HAVE THOUGHT OF THAT.
OKAY, JULIE! AFTER ALL, WE'RE HERE TO LEARN TO CHALLENGE OURSELVES!
!
BUT THEN...THAT MEANS I HAVE THE LEAD ROLE! SNOW WHITE!
?!
?
BOOM
MY GOODNESS, CARLA'S ALREADY GETTING IN CHARACTER!
THE SCENE WHERE SNOW WHITE FALLS UNCONSCIOUS AFTER BITING THE APPLE, IT'S JUST LIKE THIS, ISN'T IT?

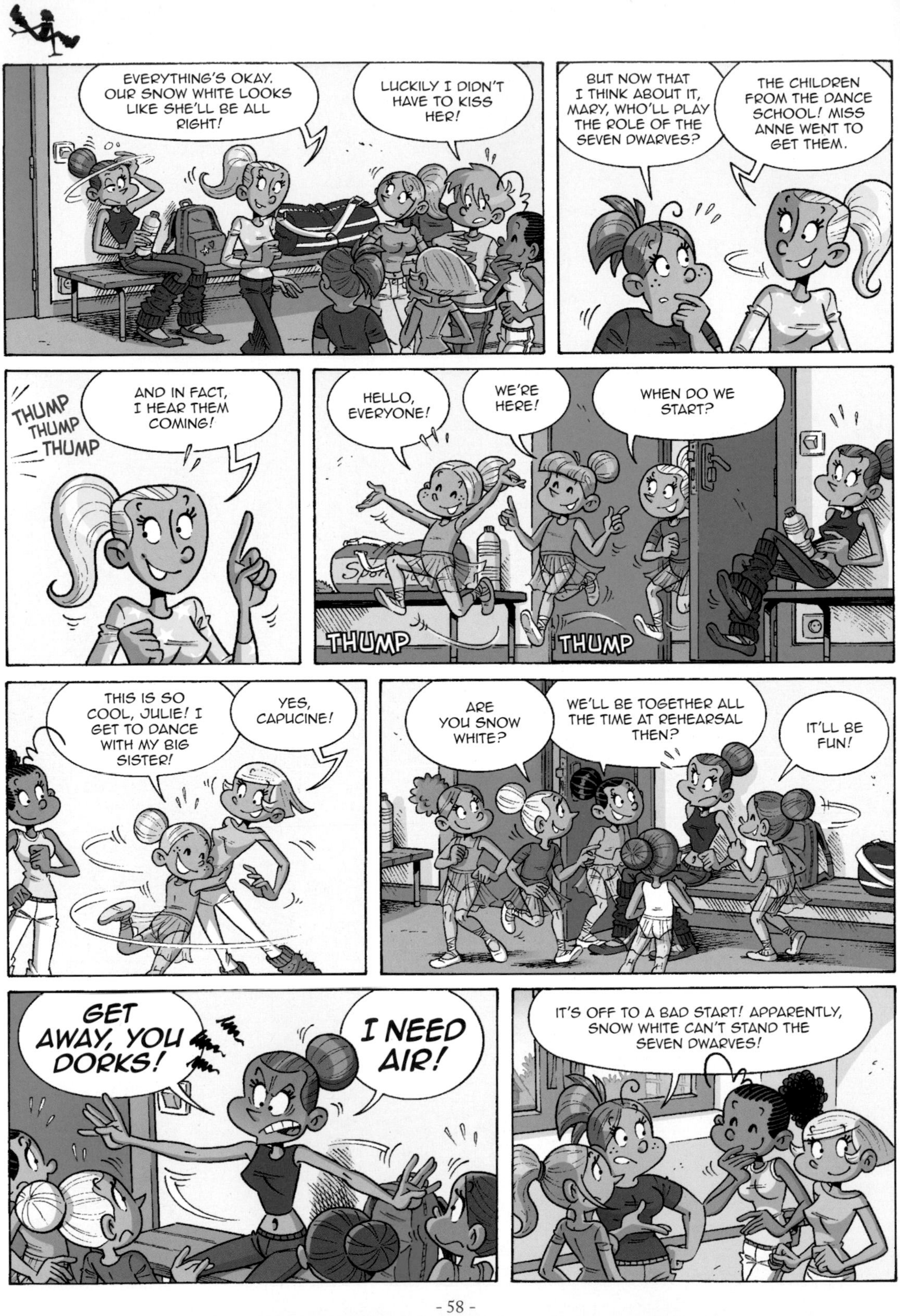
EVERYTHING'S OKAY. OUR SNOW WHITE LOOKS LIKE SHE'LL BE ALL RIGHT!
LUCKILY I DIDN'T HAVE TO KISS HER!
BUT NOW THAT I THINK ABOUT IT, MARY, WHO'LL PLAY THE ROLE OF THE SEVEN DWARVES?
THE CHILDREN FROM THE DANCE SCHOOL! MISS ANNE WENT TO GET THEM.
THUMP THUMP THUMP
AND IN FACT, I HEAR THEM COMING!
HELLO, EVERYONE!
WE'RE HERE!
WHEN DO WE START?
THUMP
THUMP
THIS IS SO COOL, JULIE! I GET TO DANCE WITH MY BIG SISTER!
YES, CAPUCINE!
ARE YOU SNOW WHITE?
WE'LL BE TOGETHER ALL THE TIME AT REHEARSAL THEN?
IT'LL BE FUN!
GET AWAY, YOU DORKS!
I NEED AIR!
IT'S OFF TO A BAD START! APPARENTLY, SNOW WHITE CAN'T STAND THE SEVEN DWARVES!

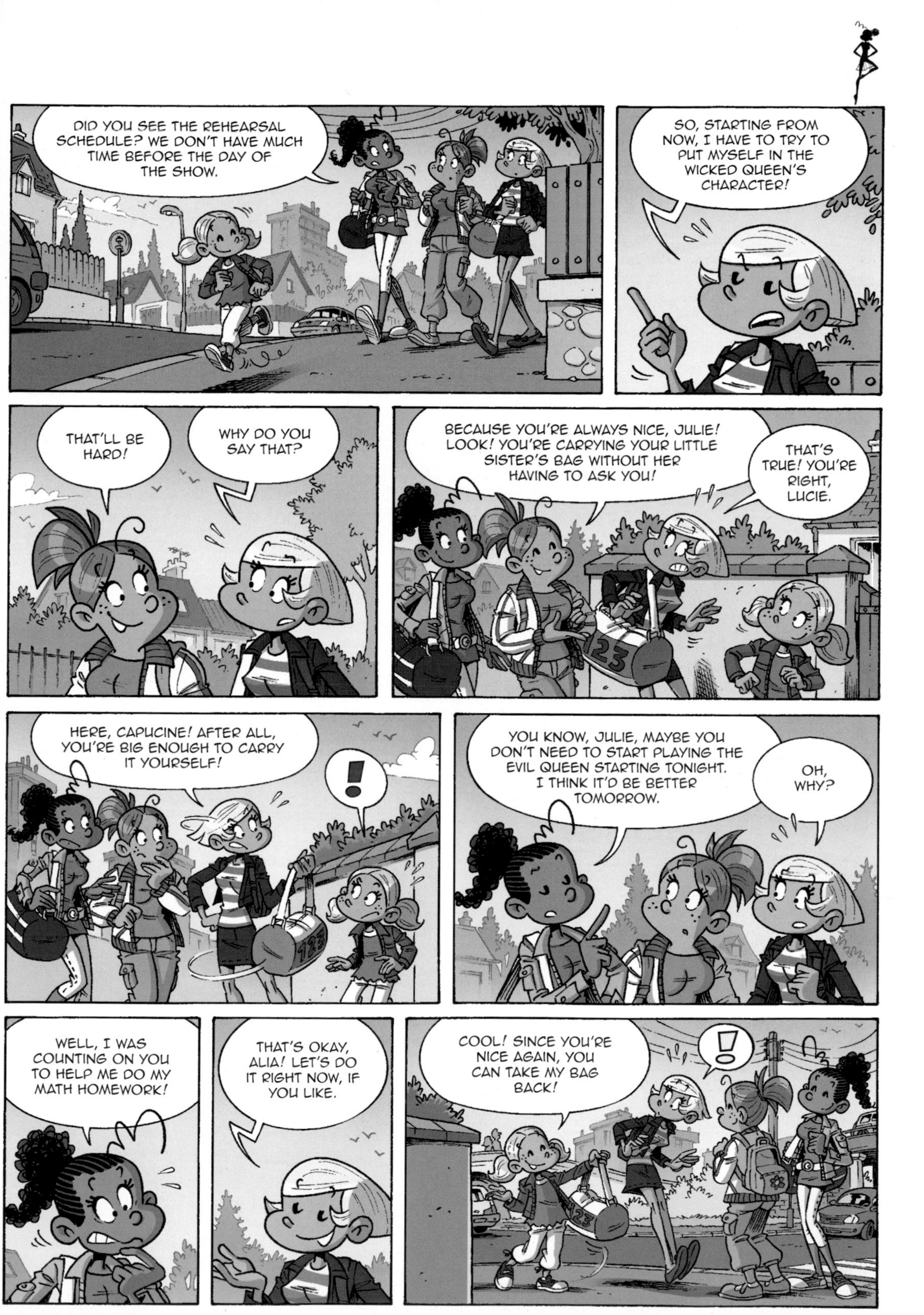
DID YOU SEE THE REHEARSAL SCHEDULE? WE DON'T HAVE MUCH TIME BEFORE THE DAY OF THE SHOW.
SO, STARTING FROM NOW, I HAVE TO TRY TO PUT MYSELF IN THE WICKED QUEEN'S CHARACTER!
THAT'LL BE HARD!
WHY DO YOU SAY THAT?
BECAUSE YOU'RE ALWAYS NICE, JULIE! LOOK! YOU'RE CARRYING YOUR LITTLE SISTER'S BAG WITHOUT HER HAVING TO ASK YOU!
THAT'S TRUE! YOU'RE RIGHT, LUCIE.
HERE, CAPUCINE! AFTER ALL, YOU'RE BIG ENOUGH TO CARRY IT YOURSELF!
!
123
YOU KNOW, JULIE, MAYBE YOU DON'T NEED TO START PLAYING THE EVIL QUEEN STARTING TONIGHT. I THINK IT'D BE BETTER TOMORROW.
OH, WHY?
WELL, I WAS COUNTING ON YOU TO HELP ME DO MY MATH HOMEWORK!
THAT'S OKAY, ALIA! LET'S DO IT RIGHT NOW, IF YOU LIKE.
COOL! SINCE YOU'RE NICE AGAIN, YOU CAN TAKE MY BAG BACK!
!

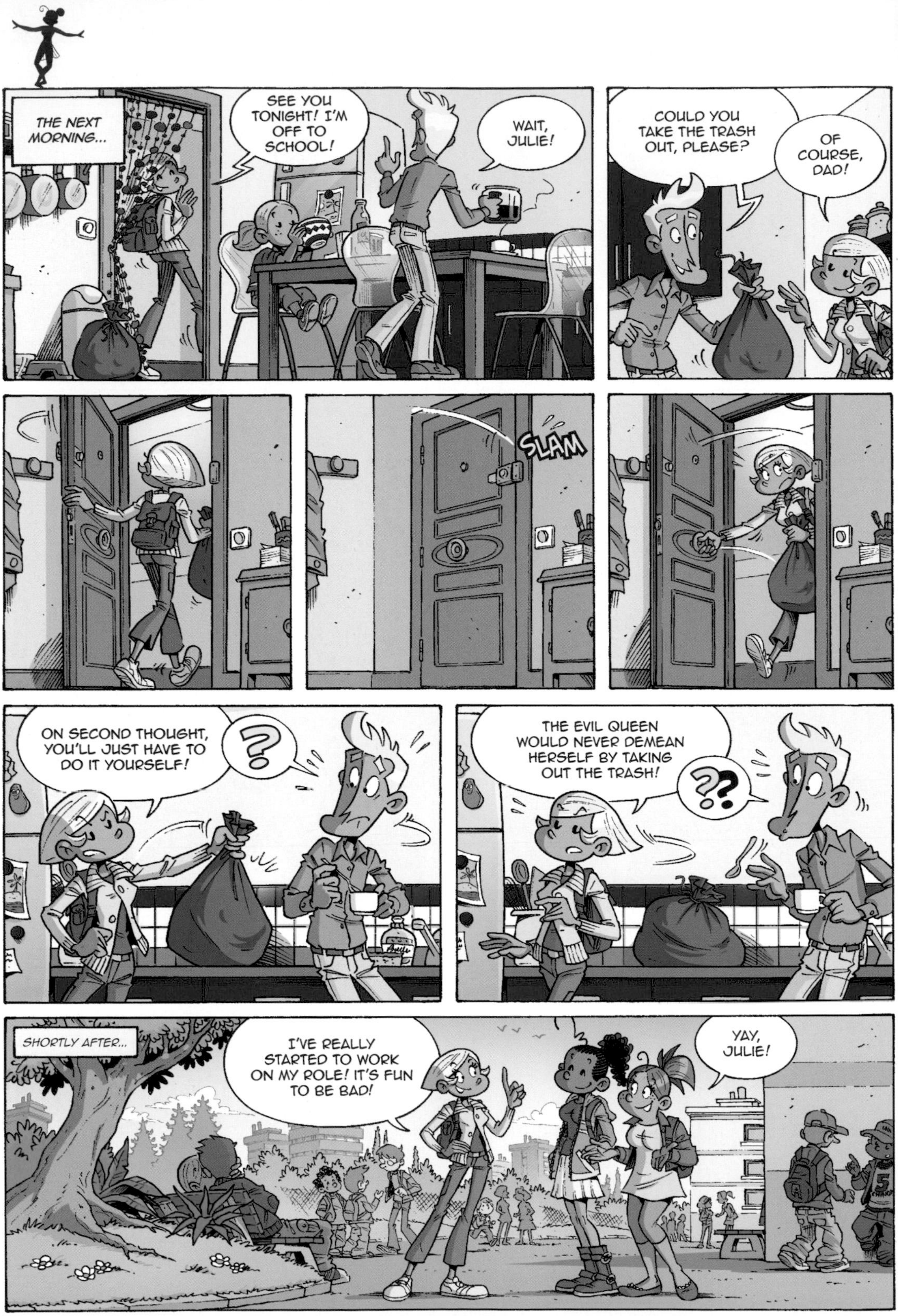
THE NEXT MORNING...
SEE YOU TONIGHT! I'M OFF TO SCHOOL!
WAIT, JULIE!
COULD YOU TAKE THE TRASH OUT, PLEASE?
OF COURSE, DAD!
SLAM
ON SECOND THOUGHT, YOU'LL JUST HAVE TO DO IT YOURSELF!
?
THE EVIL QUEEN WOULD NEVER DEMEAN HERSELF BY TAKING OUT THE TRASH!
??
SHORTLY AFTER...
I'VE REALLY STARTED TO WORK ON MY ROLE! IT'S FUN TO BE BAD!
YAY, JULIE!

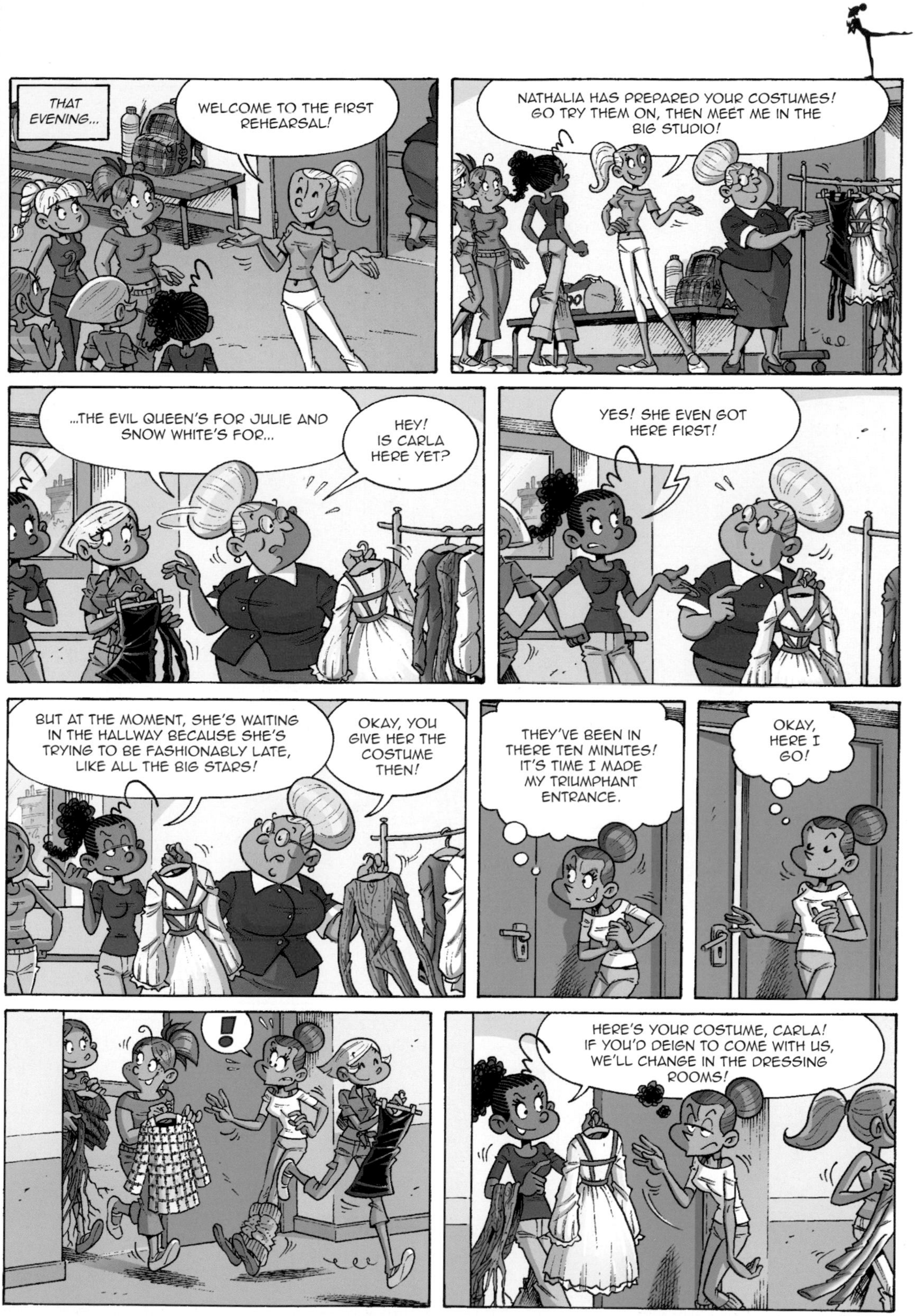

THAT EVENING...
WELCOME TO THE FIRST REHEARSAL!
NATHALIA HAS PREPARED YOUR COSTUMES! GO TRY THEM ON, THEN MEET ME IN THE BIG STUDIO!
...THE EVIL QUEEN'S FOR JULIE AND SNOW WHITE'S FOR...
HEY! IS CARLA HERE YET?
YES! SHE EVEN GOT HERE FIRST!
BUT AT THE MOMENT, SHE'S WAITING IN THE HALLWAY BECAUSE SHE'S TRYING TO BE FASHIONABLY LATE, LIKE ALL THE BIG STARS!
OKAY, YOU GIVE HER THE COSTUME THEN!
THEY'VE BEEN IN THERE TEN MINUTES! IT'S TIME I MADE MY TRIUMPHANT ENTRANCE.
OKAY, HERE I GO!
!
HERE'S YOUR COSTUME, CARLA! IF YOU'D DEIGN TO COME WITH US, WE'LL CHANGE IN THE DRESSING ROOMS!

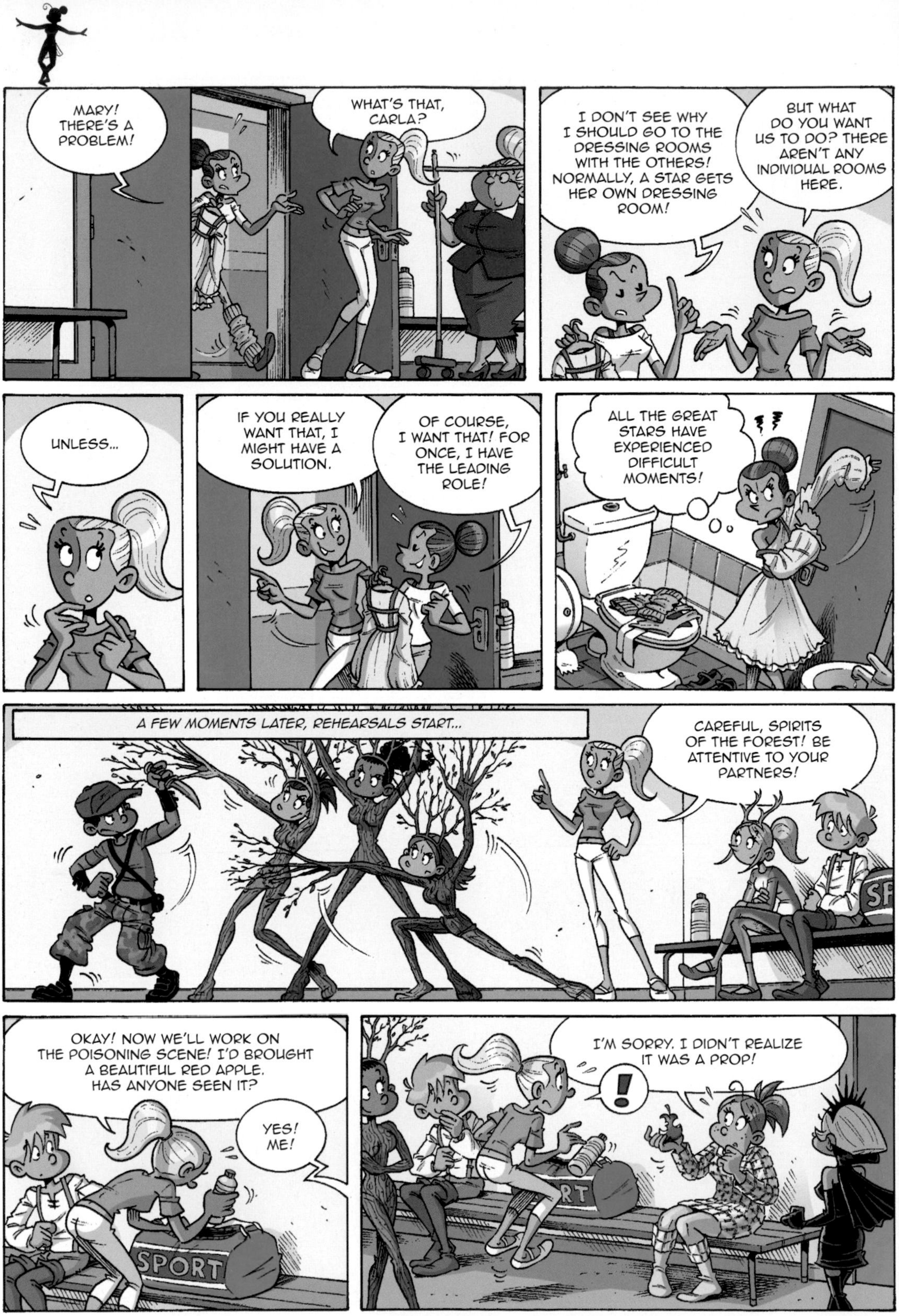
MARY! THERE'S A PROBLEM!
WHAT'S THAT, CARLA?
I DON'T SEE WHY I SHOULD GO TO THE DRESSING ROOMS WITH THE OTHERS! NORMALLY, A STAR GETS HER OWN DRESSING ROOM!
BUT WHAT DO YOU WANT US TO DO? THERE AREN'T ANY INDIVIDUAL ROOMS HERE.
UNLESS...
IF YOU REALLY WANT THAT, I MIGHT HAVE A SOLUTION.
OF COURSE, I WANT THAT! FOR ONCE, I HAVE THE LEADING ROLE!
ALL THE GREAT STARS HAVE EXPERIENCED DIFFICULT MOMENTS!
A FEW MOMENTS LATER, REHEARSALS START...
CAREFUL, SPIRITS OF THE FOREST! BE ATTENTIVE TO YOUR PARTNERS!
SPORT
OKAY! NOW WE'LL WORK ON THE POISONING SCENE! I'D BROUGHT A BEAUTIFUL RED APPLE. HAS ANYONE SEEN IT?
YES! ME!
SPORT
I'M SORRY. I DIDN'T REALIZE IT WAS A PROP!
!

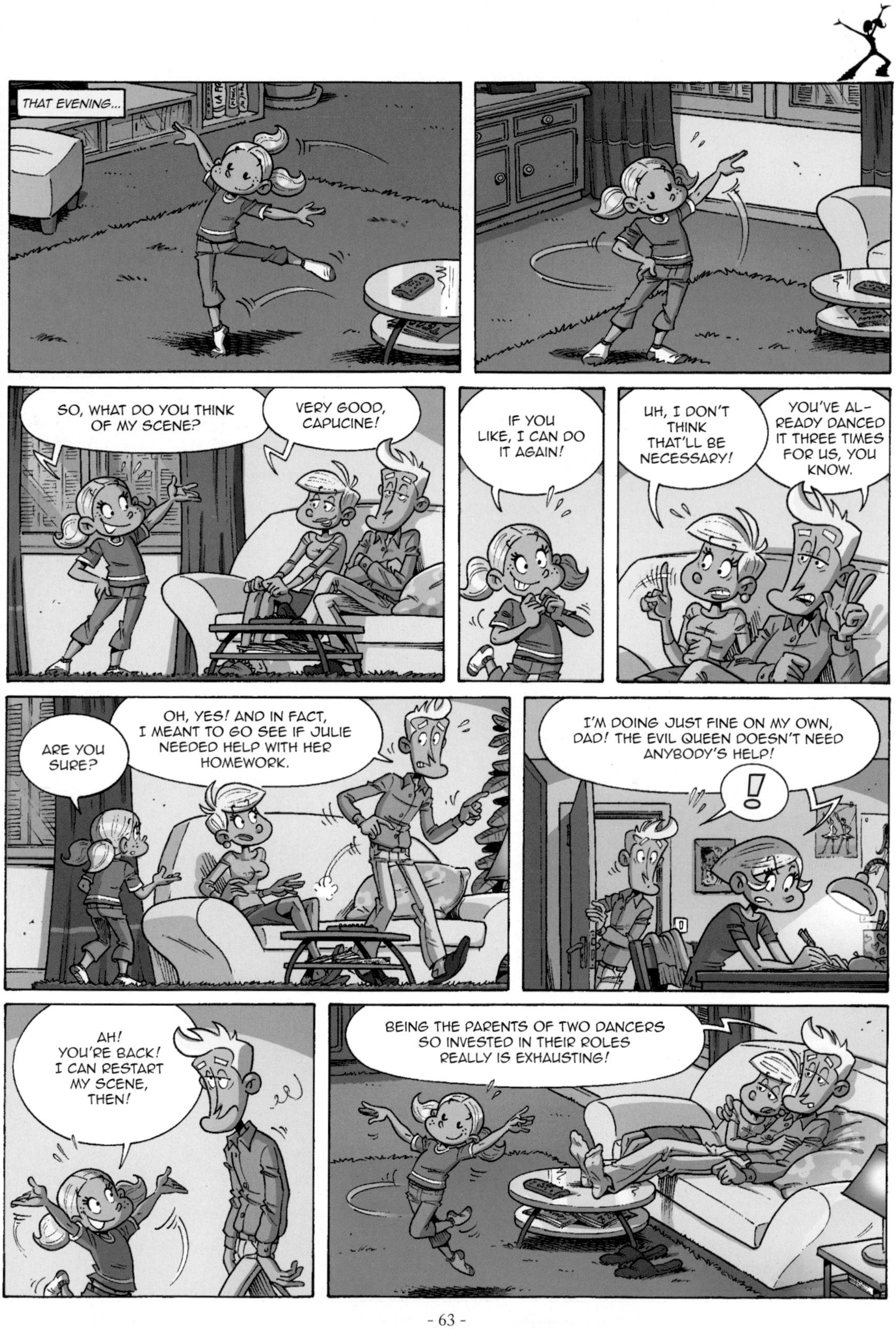
THAT EVENING...
SO, WHAT DO YOU THINK OF MY SCENE?
VERY GOOD, CAPUCINE!
IF YOU LIKE, I CAN DO IT AGAIN!
UH, I DON'T THINK THAT'LL BE NECESSARY!
YOU'VE AL-READY DANCED IT THREE TIMES FOR US, YOU KNOW.
ARE YOU SURE?
OH, YES! AND IN FACT, I MEANT TO GO SEE IF JULIE NEEDED HELP WITH HER HOMEWORK.
I'M DOING JUST FINE ON MY OWN, DAD! THE EVIL QUEEN DOESN'T NEED ANYBODY'S HELP!
!
AH! YOU'RE BACK! I CAN RESTART MY SCENE, THEN!
BEING THE PARENTS OF TWO DANCERS SO INVESTED IN THEIR ROLES REALLY IS EXHAUSTING!

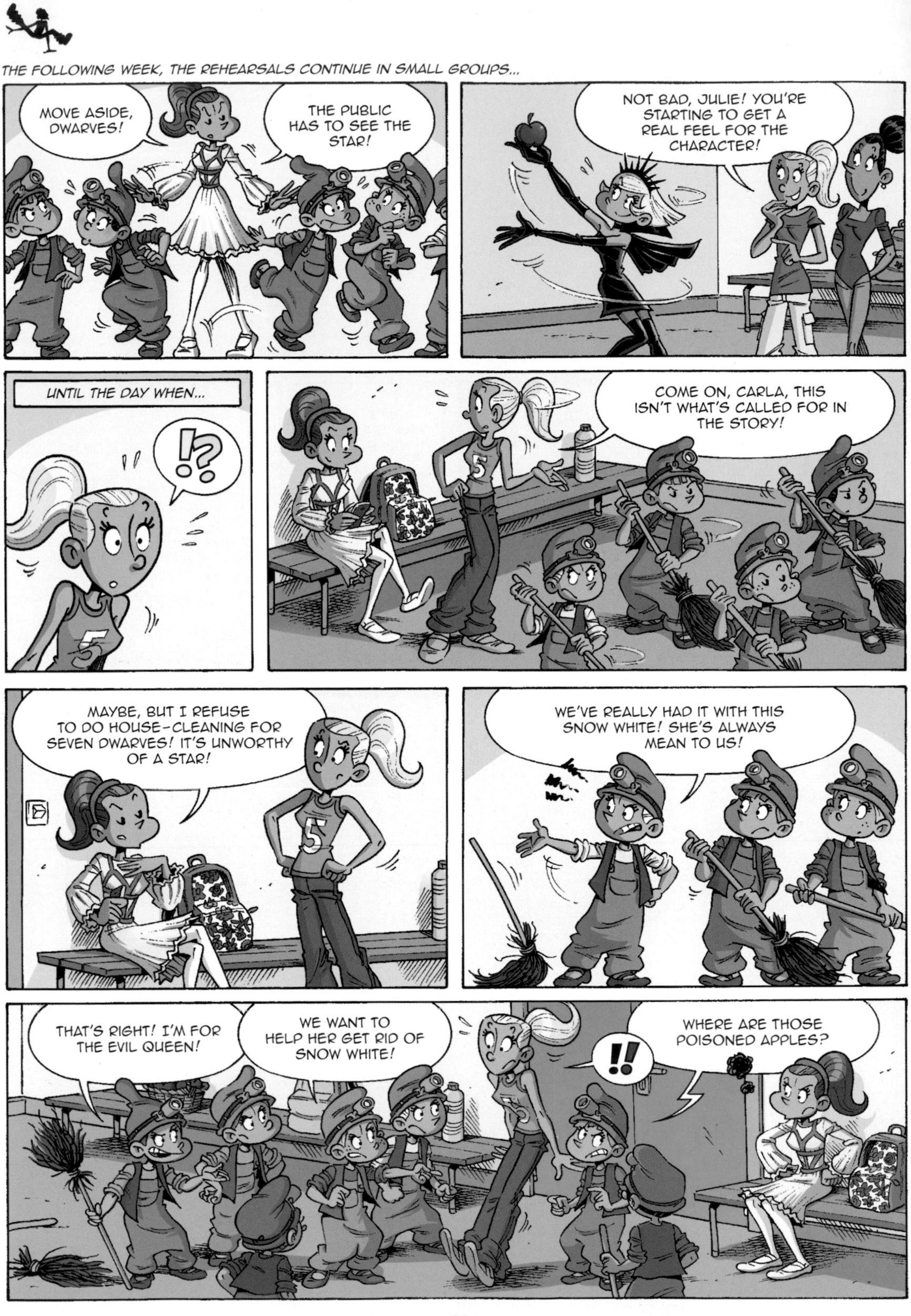
THE FOLLOWING WEEK, THE REHEARSALS CONTINUE IN SMALL GROUPS...
MOVE ASIDE, DWARVES!
THE PUBLIC HAS TO SEE THE STAR!
NOT BAD, JULIE! YOU'RE STARTING TO GET A REAL FEEL FOR THE CHARACTER!
UNTIL THE DAY WHEN...
!?
COME ON, CARLA, THIS ISN'T WHAT'S CALLED FOR IN THE STORY!
MAYBE, BUT I REFUSE TO DO HOUSE-CLEANING FOR SEVEN DWARVES! IT'S UNWORTHY OF A STAR!
WE'VE REALLY HAD IT WITH THIS SNOW WHITE! SHE'S ALWAYS MEAN TO US!
THAT'S RIGHT! I'M FOR THE EVIL QUEEN!
WE WANT TO HELP HER GET RID OF SNOW WHITE!
!!
WHERE ARE THOSE POISONED APPLES?

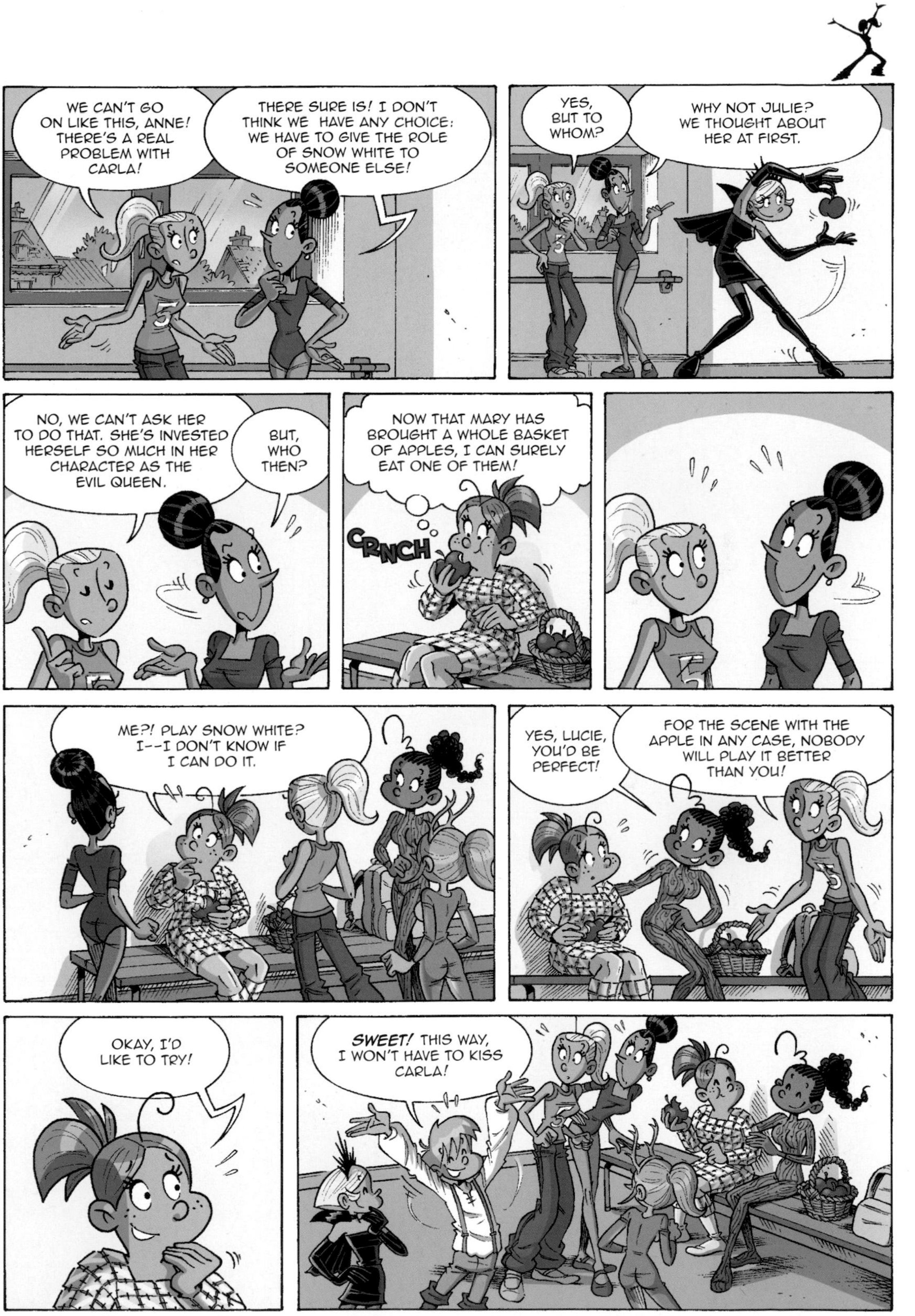
WE CAN'T GO ON LIKE THIS, ANNE! THERE'S A REAL PROBLEM WITH CARLA!
THERE SURE IS! I DON'T THINK WE HAVE ANY CHOICE: WE HAVE TO GIVE THE ROLE OF SNOW WHITE TO SOMEONE ELSE!
YES, BUT TO WHOM?
WHY NOT JULIE? WE THOUGHT ABOUT HER AT FIRST.
NO, WE CAN'T ASK HER TO DO THAT. SHE'S INVESTED HERSELF SO MUCH IN HER CHARACTER AS THE EVIL QUEEN.
BUT, WHO THEN?
NOW THAT MARY HAS BROUGHT A WHOLE BASKET OF APPLES, I CAN SURELY EAT ONE OF THEM!
CRNCH
ME?! PLAY SNOW WHITE? I--I DON'T KNOW IF I CAN DO IT.
YES, LUCIE, YOU'D BE PERFECT!
FOR THE SCENE WITH THE APPLE IN ANY CASE, NOBODY WILL PLAY IT BETTER THAN YOU!
OKAY, I'D LIKE TO TRY!
SWEET! THIS WAY, I WON'T HAVE TO KISS CARLA!

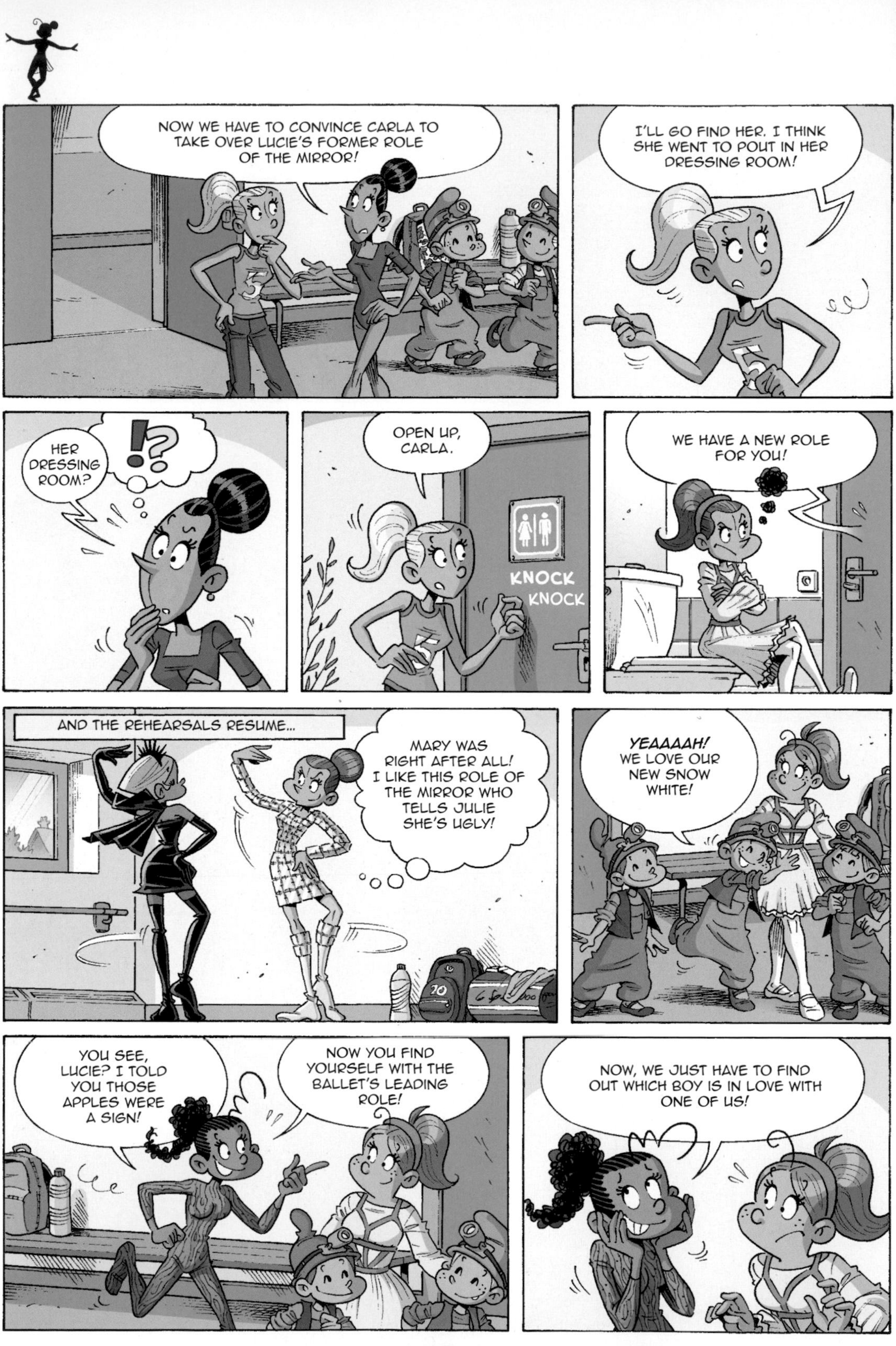
NOW WE HAVE TO CONVINCE CARLA TO TAKE OVER LUCIE'S FORMER ROLE OF THE MIRROR!
I'LL GO FIND HER. I THINK SHE WENT TO POUT IN HER DRESSING ROOM!
HER DRESSING ROOM?
!?
OPEN UP, CARLA.
KNOCK
KNOCK
WE HAVE A NEW ROLE FOR YOU!
AND THE REHEARSALS RESUME...
MARY WAS RIGHT AFTER ALL! I LIKE THIS ROLE OF THE MIRROR WHO TELLS JULIE SHE'S UGLY!
YEAAAAH! WE LOVE OUR NEW SNOW WHITE!
YOU SEE, LUCIE? I TOLD YOU THOSE APPLES WERE A SIGN!
NOW YOU FIND YOURSELF WITH THE BALLET'S LEADING ROLE!
NOW, WE JUST HAVE TO FIND OUT WHICH BOY IS IN LOVE WITH ONE OF US!

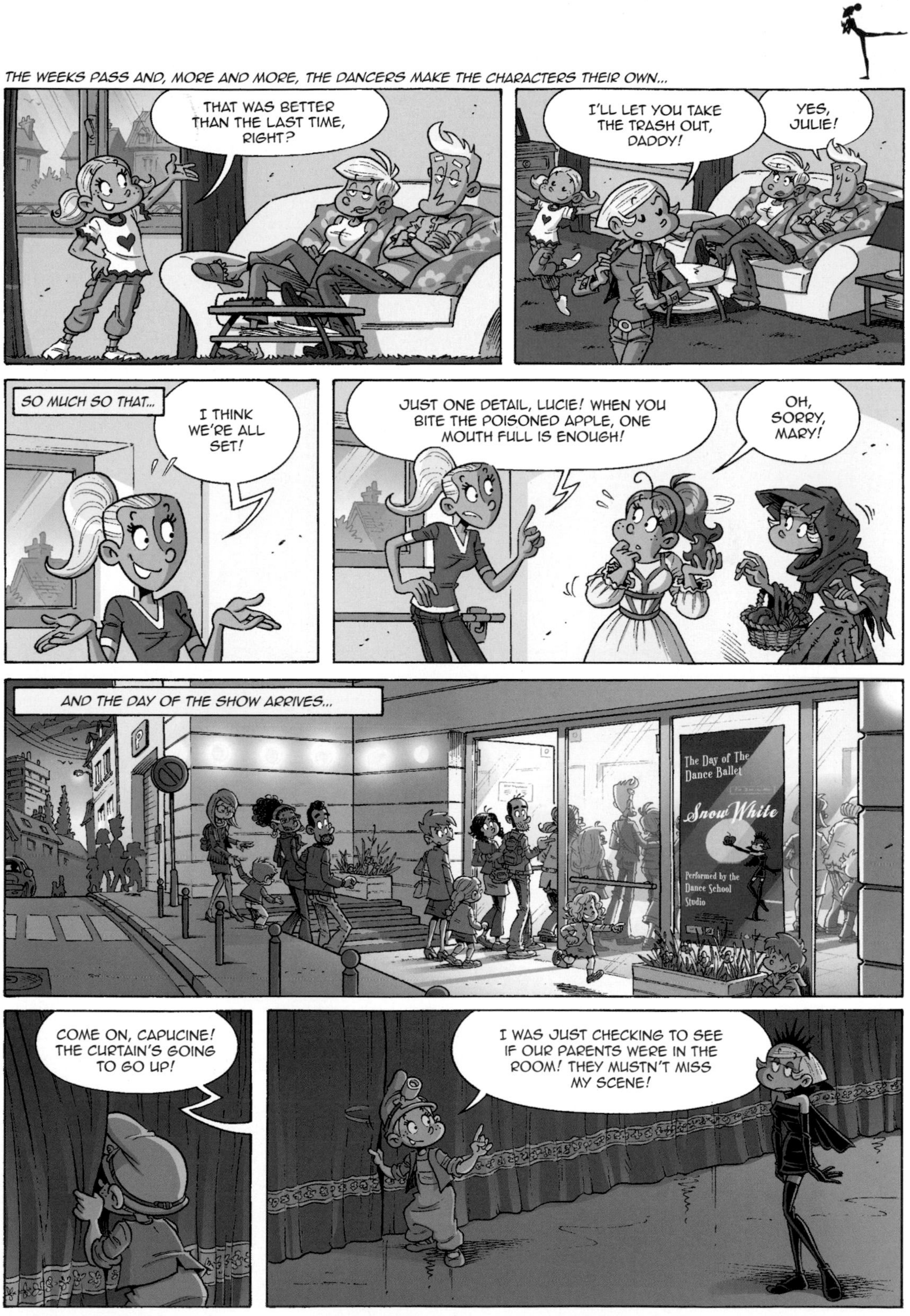
THE WEEKS PASS AND, MORE AND MORE, THE DANCERS MAKE THE CHARACTERS THEIR OWN...
THAT WAS BETTER THAN THE LAST TIME, RIGHT?
I'LL LET YOU TAKE THE TRASH OUT, DADDY!
YES, JULIE!
SO MUCH SO THAT...
I THINK WE'RE ALL SET!
JUST ONE DETAIL, LUCIE! WHEN YOU BITE THE POISONED APPLE, ONE MOUTH FULL IS ENOUGH!
OH, SORRY, MARY!
AND THE DAY OF THE SHOW ARRIVES...
The Day of The Dance Ballet
Snow White
Performed by the Dance School Studio
COME ON, CAPUCINE! THE CURTAIN'S GOING TO GO UP!
I WAS JUST CHECKING TO SEE IF OUR PARENTS WERE IN THE ROOM! THEY MUSTN'T MISS MY SCENE!

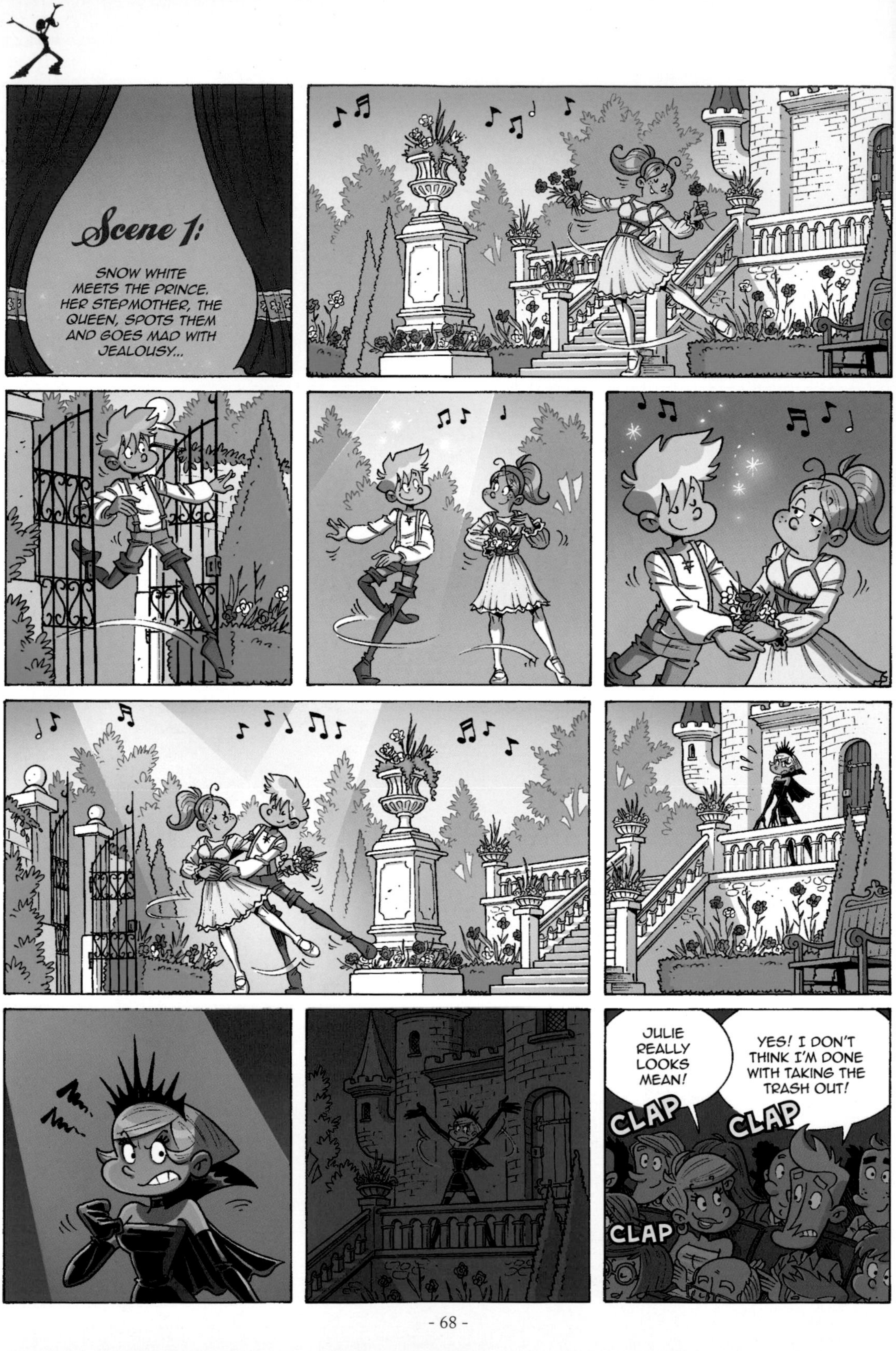

Scene 1:
SNOW WHITE MEETS THE PRINCE. HER STEPMOTHER, THE QUEEN, SPOTS THEM AND GOES MAD WITH JEALOUSY...
JULIE REALLY LOOKS MEAN!
YES! I DON'T THINK I'M DONE WITH TAKING THE TRASH OUT!
CLAP
CLAP
CLAP

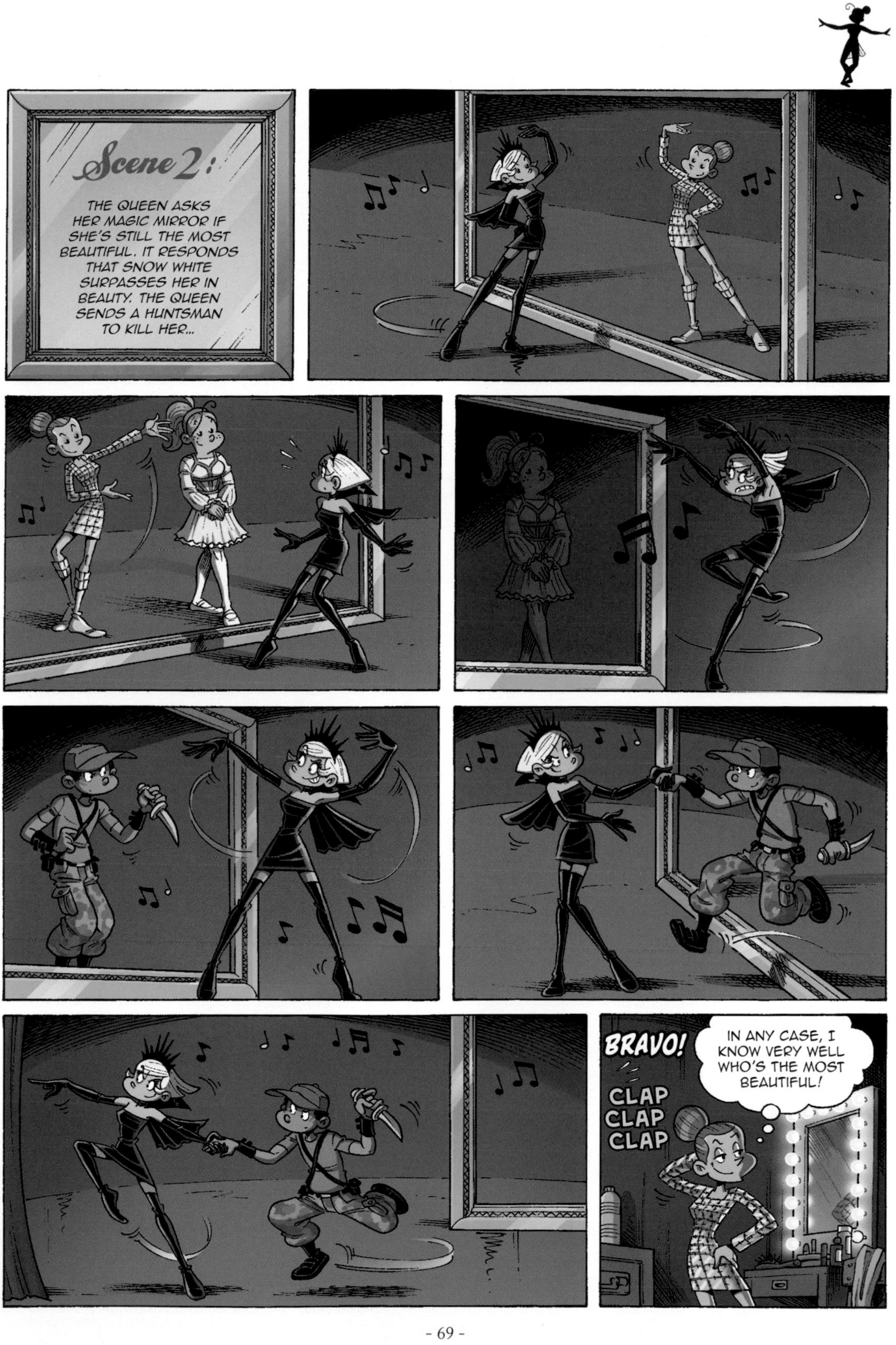
Scene 2:
THE QUEEN ASKS HER MAGIC MIRROR IF SHE'S STILL THE MOST BEAUTIFUL. IT RESPONDS THAT SNOW WHITE SURPASSES HER IN BEAUTY. THE QUEEN SENDS A HUNTSMAN TO KILL HER...
BRAVO!
CLAP
CLAP
CLAP
IN ANY CASE, I KNOW VERY WELL WHO'S THE MOST BEAUTIFUL!

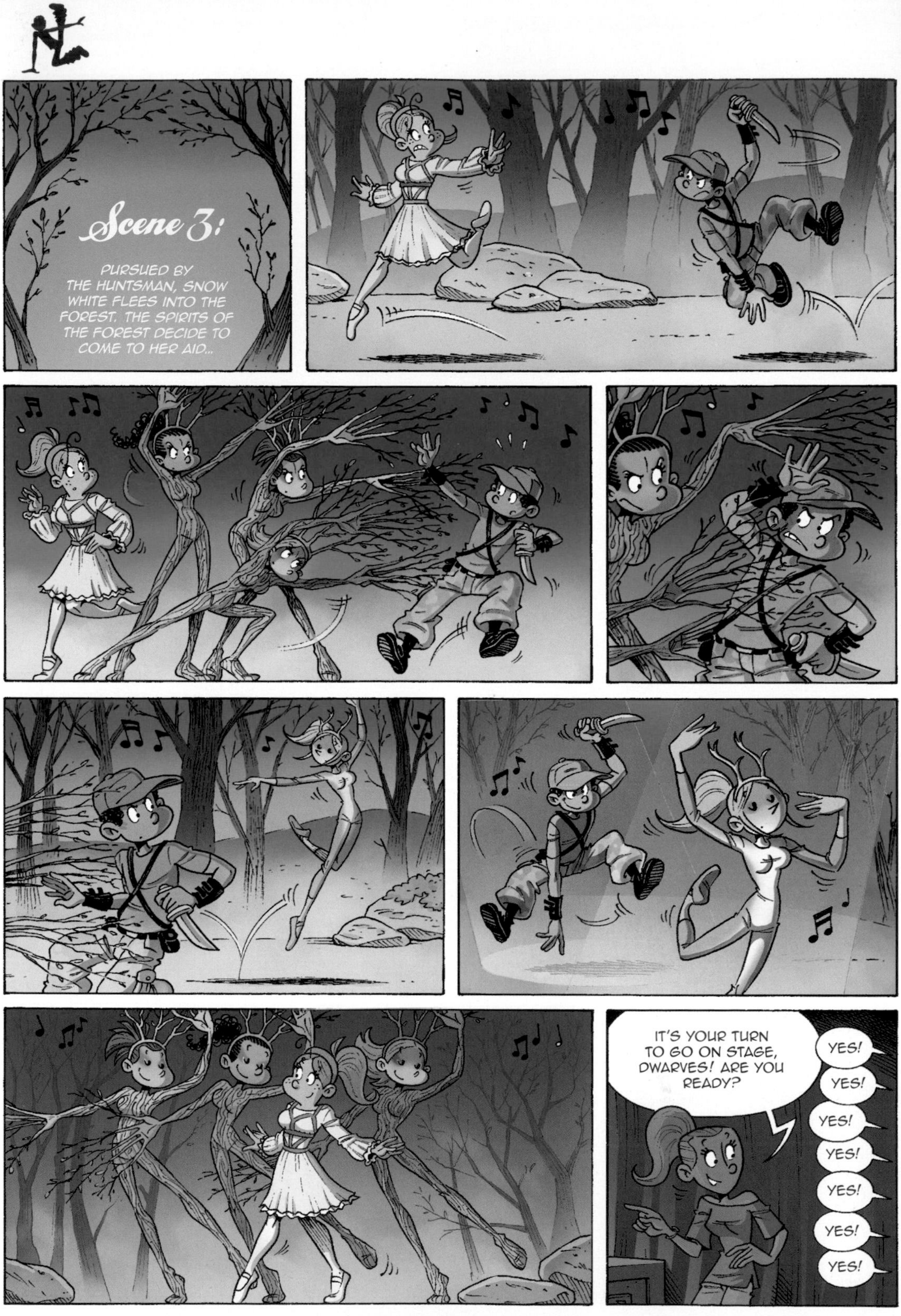
Scene 3:
PURSUED BY THE HUNTSMAN, SNOW WHITE FLEES INTO THE FOREST. THE SPIRITS OF THE FOREST DECIDE TO COME TO HER AID...
IT'S YOUR TURN TO GO ON STAGE, DWARVES! ARE YOU READY?
YES!
YES!
YES!
YES!
YES!
YES!
YES!

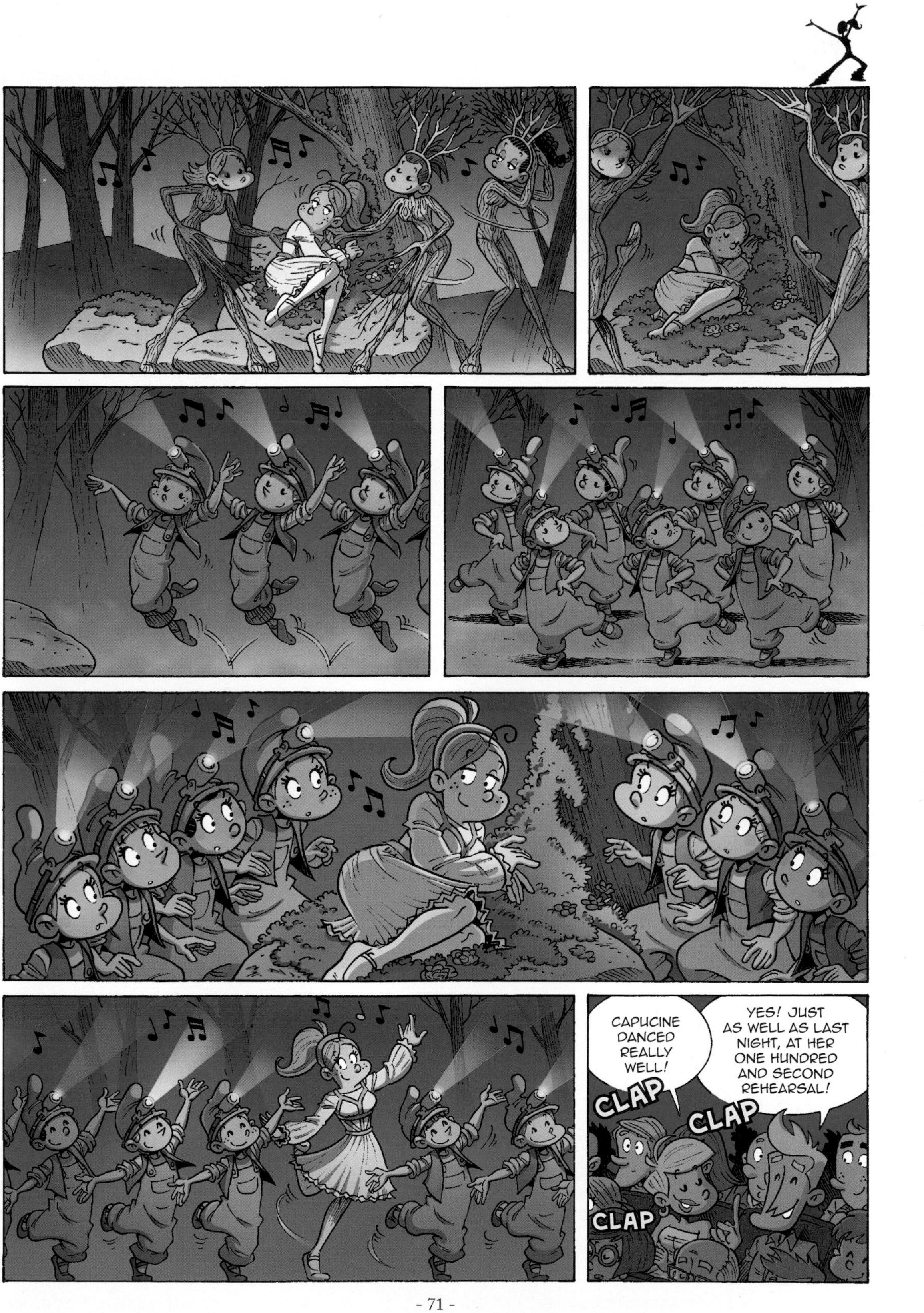
CAPUCINE DANCED REALLY WELL!
YES! JUST AS WELL AS LAST NIGHT, AT HER ONE HUNDRED AND SECOND REHEARSAL!
CLAP
CLAP
CLAP

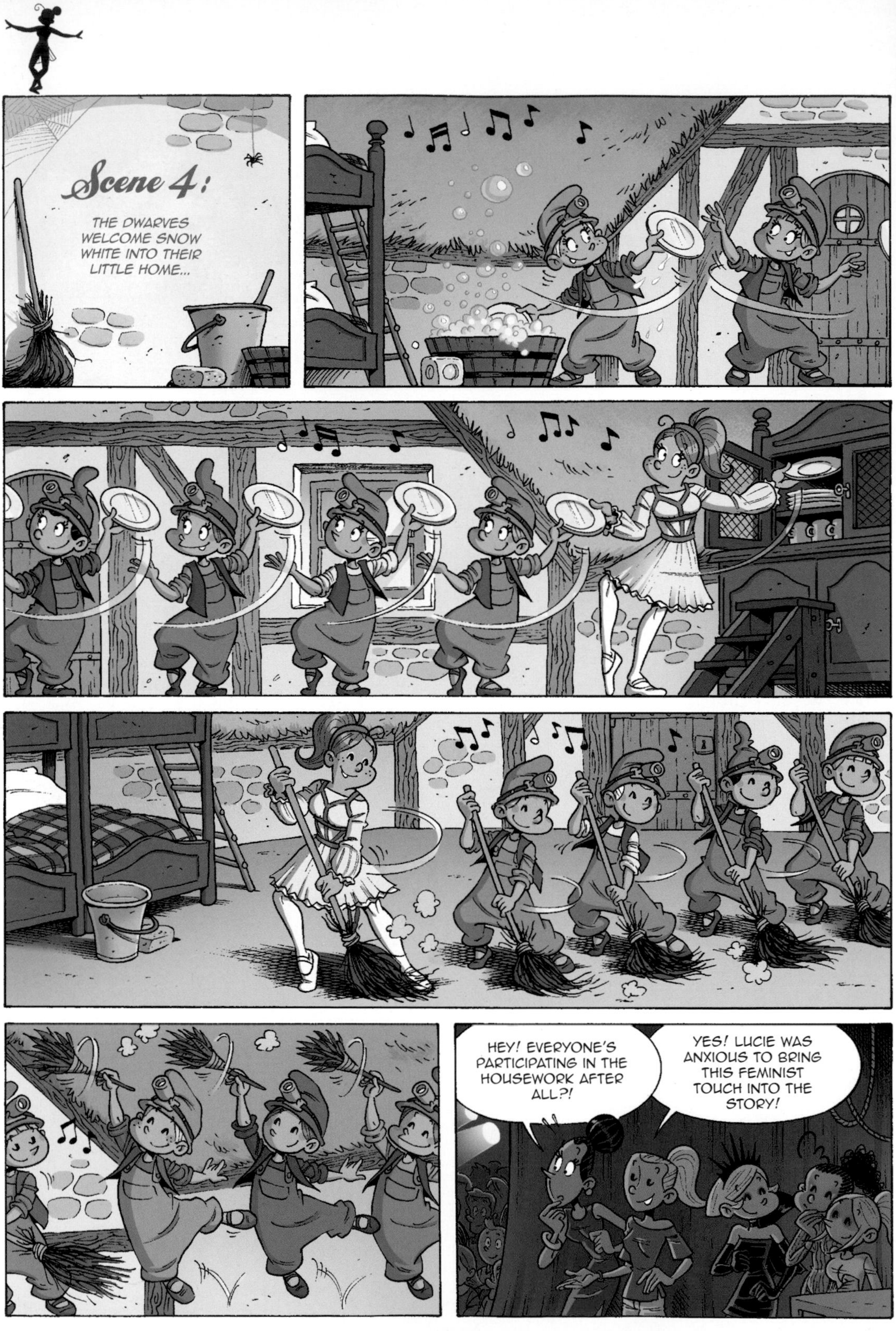
Scene 4:
THE DWARVES WELCOME SNOW WHITE INTO THEIR LITTLE HOME...
HEY! EVERYONE'S PARTICIPATING IN THE HOUSEWORK AFTER ALL?!
YES! LUCIE WAS ANXIOUS TO BRING THIS FEMINIST TOUCH INTO THE STORY!

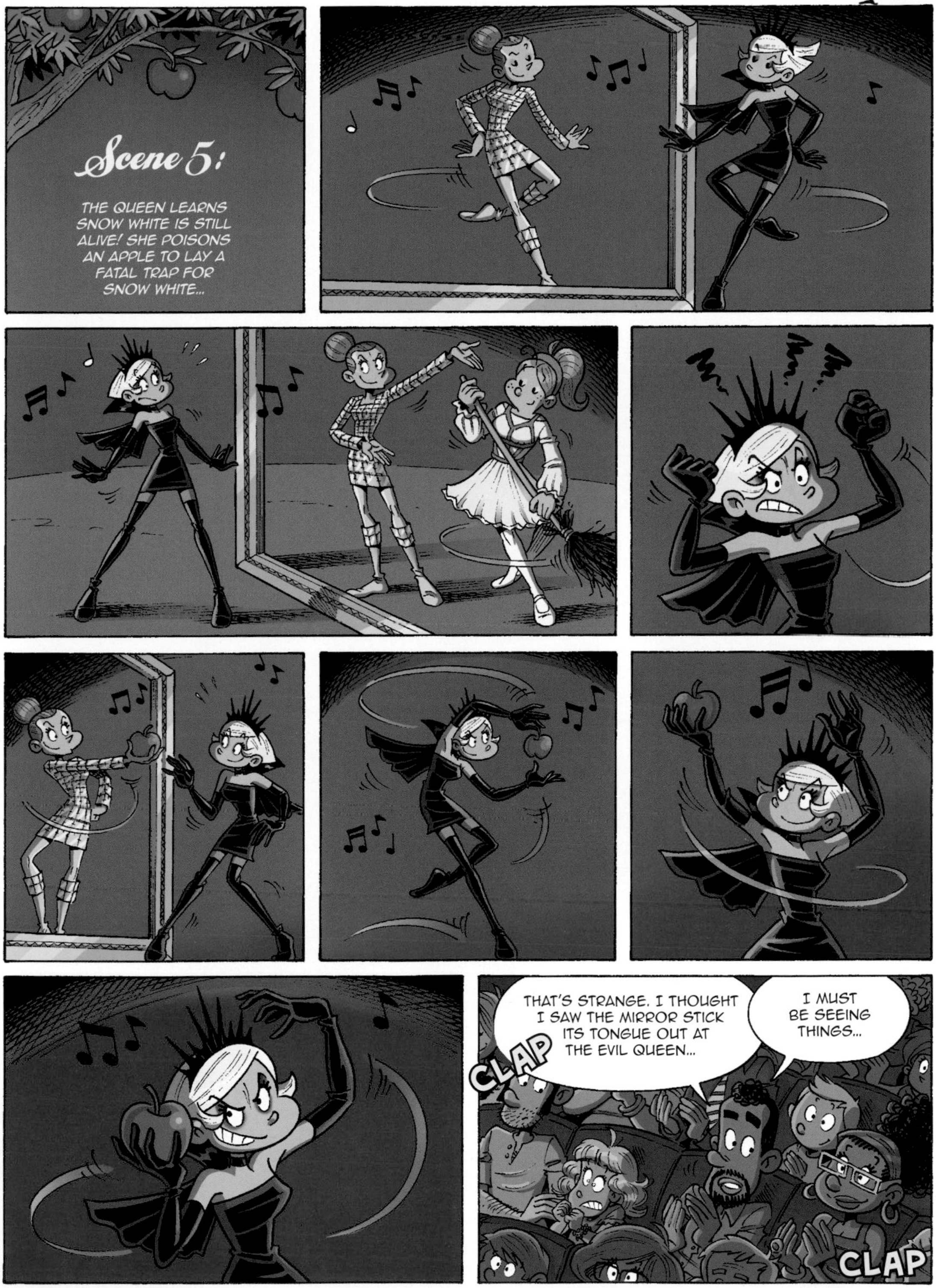
Scene 5:
THE QUEEN LEARNS SNOW WHITE IS STILL ALIVE! SHE POISONS AN APPLE TO LAY A FATAL TRAP FOR SNOW WHITE...
CLAP
THAT'S STRANGE. I THOUGHT I SAW THE MIRROR STICK ITS TONGUE OUT AT THE EVIL QUEEN...
I MUST BE SEEING THINGS...
CLAP

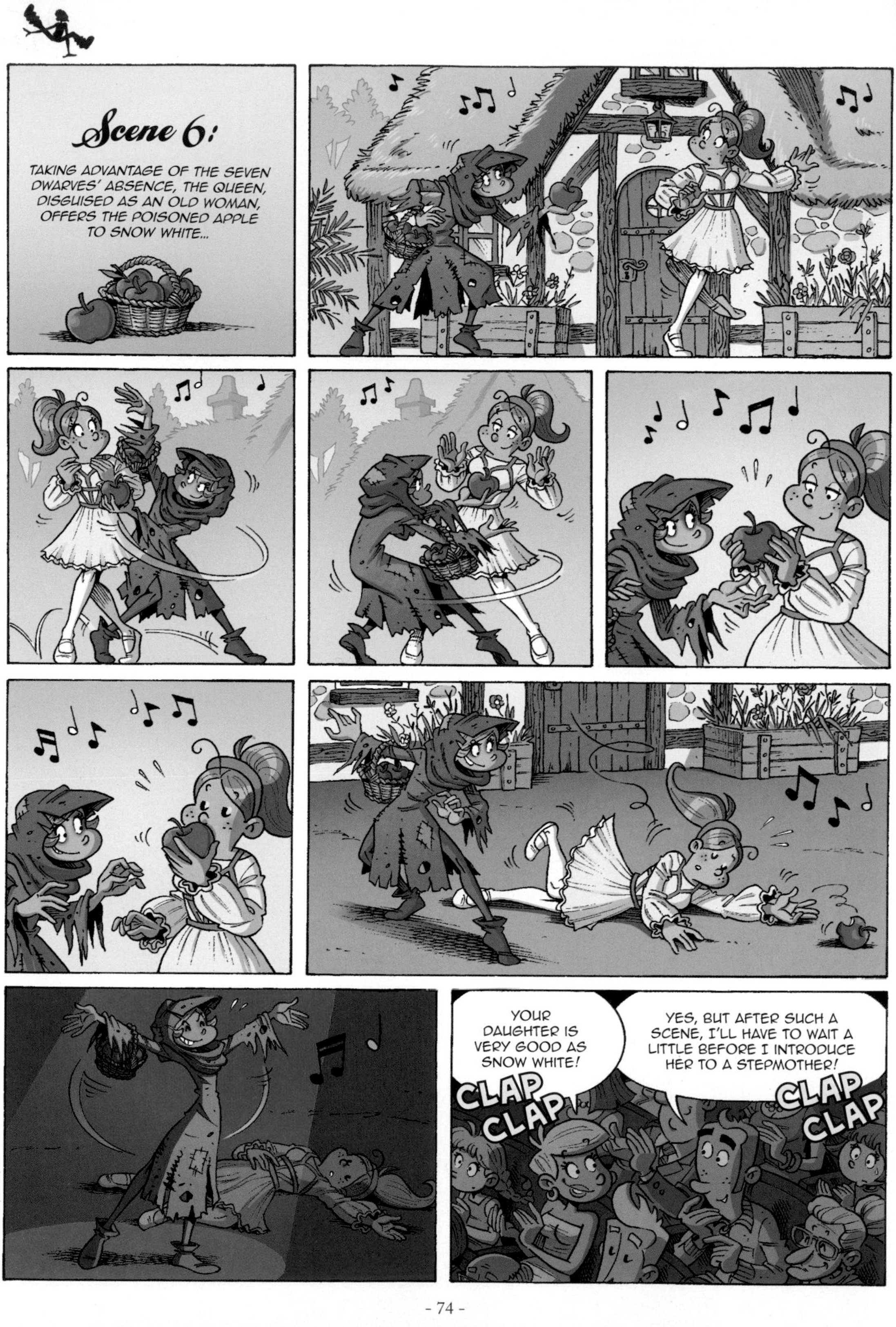
Scene 6:
TAKING ADVANTAGE OF THE SEVEN DWARVES' ABSENCE, THE QUEEN, DISGUISED AS AN OLD WOMAN, OFFERS THE POISONED APPLE TO SNOW WHITE...
YOUR DAUGHTER IS VERY GOOD AS SNOW WHITE!
YES, BUT AFTER SUCH A SCENE, I'LL HAVE TO WAIT A LITTLE BEFORE I INTRODUCE HER TO A STEPMOTHER!
CLAP CLAP
CLAP CLAP

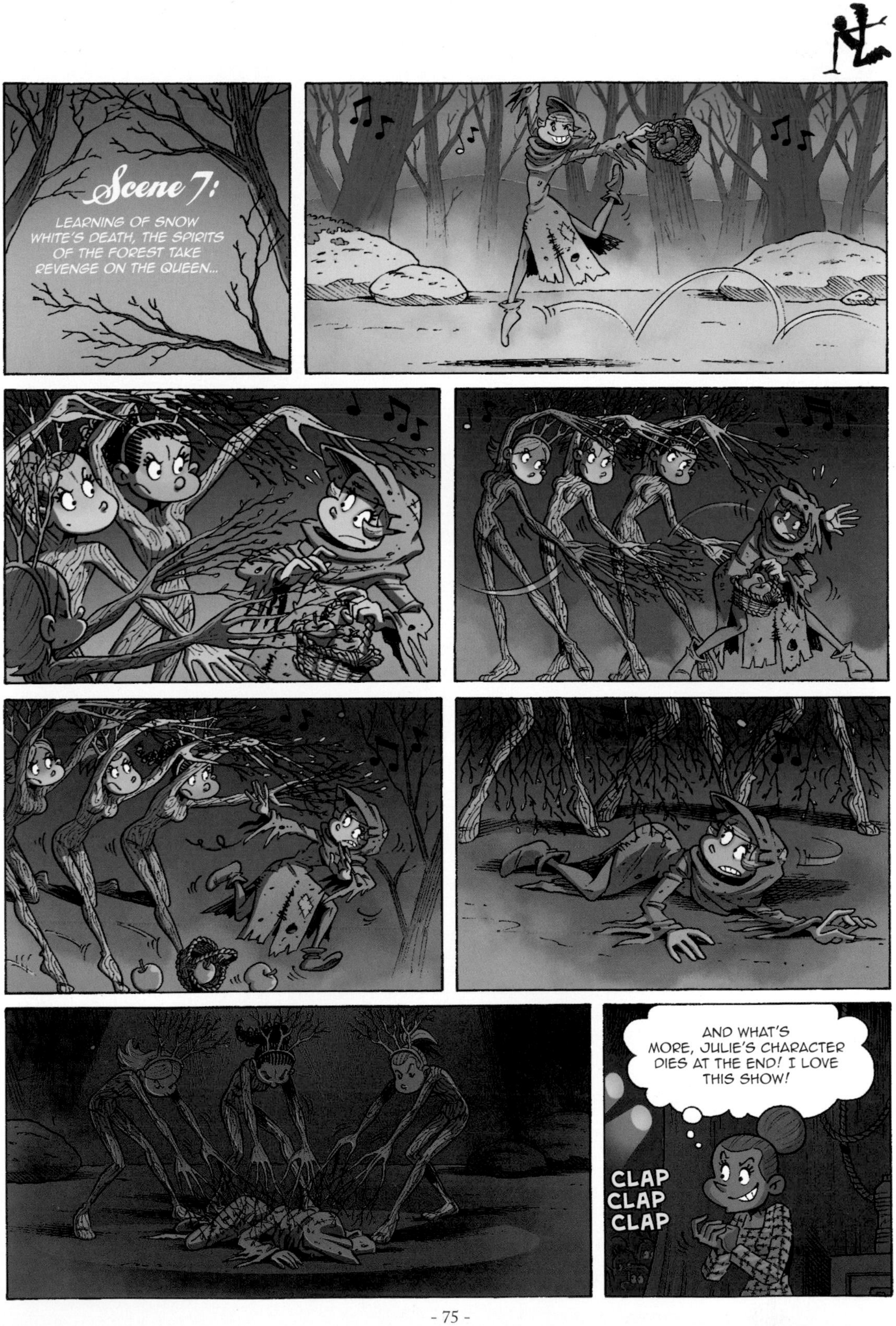
Scene 7:
LEARNING OF SNOW WHITE'S DEATH, THE SPIRITS OF THE FOREST TAKE REVENGE ON THE QUEEN...
AND WHAT'S MORE, JULIE'S CHARACTER DIES AT THE END! I LOVE THIS SHOW!
CLAP CLAP CLAP

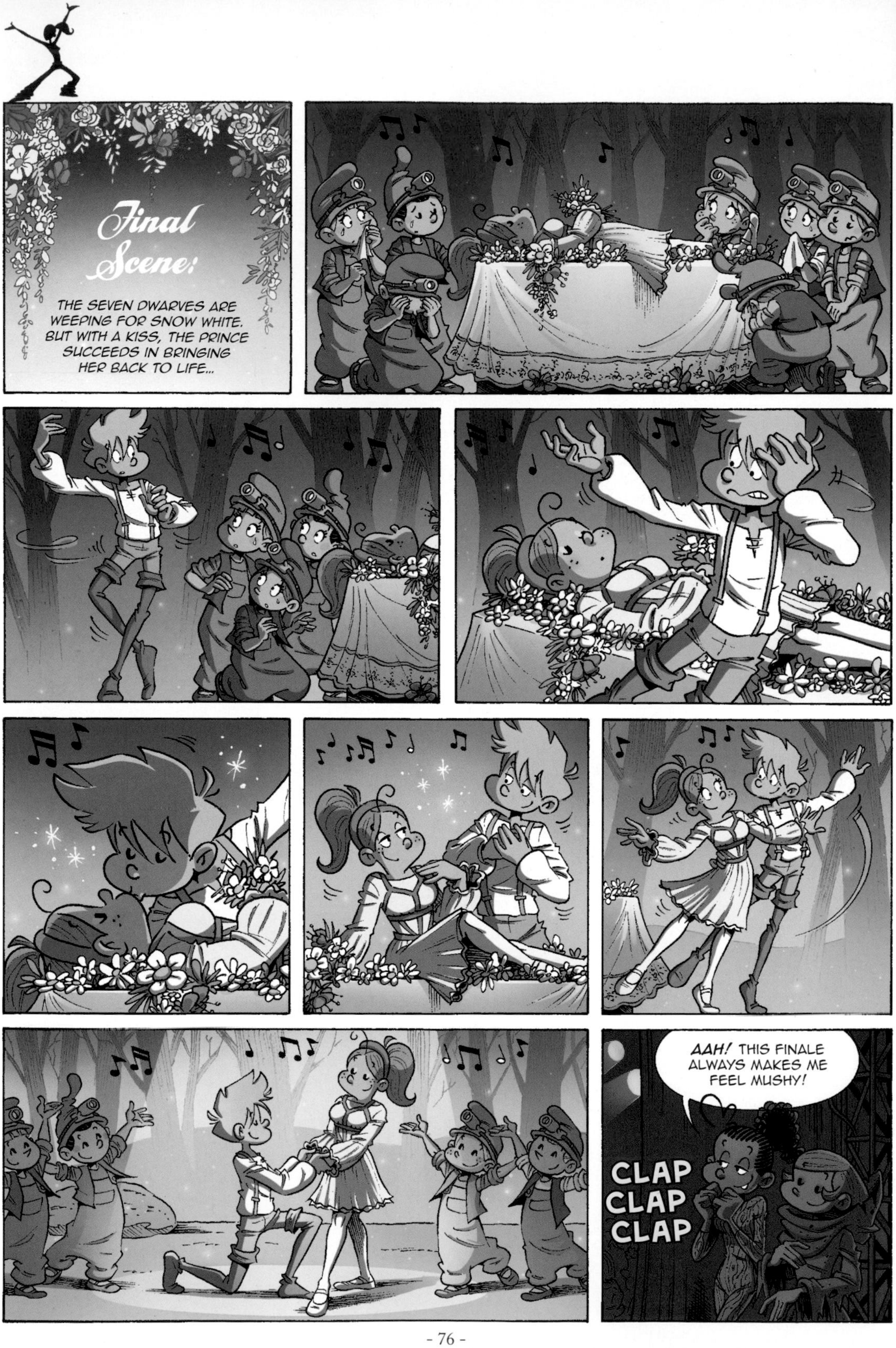
Final Scene:
THE SEVEN DWARVES ARE WEEPING FOR SNOW WHITE. BUT WITH A KISS, THE PRINCE SUCCEEDS IN BRINGING HER BACK TO LIFE...
AAH! THIS FINALE ALWAYS MAKES ME FEEL MUSHY!
CLAP CLAP CLAP

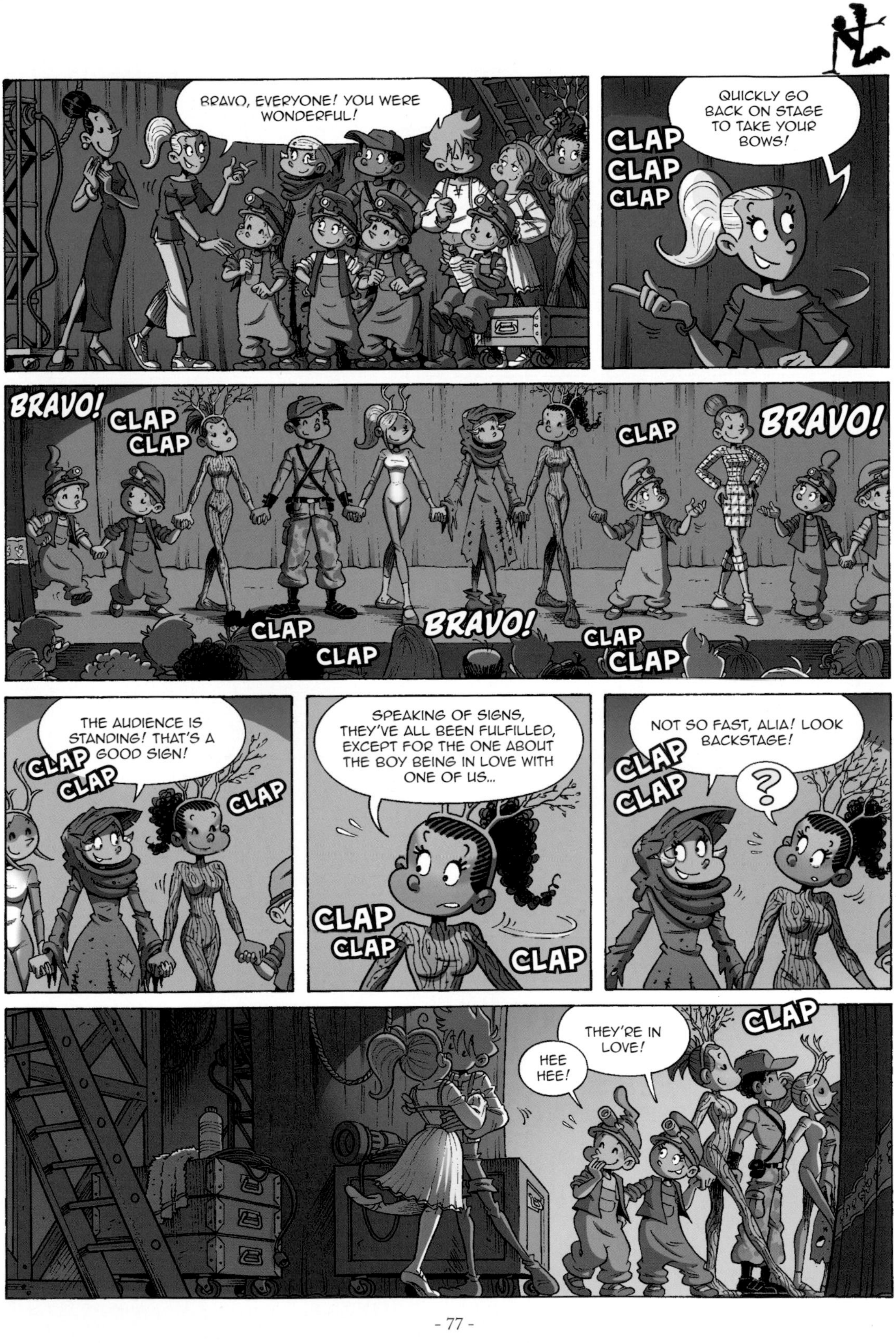
BRAVO, EVERYONE! YOU WERE WONDERFUL!
CLAP
CLAP
CLAP
QUICKLY GO BACK ON STAGE TO TAKE YOUR BOWS!
BRAVO!
CLAP
CLAP
CLAP
BRAVO!
CLAP
BRAVO!
CLAP
CLAP
CLAP
THE AUDIENCE IS STANDING! THAT'S A GOOD SIGN!
CLAP
CLAP
CLAP
SPEAKING OF SIGNS, THEY'VE ALL BEEN FULFILLED, EXCEPT FOR THE ONE ABOUT THE BOY BEING IN LOVE WITH ONE OF US...
CLAP
CLAP
CLAP
NOT SO FAST, ALIA! LOOK BACKSTAGE!
CLAP
CLAP
?
HEE HEE!
THEY'RE IN LOVE!
CLAP

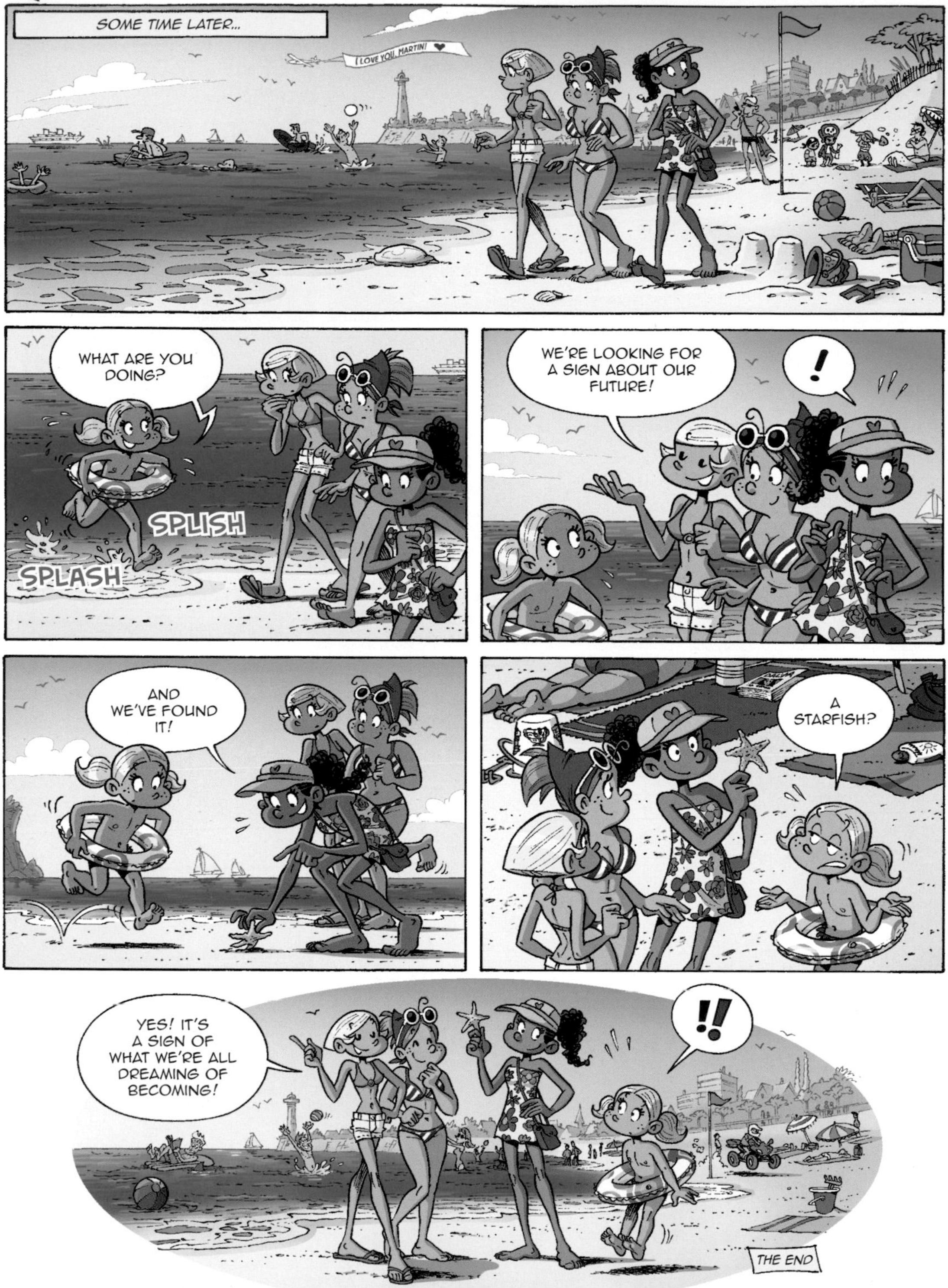
SOME TIME LATER...
I LOVE YOU, MARTIN!
WHAT ARE YOU DOING?
SPLISH
SPLASH
WE'RE LOOKING FOR A SIGN ABOUT OUR FUTURE!
!
AND WE'VE FOUND IT!
A STARFISH?
YES! IT'S A SIGN OF WHAT WE'RE ALL DREAMING OF BECOMING!
!!
THE END

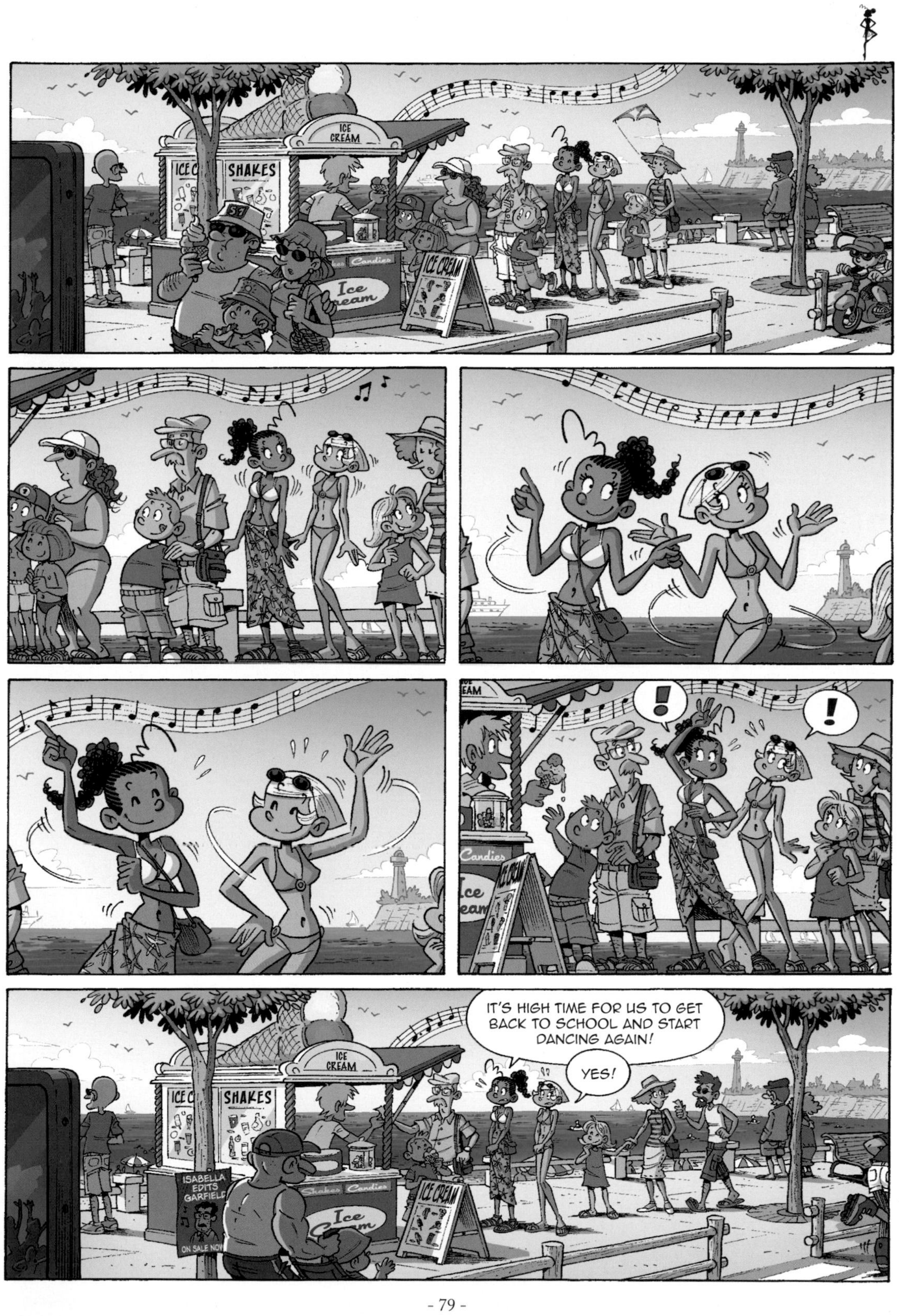
ICE CREAM
ICE CREAM
SHAKES
Candies
ICE CREAM
Ice Cream
!
!
ICE CREAM
SHAKES
ISABELLA EDITS GARFIELD
ON SALE NOW
Shakes Candies
Ice Cream
ICE CREAM
IT'S HIGH TIME FOR US TO GET BACK TO SCHOOL AND START DANCING AGAIN!
YES!

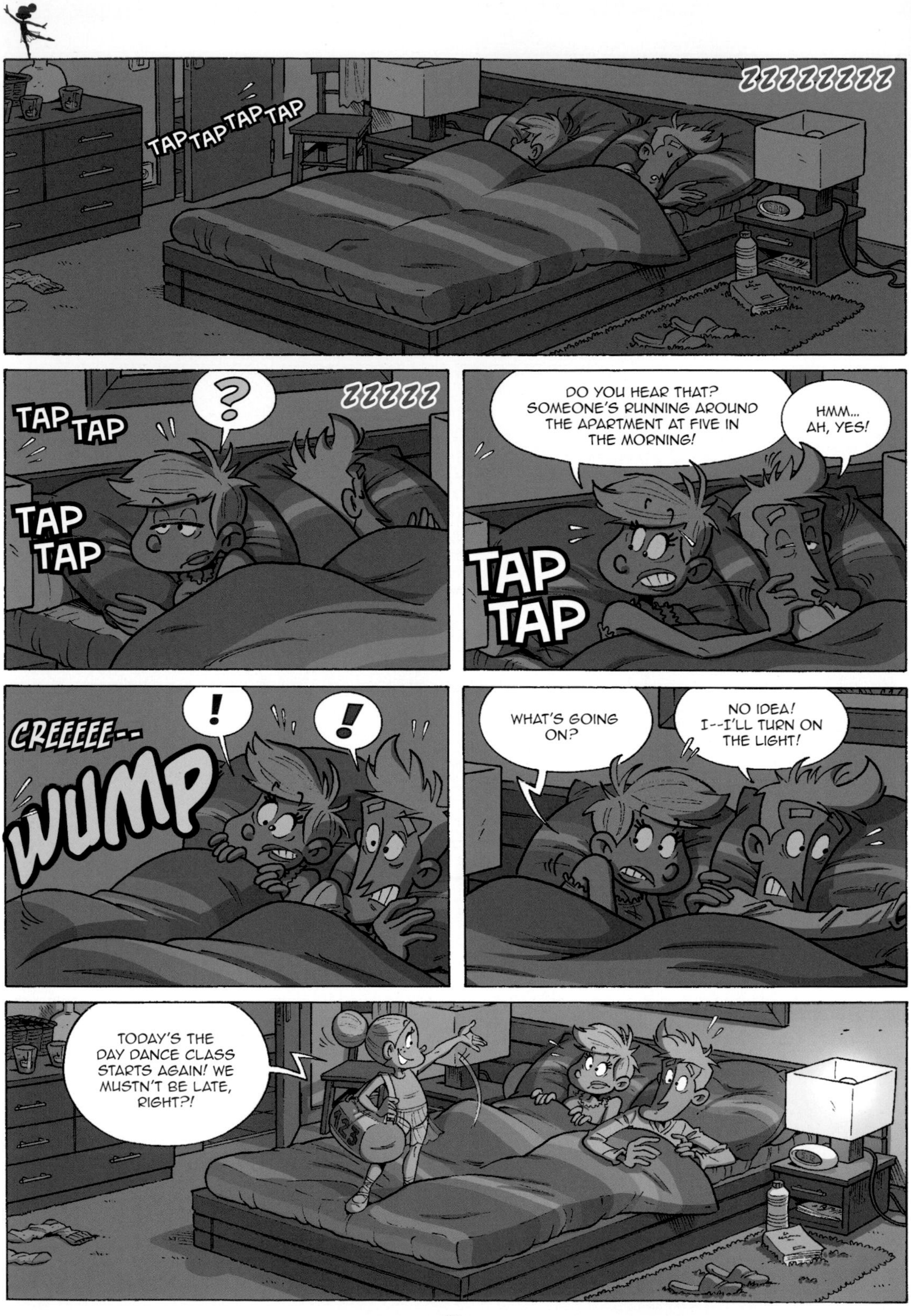
TAP TAP TAP TAP
ZZZZZZZZ
TAP TAP
?
ZZZZZ
TAP TAP
DO YOU HEAR THAT? SOMEONE'S RUNNING AROUND THE APARTMENT AT FIVE IN THE MORNING!
HMM... AH, YES!
TAP TAP
CREEEEE--
WUMP
!
!
WHAT'S GOING ON?
NO IDEA! I--I'LL TURN ON THE LIGHT!
TODAY'S THE DAY DANCE CLASS STARTS AGAIN! WE MUSTN'T BE LATE, RIGHT?!
123

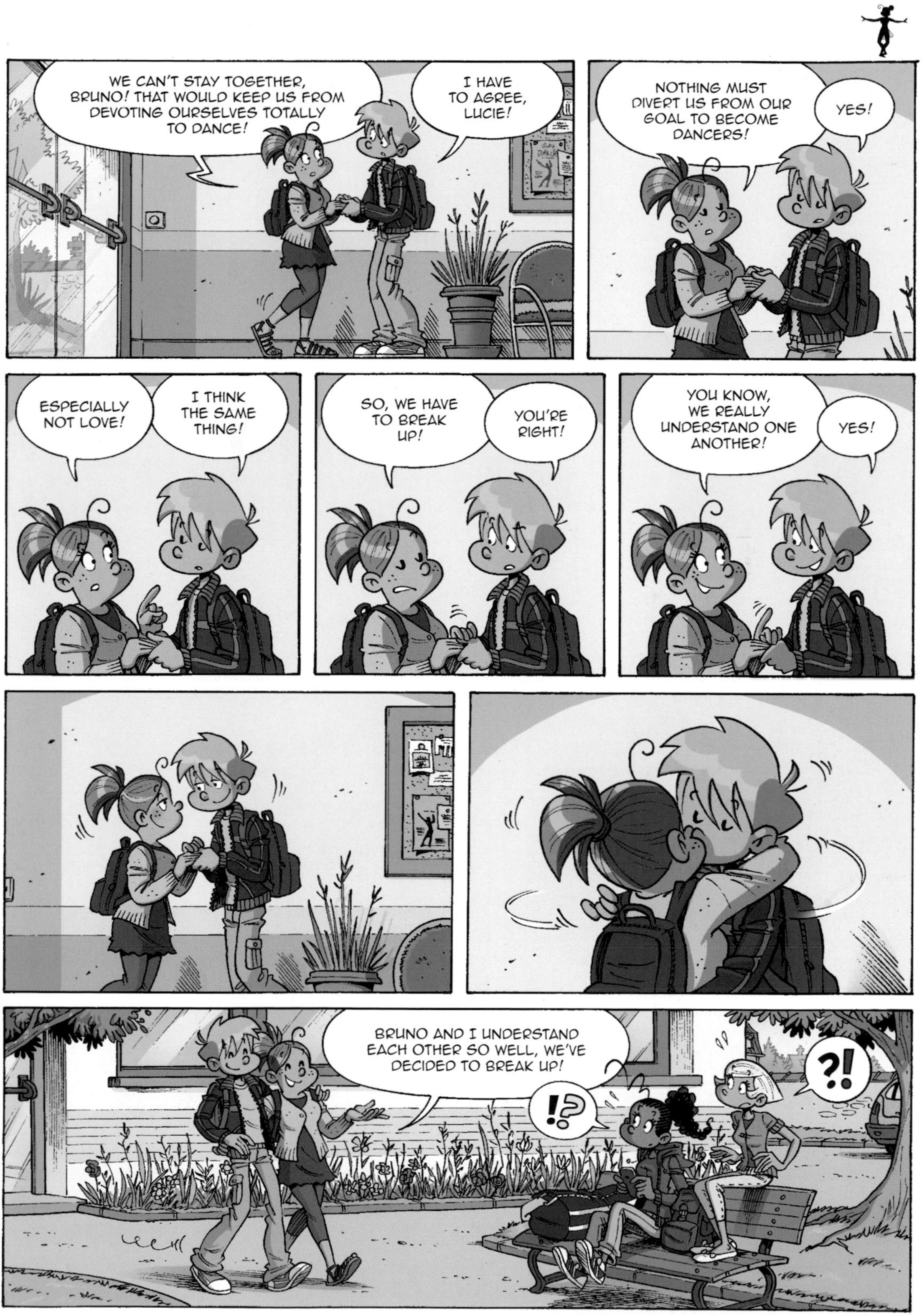
WE CAN'T STAY TOGETHER, BRUNO! THAT WOULD KEEP US FROM DEVOTING OURSELVES TOTALLY TO DANCE!
I HAVE TO AGREE, LUCIE!
NOTHING MUST DIVERT US FROM OUR GOAL TO BECOME DANCERS!
YES!
ESPECIALLY NOT LOVE!
I THINK THE SAME THING!
SO, WE HAVE TO BREAK UP!
YOU'RE RIGHT!
YOU KNOW, WE REALLY UNDERSTAND ONE ANOTHER!
YES!
BRUNO AND I UNDERSTAND EACH OTHER SO WELL, WE'VE DECIDED TO BREAK UP!
!?
?!

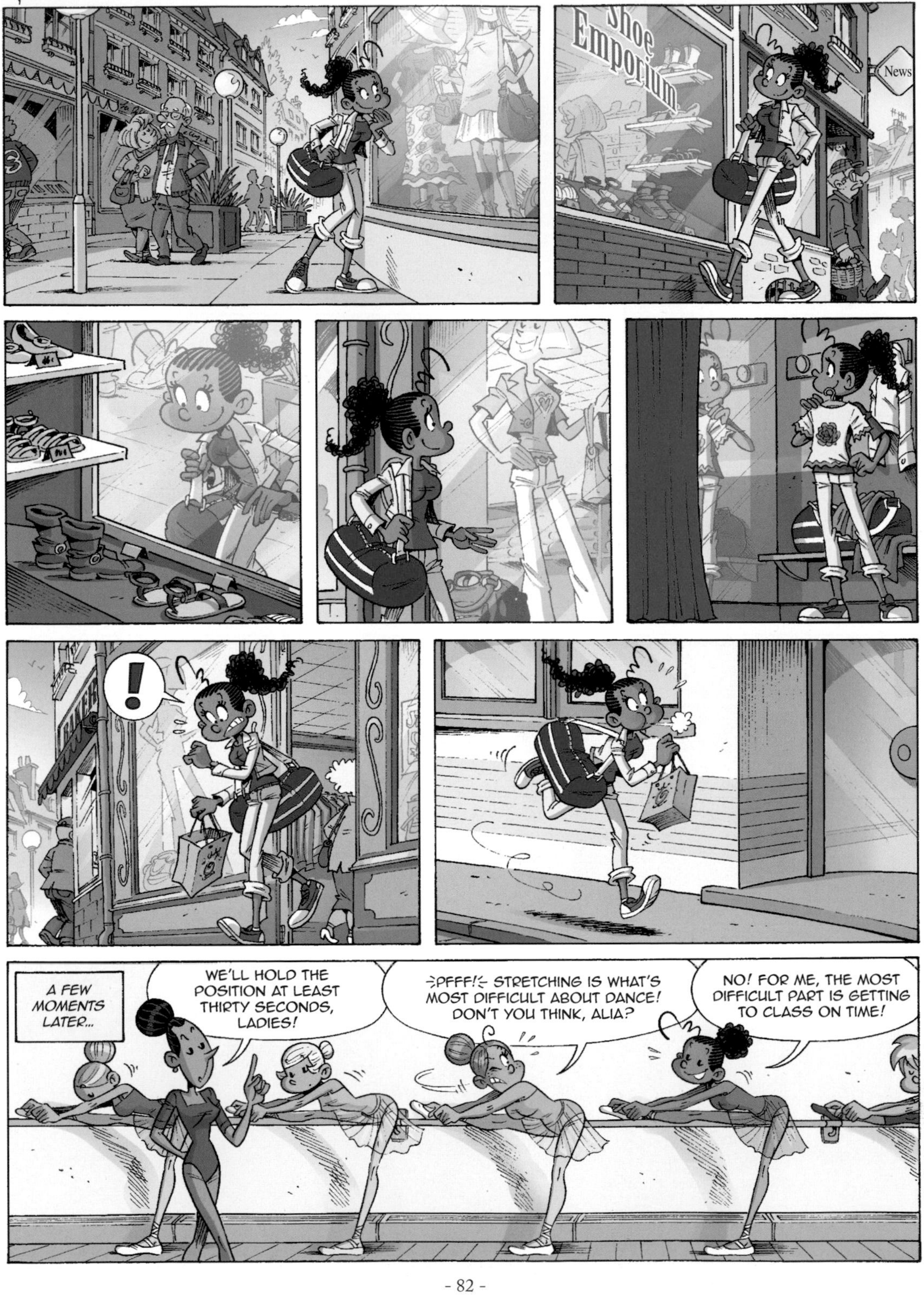

Shoe Emporium
News
!
A FEW MOMENTS LATER...
WE'LL HOLD THE POSITION AT LEAST THIRTY SECONDS, LADIES!
PFFF! STRETCHING IS WHAT'S MOST DIFFICULT ABOUT DANCE! DON'T YOU THINK, ALIA?
NO! FOR ME, THE MOST DIFFICULT PART IS GETTING TO CLASS ON TIME!

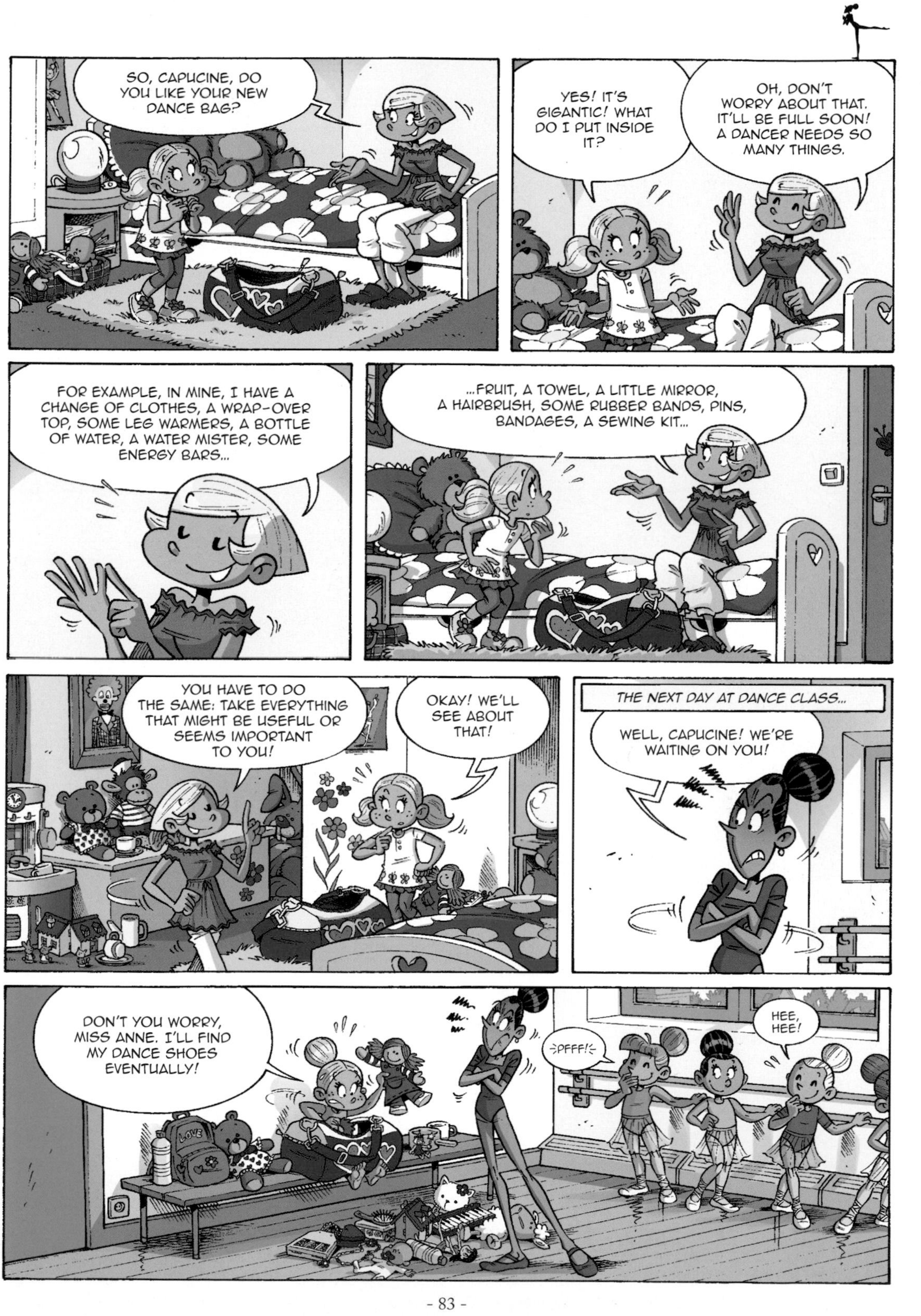
SO, CAPUCINE, DO YOU LIKE YOUR NEW DANCE BAG?
YES! IT'S GIGANTIC! WHAT DO I PUT INSIDE IT?
OH, DON'T WORRY ABOUT THAT. IT'LL BE FULL SOON! A DANCER NEEDS SO MANY THINGS.
FOR EXAMPLE, IN MINE, I HAVE A CHANGE OF CLOTHES, A WRAP-OVER TOP, SOME LEG WARMERS, A BOTTLE OF WATER, A WATER MISTER, SOME ENERGY BARS...
...FRUIT, A TOWEL, A LITTLE MIRROR, A HAIRBRUSH, SOME RUBBER BANDS, PINS, BANDAGES, A SEWING KIT...
YOU HAVE TO DO THE SAME: TAKE EVERYTHING THAT MIGHT BE USEFUL OR SEEMS IMPORTANT TO YOU!
OKAY! WE'LL SEE ABOUT THAT!
THE NEXT DAY AT DANCE CLASS...
WELL, CAPUCINE! WE'RE WAITING ON YOU!
DON'T YOU WORRY, MISS ANNE. I'LL FIND MY DANCE SHOES EVENTUALLY!
PFFF!
HEE, HEE!
LOVE

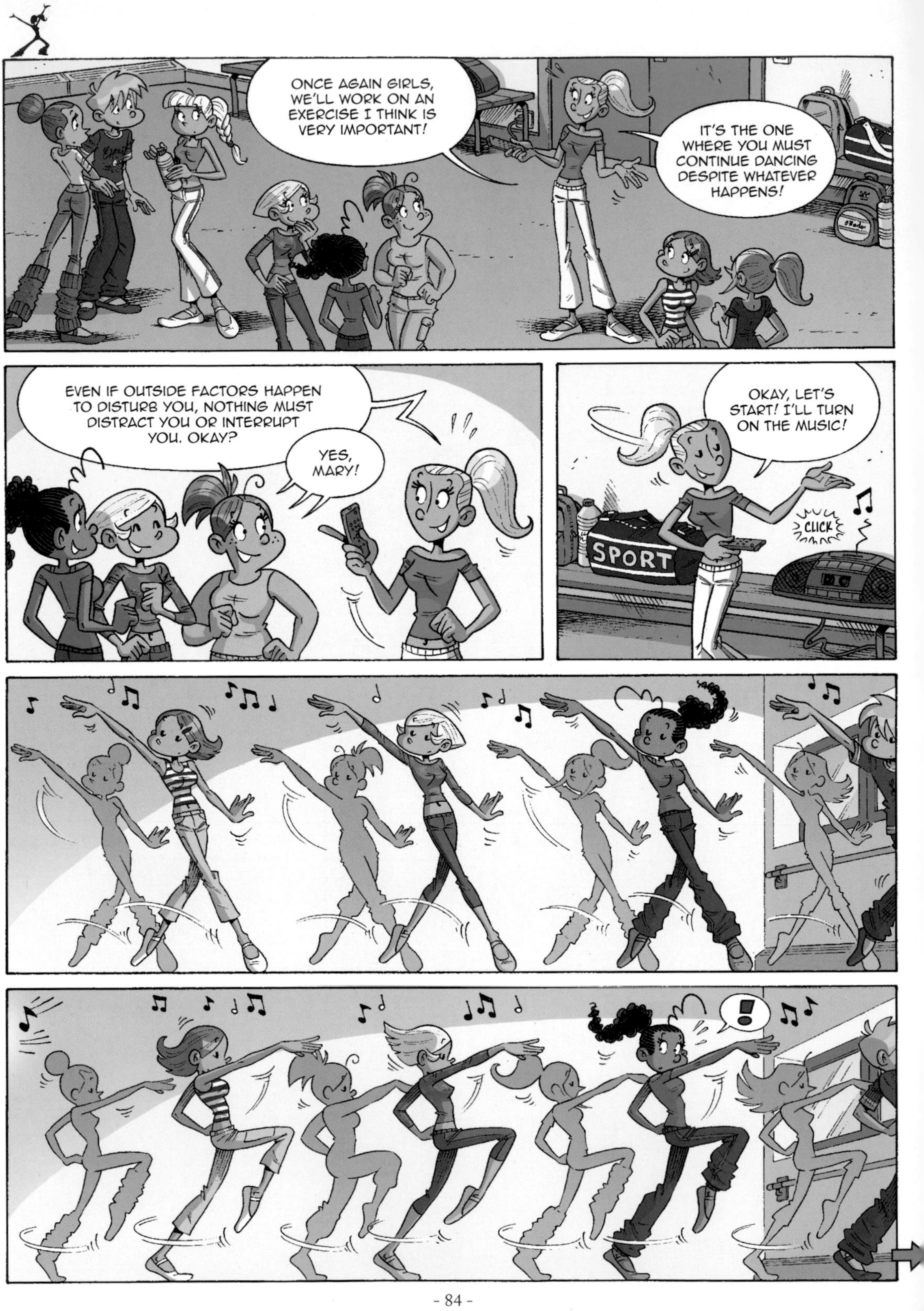
ONCE AGAIN GIRLS, WE'LL WORK ON AN EXERCISE I THINK IS VERY IMPORTANT!
IT'S THE ONE WHERE YOU MUST CONTINUE DANCING DESPITE WHATEVER HAPPENS!
EVEN IF OUTSIDE FACTORS HAPPEN TO DISTURB YOU, NOTHING MUST DISTRACT YOU OR INTERRUPT YOU. OKAY?
YES, MARY!
OKAY, LET'S START! I'LL TURN ON THE MUSIC!
CLICK
SPORT
!

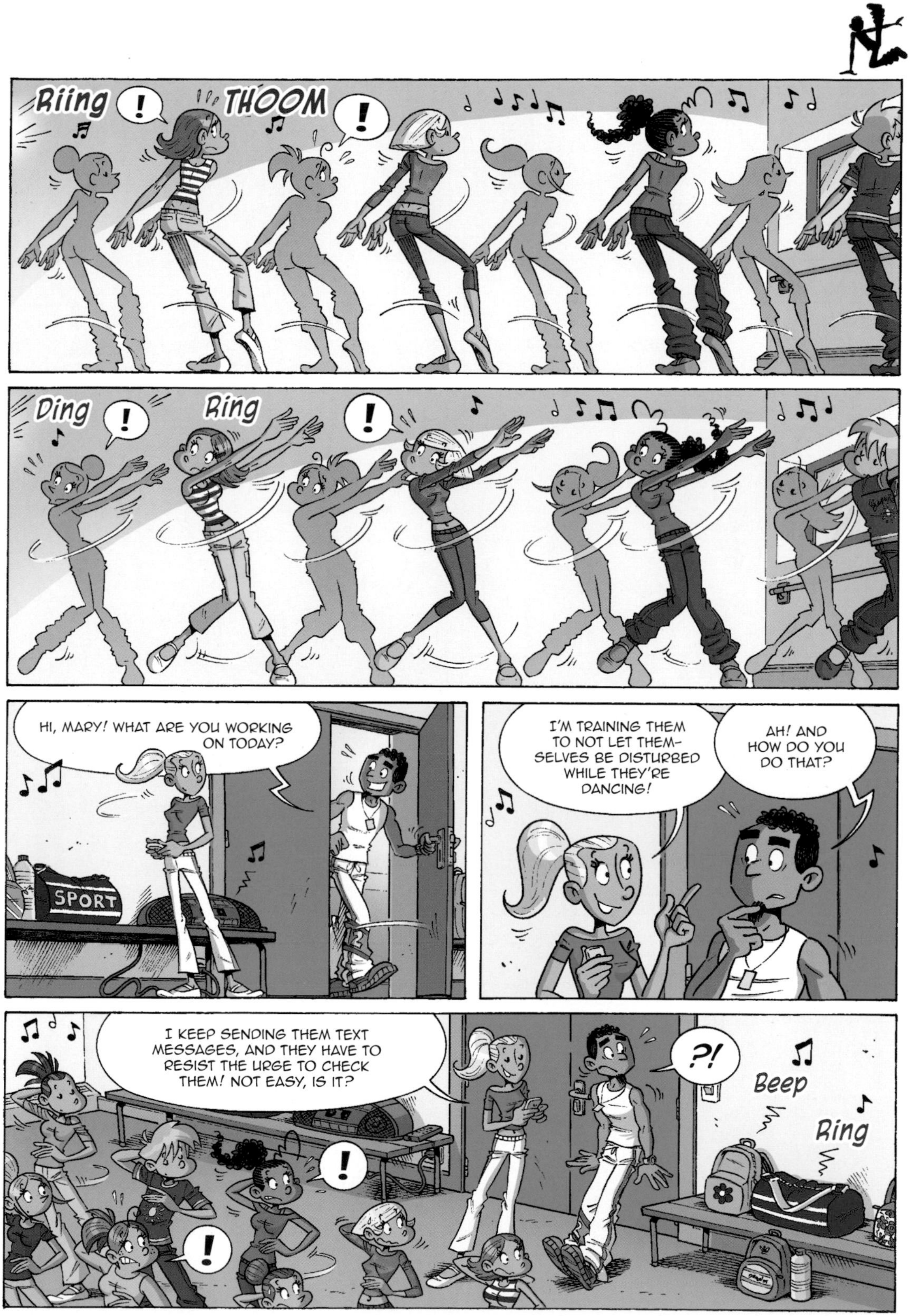
Riing
!
THOOM
!
Ding
!
Ring
!
HI, MARY! WHAT ARE YOU WORKING ON TODAY?
SPORT
I'M TRAINING THEM TO NOT LET THEM-SELVES BE DISTURBED WHILE THEY'RE DANCING!
AH! AND HOW DO YOU DO THAT?
I KEEP SENDING THEM TEXT MESSAGES, AND THEY HAVE TO RESIST THE URGE TO CHECK THEM! NOT EASY, IS IT?
?!
Beep
Ring
!
!

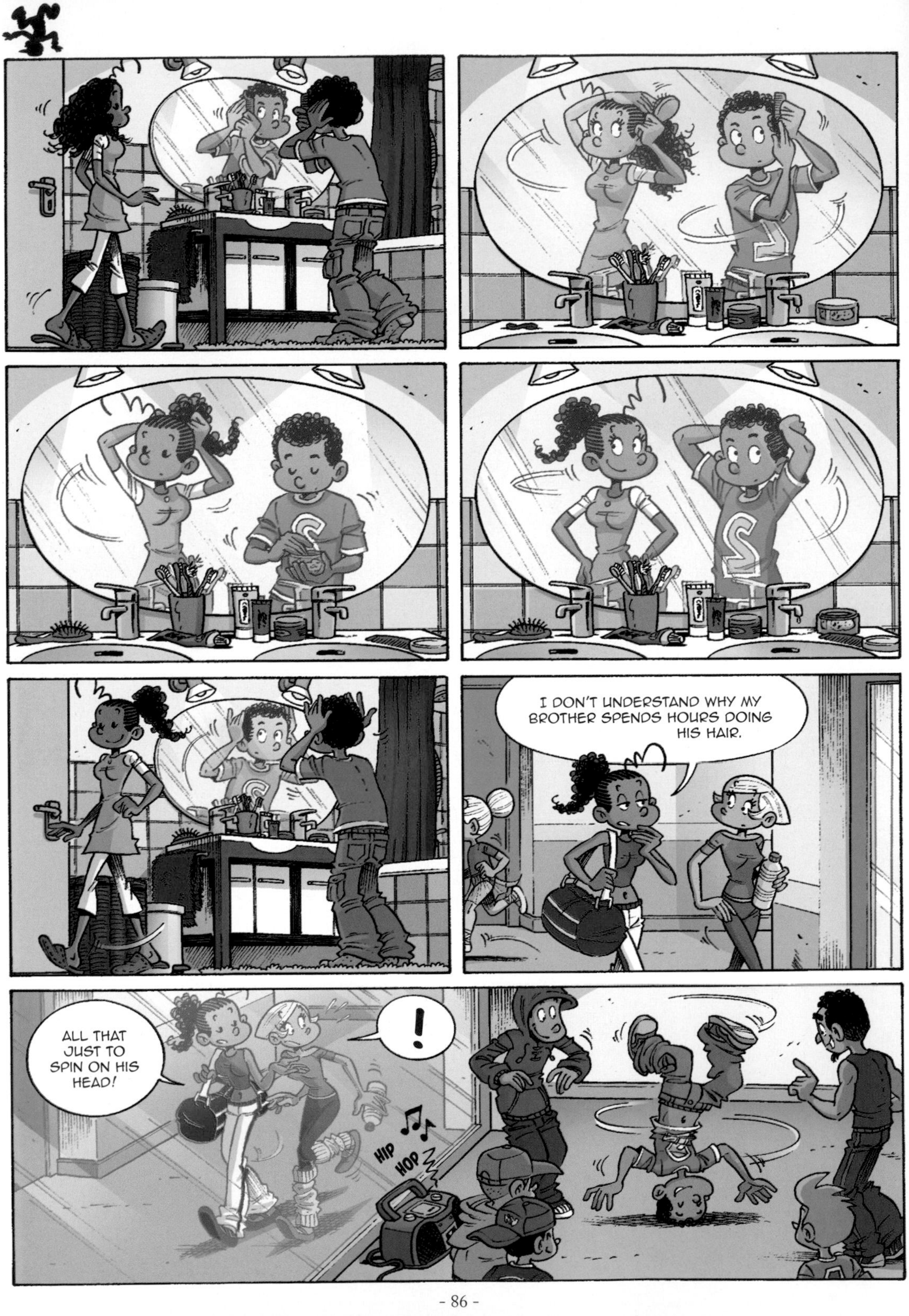
I DON'T UNDERSTAND WHY MY BROTHER SPENDS HOURS DOING HIS HAIR.
ALL THAT JUST TO SPIN ON HIS HEAD!
!
HIP HOP

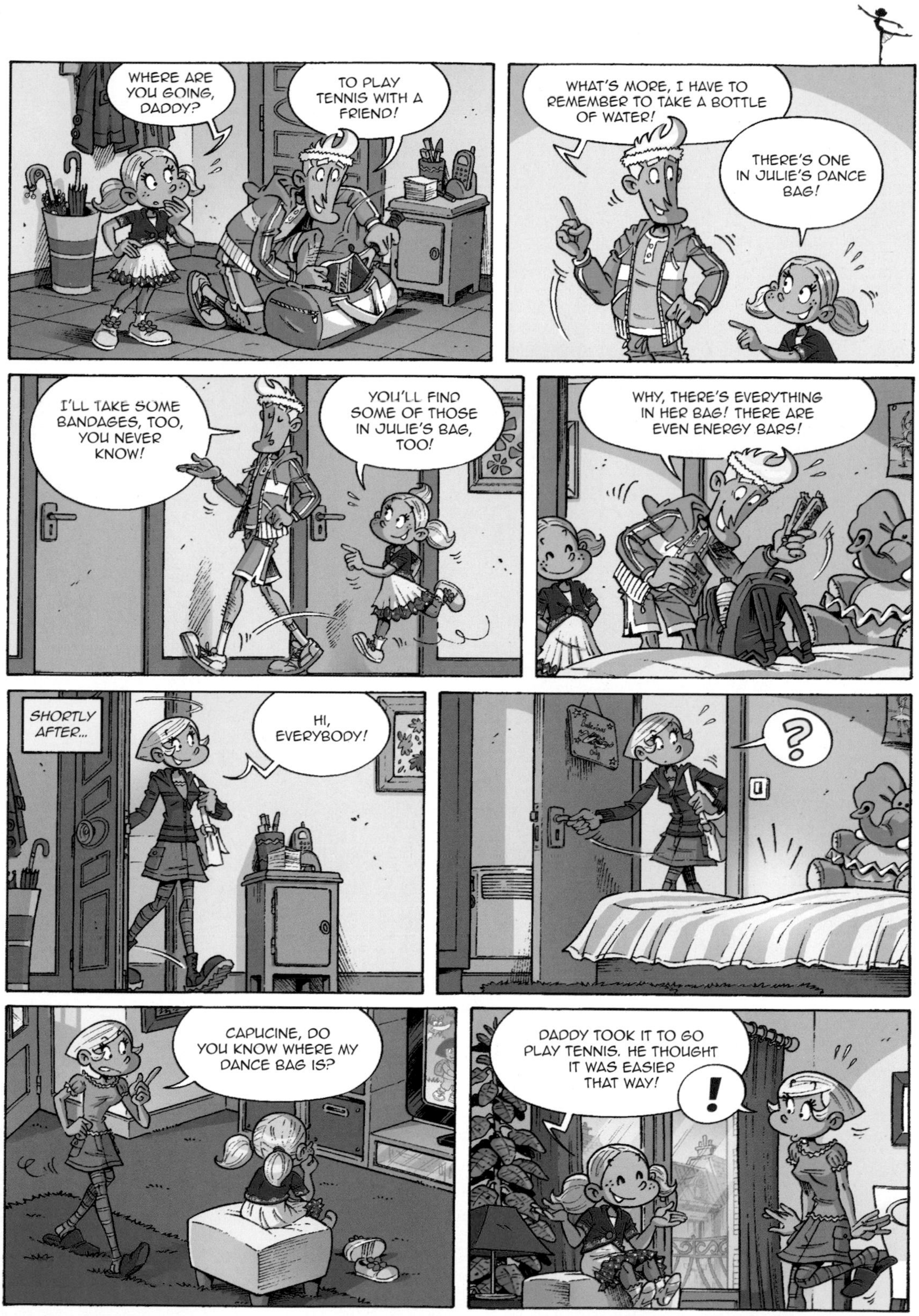
WHERE ARE YOU GOING, DADDY?
TO PLAY TENNIS WITH A FRIEND!
WHAT'S MORE, I HAVE TO REMEMBER TO TAKE A BOTTLE OF WATER!
THERE'S ONE IN JULIE'S DANCE BAG!
I'LL TAKE SOME BANDAGES, TOO, YOU NEVER KNOW!
YOU'LL FIND SOME OF THOSE IN JULIE'S BAG, TOO!
WHY, THERE'S EVERYTHING IN HER BAG! THERE ARE EVEN ENERGY BARS!
SHORTLY AFTER...
HI, EVERYBODY!
?
CAPUCINE, DO YOU KNOW WHERE MY DANCE BAG IS?
DADDY TOOK IT TO GO PLAY TENNIS. HE THOUGHT IT WAS EASIER THAT WAY!
!

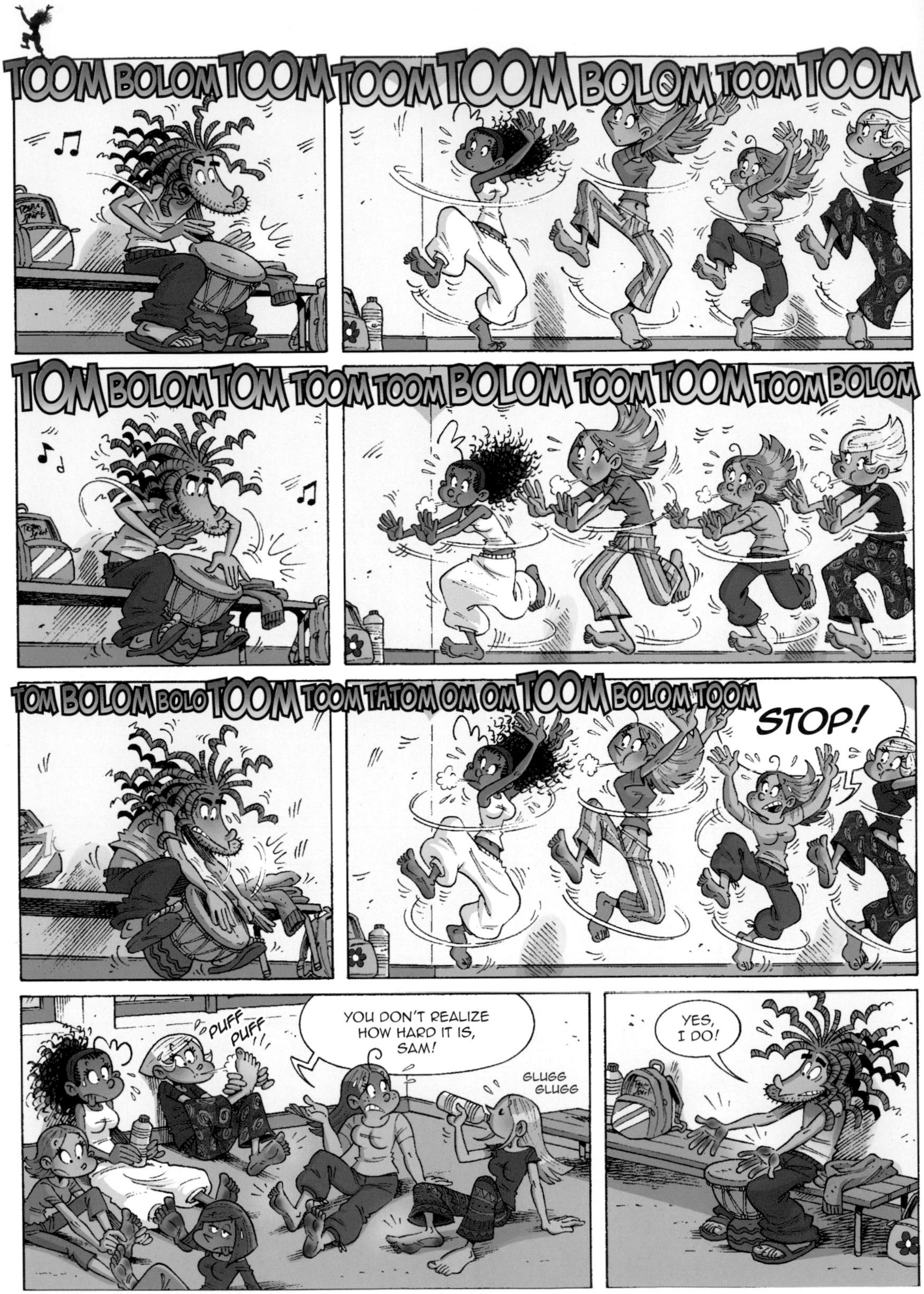
TOOM BOLOM TOOM TOOM TOOM BOLOM TOOM TOOM
TOM BOLOM TOM TOOM TOOM BOLOM TOOM TOOM TOOM BOLOM
TOM BOLOM BOLO TOOM TOOM TATOM OM OM TOOM BOLOM TOOM
STOP!
PUFF PUFF
YOU DON'T REALIZE HOW HARD IT IS, SAM!
GLUGG GLUGG
YES, I DO!

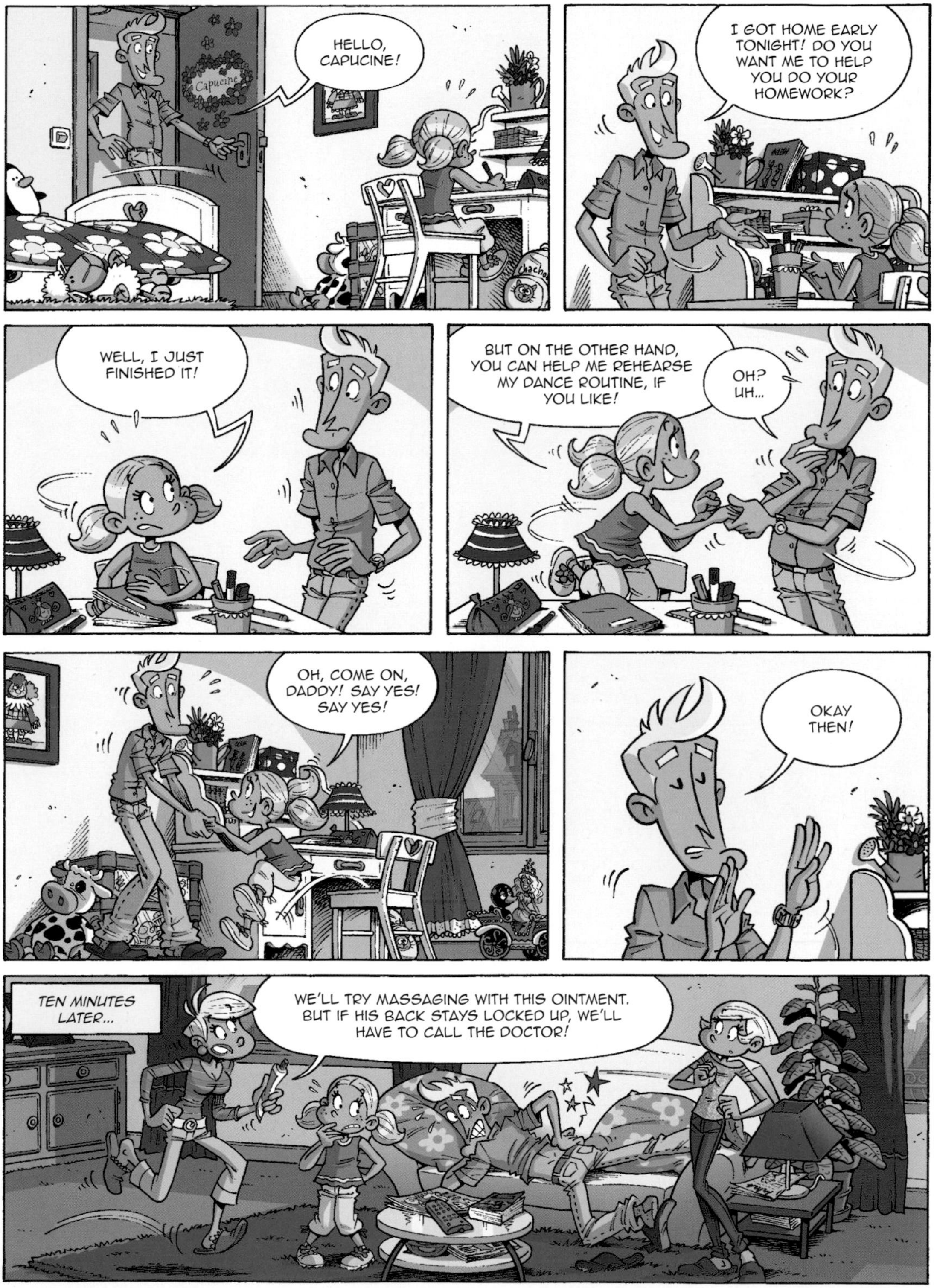
HELLO, CAPUCINE!
I GOT HOME EARLY TONIGHT! DO YOU WANT ME TO HELP YOU DO YOUR HOMEWORK?
WELL, I JUST FINISHED IT!
BUT ON THE OTHER HAND, YOU CAN HELP ME REHEARSE MY DANCE ROUTINE, IF YOU LIKE!
OH? UH...
OH, COME ON, DADDY! SAY YES! SAY YES!
OKAY THEN!
TEN MINUTES LATER...
WE'LL TRY MASSAGING WITH THIS OINTMENT. BUT IF HIS BACK STAYS LOCKED UP, WE'LL HAVE TO CALL THE DOCTOR!

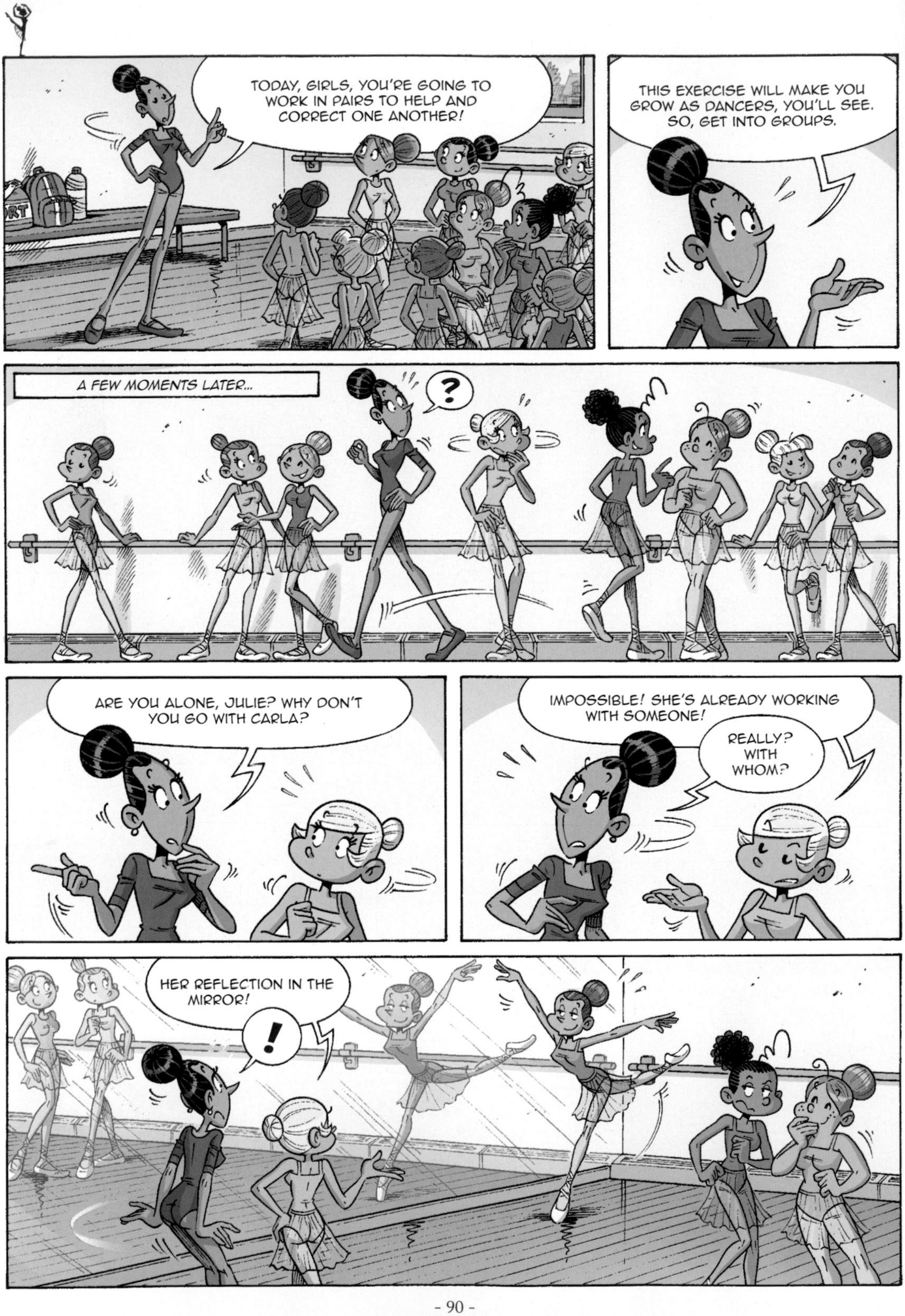
TODAY, GIRLS, YOU'RE GOING TO WORK IN PAIRS TO HELP AND CORRECT ONE ANOTHER!
THIS EXERCISE WILL MAKE YOU GROW AS DANCERS, YOU'LL SEE. SO, GET INTO GROUPS.
A FEW MOMENTS LATER...
?
ARE YOU ALONE, JULIE? WHY DON'T YOU GO WITH CARLA?
IMPOSSIBLE! SHE'S ALREADY WORKING WITH SOMEONE!
REALLY? WITH WHOM?
HER REFLECTION IN THE MIRROR!
!

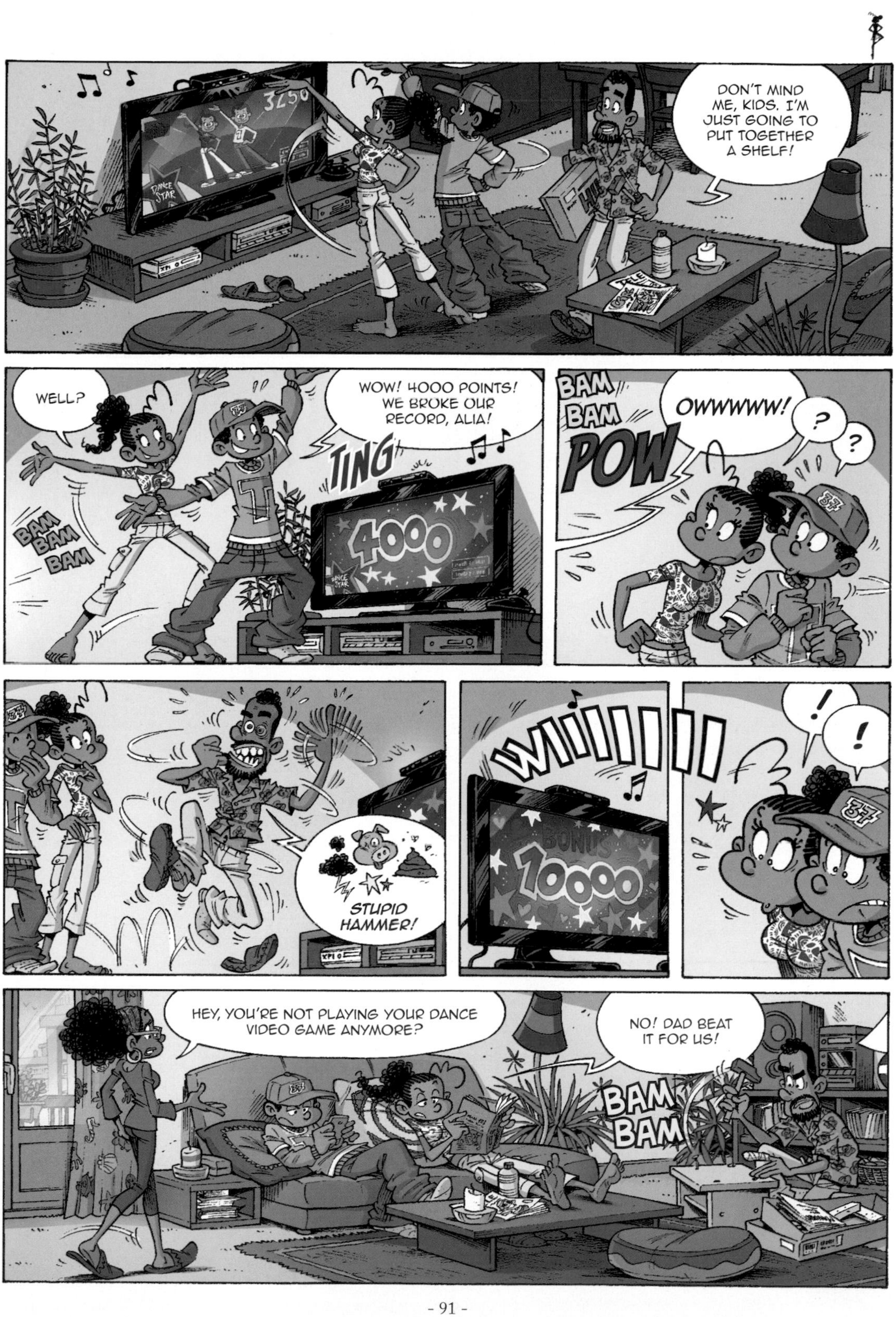
3250
DANCE STAR
DON'T MIND ME, KIDS. I'M JUST GOING TO PUT TOGETHER A SHELF!
WELL?
WOW! 4000 POINTS! WE BROKE OUR RECORD, ALIA!
TING
BAM BAM BAM
4000
BAM BAM POW
OWWWWW!
? ?
STUPID HAMMER!
WIIIIIII
BONUS 10000
! !
HEY, YOU'RE NOT PLAYING YOUR DANCE VIDEO GAME ANYMORE?
NO! DAD BEAT IT FOR US!
BAM BAM

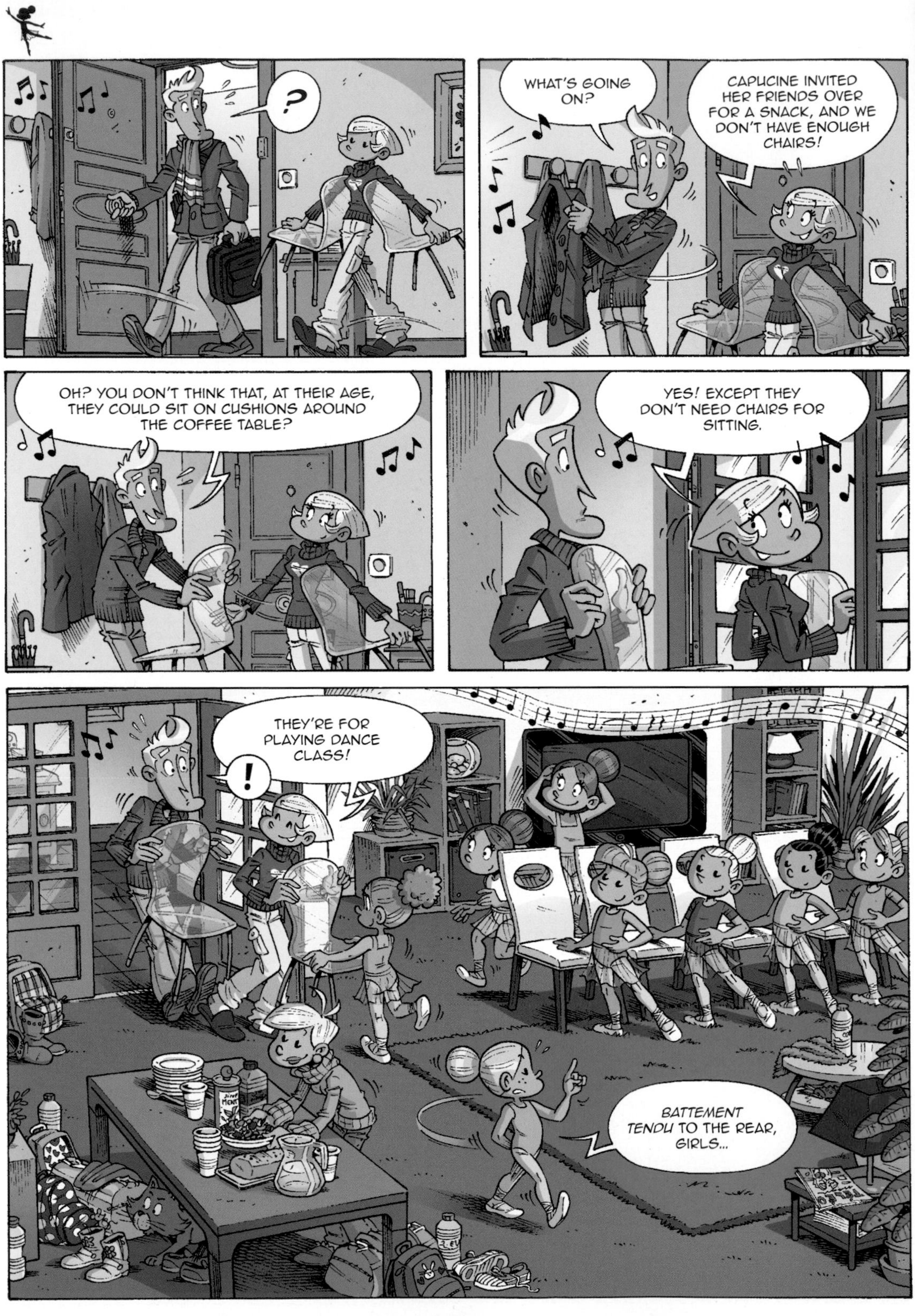
?
WHAT'S GOING ON?
CAPUCINE INVITED HER FRIENDS OVER FOR A SNACK, AND WE DON'T HAVE ENOUGH CHAIRS!
OH? YOU DON'T THINK THAT, AT THEIR AGE, THEY COULD SIT ON CUSHIONS AROUND THE COFFEE TABLE?
YES! EXCEPT THEY DON'T NEED CHAIRS FOR SITTING.
!
THEY'RE FOR PLAYING DANCE CLASS!
BATTEMENT TENDU TO THE REAR, GIRLS...

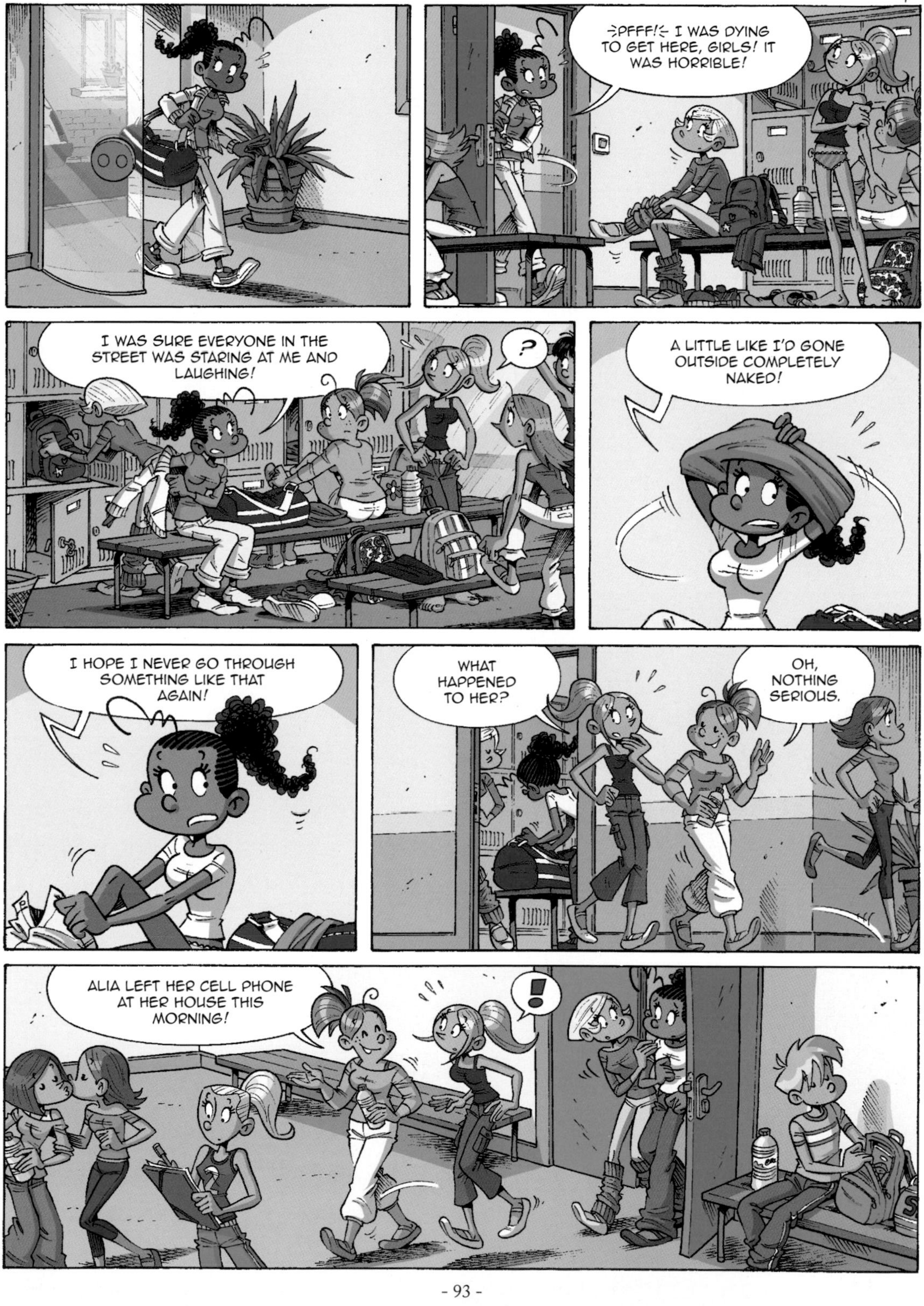
PFFF! I WAS DYING TO GET HERE, GIRLS! IT WAS HORRIBLE!
I WAS SURE EVERYONE IN THE STREET WAS STARING AT ME AND LAUGHING!
?
A LITTLE LIKE I'D GONE OUTSIDE COMPLETELY NAKED!
I HOPE I NEVER GO THROUGH SOMETHING LIKE THAT AGAIN!
WHAT HAPPENED TO HER?
OH, NOTHING SERIOUS.
ALIA LEFT HER CELL PHONE AT HER HOUSE THIS MORNING!
!

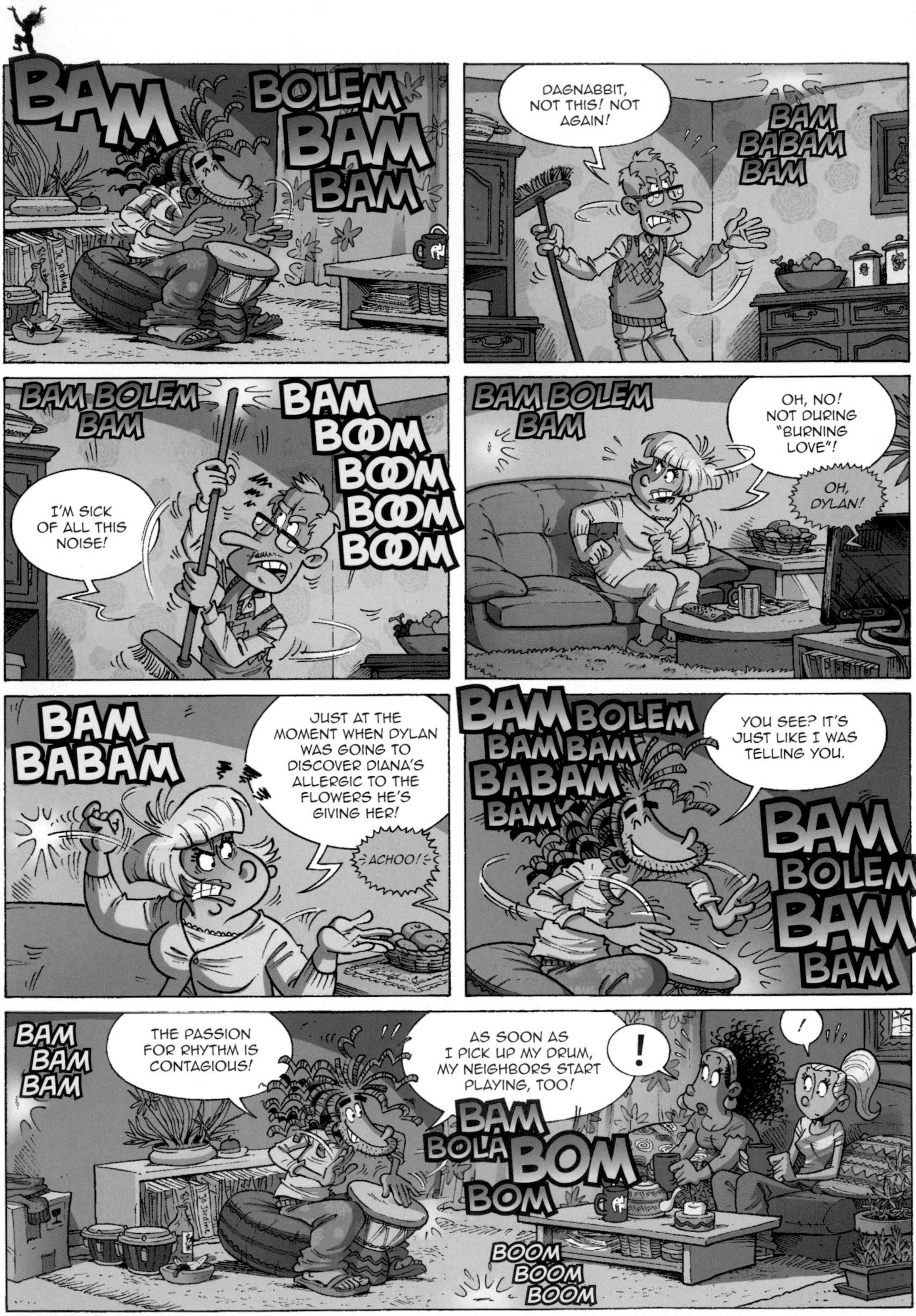
BAM
BOLEM BAM BAM
DAGNABBIT, NOT THIS! NOT AGAIN!
BAM BABAM BAM
BAM BOLEM BAM
BAM BOOM BOOM BOOM BOOM
I'M SICK OF ALL THIS NOISE!
BAM BOLEM BAM
OH, NO! NOT DURING "BURNING LOVE"!
OH, DYLAN!
BAM BABAM
JUST AT THE MOMENT WHEN DYLAN WAS GOING TO DISCOVER DIANA'S ALLERGIC TO THE FLOWERS HE'S GIVING HER!
ACHOO!
BAM BOLEM BAM BAM BABAM BAM
YOU SEE? IT'S JUST LIKE I WAS TELLING YOU.
BAM BOLEM BAM BAM
BAM BAM BAM
THE PASSION FOR RHYTHM IS CONTAGIOUS!
AS SOON AS I PICK UP MY DRUM, MY NEIGHBORS START PLAYING, TOO!
!
!
BAM BOLA BOM BOM
BOOM BOOM BOOM

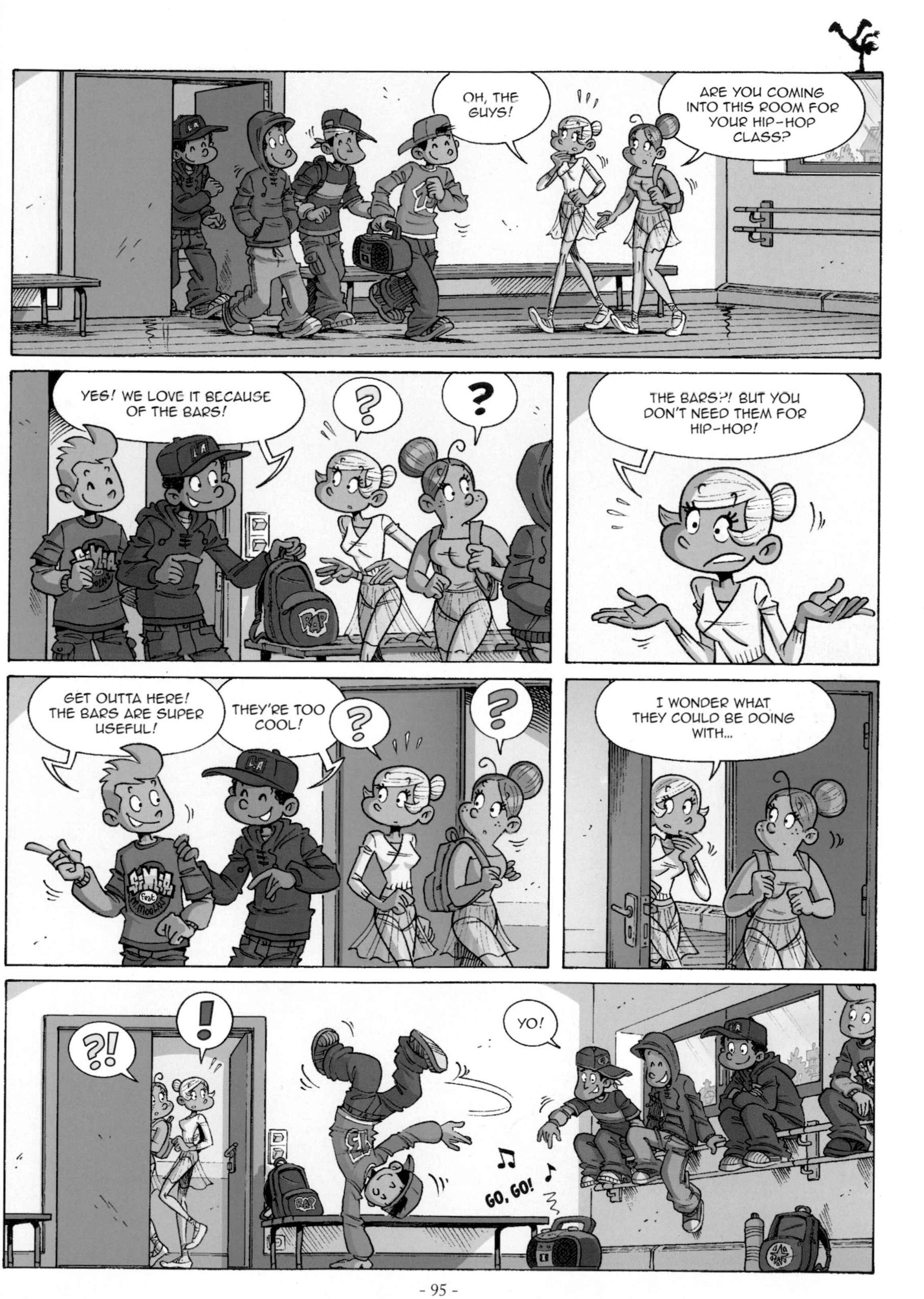
OH, THE GUYS!
ARE YOU COMING INTO THIS ROOM FOR YOUR HIP-HOP CLASS?
YES! WE LOVE IT BECAUSE OF THE BARS!
?
?
THE BARS?! BUT YOU DON'T NEED THEM FOR HIP-HOP!
GET OUTTA HERE! THE BARS ARE SUPER USEFUL!
THEY'RE TOO COOL!
?
?
I WONDER WHAT THEY COULD BE DOING WITH...
?!
!
YO!
GO, GO!

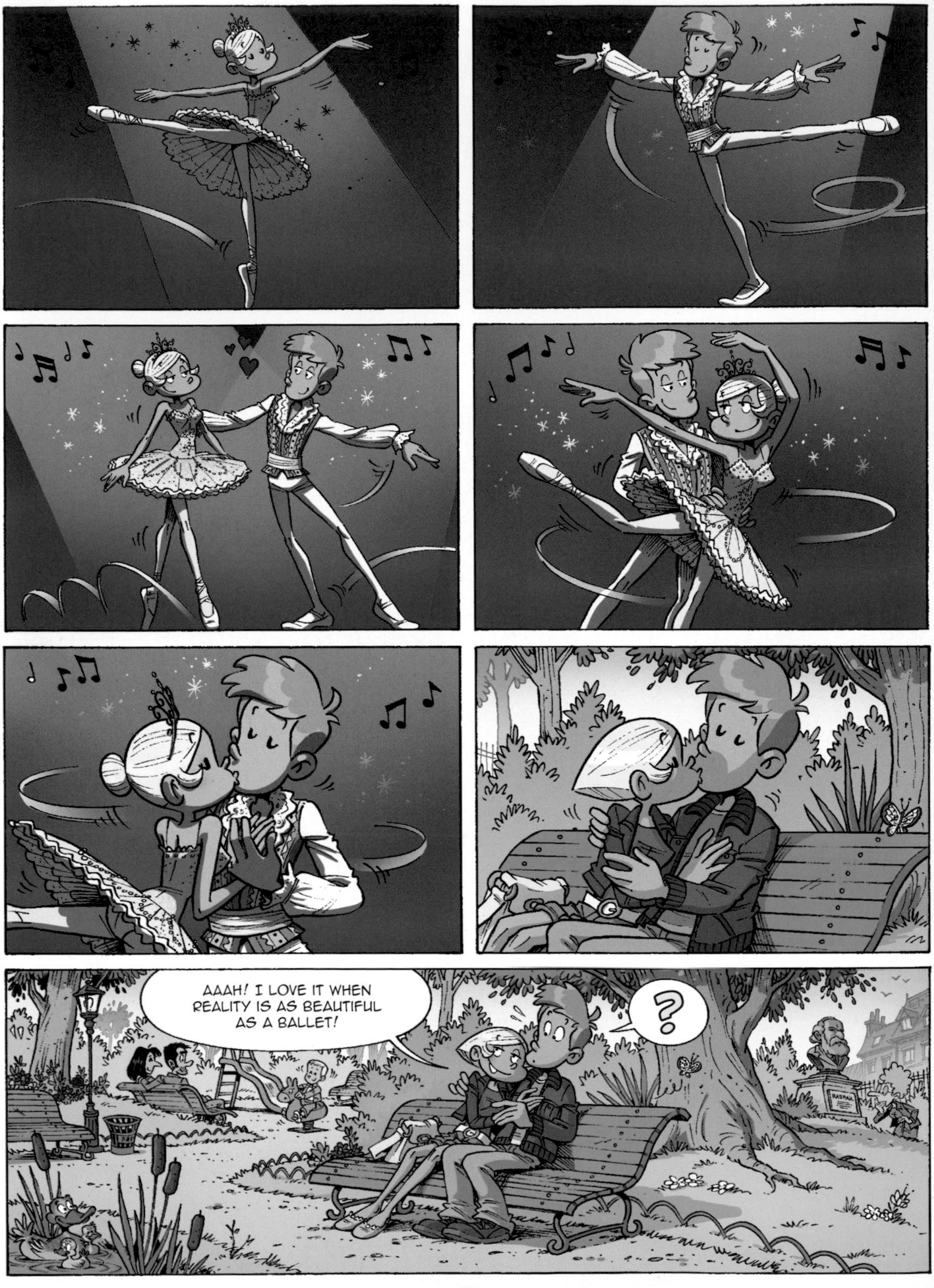
AAAH! I LOVE IT WHEN REALITY IS AS BEAUTIFUL AS A BALLET!
?

Dancing in the Rain

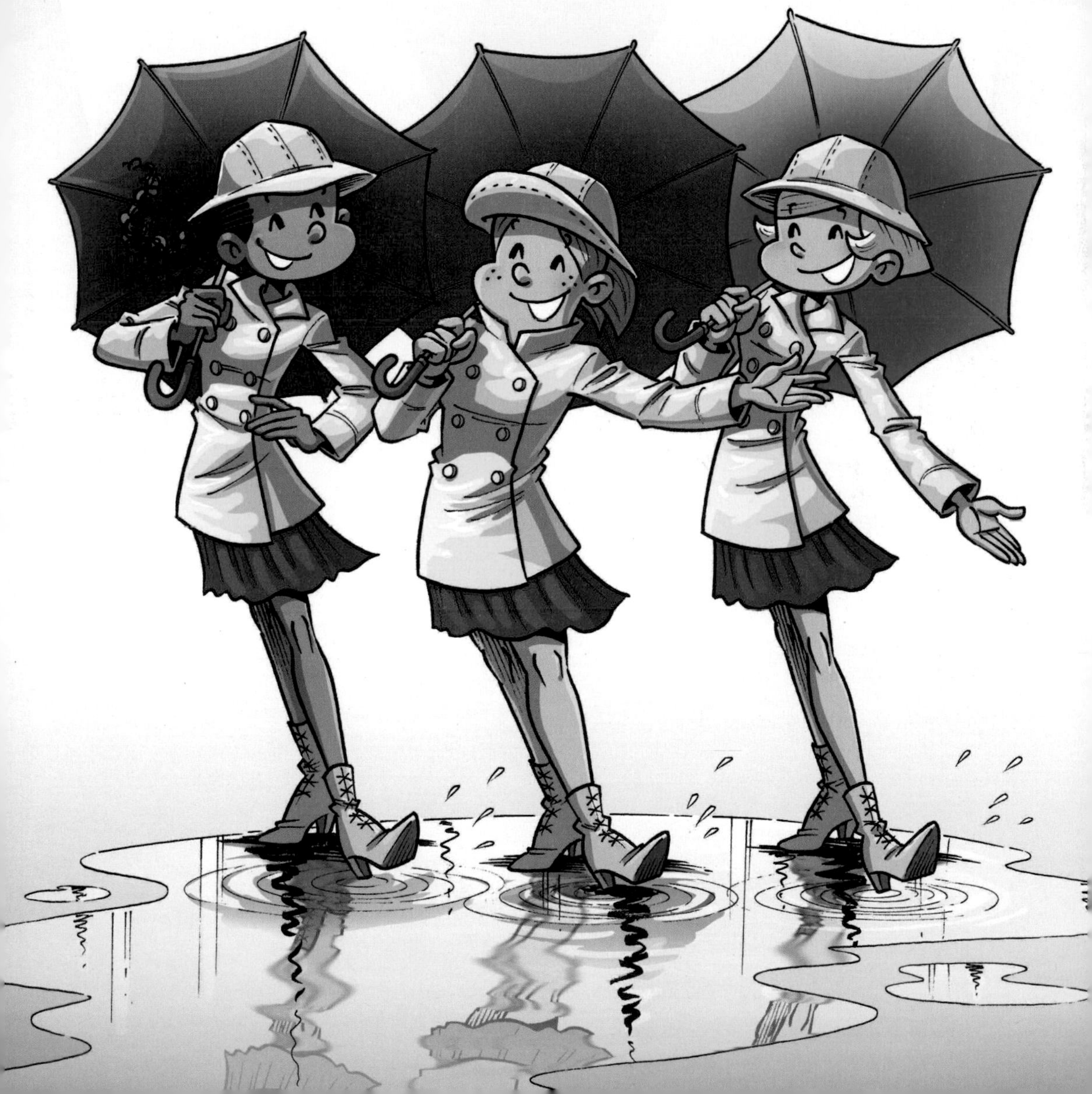

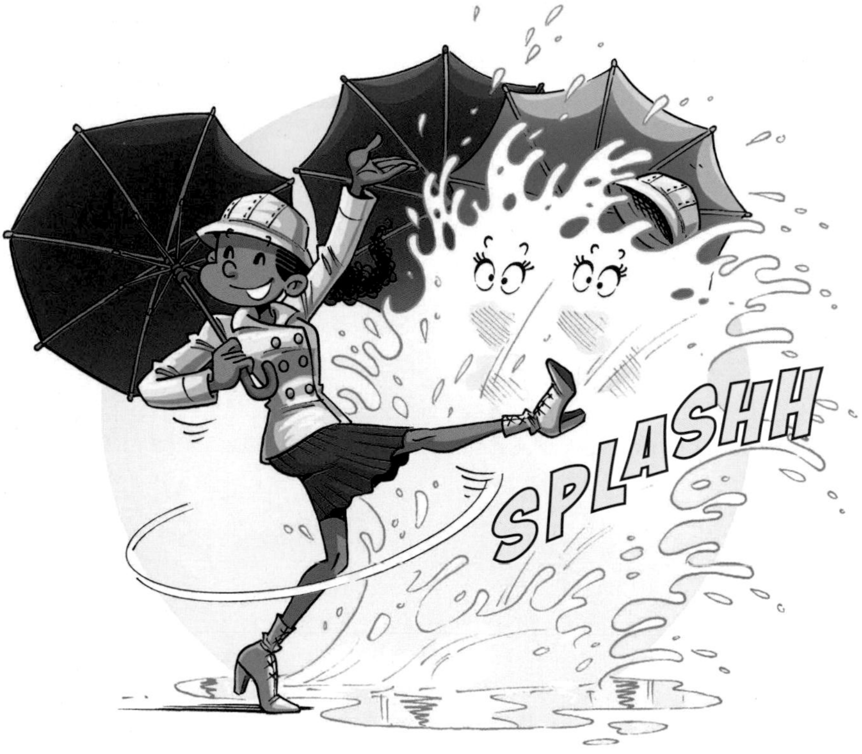
SPLASHH

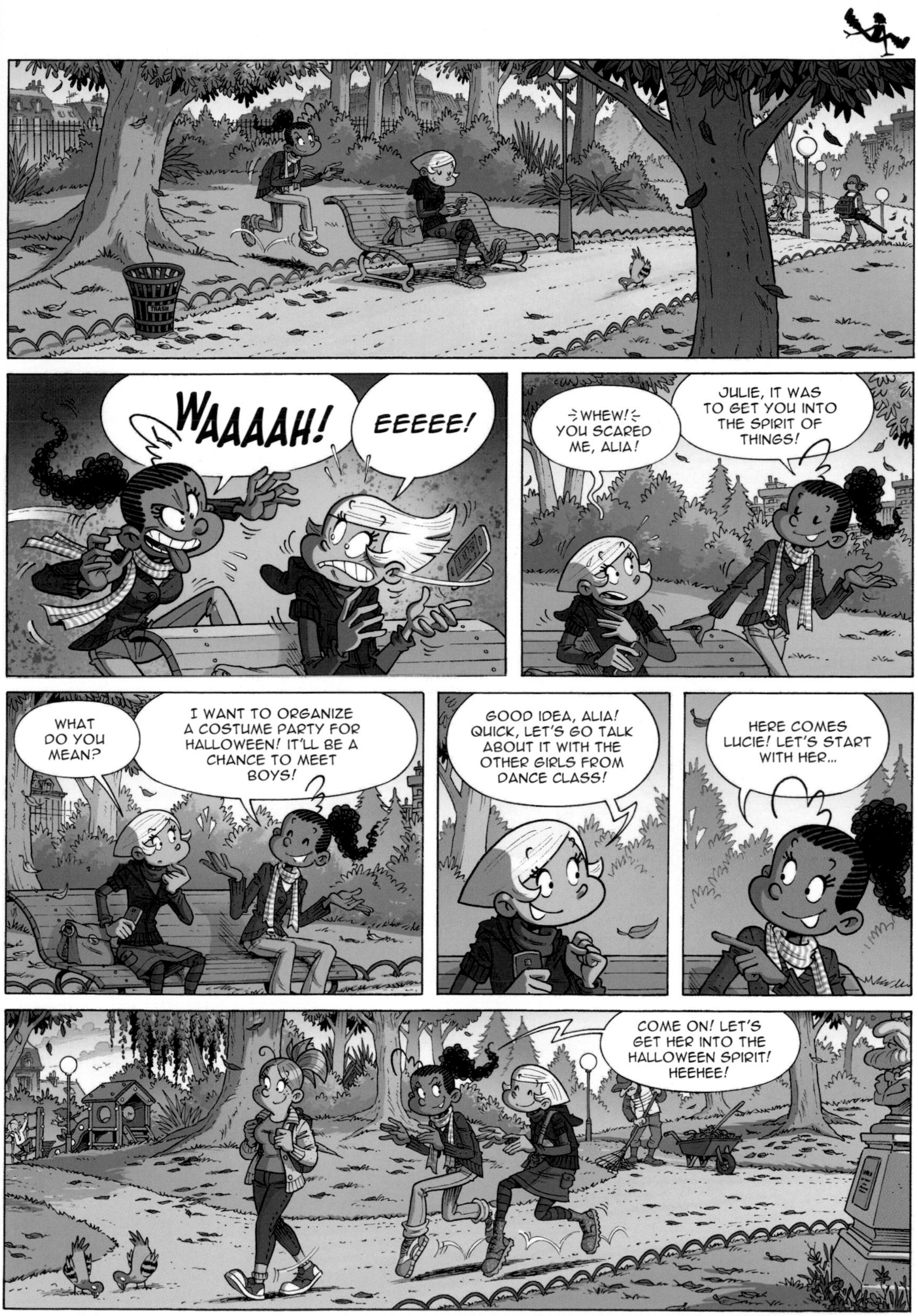
WAAAAH!
EEEEE!
WHEW! YOU SCARED ME, ALIA!
JULIE, IT WAS TO GET YOU INTO THE SPIRIT OF THINGS!
WHAT DO YOU MEAN?
I WANT TO ORGANIZE A COSTUME PARTY FOR HALLOWEEN! IT'LL BE A CHANCE TO MEET BOYS!
GOOD IDEA, ALIA! QUICK, LET'S GO TALK ABOUT IT WITH THE OTHER GIRLS FROM DANCE CLASS!
HERE COMES LUCIE! LET'S START WITH HER...
COME ON! LET'S GET HER INTO THE HALLOWEEN SPIRIT! HEEHEE!

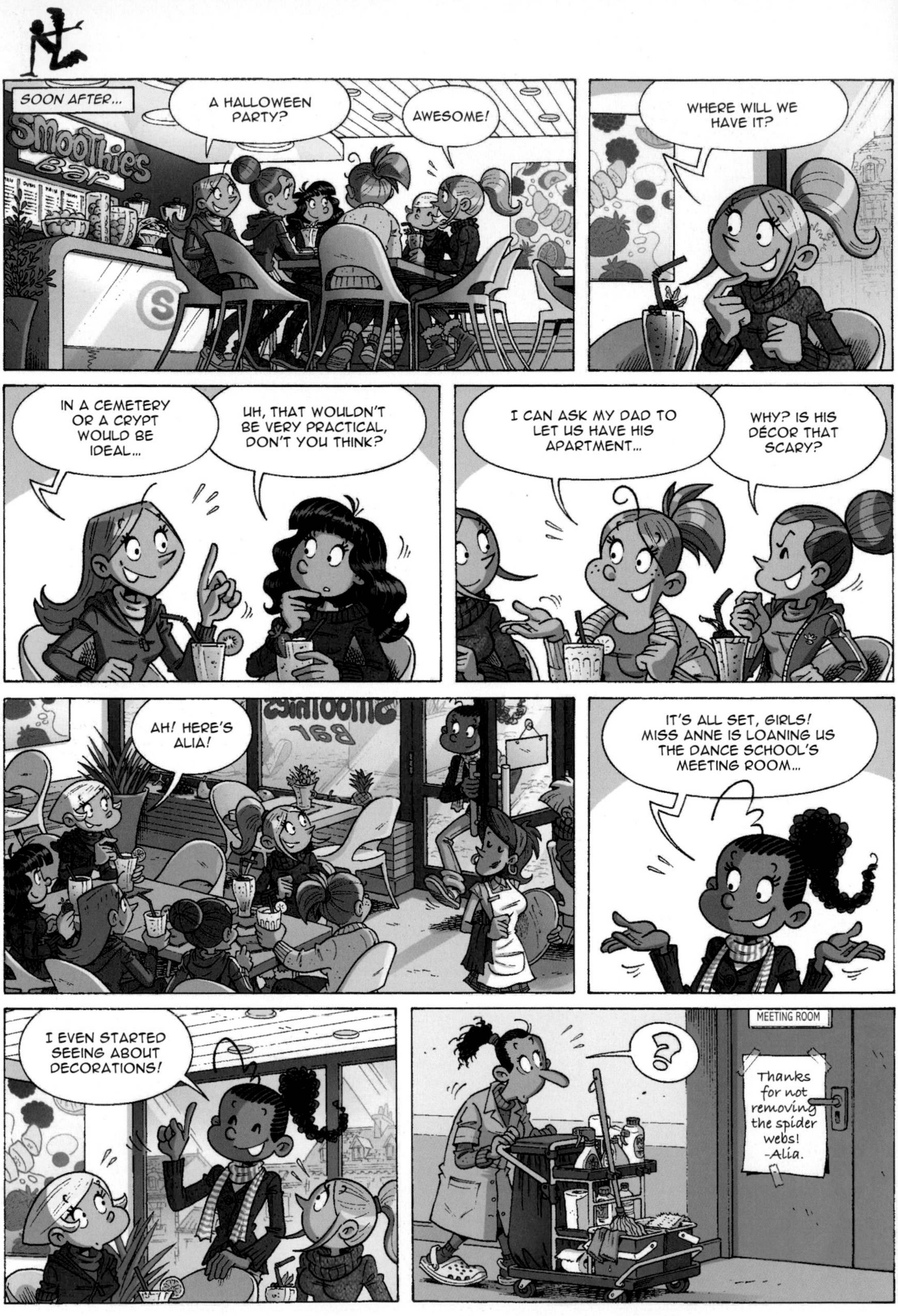
SOON AFTER...
A HALLOWEEN PARTY?
AWESOME!
WHERE WILL WE HAVE IT?
IN A CEMETERY OR A CRYPT WOULD BE IDEAL...
UH, THAT WOULDN'T BE VERY PRACTICAL, DON'T YOU THINK?
I CAN ASK MY DAD TO LET US HAVE HIS APARTMENT...
WHY? IS HIS DÉCOR THAT SCARY?
AH! HERE'S ALIA!
IT'S ALL SET, GIRLS! MISS ANNE IS LOANING US THE DANCE SCHOOL'S MEETING ROOM...
I EVEN STARTED SEEING ABOUT DECORATIONS!
?
MEETING ROOM
Thanks for not removing the spider webs! -Alia.

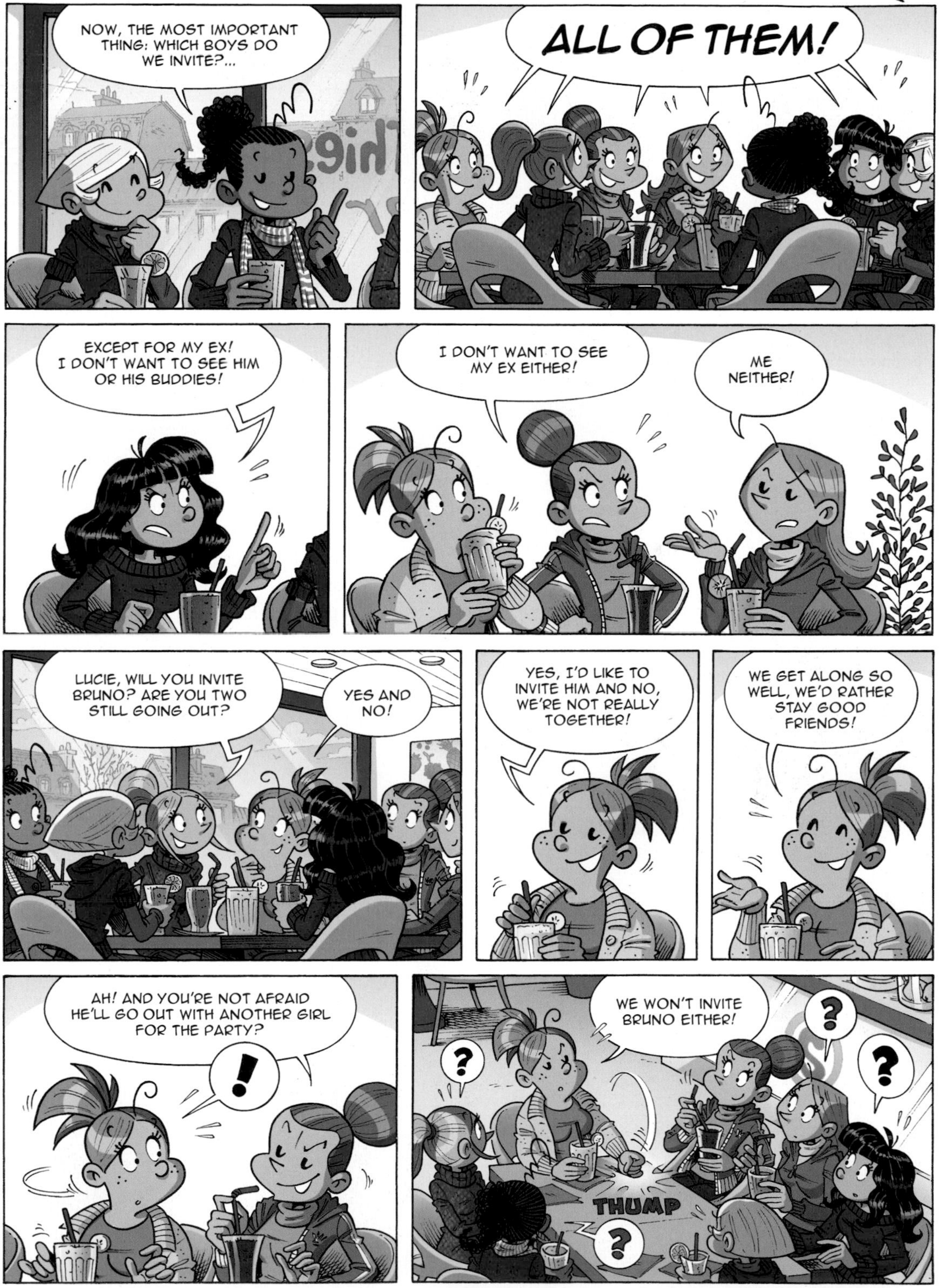
NOW, THE MOST IMPORTANT THING: WHICH BOYS DO WE INVITE?...
ALL OF THEM!
EXCEPT FOR MY EX! I DON'T WANT TO SEE HIM OR HIS BUDDIES!
I DON'T WANT TO SEE MY EX EITHER!
ME NEITHER!
LUCIE, WILL YOU INVITE BRUNO? ARE YOU TWO STILL GOING OUT?
YES AND NO!
YES, I'D LIKE TO INVITE HIM AND NO, WE'RE NOT REALLY TOGETHER!
WE GET ALONG SO WELL, WE'D RATHER STAY GOOD FRIENDS!
AH! AND YOU'RE NOT AFRAID HE'LL GO OUT WITH ANOTHER GIRL FOR THE PARTY?
!
WE WON'T INVITE BRUNO EITHER!
?
?
?
THUMP
?

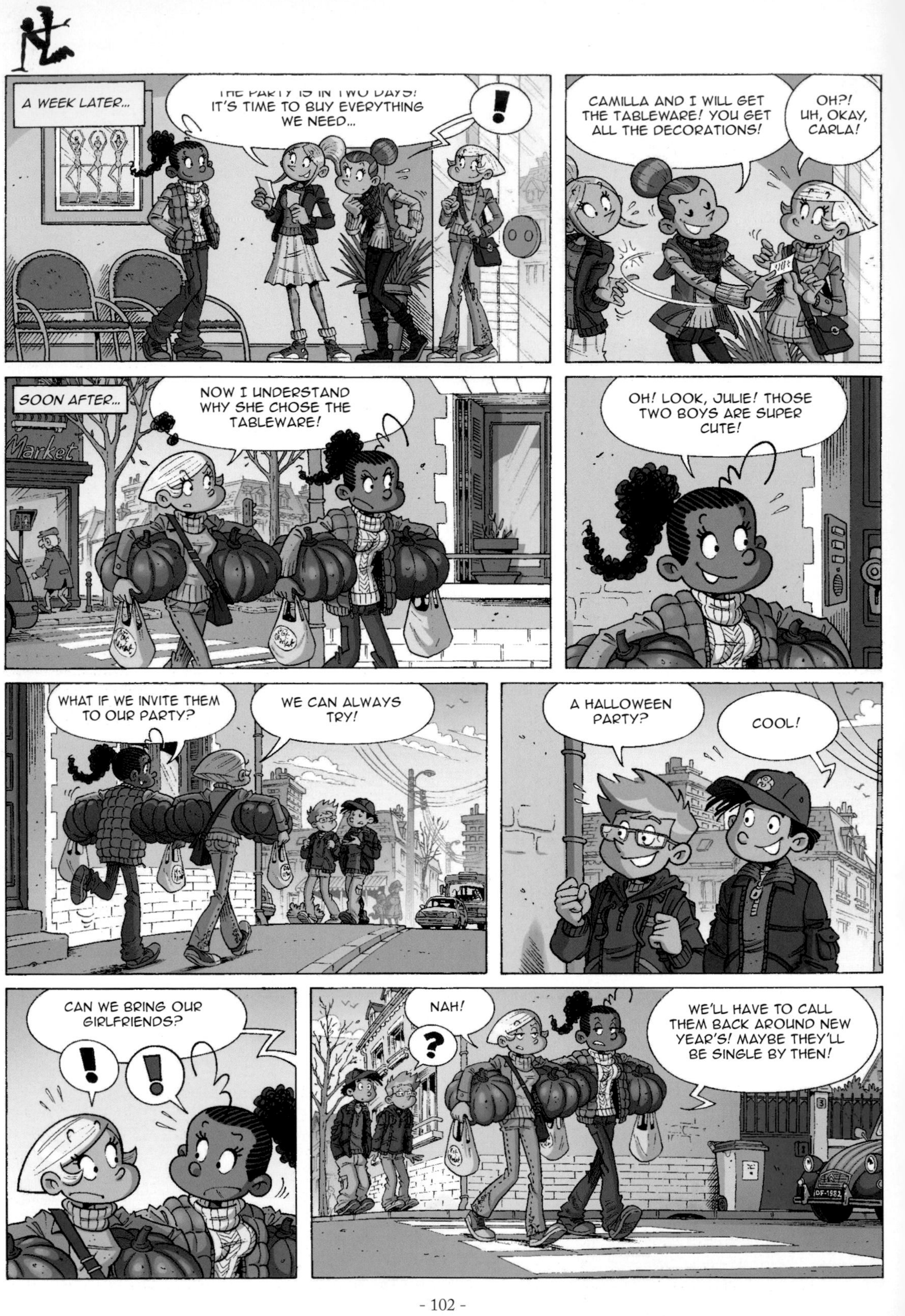
A WEEK LATER...
THE PARTY IS IN TWO DAYS! IT'S TIME TO BUY EVERYTHING WE NEED...
!
CAMILLA AND I WILL GET THE TABLEWARE! YOU GET ALL THE DECORATIONS!
OH?! UH, OKAY, CARLA!
SOON AFTER...
NOW I UNDERSTAND WHY SHE CHOSE THE TABLEWARE!
Market
OH! LOOK, JULIE! THOSE TWO BOYS ARE SUPER CUTE!
WHAT IF WE INVITE THEM TO OUR PARTY?
WE CAN ALWAYS TRY!
A HALLOWEEN PARTY?
COOL!
CAN WE BRING OUR GIRLFRIENDS?
!
!
NAH!
?
WE'LL HAVE TO CALL THEM BACK AROUND NEW YEAR'S! MAYBE THEY'LL BE SINGLE BY THEN!

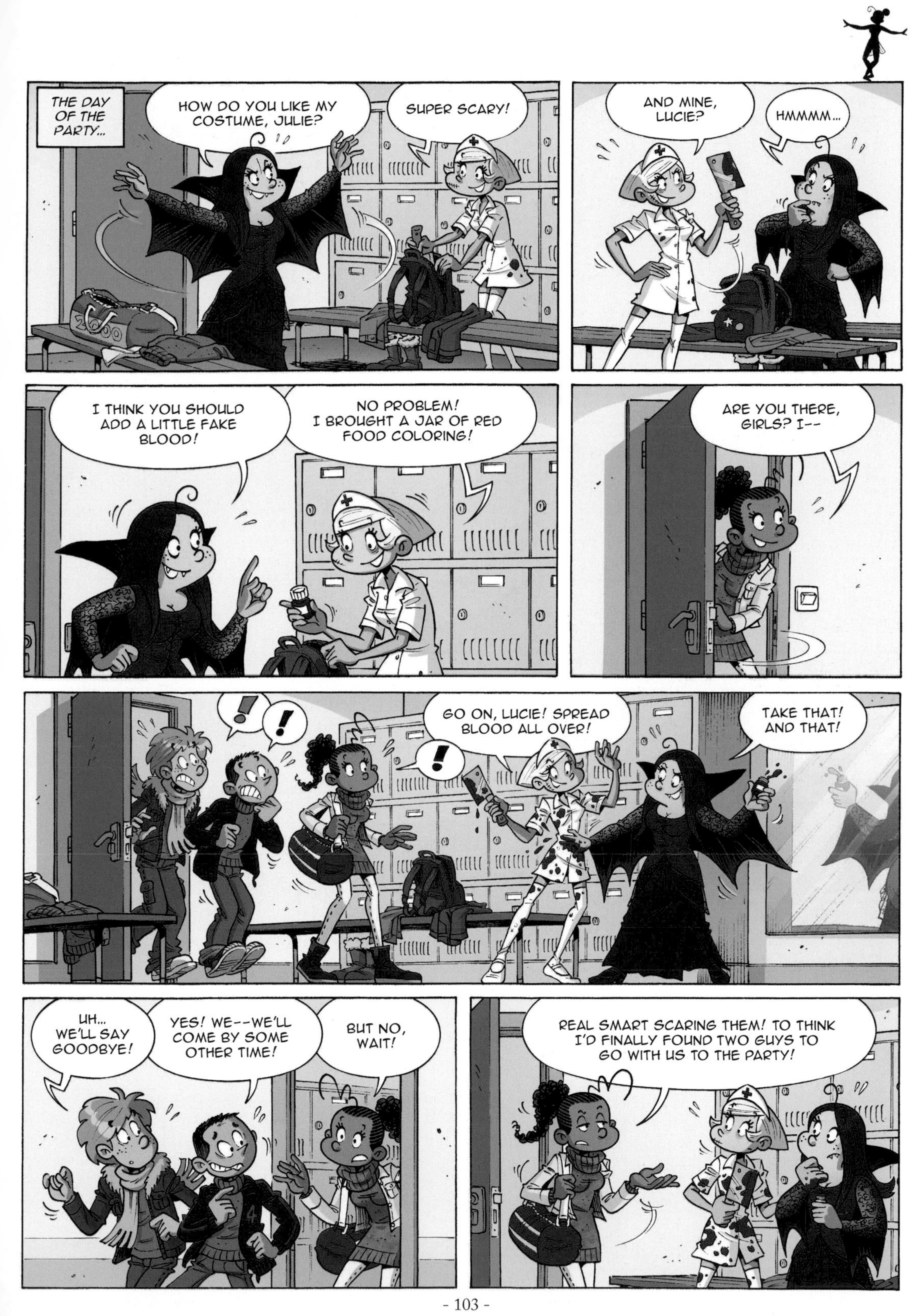
THE DAY OF THE PARTY...
HOW DO YOU LIKE MY COSTUME, JULIE?
SUPER SCARY!
AND MINE, LUCIE?
HMMMM...
I THINK YOU SHOULD ADD A LITTLE FAKE BLOOD!
NO PROBLEM! I BROUGHT A JAR OF RED FOOD COLORING!
ARE YOU THERE, GIRLS? I--
!
!
!
GO ON, LUCIE! SPREAD BLOOD ALL OVER!
TAKE THAT! AND THAT!
UH... WE'LL SAY GOODBYE!
YES! WE--WE'LL COME BY SOME OTHER TIME!
BUT NO, WAIT!
REAL SMART SCARING THEM! TO THINK I'D FINALLY FOUND TWO GUYS TO GO WITH US TO THE PARTY!

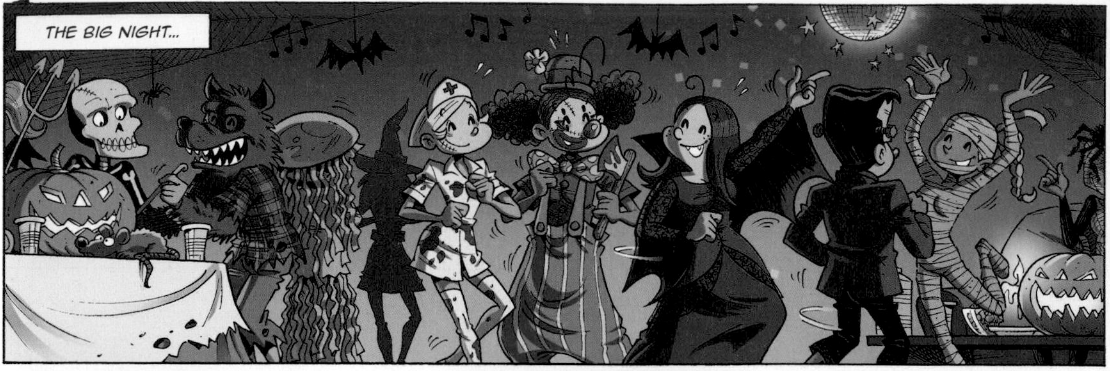
THE BIG NIGHT...

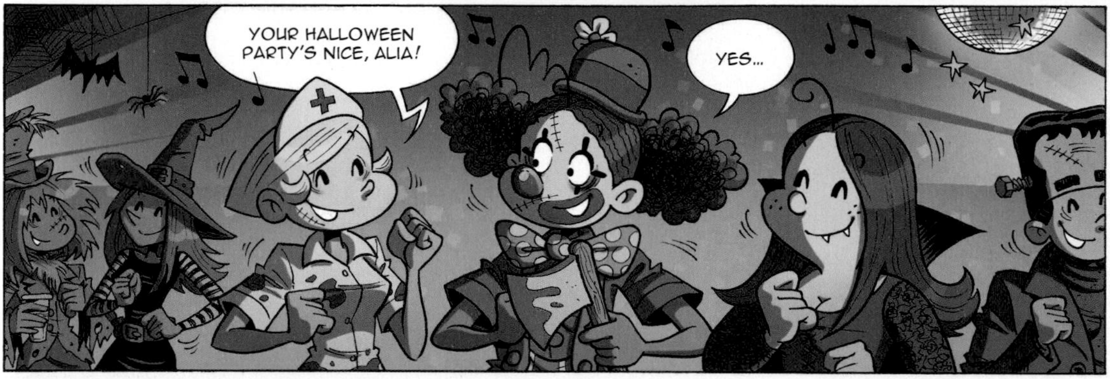
YOUR HALLOWEEN PARTY'S NICE, ALIA!
YES...

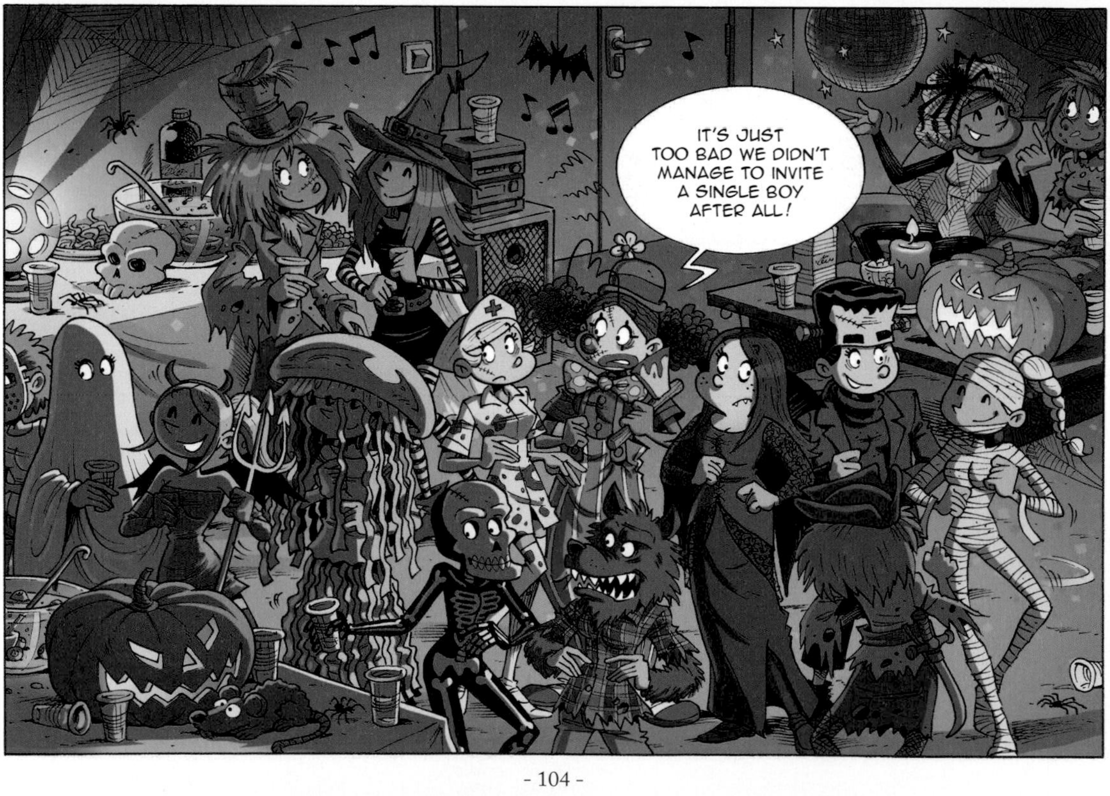
IT'S JUST TOO BAD WE DIDN'T MANAGE TO INVITE A SINGLE BOY AFTER ALL!

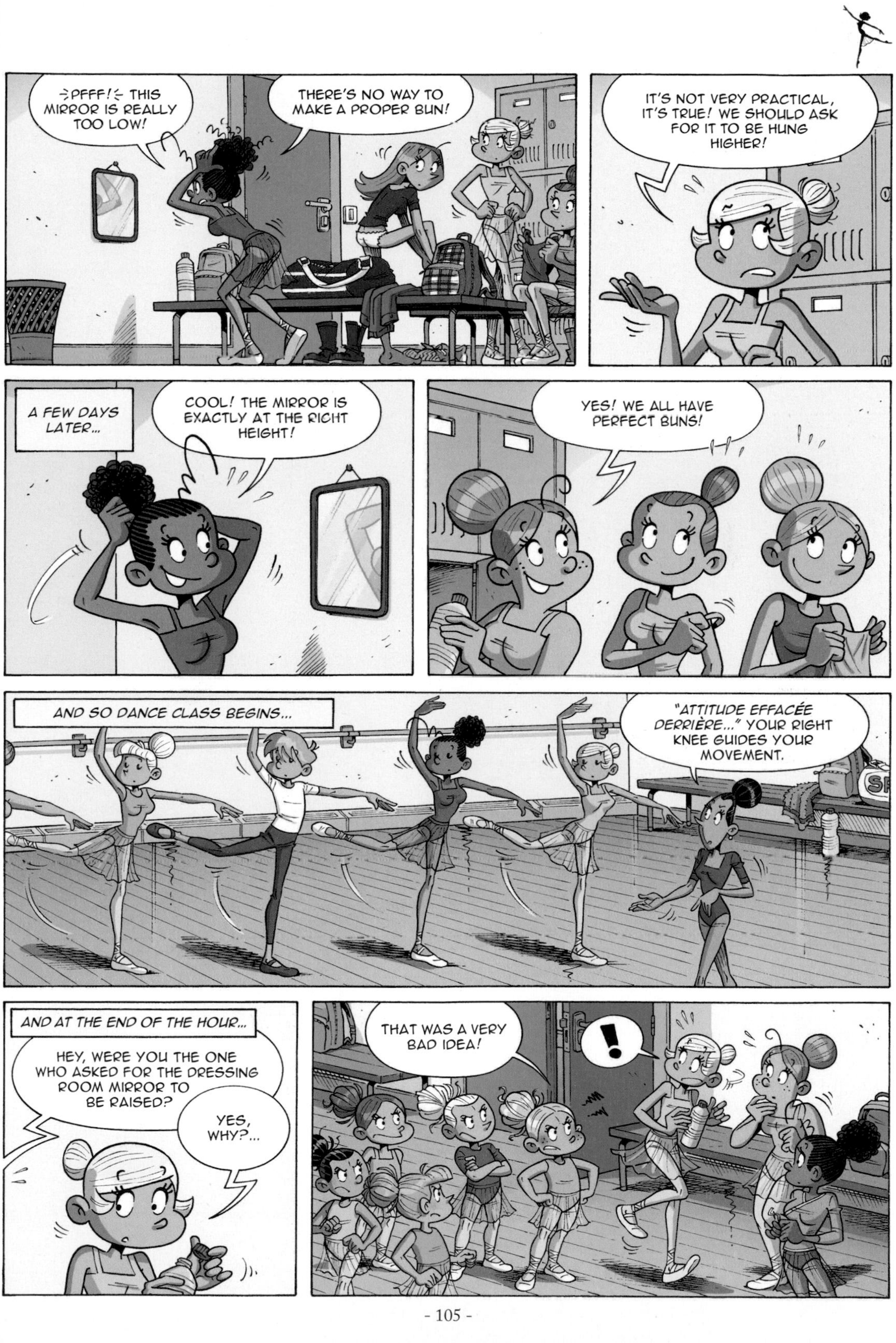

PFFF! THIS MIRROR IS REALLY TOO LOW!
THERE'S NO WAY TO MAKE A PROPER BUN!
IT'S NOT VERY PRACTICAL, IT'S TRUE! WE SHOULD ASK FOR IT TO BE HUNG HIGHER!
A FEW DAYS LATER...
COOL! THE MIRROR IS EXACTLY AT THE RIGHT HEIGHT!
YES! WE ALL HAVE PERFECT BUNS!
AND SO DANCE CLASS BEGINS...
"ATTITUDE EFFACÉE DERRIÈRE..." YOUR RIGHT KNEE GUIDES YOUR MOVEMENT.
AND AT THE END OF THE HOUR...
HEY, WERE YOU THE ONE WHO ASKED FOR THE DRESSING ROOM MIRROR TO BE RAISED?
YES, WHY?...
THAT WAS A VERY BAD IDEA!
!

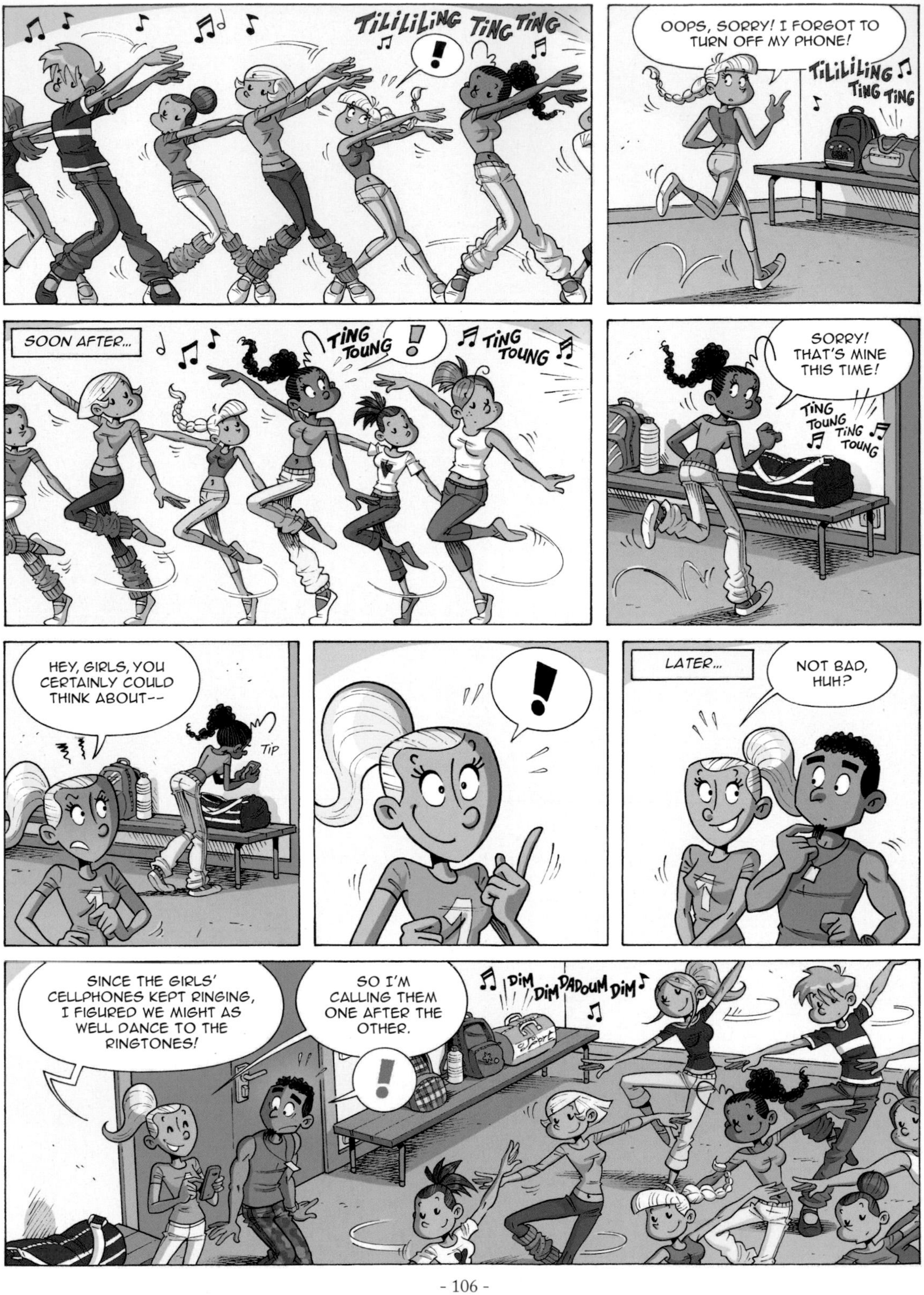
TILILILING TING TING
!
OOPS, SORRY! I FORGOT TO TURN OFF MY PHONE!
TILILILING TING TING
SOON AFTER...
TING TOUNG
!
TING TOUNG
SORRY! THAT'S MINE THIS TIME!
TING TOUNG TING TOUNG
HEY, GIRLS, YOU CERTAINLY COULD THINK ABOUT--
TIP
!
LATER...
NOT BAD, HUH?
SINCE THE GIRLS' CELLPHONES KEPT RINGING, I FIGURED WE MIGHT AS WELL DANCE TO THE RINGTONES!
SO I'M CALLING THEM ONE AFTER THE OTHER.
DIM DIM DADOUM DIM
!

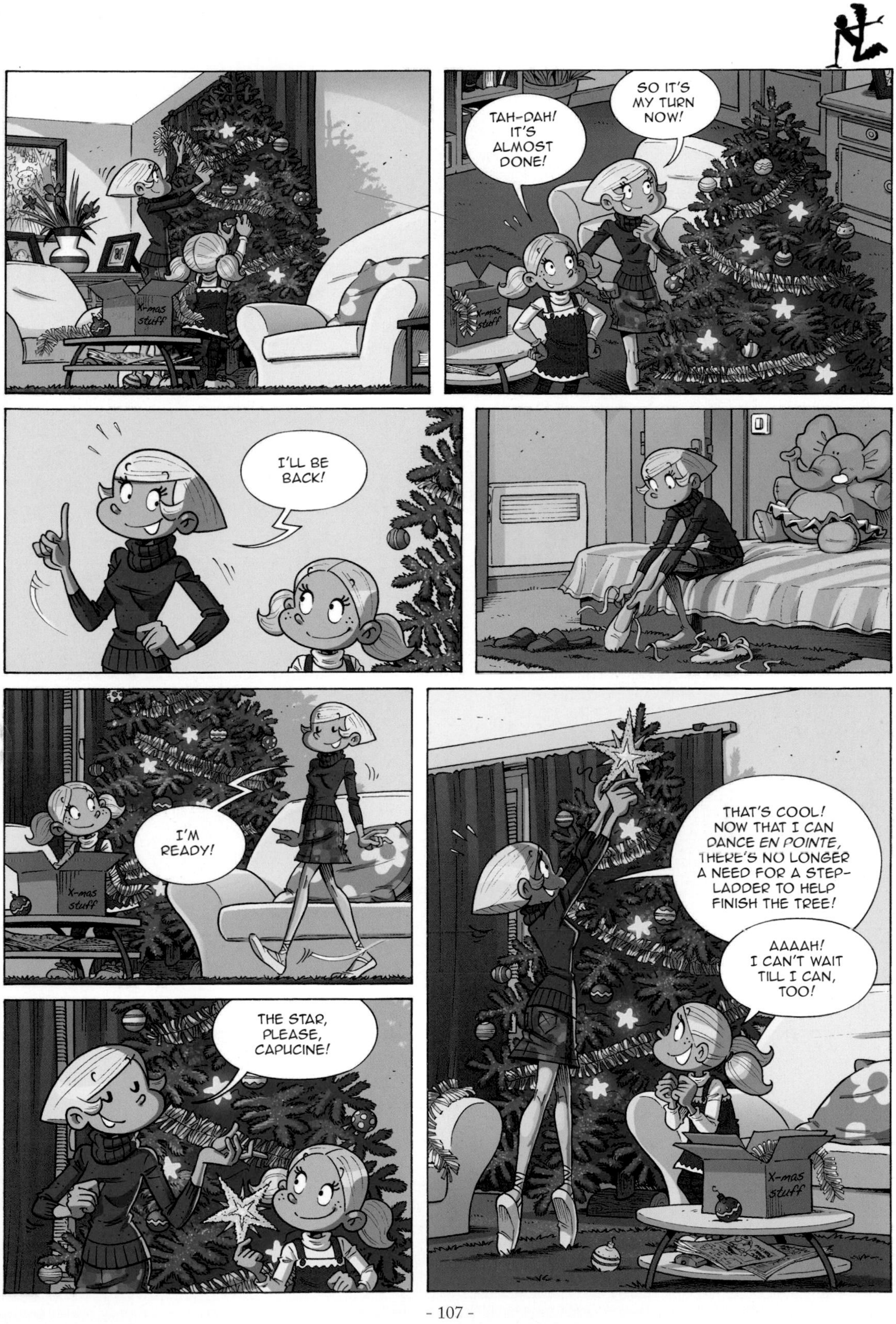
TAH-DAH! IT'S ALMOST DONE!
SO IT'S MY TURN NOW!
I'LL BE BACK!
I'M READY!
THE STAR, PLEASE, CAPUCINE!
THAT'S COOL! NOW THAT I CAN DANCE *EN POINTE*, THERE'S NO LONGER A NEED FOR A STEP-LADDER TO HELP FINISH THE TREE!
AAAAH! I CAN'T WAIT TILL I CAN, TOO!
X-mas stuff

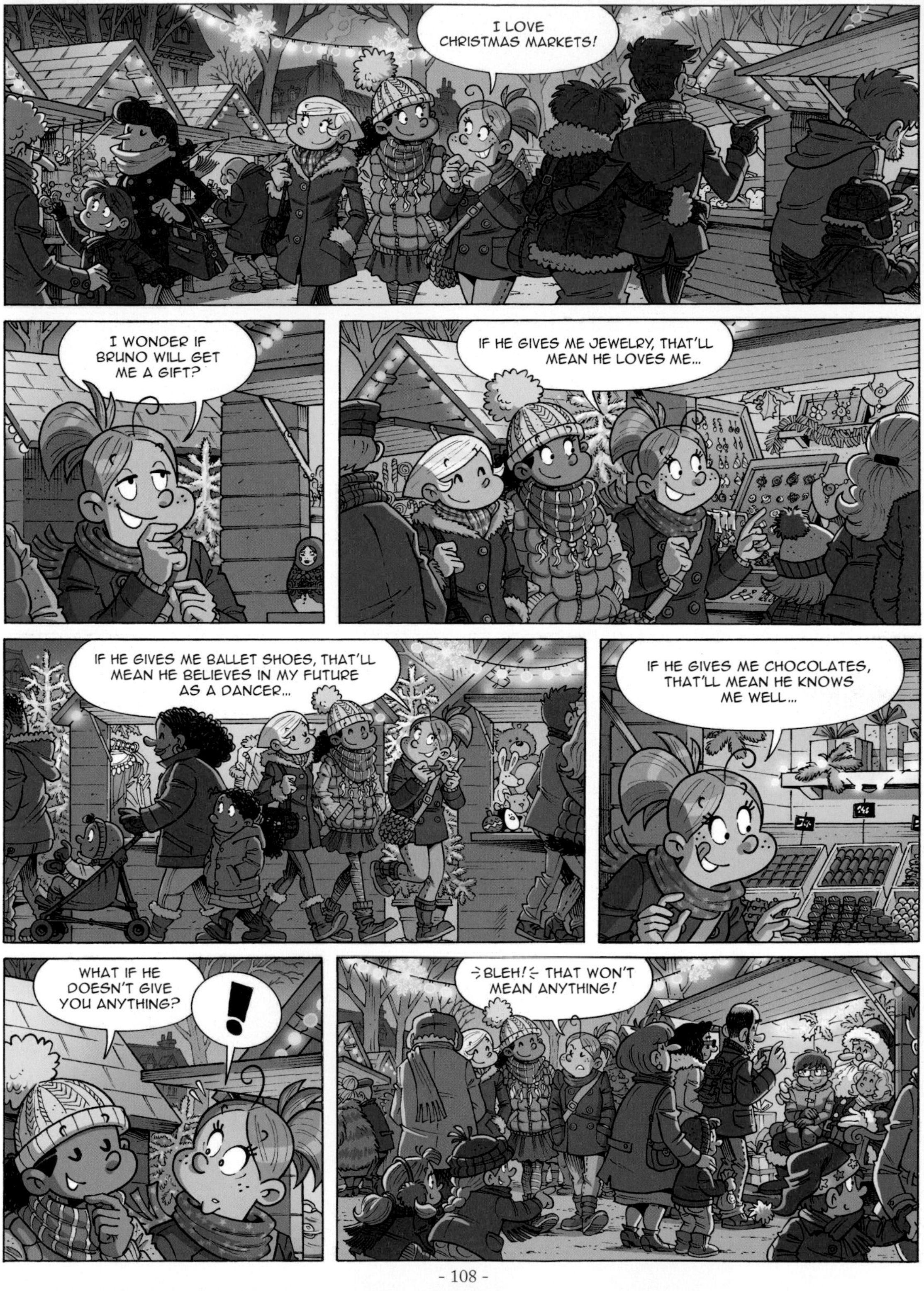
I LOVE CHRISTMAS MARKETS!
I WONDER IF BRUNO WILL GET ME A GIFT?
IF HE GIVES ME JEWELRY, THAT'LL MEAN HE LOVES ME...
IF HE GIVES ME BALLET SHOES, THAT'LL MEAN HE BELIEVES IN MY FUTURE AS A DANCER...
IF HE GIVES ME CHOCOLATES, THAT'LL MEAN HE KNOWS ME WELL...
WHAT IF HE DOESN'T GIVE YOU ANYTHING?
!
BLEH! THAT WON'T MEAN ANYTHING!

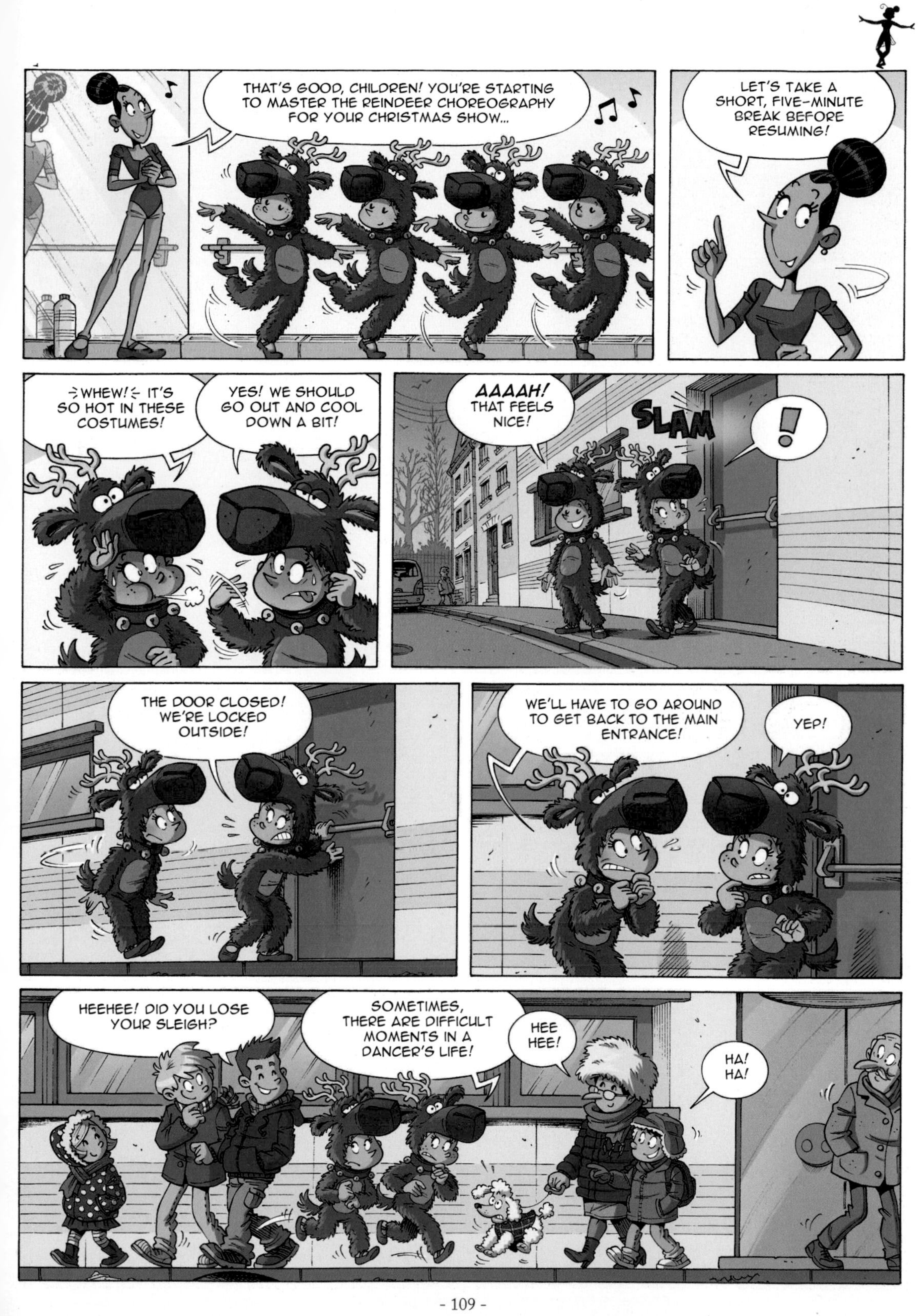
THAT'S GOOD, CHILDREN! YOU'RE STARTING TO MASTER THE REINDEER CHOREOGRAPHY FOR YOUR CHRISTMAS SHOW...
LET'S TAKE A SHORT, FIVE-MINUTE BREAK BEFORE RESUMING!
WHEW! IT'S SO HOT IN THESE COSTUMES!
YES! WE SHOULD GO OUT AND COOL DOWN A BIT!
AAAAH! THAT FEELS NICE!
SLAM
!
THE DOOR CLOSED! WE'RE LOCKED OUTSIDE!
WE'LL HAVE TO GO AROUND TO GET BACK TO THE MAIN ENTRANCE!
YEP!
HEEHEE! DID YOU LOSE YOUR SLEIGH?
SOMETIMES, THERE ARE DIFFICULT MOMENTS IN A DANCER'S LIFE!
HEE HEE!
HA! HA!

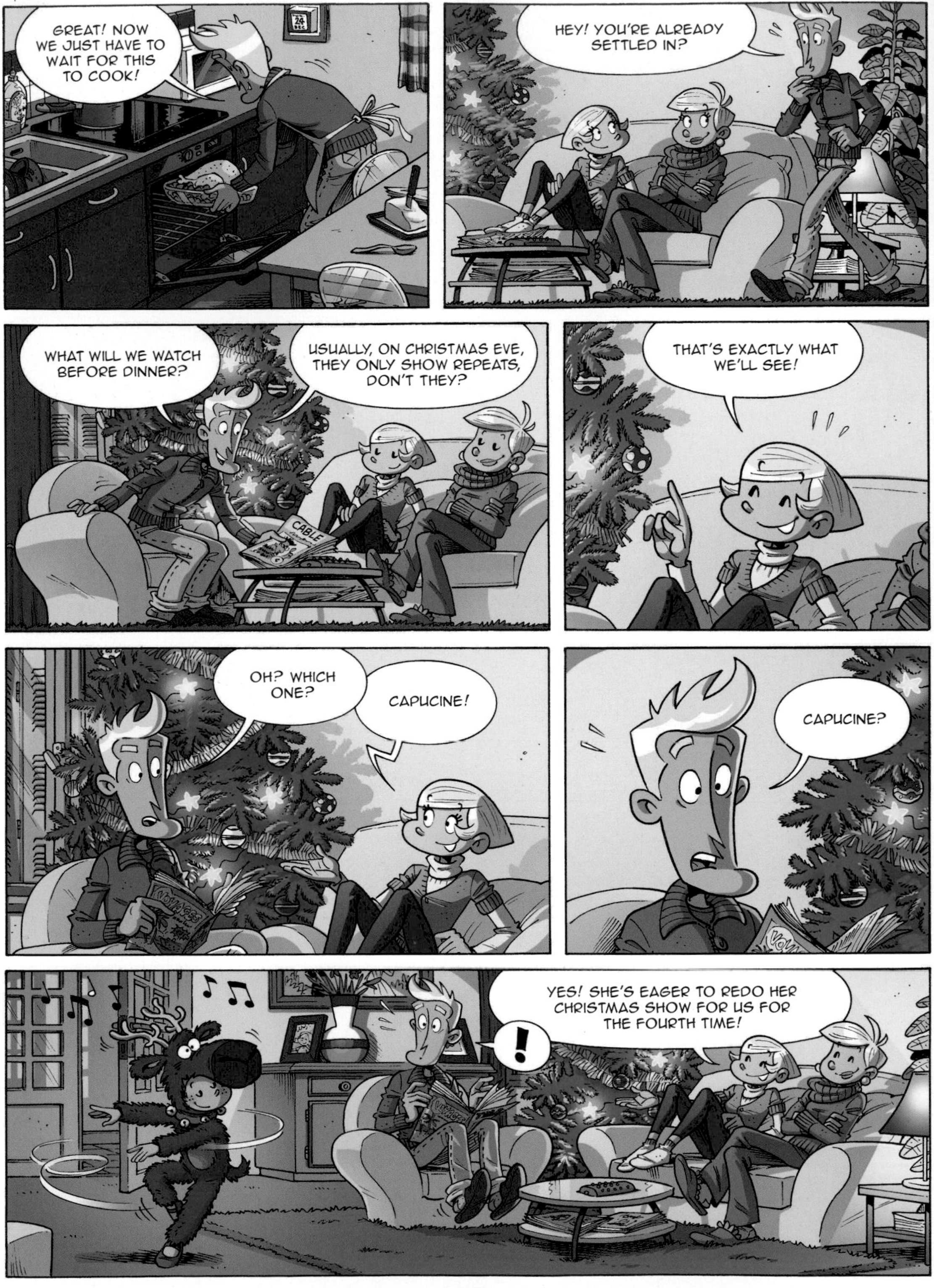
GREAT! NOW WE JUST HAVE TO WAIT FOR THIS TO COOK!
HEY! YOU'RE ALREADY SETTLED IN?
WHAT WILL WE WATCH BEFORE DINNER?
USUALLY, ON CHRISTMAS EVE, THEY ONLY SHOW REPEATS, DON'T THEY?
CABLE
THAT'S EXACTLY WHAT WE'LL SEE!
OH? WHICH ONE?
CAPUCINE!
CAPUCINE?
!
YES! SHE'S EAGER TO REDO HER CHRISTMAS SHOW FOR US FOR THE FOURTH TIME!

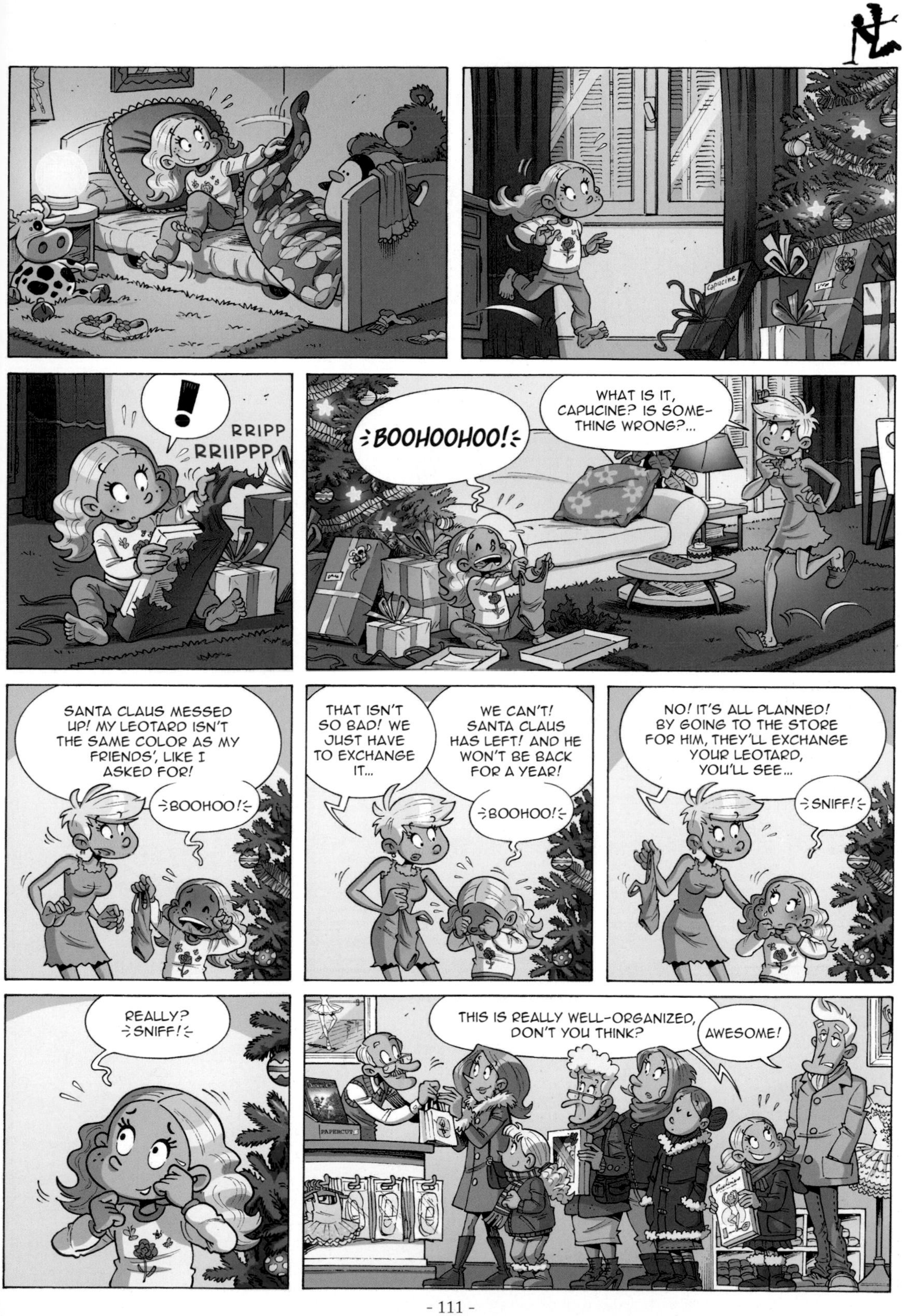
RRIPP
RRIIPPP
Capucine
BOOHOOHOO!
WHAT IS IT, CAPUCINE? IS SOMETHING WRONG?...
SANTA CLAUS MESSED UP! MY LEOTARD ISN'T THE SAME COLOR AS MY FRIENDS', LIKE I ASKED FOR!
BOOHOO!
THAT ISN'T SO BAD! WE JUST HAVE TO EXCHANGE IT...
WE CAN'T! SANTA CLAUS HAS LEFT! AND HE WON'T BE BACK FOR A YEAR!
BOOHOO!
NO! IT'S ALL PLANNED! BY GOING TO THE STORE FOR HIM, THEY'LL EXCHANGE YOUR LEOTARD, YOU'LL SEE...
SNIFF!
REALLY? SNIFF!
THIS IS REALLY WELL-ORGANIZED, DON'T YOU THINK?
AWESOME!
PAPERCUT

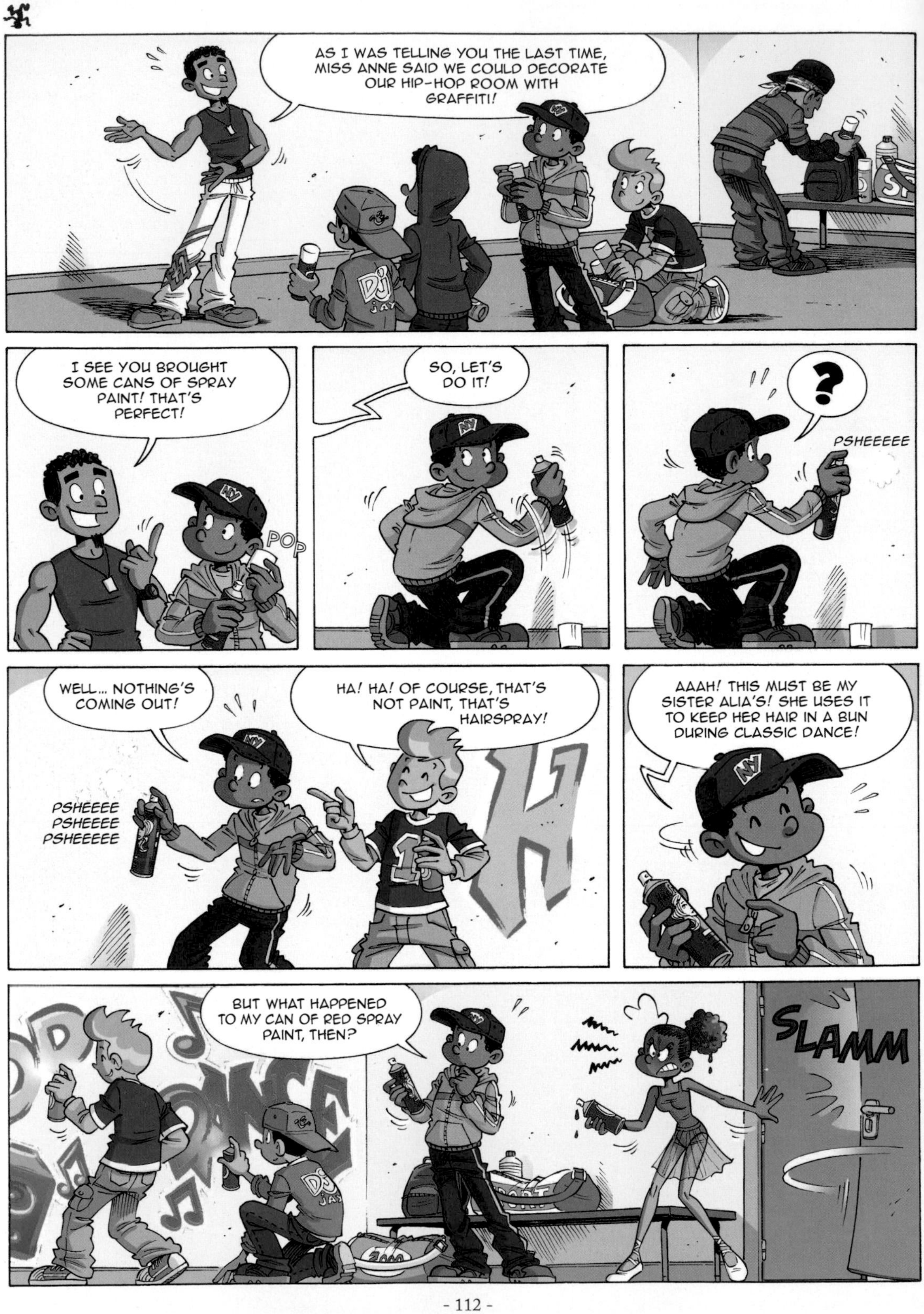

AS I WAS TELLING YOU THE LAST TIME, MISS ANNE SAID WE COULD DECORATE OUR HIP-HOP ROOM WITH GRAFFITI!
I SEE YOU BROUGHT SOME CANS OF SPRAY PAINT! THAT'S PERFECT!
POP
SO, LET'S DO IT!
?
PSHEEEEE
WELL... NOTHING'S COMING OUT!
PSHEEEE
PSHEEEE
PSHEEEEE
HA! HA! OF COURSE, THAT'S NOT PAINT, THAT'S HAIRSPRAY!
AAAH! THIS MUST BE MY SISTER ALIA'S! SHE USES IT TO KEEP HER HAIR IN A BUN DURING CLASSIC DANCE!
BUT WHAT HAPPENED TO MY CAN OF RED SPRAY PAINT, THEN?
SLAMM

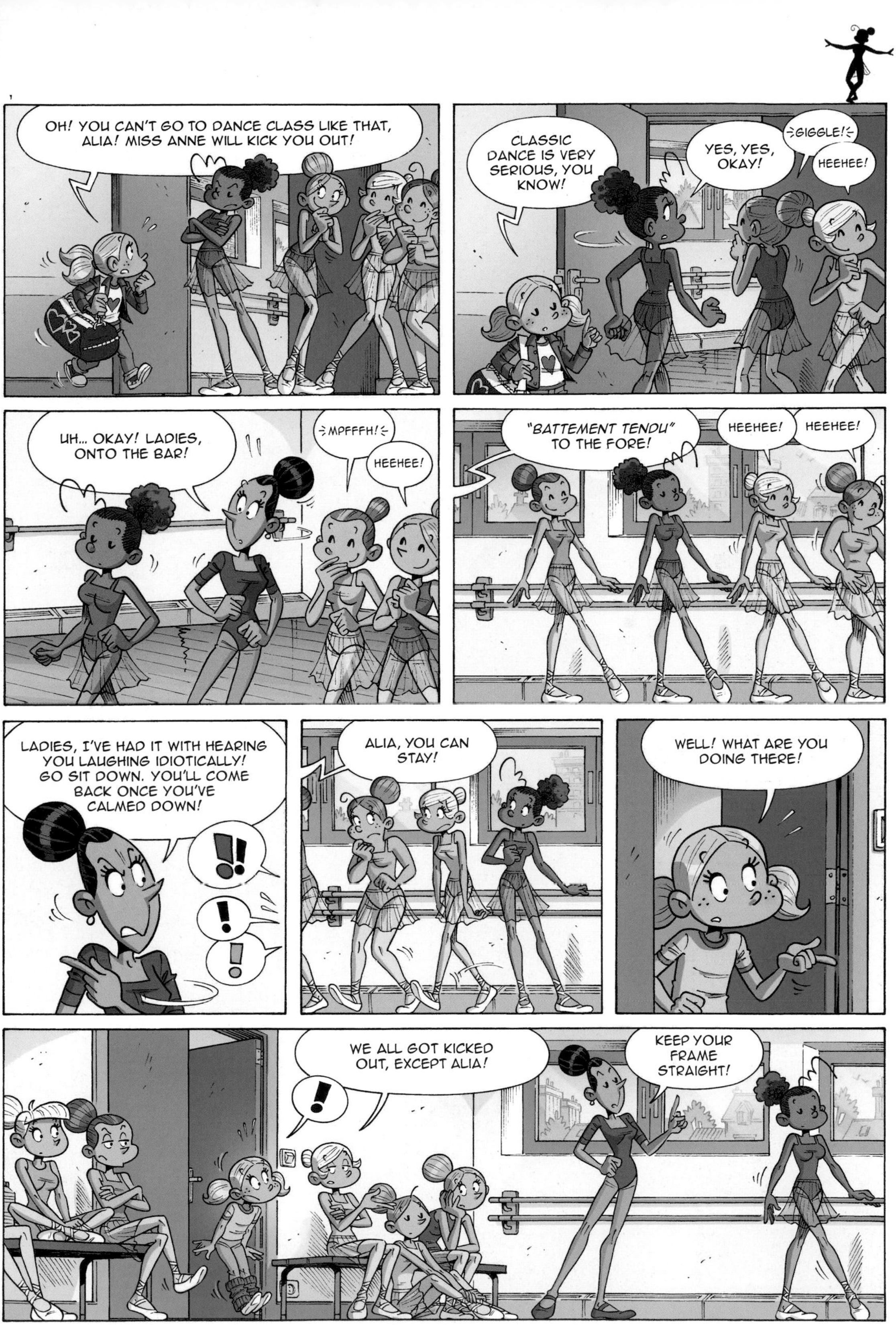
OH! YOU CAN'T GO TO DANCE CLASS LIKE THAT, ALIA! MISS ANNE WILL KICK YOU OUT!
CLASSIC DANCE IS VERY SERIOUS, YOU KNOW!
YES, YES, OKAY!
GIGGLE!
HEEHEE!
UH... OKAY! LADIES, ONTO THE BAR!
MPFFFH!
HEEHEE!
"BATTEMENT TENDU" TO THE FORE!
HEEHEE!
HEEHEE!
LADIES, I'VE HAD IT WITH HEARING YOU LAUGHING IDIOTICALLY! GO SIT DOWN. YOU'LL COME BACK ONCE YOU'VE CALMED DOWN!
!!
!
!
ALIA, YOU CAN STAY!
WELL! WHAT ARE YOU DOING THERE!
!
WE ALL GOT KICKED OUT, EXCEPT ALIA!
KEEP YOUR FRAME STRAIGHT!

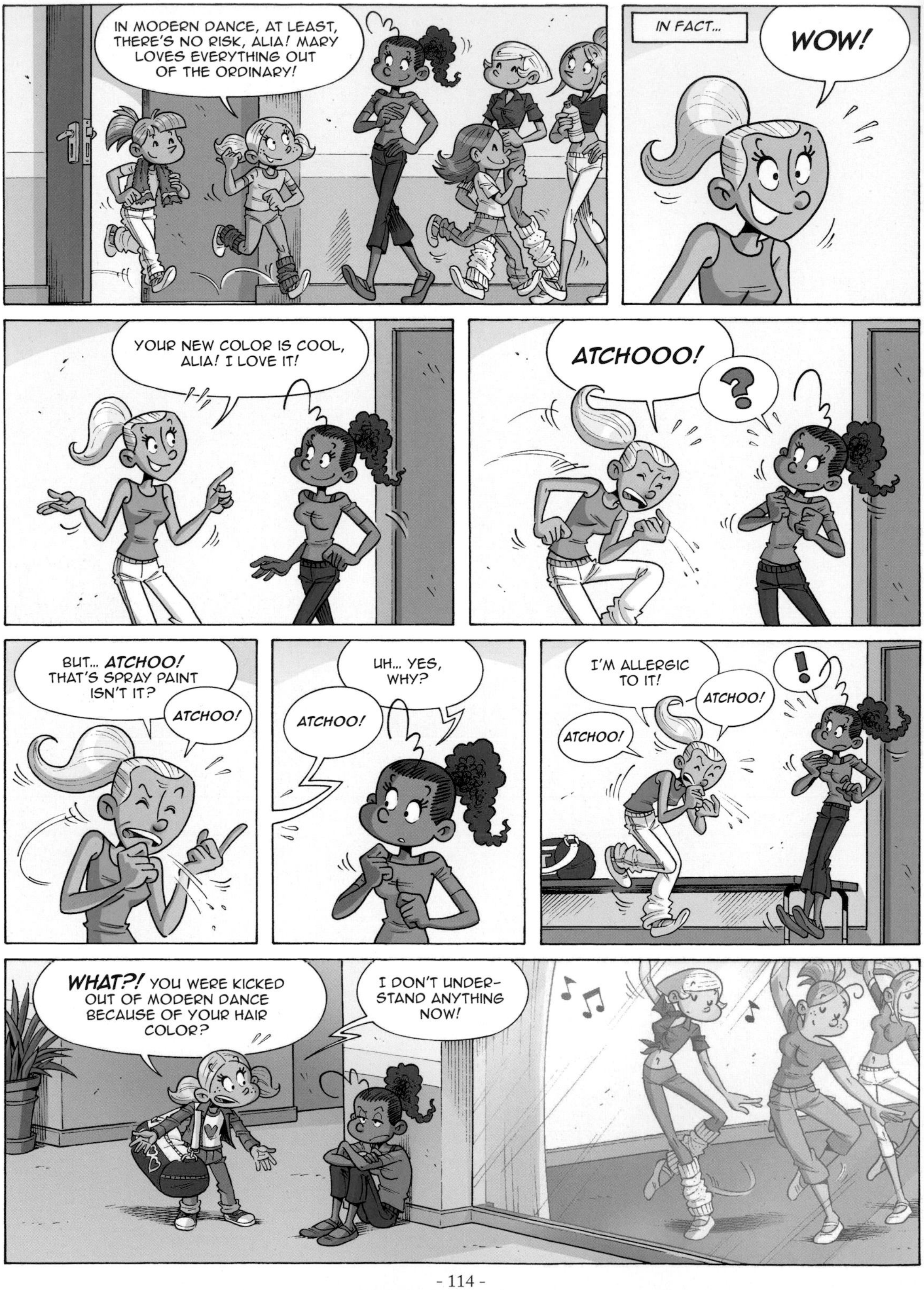
IN MODERN DANCE, AT LEAST, THERE'S NO RISK, ALIA! MARY LOVES EVERYTHING OUT OF THE ORDINARY!
IN FACT...
WOW!
YOUR NEW COLOR IS COOL, ALIA! I LOVE IT!
ATCHOOO!
?
BUT... ATCHOO! THAT'S SPRAY PAINT ISN'T IT?
ATCHOO!
UH... YES, WHY?
ATCHOO!
I'M ALLERGIC TO IT!
ATCHOO!
ATCHOO!
!
WHAT?! YOU WERE KICKED OUT OF MODERN DANCE BECAUSE OF YOUR HAIR COLOR?
I DON'T UNDER-STAND ANYTHING NOW!

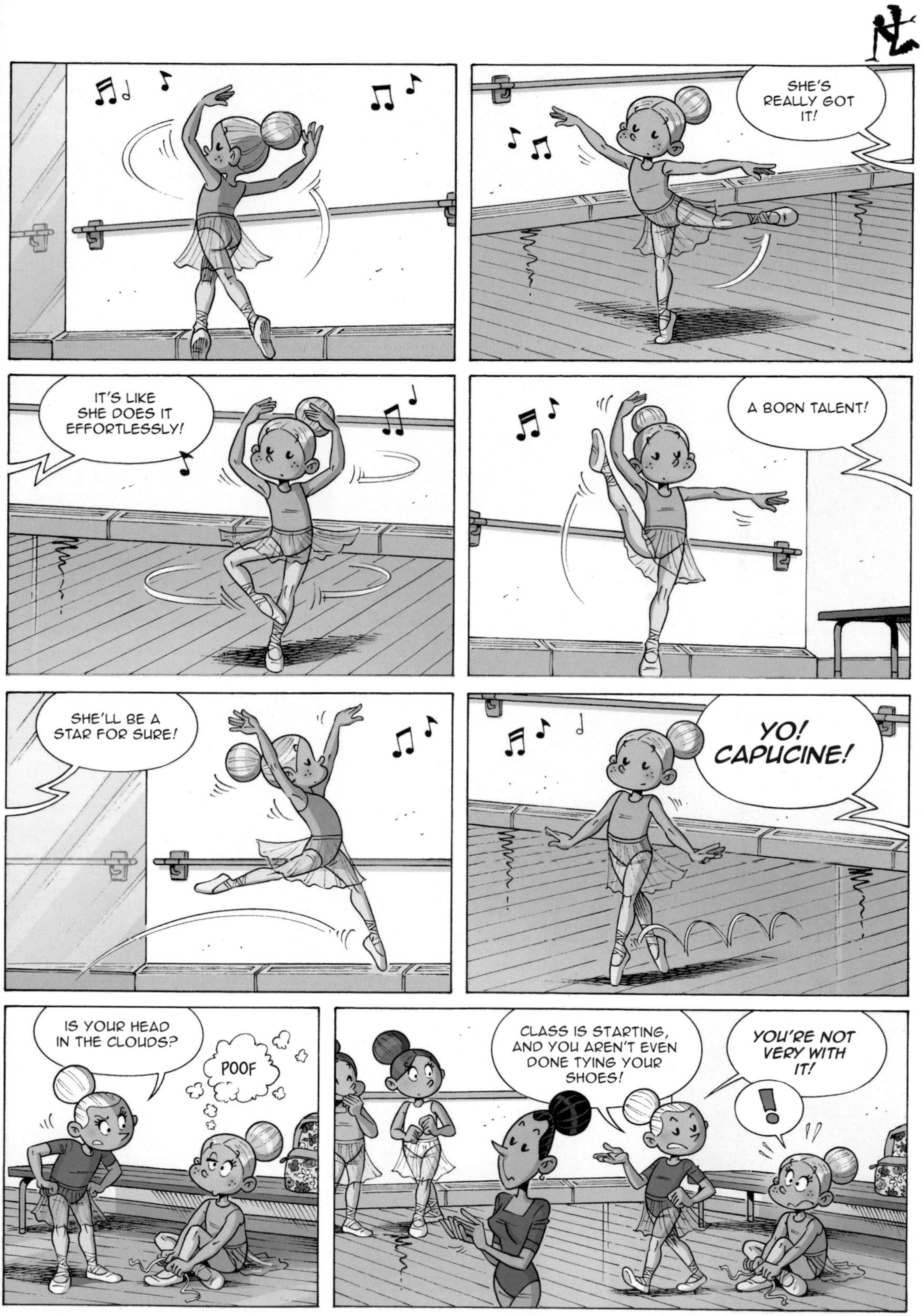
SHE'S REALLY GOT IT!
IT'S LIKE SHE DOES IT EFFORTLESSLY!
A BORN TALENT!
SHE'LL BE A STAR FOR SURE!
YO! CAPUCINE!
IS YOUR HEAD IN THE CLOUDS?
POOF
CLASS IS STARTING, AND YOU AREN'T EVEN DONE TYING YOUR SHOES!
YOU'RE NOT VERY WITH IT!
!

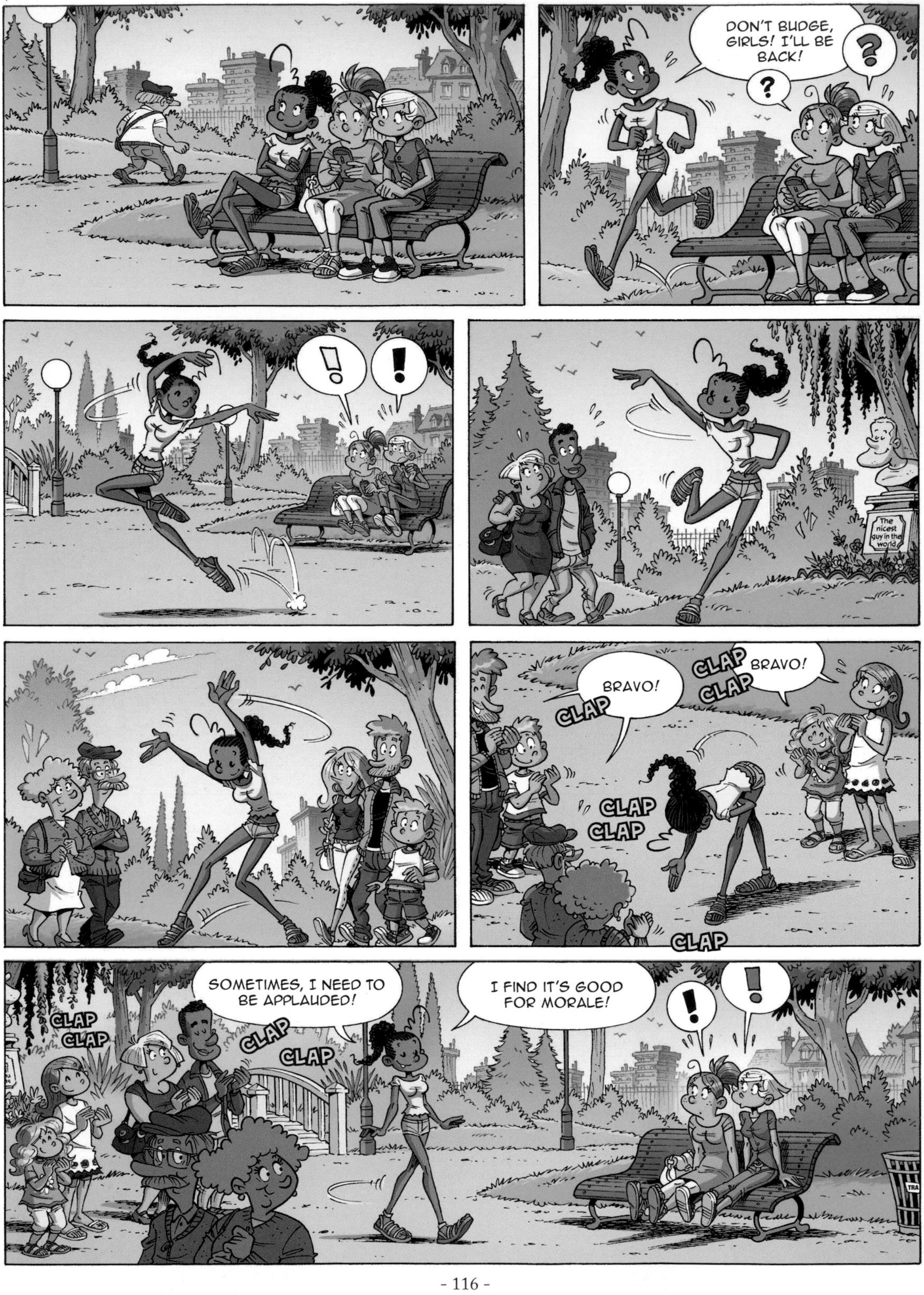
DON'T BUDGE, GIRLS! I'LL BE BACK!
?
?
!
!
The nicest guy in the world
CLAP
BRAVO!
CLAP
CLAP
BRAVO!
CLAP
CLAP
CLAP
CLAP
CLAP
SOMETIMES, I NEED TO BE APPLAUDED!
CLAP
CLAP
I FIND IT'S GOOD FOR MORALE!
!
!

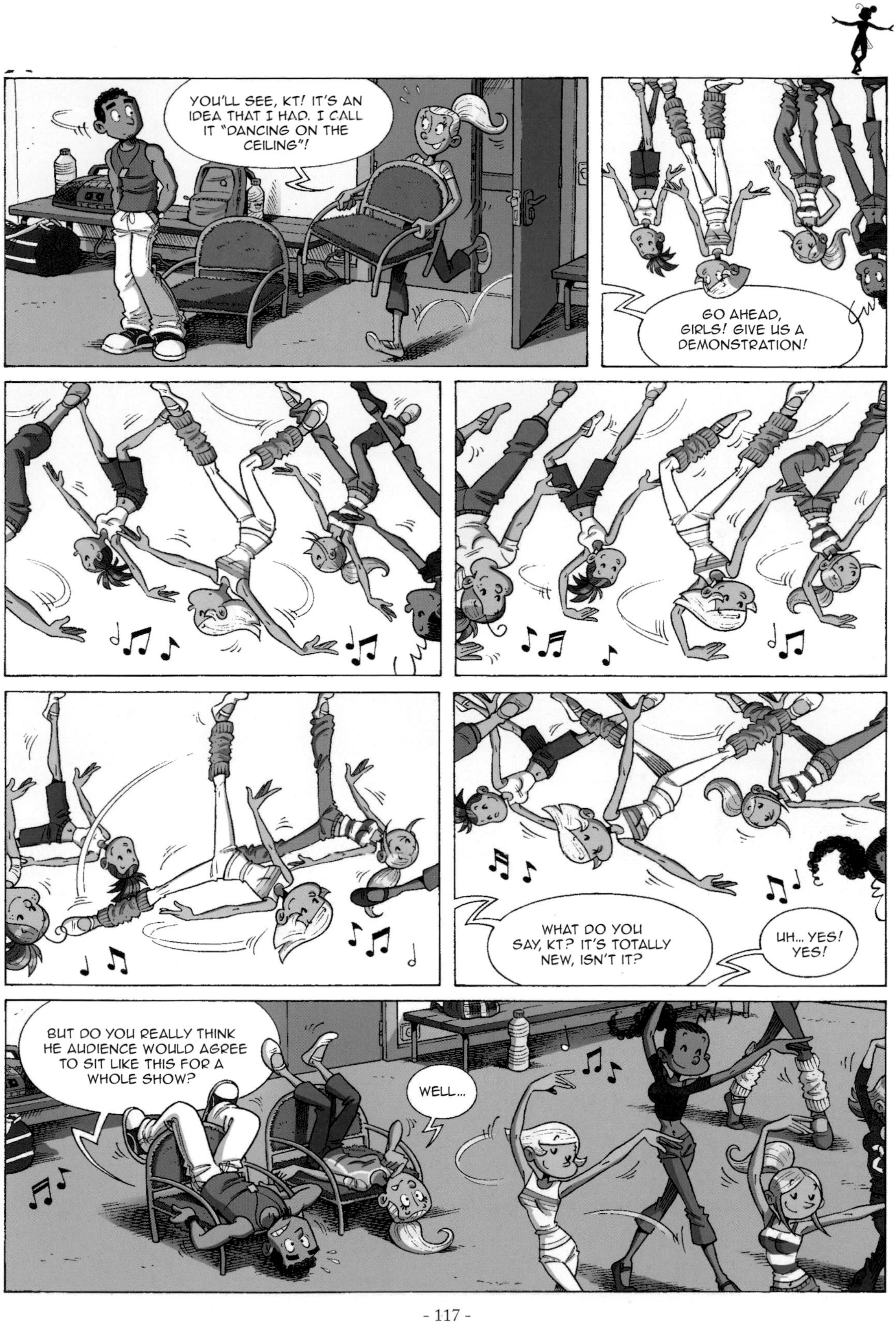
YOU'LL SEE, KT! IT'S AN IDEA THAT I HAD. I CALL IT "DANCING ON THE CEILING"!
GO AHEAD, GIRLS! GIVE US A DEMONSTRATION!
WHAT DO YOU SAY, KT? IT'S TOTALLY NEW, ISN'T IT?
UH... YES! YES!
BUT DO YOU REALLY THINK HE AUDIENCE WOULD AGREE TO SIT LIKE THIS FOR A WHOLE SHOW?
WELL...

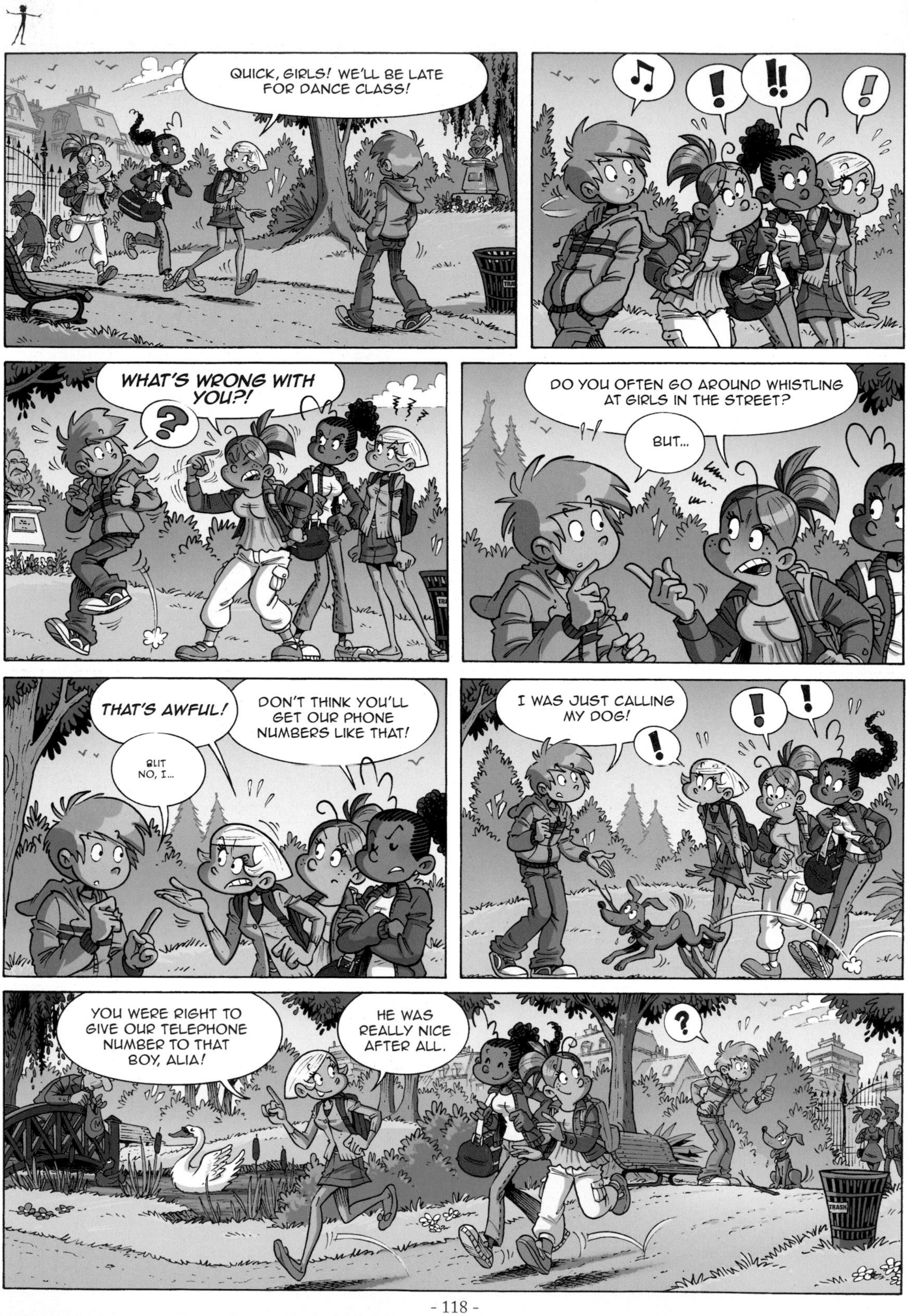
QUICK, GIRLS! WE'LL BE LATE FOR DANCE CLASS!
♫
!
!!
!
?
WHAT'S WRONG WITH YOU?!
DO YOU OFTEN GO AROUND WHISTLING AT GIRLS IN THE STREET?
BUT...
THAT'S AWFUL!
BUT NO, I...
DON'T THINK YOU'LL GET OUR PHONE NUMBERS LIKE THAT!
I WAS JUST CALLING MY DOG!
!
!
!
YOU WERE RIGHT TO GIVE OUR TELEPHONE NUMBER TO THAT BOY, ALIA!
HE WAS REALLY NICE AFTER ALL.
?
TRASH

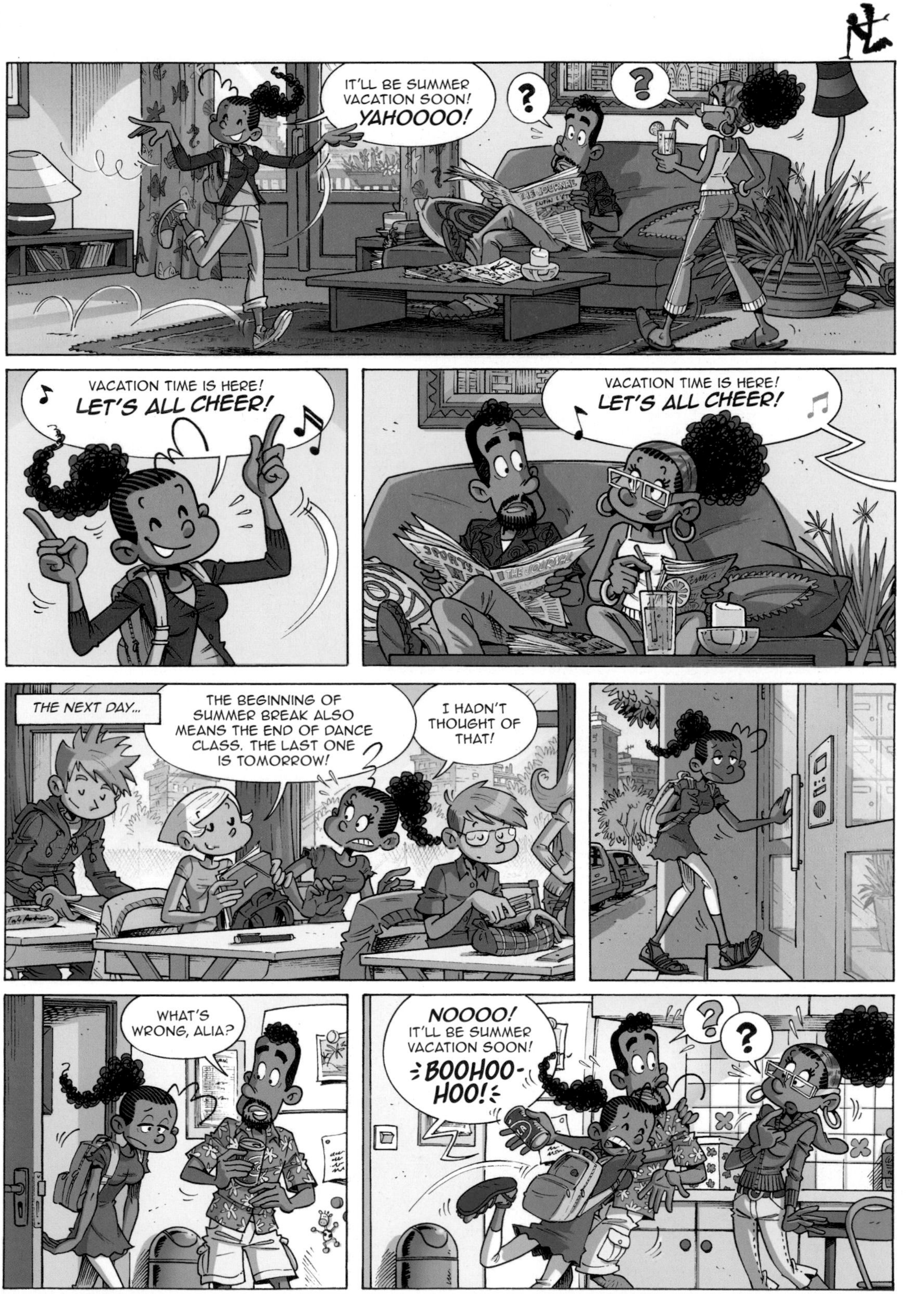
IT'LL BE SUMMER VACATION SOON! YAHOOOO!
?
?
VACATION TIME IS HERE! LET'S ALL CHEER!
VACATION TIME IS HERE! LET'S ALL CHEER!
THE JOURNAL
SPORTS
THE JOURNAL
THE NEXT DAY...
THE BEGINNING OF SUMMER BREAK ALSO MEANS THE END OF DANCE CLASS. THE LAST ONE IS TOMORROW!
I HADN'T THOUGHT OF THAT!
WHAT'S WRONG, ALIA?
NOOOO! IT'LL BE SUMMER VACATION SOON! BOOHOO-HOO!
?
?

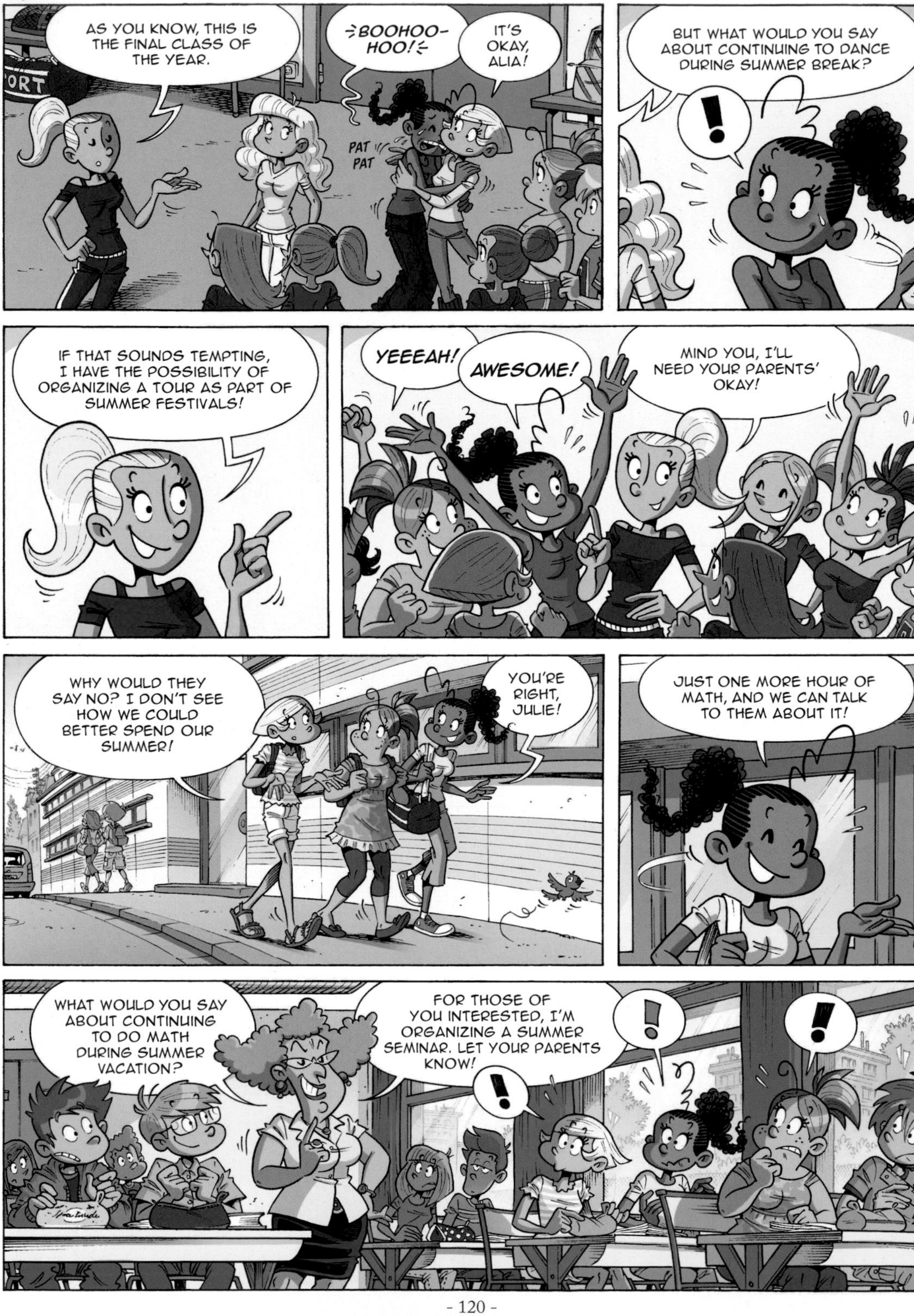

AS YOU KNOW, THIS IS THE FINAL CLASS OF THE YEAR.
BOOHOO-HOO!
IT'S OKAY, ALIA!
PAT PAT
BUT WHAT WOULD YOU SAY ABOUT CONTINUING TO DANCE DURING SUMMER BREAK?
!
IF THAT SOUNDS TEMPTING, I HAVE THE POSSIBILITY OF ORGANIZING A TOUR AS PART OF SUMMER FESTIVALS!
YEEEAH!
AWESOME!
MIND YOU, I'LL NEED YOUR PARENTS' OKAY!
WHY WOULD THEY SAY NO? I DON'T SEE HOW WE COULD BETTER SPEND OUR SUMMER!
YOU'RE RIGHT, JULIE!
JUST ONE MORE HOUR OF MATH, AND WE CAN TALK TO THEM ABOUT IT!
WHAT WOULD YOU SAY ABOUT CONTINUING TO DO MATH DURING SUMMER VACATION?
FOR THOSE OF YOU INTERESTED, I'M ORGANIZING A SUMMER SEMINAR. LET YOUR PARENTS KNOW!
!
!
!

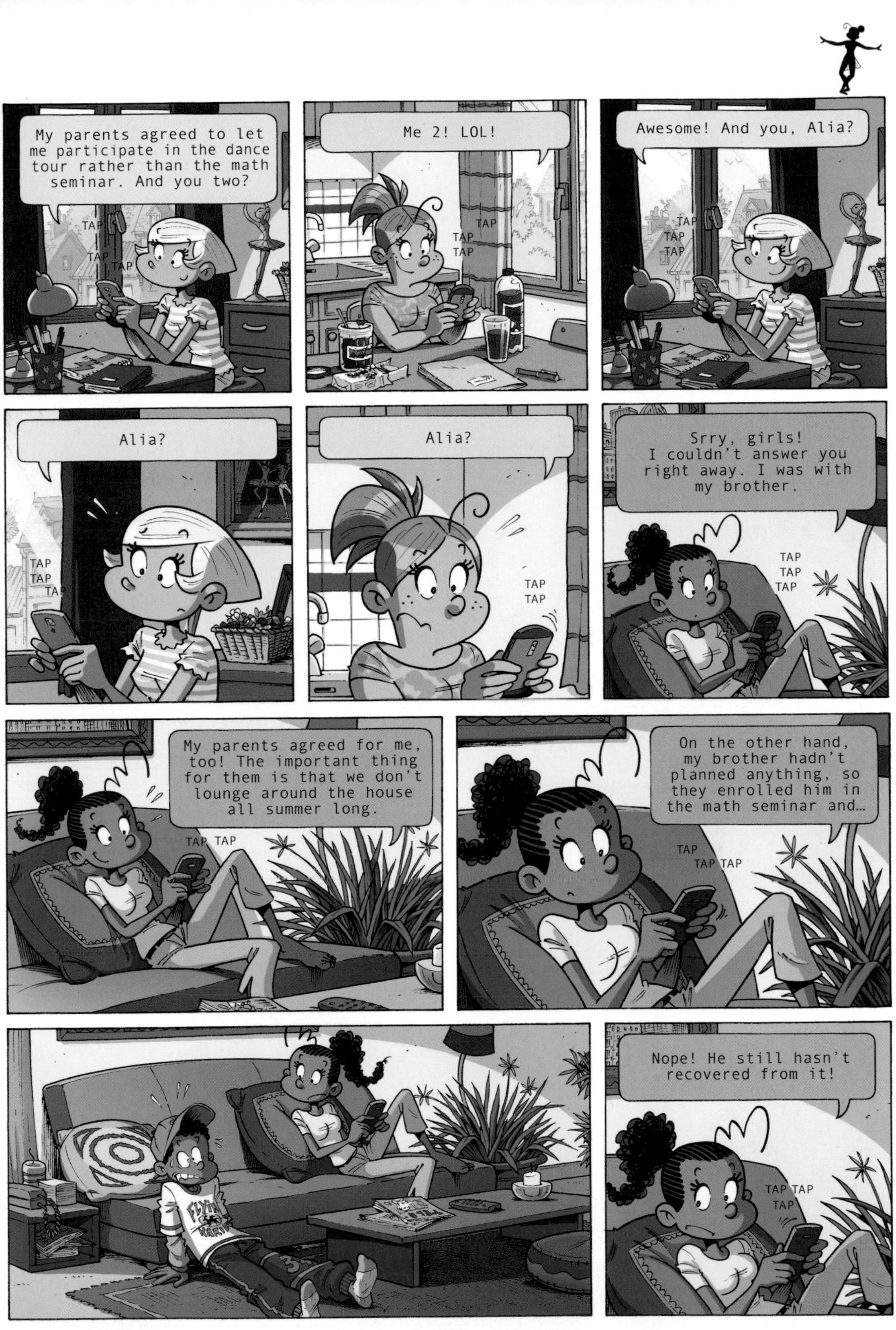

My parents agreed to let me participate in the dance tour rather than the math seminar. And you two?
TAP TAP TAP
Me 2! LOL!
TAP TAP TAP
Awesome! And you, Alia?
TAP TAP TAP
Alia?
TAP TAP TAP
Alia?
TAP TAP
Srry, girls! I couldn't answer you right away. I was with my brother.
TAP TAP TAP
My parents agreed for me, too! The important thing for them is that we don't lounge around the house all summer long.
TAP TAP
On the other hand, my brother hadn't planned anything, so they enrolled him in the math seminar and...
TAP TAP TAP
Nope! He still hasn't recovered from it!
TAP TAP TAP

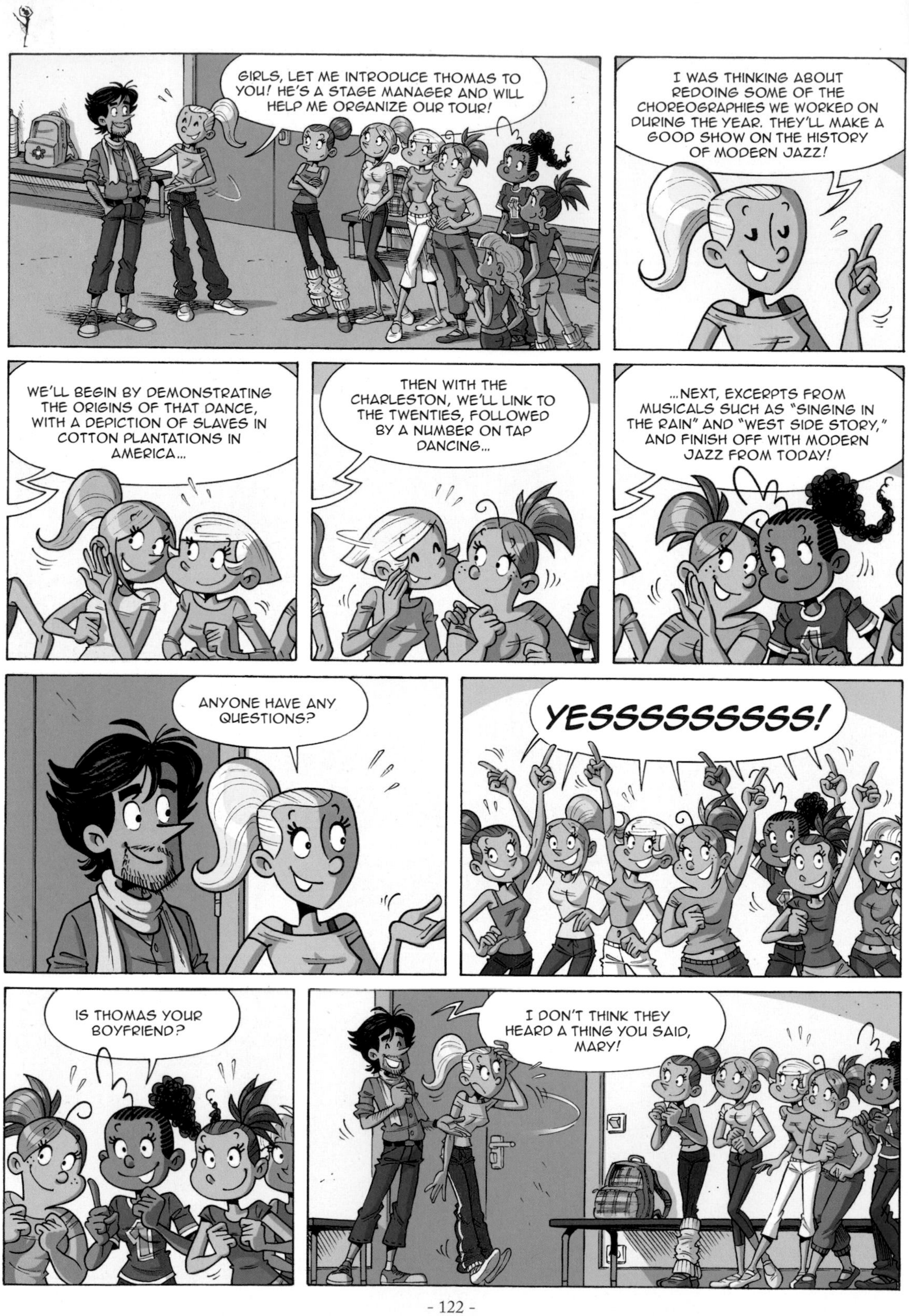
GIRLS, LET ME INTRODUCE THOMAS TO YOU! HE'S A STAGE MANAGER AND WILL HELP ME ORGANIZE OUR TOUR!
I WAS THINKING ABOUT REDOING SOME OF THE CHOREOGRAPHIES WE WORKED ON DURING THE YEAR. THEY'LL MAKE A GOOD SHOW ON THE HISTORY OF MODERN JAZZ!
WE'LL BEGIN BY DEMONSTRATING THE ORIGINS OF THAT DANCE, WITH A DEPICTION OF SLAVES IN COTTON PLANTATIONS IN AMERICA...
THEN WITH THE CHARLESTON, WE'LL LINK TO THE TWENTIES, FOLLOWED BY A NUMBER ON TAP DANCING...
...NEXT, EXCERPTS FROM MUSICALS SUCH AS "SINGING IN THE RAIN" AND "WEST SIDE STORY," AND FINISH OFF WITH MODERN JAZZ FROM TODAY!
ANYONE HAVE ANY QUESTIONS?
YESSSSSSSSS!
IS THOMAS YOUR BOYFRIEND?
I DON'T THINK THEY HEARD A THING YOU SAID, MARY!

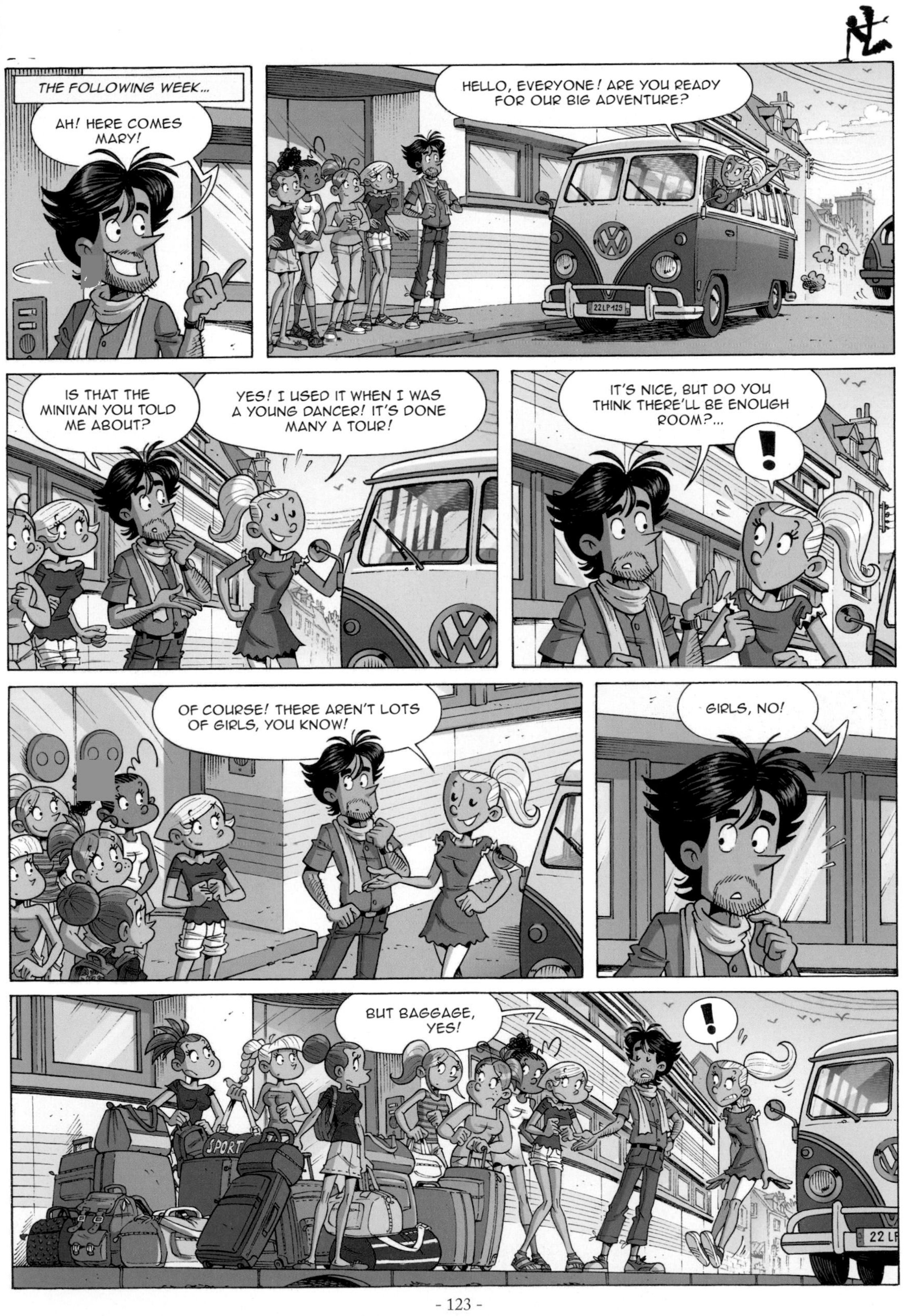
THE FOLLOWING WEEK...
AH! HERE COMES MARY!
HELLO, EVERYONE! ARE YOU READY FOR OUR BIG ADVENTURE?
IS THAT THE MINIVAN YOU TOLD ME ABOUT?
YES! I USED IT WHEN I WAS A YOUNG DANCER! IT'S DONE MANY A TOUR!
IT'S NICE, BUT DO YOU THINK THERE'LL BE ENOUGH ROOM?...
!
OF COURSE! THERE AREN'T LOTS OF GIRLS, YOU KNOW!
GIRLS, NO!
BUT BAGGAGE, YES!
!
SPORT

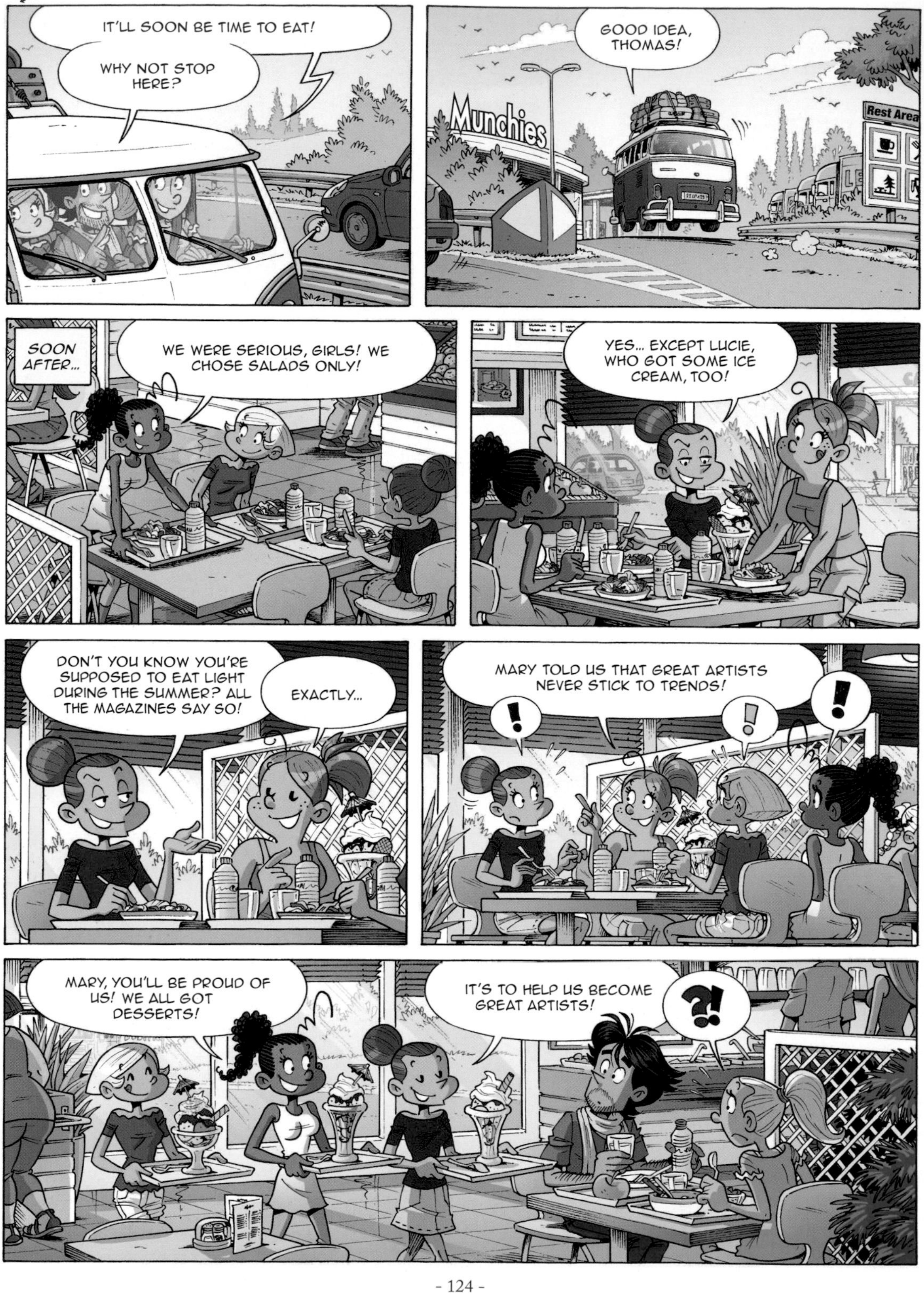
IT'LL SOON BE TIME TO EAT!
WHY NOT STOP HERE?
GOOD IDEA, THOMAS!
Munchies
Rest Area
SOON AFTER...
WE WERE SERIOUS, GIRLS! WE CHOSE SALADS ONLY!
YES... EXCEPT LUCIE, WHO GOT SOME ICE CREAM, TOO!
DON'T YOU KNOW YOU'RE SUPPOSED TO EAT LIGHT DURING THE SUMMER? ALL THE MAGAZINES SAY SO!
EXACTLY...
MARY TOLD US THAT GREAT ARTISTS NEVER STICK TO TRENDS!
!
!
!
MARY, YOU'LL BE PROUD OF US! WE ALL GOT DESSERTS!
IT'S TO HELP US BECOME GREAT ARTISTS!
?!

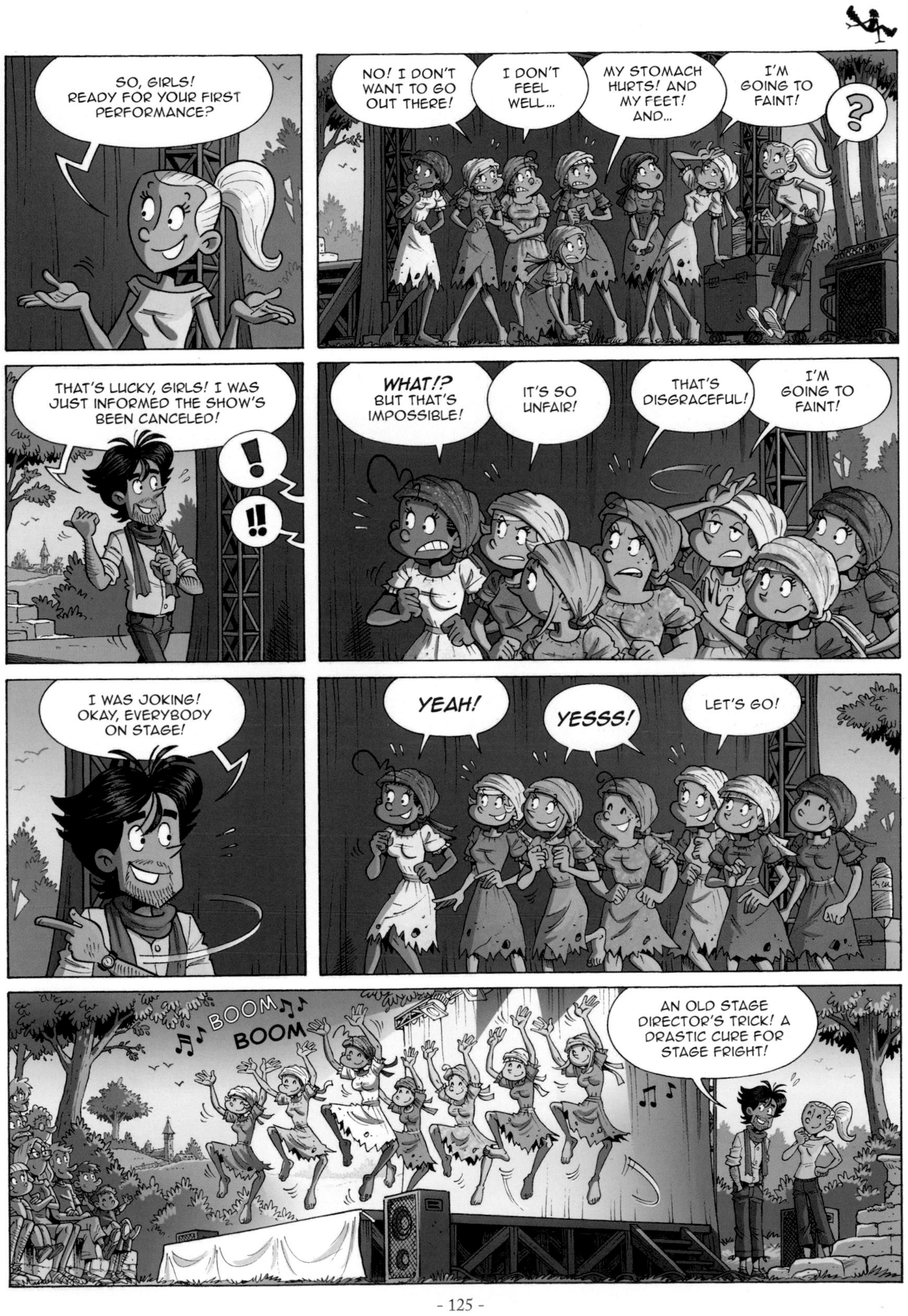
SO, GIRLS! READY FOR YOUR FIRST PERFORMANCE?
NO! I DON'T WANT TO GO OUT THERE!
I DON'T FEEL WELL...
MY STOMACH HURTS! AND MY FEET! AND...
I'M GOING TO FAINT!
?
THAT'S LUCKY, GIRLS! I WAS JUST INFORMED THE SHOW'S BEEN CANCELED!
!
!!
WHAT!? BUT THAT'S IMPOSSIBLE!
IT'S SO UNFAIR!
THAT'S DISGRACEFUL!
I'M GOING TO FAINT!
I WAS JOKING! OKAY, EVERYBODY ON STAGE!
YEAH!
YESSS!
LET'S GO!
BOOM
BOOM
AN OLD STAGE DIRECTOR'S TRICK! A DRASTIC CURE FOR STAGE FRIGHT!

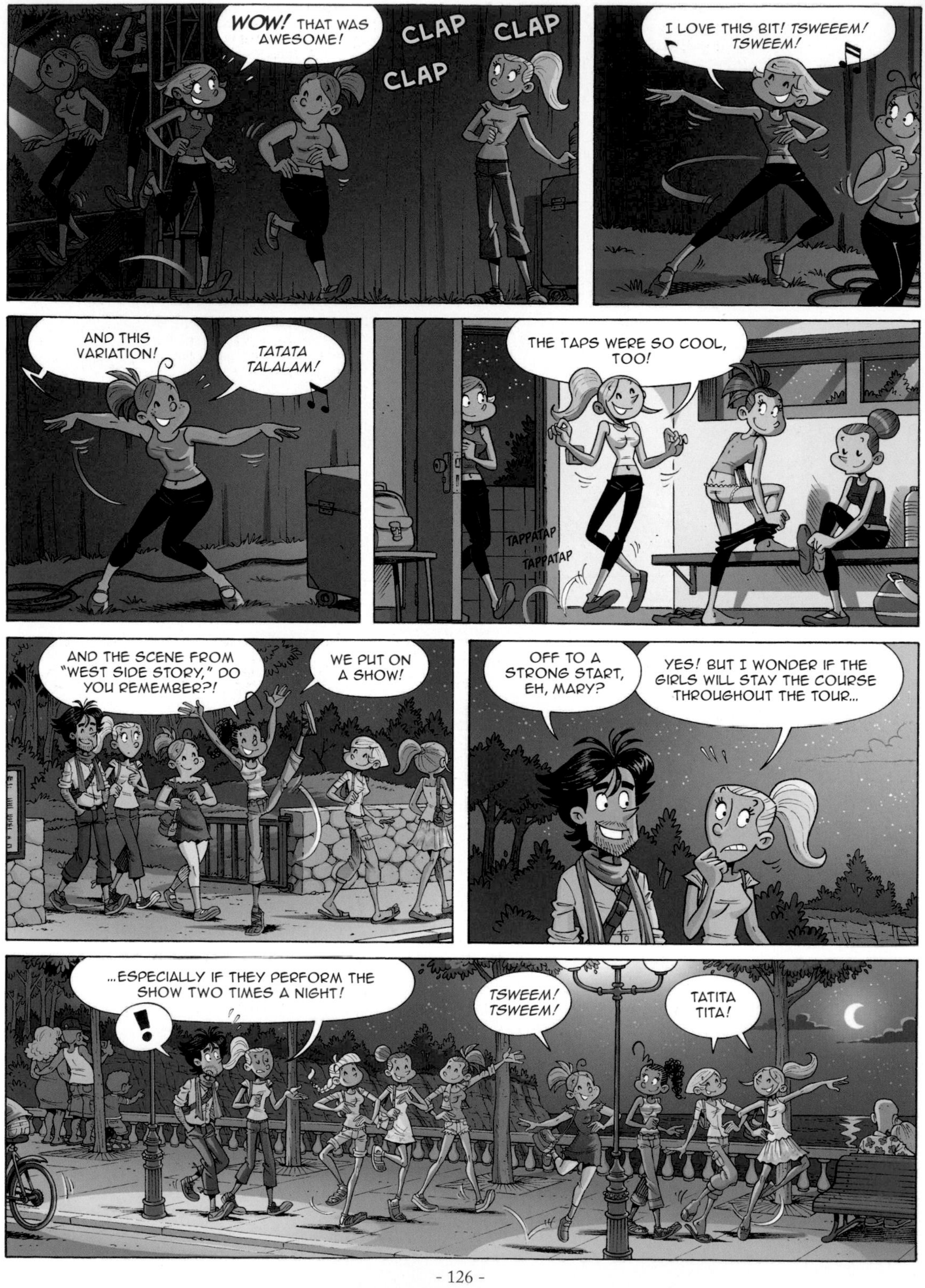
WOW! THAT WAS AWESOME!
CLAP
CLAP
CLAP
I LOVE THIS BIT! TSWEEEM! TSWEEM!
AND THIS VARIATION!
TATATA TALALAM!
THE TAPS WERE SO COOL, TOO!
TAPPATAP
TAPPATAP
AND THE SCENE FROM "WEST SIDE STORY," DO YOU REMEMBER?!
WE PUT ON A SHOW!
OFF TO A STRONG START, EH, MARY?
YES! BUT I WONDER IF THE GIRLS WILL STAY THE COURSE THROUGHOUT THE TOUR...
...ESPECIALLY IF THEY PERFORM THE SHOW TWO TIMES A NIGHT!
!
TSWEEM! TSWEEM!
TATITA TITA!

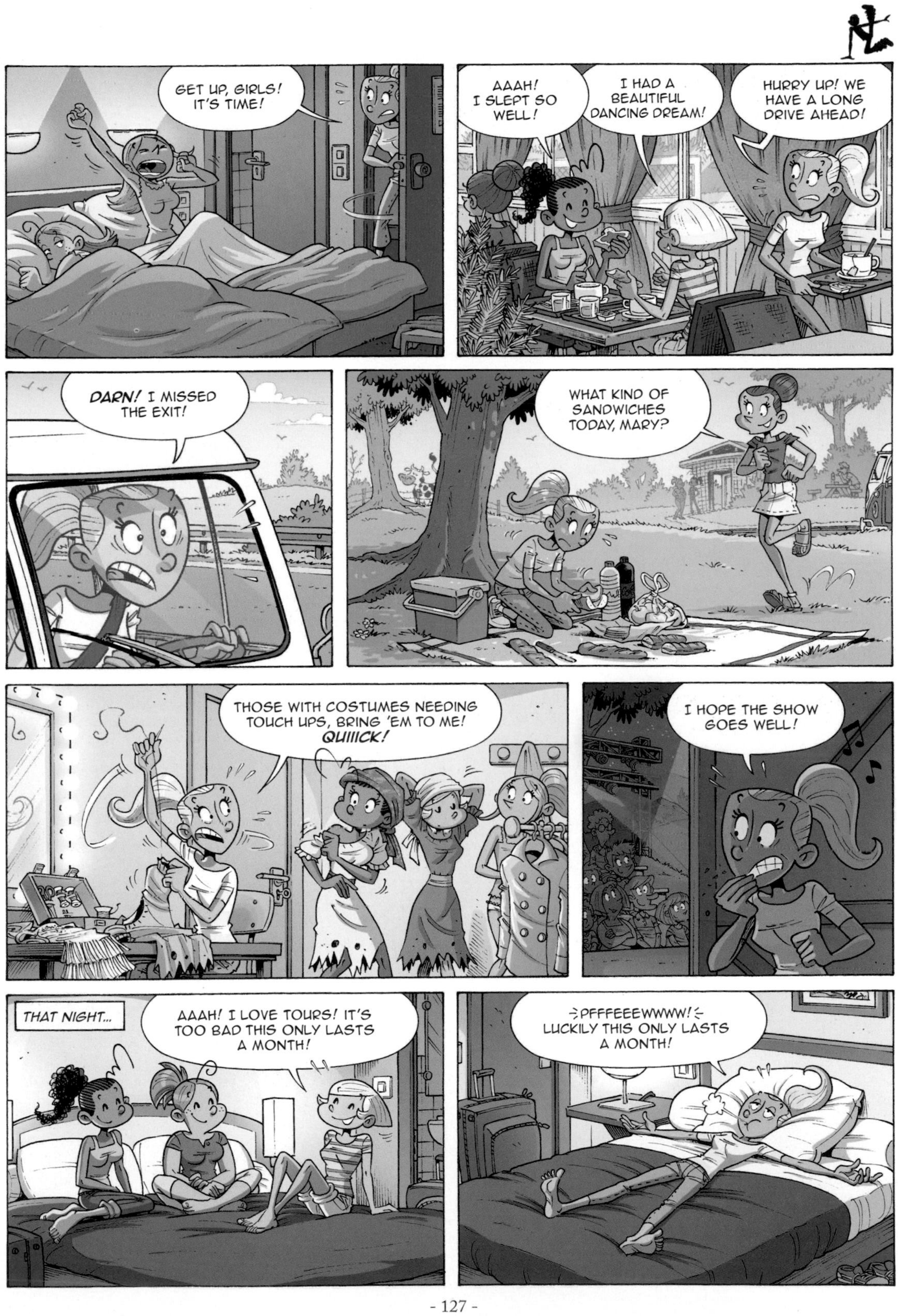
GET UP, GIRLS! IT'S TIME!
AAAH! I SLEPT SO WELL!
I HAD A BEAUTIFUL DANCING DREAM!
HURRY UP! WE HAVE A LONG DRIVE AHEAD!
DARN! I MISSED THE EXIT!
WHAT KIND OF SANDWICHES TODAY, MARY?
THOSE WITH COSTUMES NEEDING TOUCH UPS, BRING 'EM TO ME! QUIIICK!
I HOPE THE SHOW GOES WELL!
THAT NIGHT...
AAAH! I LOVE TOURS! IT'S TOO BAD THIS ONLY LASTS A MONTH!
PFFFEEEWWWW! LUCKILY THIS ONLY LASTS A MONTH!

CLAP CLAP

CLAP CLAP

CLAP

CLAP

BRAVO!

BRAVO!

WOW! THAT WAS AWESOME!

THOSE DANCERS ARE SO CUTE!

CLAP

CLAP

CLAP

I'D LIKE TO SEE THEM AGAIN!

ME, TOO!

LOOK! TOMORROW NIGHT, THEY'RE DANCING KIND OF FAR FROM HERE! YOU THINK WE CAN GET THERE BY SCOOTER?

YES! THAT SHOULD BE DOABLE BY LEAVING AT DAYBREAK!

the Dance Class
HISTORY OF JAZZ TOUR

THEY'RE WORTH THE EFFORT!

THE NEXT DAY...

I COULDN'T WAIT TO SEE THEM AGAIN, I DIDN'T SLEEP A WINK ALL NIGHT!

ME EITHER!

VRRRRR

COOL! WE'RE HERE FIRST!

EVEN BETTER! WE'LL BE ABLE TO REST A BIT WHILE WAITING FOR THE SHOW!

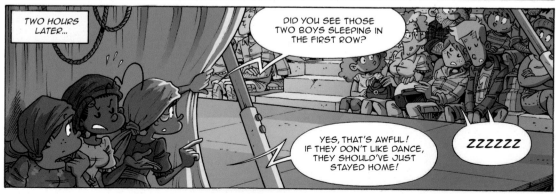

TWO HOURS LATER...

DID YOU SEE THOSE TWO BOYS SLEEPING IN THE FIRST ROW?

YES, THAT'S AWFUL! IF THEY DON'T LIKE DANCE, THEY SHOULD'VE JUST STAYED HOME!

ZZZZZZ

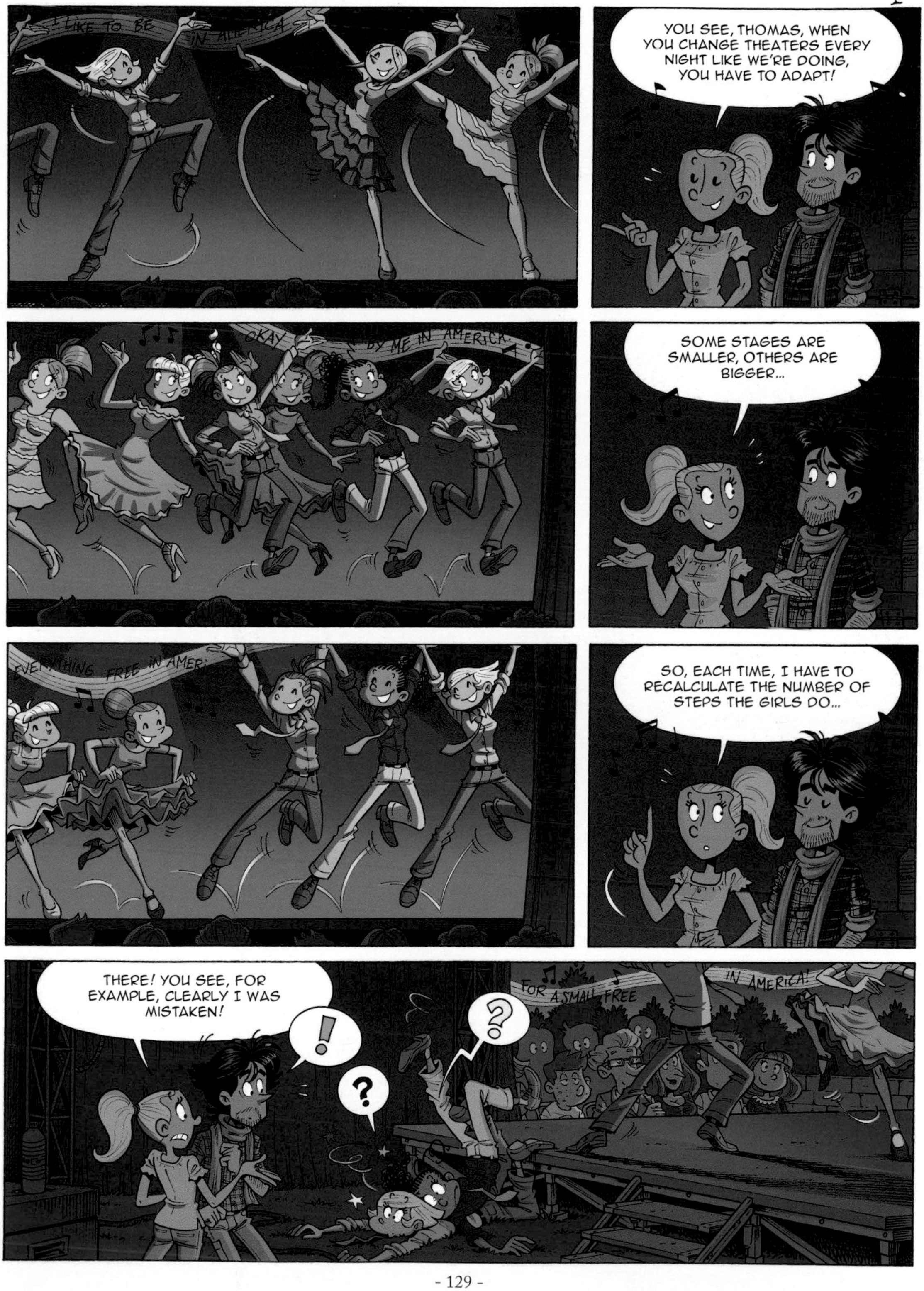

I LIKE TO BE
IN AMERICA
YOU SEE, THOMAS, WHEN YOU CHANGE THEATERS EVERY NIGHT LIKE WE'RE DOING, YOU HAVE TO ADAPT!
OKAY
BY ME IN AMERICA
SOME STAGES ARE SMALLER, OTHERS ARE BIGGER...
FREE IN AMER
SO, EACH TIME, I HAVE TO RECALCULATE THE NUMBER OF STEPS THE GIRLS DO...
THERE! YOU SEE, FOR EXAMPLE, CLEARLY I WAS MISTAKEN!
FOR A SMALL FREE
IN AMERICA!
!
?
?

ZWIIIIPP

CAREFUL, GIRLS! THE STAGE FLOOR IS VERY SLIPPERY!

IT IS! I MUSTN'T FALL WHILE DANCING!

DON'T WORRY! I'LL TEACH YOU A DANCER SECRET!

WHEN THE FLOOR IS SLIPPERY, YOU JUST HAVE TO POUR SOME SODA ON IT. THE SUGAR CREATES A FINE ADHESIVE FILM UNDER YOUR SHOES!

AWESOME! LET'S DO THAT!

I SAW A VENDING MACHINE AT THE THEATER ENTRANCE!

SOON AFTER...

THAT'S PERFECT, GIRLS!

PLOOP PLOOP

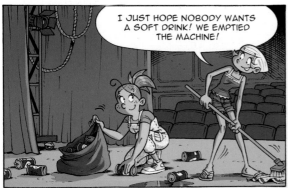

I JUST HOPE NOBODY WANTS A SOFT DRINK! WE EMPTIED THE MACHINE!

AT THE ENTRANCE...

RAAAH! A HUNDRED MILES BY SCOOTER AND NOT EVEN A SODA TO QUENCH MY THIRST!

≳ PFFF ≲

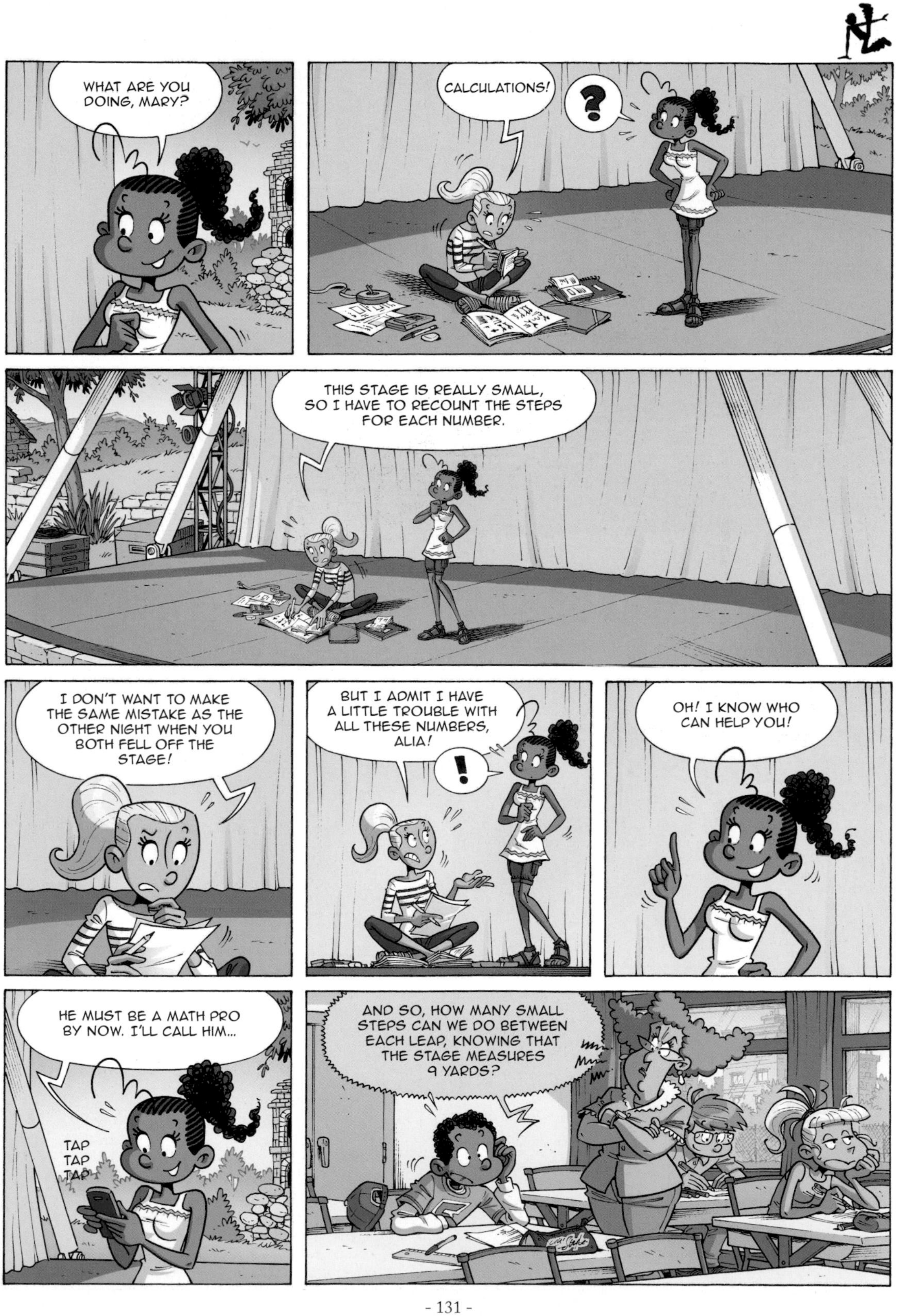
WHAT ARE YOU DOING, MARY?
CALCULATIONS!
?
THIS STAGE IS REALLY SMALL, SO I HAVE TO RECOUNT THE STEPS FOR EACH NUMBER.
I DON'T WANT TO MAKE THE SAME MISTAKE AS THE OTHER NIGHT WHEN YOU BOTH FELL OFF THE STAGE!
BUT I ADMIT I HAVE A LITTLE TROUBLE WITH ALL THESE NUMBERS, ALIA!
!
OH! I KNOW WHO CAN HELP YOU!
HE MUST BE A MATH PRO BY NOW. I'LL CALL HIM...
TAP TAP TAP
AND SO, HOW MANY SMALL STEPS CAN WE DO BETWEEN EACH LEAP, KNOWING THAT THE STAGE MEASURES 9 YARDS?

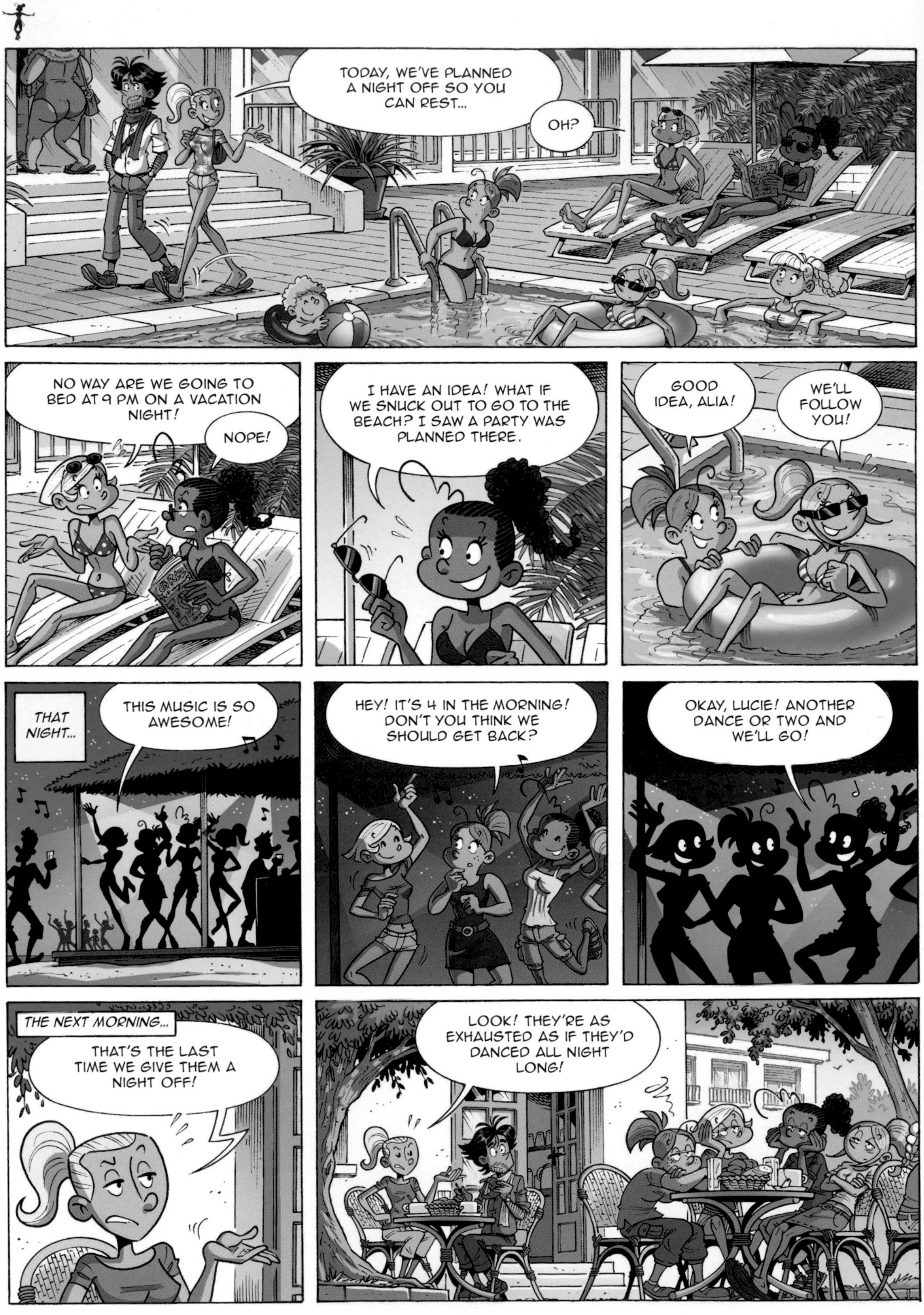
TODAY, WE'VE PLANNED A NIGHT OFF SO YOU CAN REST...
OH?
NO WAY ARE WE GOING TO BED AT 9 PM ON A VACATION NIGHT!
NOPE!
I HAVE AN IDEA! WHAT IF WE SNUCK OUT TO GO TO THE BEACH? I SAW A PARTY WAS PLANNED THERE.
GOOD IDEA, ALIA!
WE'LL FOLLOW YOU!
THAT NIGHT...
THIS MUSIC IS SO AWESOME!
HEY! IT'S 4 IN THE MORNING! DON'T YOU THINK WE SHOULD GET BACK?
OKAY, LUCIE! ANOTHER DANCE OR TWO AND WE'LL GO!
THE NEXT MORNING...
THAT'S THE LAST TIME WE GIVE THEM A NIGHT OFF!
LOOK! THEY'RE AS EXHAUSTED AS IF THEY'D DANCED ALL NIGHT LONG!

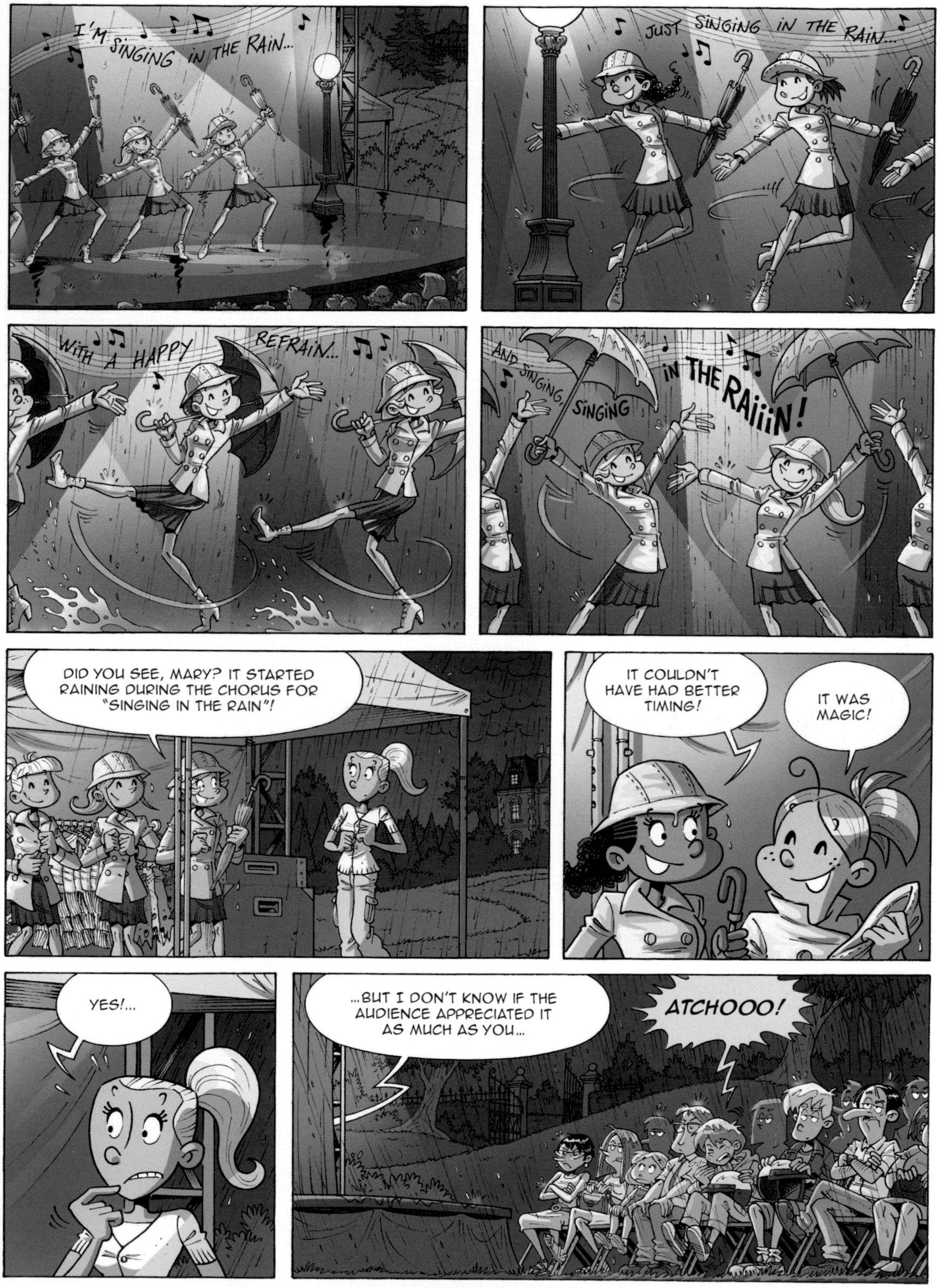
I'M SINGING IN THE RAIN...
JUST SINGING IN THE RAIN...
WITH A HAPPY REFRAIN...
AND SINGING, SINGING IN THE RAIiiN!
DID YOU SEE, MARY? IT STARTED RAINING DURING THE CHORUS FOR "SINGING IN THE RAIN"!
IT COULDN'T HAVE HAD BETTER TIMING!
IT WAS MAGIC!
YES!...
...BUT I DON'T KNOW IF THE AUDIENCE APPRECIATED IT AS MUCH AS YOU...
ATCHOOO!

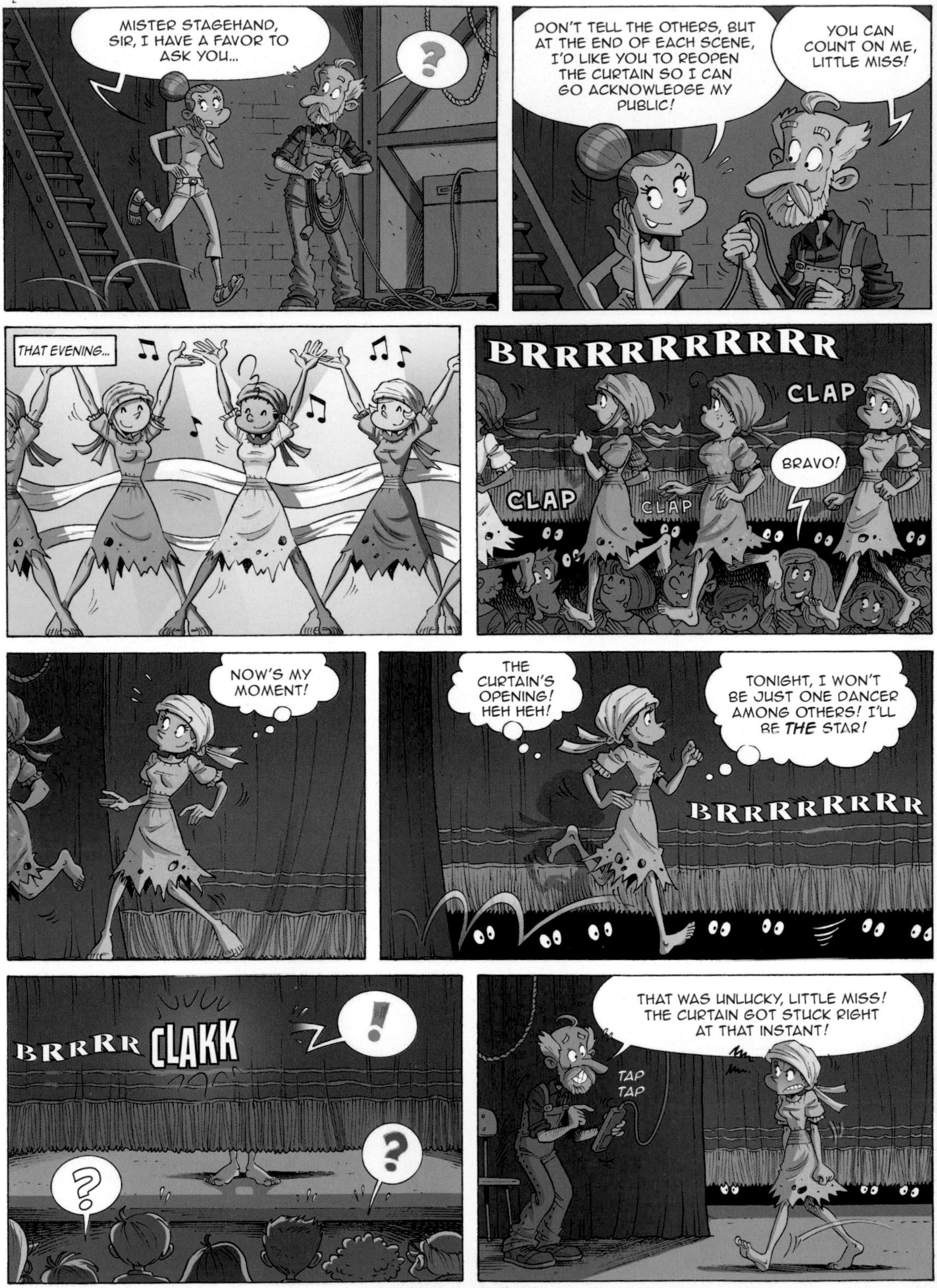

MISTER STAGEHAND, SIR, I HAVE A FAVOR TO ASK YOU...
?
DON'T TELL THE OTHERS, BUT AT THE END OF EACH SCENE, I'D LIKE YOU TO REOPEN THE CURTAIN SO I CAN GO ACKNOWLEDGE MY PUBLIC!
YOU CAN COUNT ON ME, LITTLE MISS!
THAT EVENING...
BRRRRRRRRRRR
CLAP
CLAP
CLAP
BRAVO!
NOW'S MY MOMENT!
THE CURTAIN'S OPENING! HEH HEH!
TONIGHT, I WON'T BE JUST ONE DANCER AMONG OTHERS! I'LL BE *THE* STAR!
BRRRRRRRRR
BRRRRR CLAKK
!
?
?
THAT WAS UNLUCKY, LITTLE MISS! THE CURTAIN GOT STUCK RIGHT AT THAT INSTANT!
TAP TAP

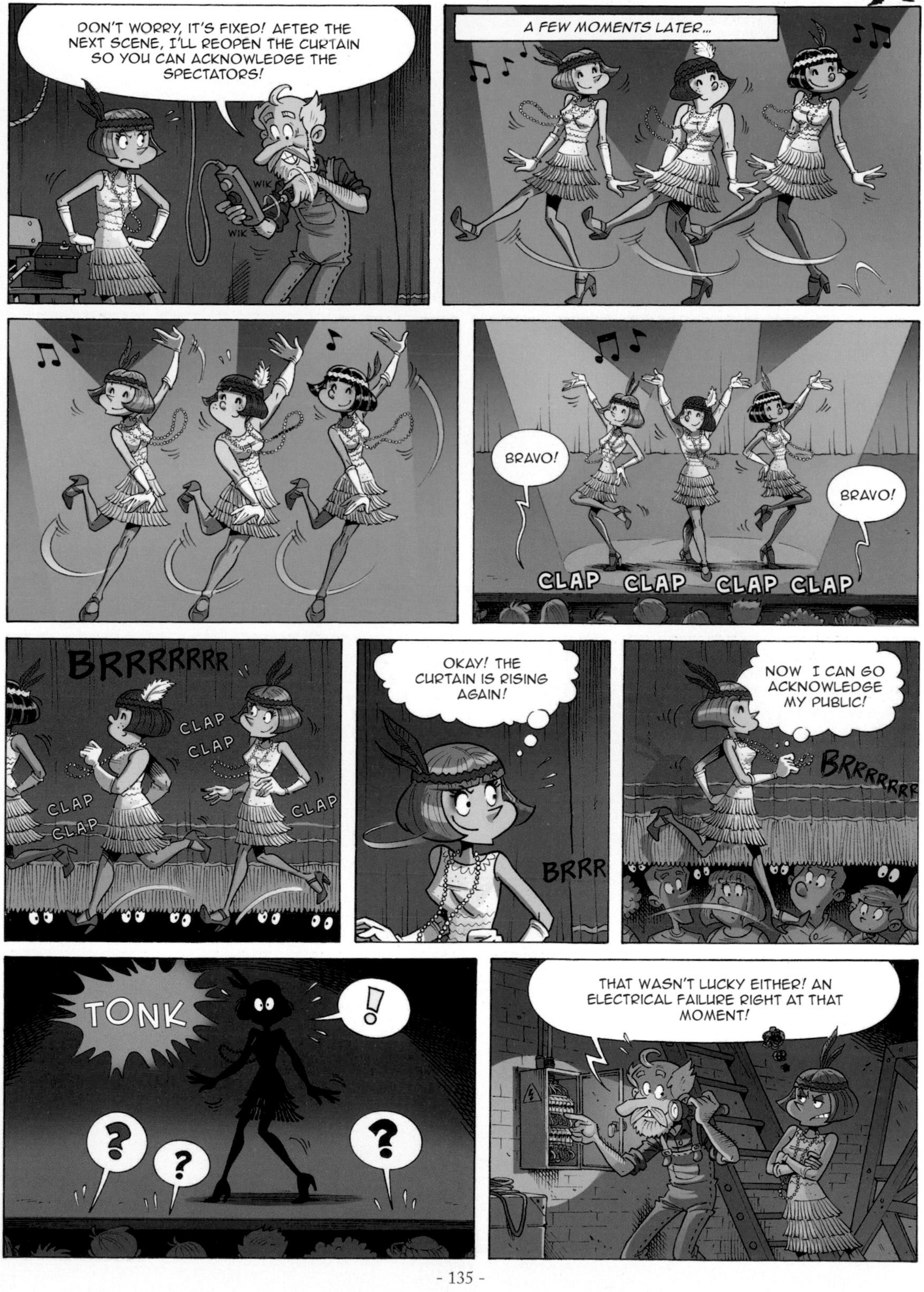
DON'T WORRY, IT'S FIXED! AFTER THE NEXT SCENE, I'LL REOPEN THE CURTAIN SO YOU CAN ACKNOWLEDGE THE SPECTATORS!
WIK
WIK
A FEW MOMENTS LATER...
BRAVO!
BRAVO!
CLAP CLAP CLAP CLAP
BRRRRRRR
CLAP
CLAP
CLAP
CLAP
CLAP
OKAY! THE CURTAIN IS RISING AGAIN!
BRRR
NOW I CAN GO ACKNOWLEDGE MY PUBLIC!
BRRRRRRR
TONK
!
?
?
?
THAT WASN'T LUCKY EITHER! AN ELECTRICAL FAILURE RIGHT AT THAT MOMENT!

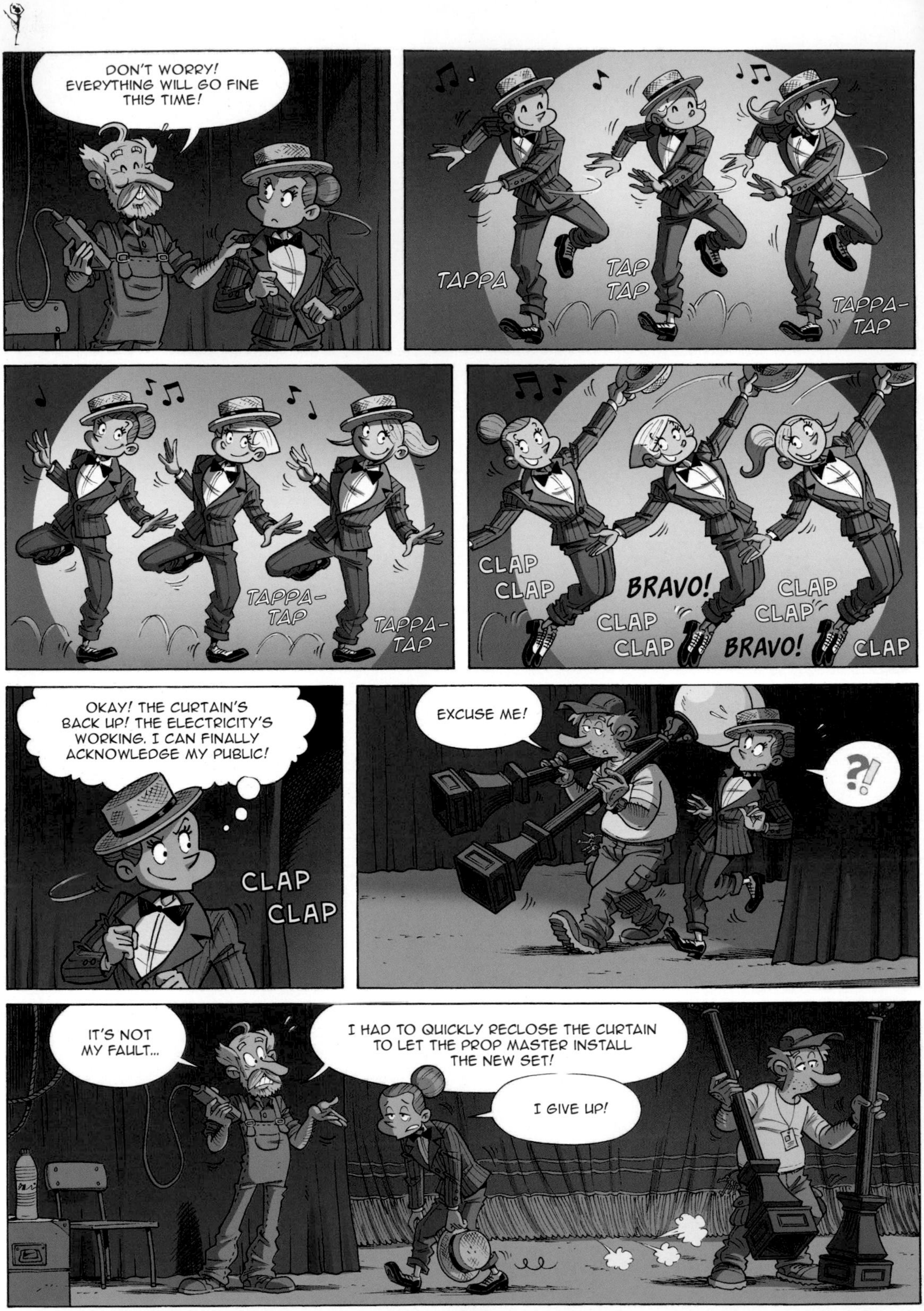
DON'T WORRY! EVERYTHING WILL GO FINE THIS TIME!
TAPPA
TAP TAP
TAPPA-TAP
TAPPA-TAP
TAPPA-TAP
CLAP CLAP
CLAP CLAP
BRAVO!
CLAP CLAP
BRAVO!
CLAP
OKAY! THE CURTAIN'S BACK UP! THE ELECTRICITY'S WORKING. I CAN FINALLY ACKNOWLEDGE MY PUBLIC!
CLAP CLAP
EXCUSE ME!
?!
IT'S NOT MY FAULT...
I HAD TO QUICKLY RECLOSE THE CURTAIN TO LET THE PROP MASTER INSTALL THE NEW SET!
I GIVE UP!

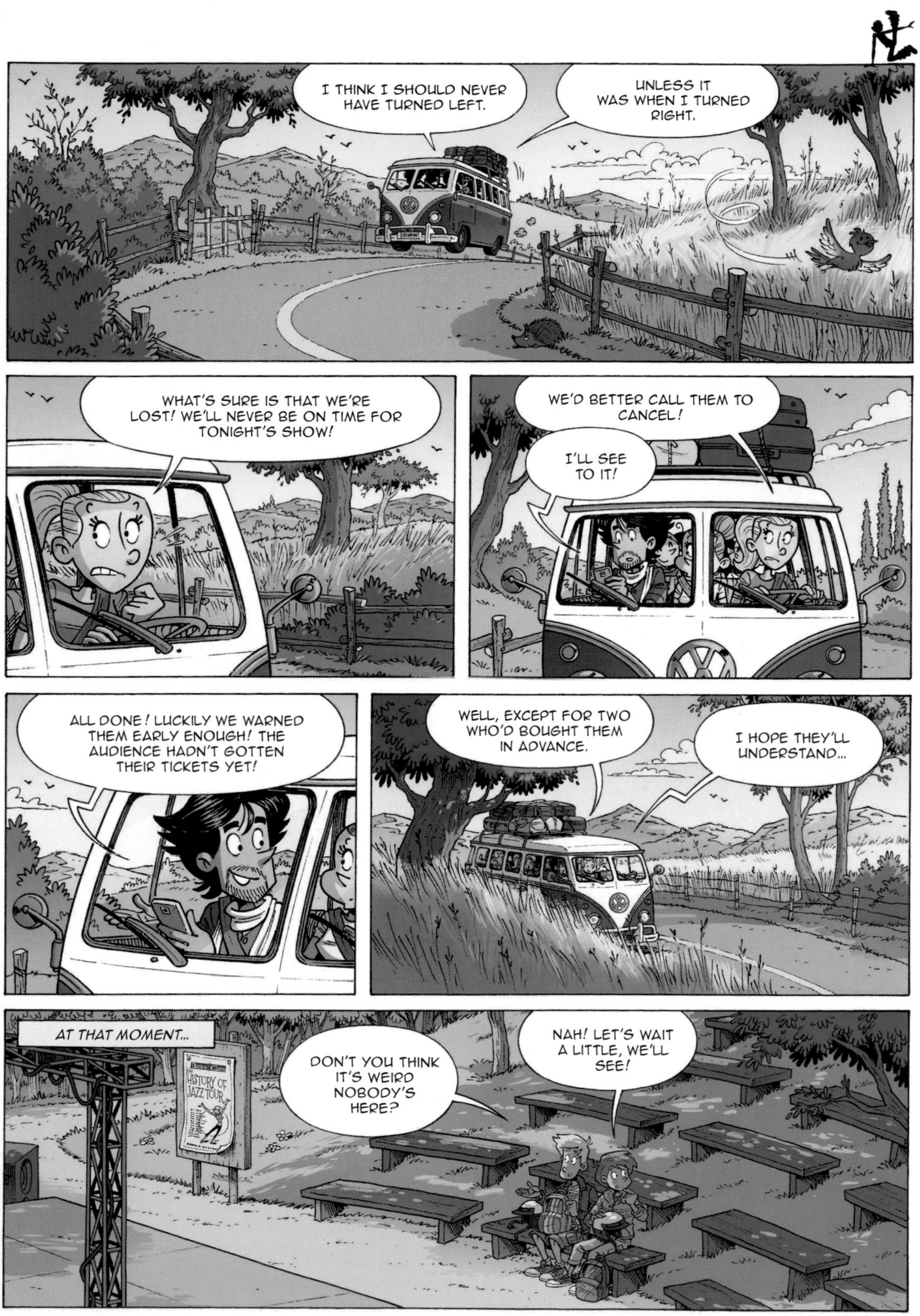
I THINK I SHOULD NEVER HAVE TURNED LEFT.
UNLESS IT WAS WHEN I TURNED RIGHT.
WHAT'S SURE IS THAT WE'RE LOST! WE'LL NEVER BE ON TIME FOR TONIGHT'S SHOW!
WE'D BETTER CALL THEM TO CANCEL!
I'LL SEE TO IT!
ALL DONE! LUCKILY WE WARNED THEM EARLY ENOUGH! THE AUDIENCE HADN'T GOTTEN THEIR TICKETS YET!
WELL, EXCEPT FOR TWO WHO'D BOUGHT THEM IN ADVANCE.
I HOPE THEY'LL UNDERSTAND...
AT THAT MOMENT...
HISTORY OF JAZZ TOUR
DON'T YOU THINK IT'S WEIRD NOBODY'S HERE?
NAH! LET'S WAIT A LITTLE, WE'LL SEE!

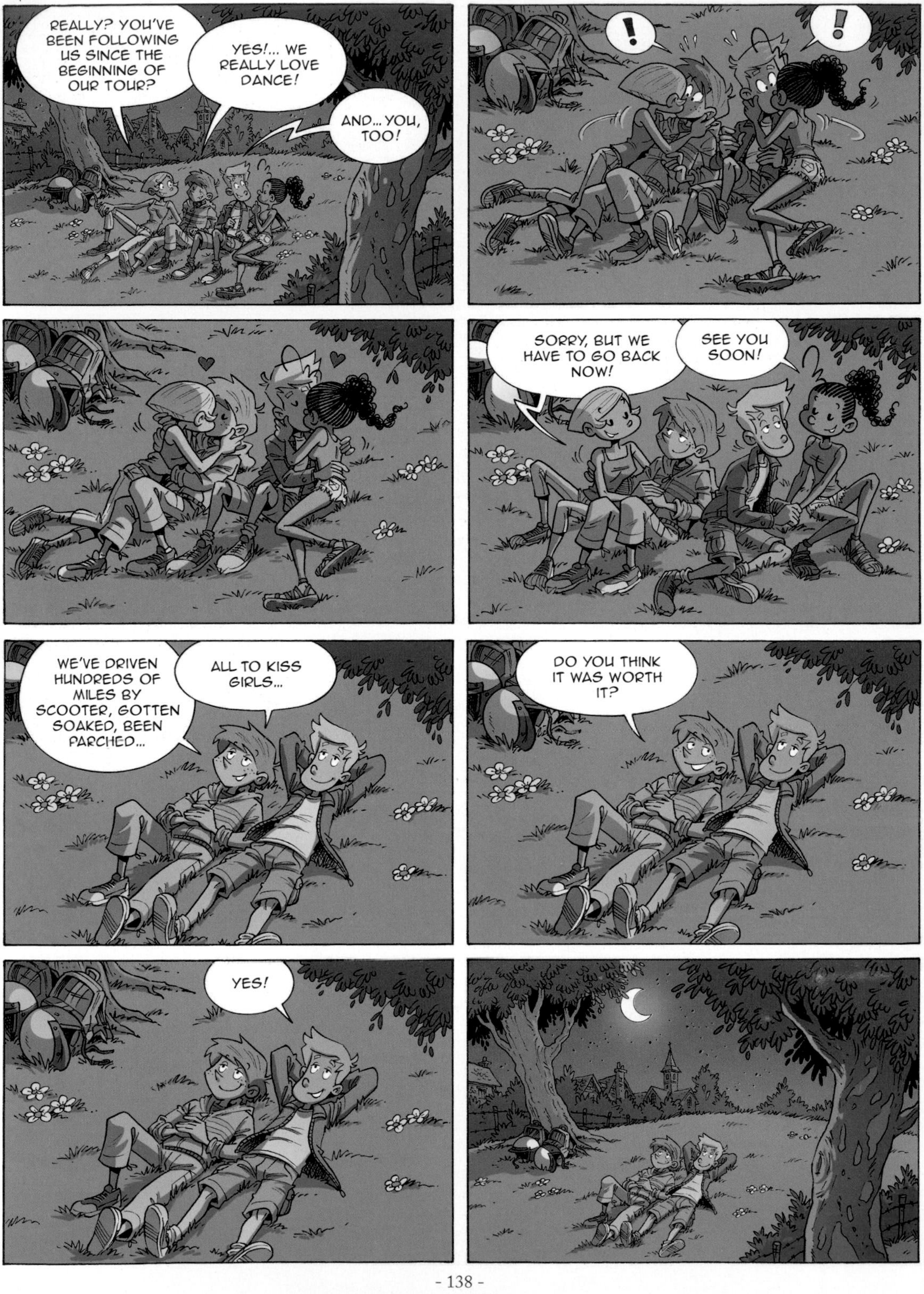
REALLY? YOU'VE BEEN FOLLOWING US SINCE THE BEGINNING OF OUR TOUR?
YES!... WE REALLY LOVE DANCE!
AND... YOU, TOO!
!
!
SORRY, BUT WE HAVE TO GO BACK NOW!
SEE YOU SOON!
WE'VE DRIVEN HUNDREDS OF MILES BY SCOOTER, GOTTEN SOAKED, BEEN PARCHED...
ALL TO KISS GIRLS...
DO YOU THINK IT WAS WORTH IT?
YES!

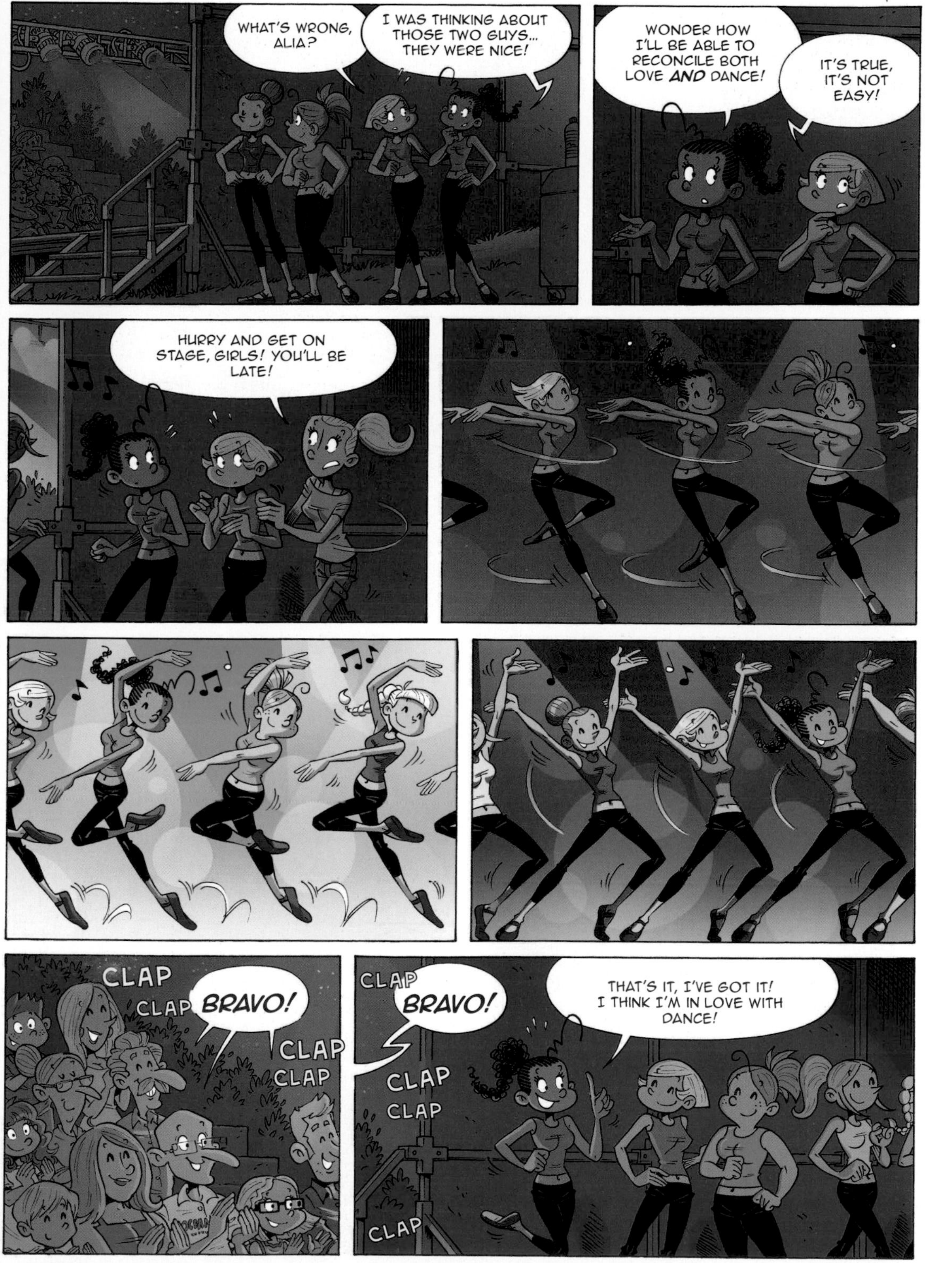
WHAT'S WRONG, ALIA?
I WAS THINKING ABOUT THOSE TWO GUYS... THEY WERE NICE!
WONDER HOW I'LL BE ABLE TO RECONCILE BOTH LOVE AND DANCE!
IT'S TRUE, IT'S NOT EASY!
HURRY AND GET ON STAGE, GIRLS! YOU'LL BE LATE!
CLAP
CLAP
BRAVO!
CLAP
CLAP
CLAP
BRAVO!
CLAP
CLAP
CLAP
THAT'S IT, I'VE GOT IT! I THINK I'M IN LOVE WITH DANCE!

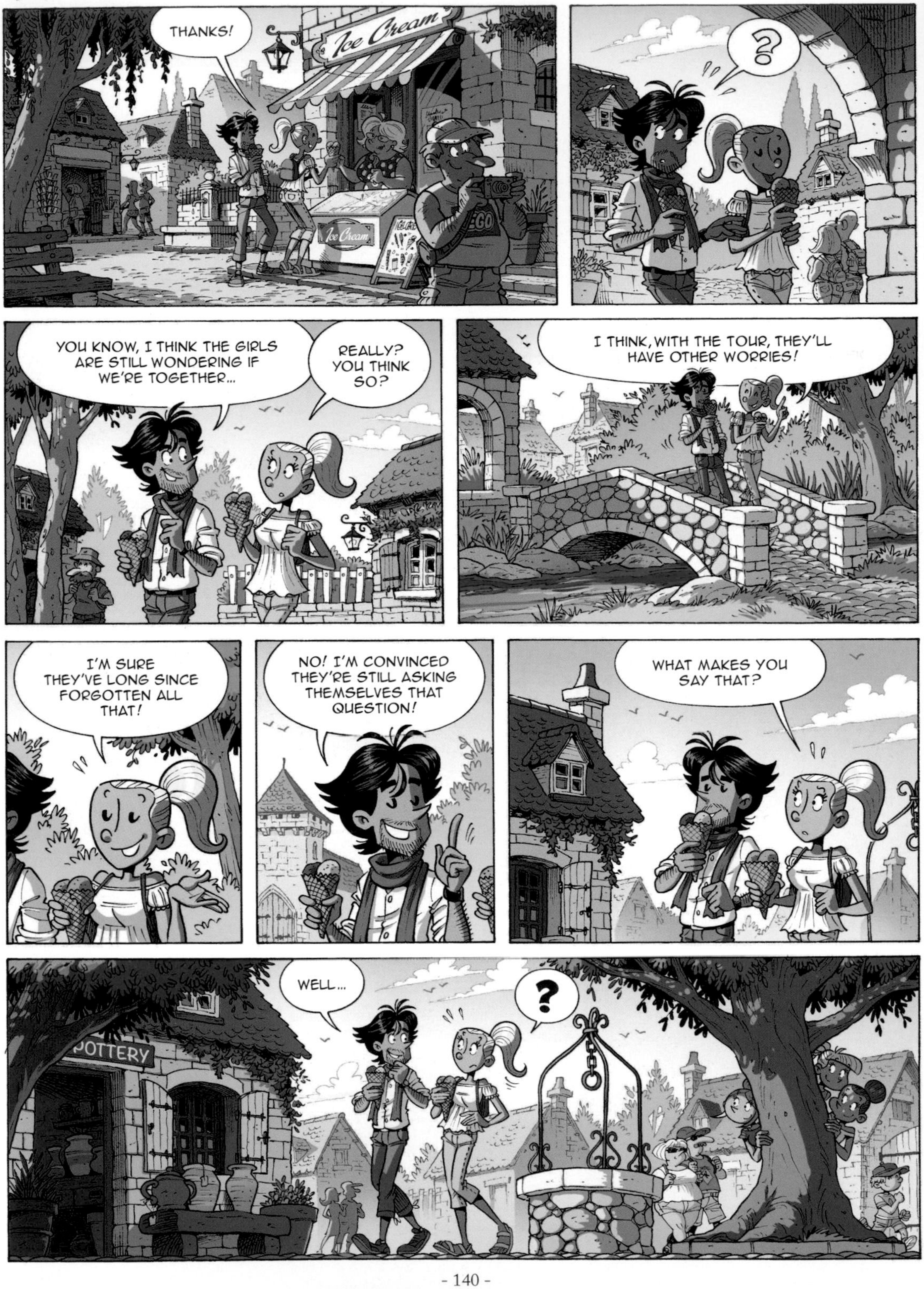
Ice Cream
THANKS!
Ice Cream
?
YOU KNOW, I THINK THE GIRLS ARE STILL WONDERING IF WE'RE TOGETHER...
REALLY? YOU THINK SO?
I THINK, WITH THE TOUR, THEY'LL HAVE OTHER WORRIES!
I'M SURE THEY'VE LONG SINCE FORGOTTEN ALL THAT!
NO! I'M CONVINCED THEY'RE STILL ASKING THEMSELVES THAT QUESTION!
WHAT MAKES YOU SAY THAT?
POTTERY
WELL...
?

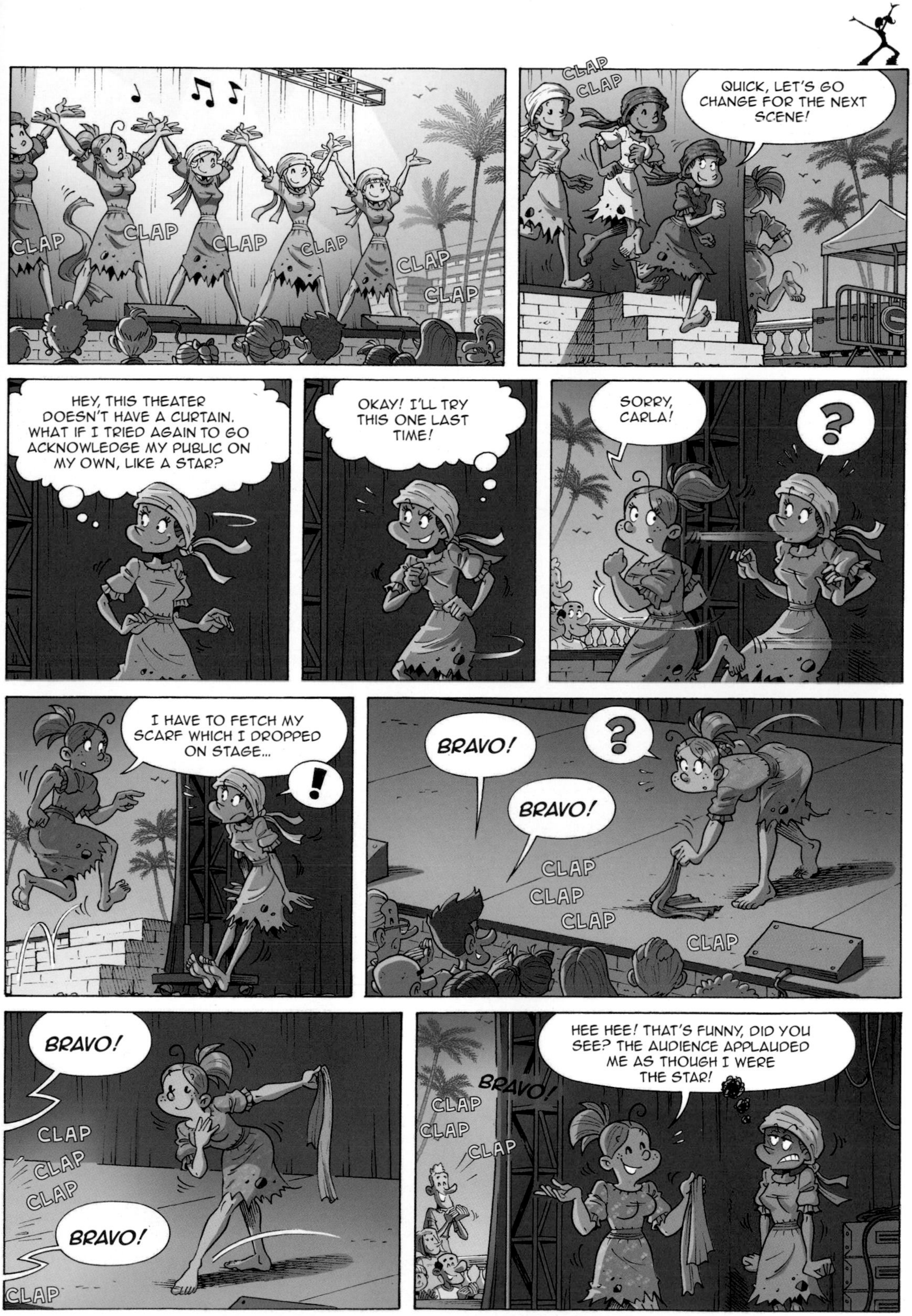
CLAP
CLAP
CLAP
CLAP
CLAP
CLAP
CLAP
CLAP
QUICK, LET'S GO CHANGE FOR THE NEXT SCENE!
HEY, THIS THEATER DOESN'T HAVE A CURTAIN. WHAT IF I TRIED AGAIN TO GO ACKNOWLEDGE MY PUBLIC ON MY OWN, LIKE A STAR?
OKAY! I'LL TRY THIS ONE LAST TIME!
SORRY, CARLA!
?
I HAVE TO FETCH MY SCARF WHICH I DROPPED ON STAGE...
!
BRAVO!
?
BRAVO!
CLAP
CLAP
CLAP
CLAP
BRAVO!
CLAP
CLAP
CLAP
BRAVO!
CLAP
HEE HEE! THAT'S FUNNY, DID YOU SEE? THE AUDIENCE APPLAUDED ME AS THOUGH I WERE THE STAR!
BRAVO!
CLAP
CLAP
CLAP

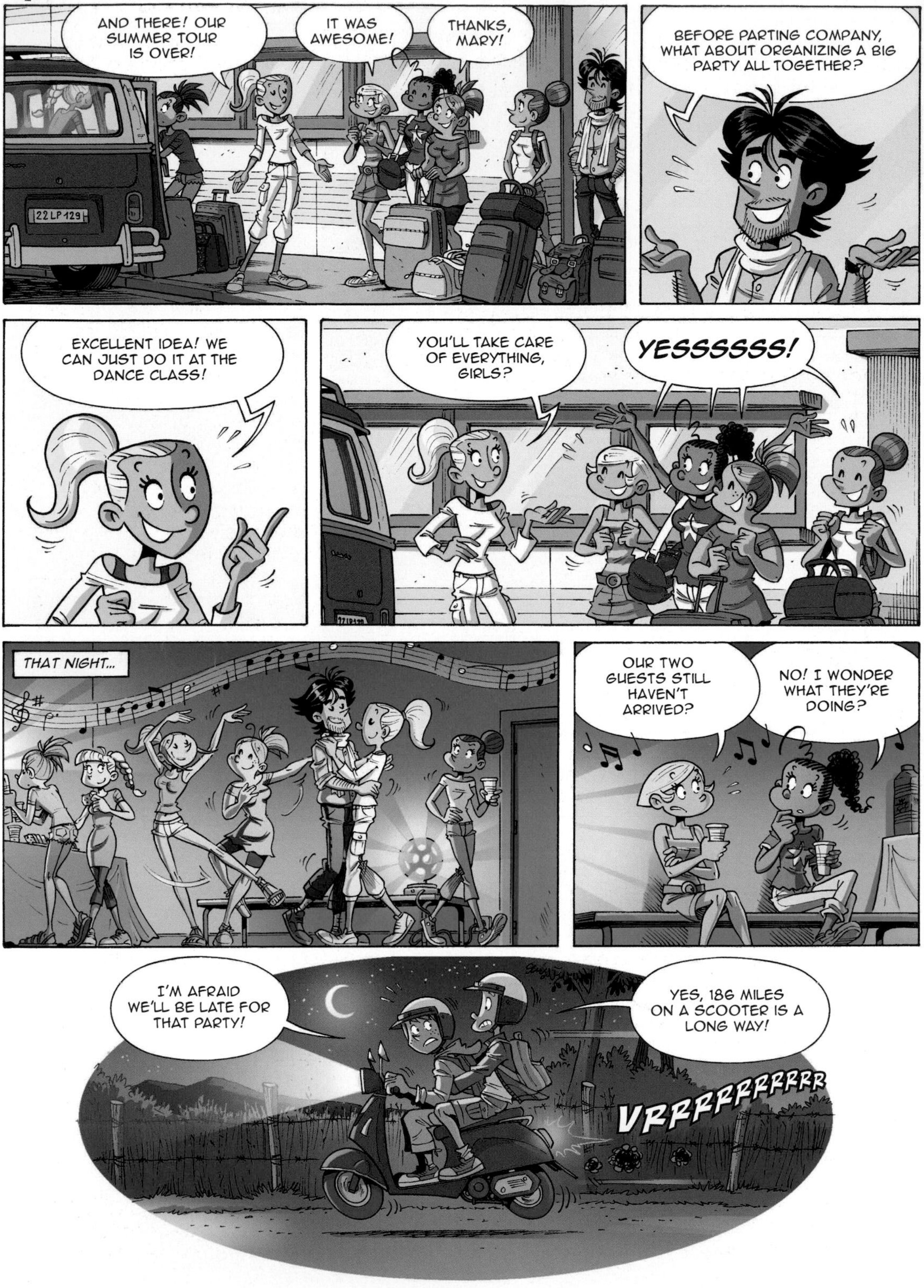
AND THERE! OUR SUMMER TOUR IS OVER!
IT WAS AWESOME!
THANKS, MARY!
22 LP 129
BEFORE PARTING COMPANY, WHAT ABOUT ORGANIZING A BIG PARTY ALL TOGETHER?
EXCELLENT IDEA! WE CAN JUST DO IT AT THE DANCE CLASS!
YOU'LL TAKE CARE OF EVERYTHING, GIRLS?
YESSSSSS!
THAT NIGHT...
OUR TWO GUESTS STILL HAVEN'T ARRIVED?
NO! I WONDER WHAT THEY'RE DOING?
I'M AFRAID WE'LL BE LATE FOR THAT PARTY!
YES, 186 MILES ON A SCOOTER IS A LONG WAY!
VRRRRRRRRRR

WATCH OUT FOR PAPERCUTZ

Welcome to the third toe-tapping edition of DANCE CLASS 3 IN 1, by Béka and Crip. I'm Jim Salicrup, the Editor-in-Chief with two left feet, choreographing the moves of Papercutz, that non-dancing troupe dedicated to publishing great graphic novels for all ages. We hope you enjoyed this collected edition of DANCE CLASS, which featured "School Night Fever," "Snow White and the Seven Dwarves," and "Dancing in the Rain." "School Night Fever" always sounded to me like an illness you might get from "Dancing in the Rain." But seriously, folks, why would anyone ever consider dancing in the rain? Aside from getting sick, they could also slip and fall.

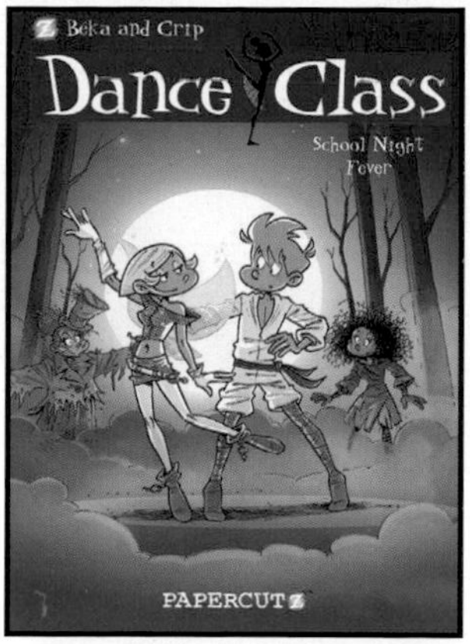

Béka and Crip
Dance Class
School Night Fever
PAPERCUTZ

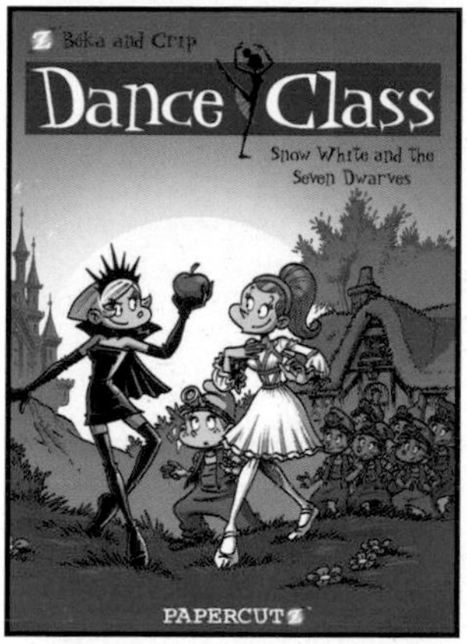

Béka and Crip
Dance Class
Snow White and the Seven Dwarves
PAPERCUTZ

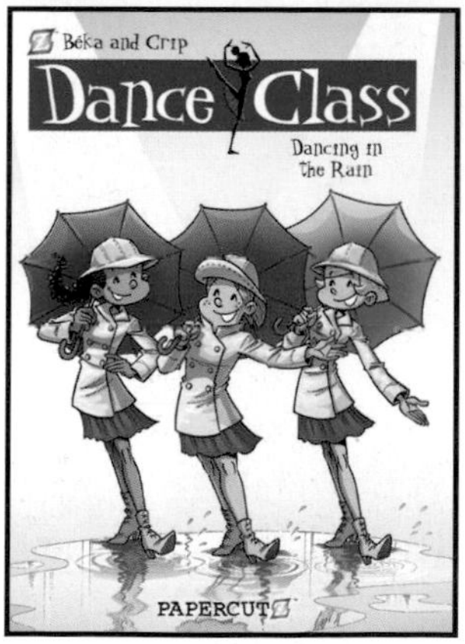

Béka and Crip
Dance Class
Dancing in the Rain
PAPERCUTZ

But who says dance students are logical? Take Julie, Alia, Lucie, and the rest of the DANCE CLASS students. After a rigorous day of dance rehearsals, when the girls are given the night off, what do they decide to do...? That's right... they dance! Why? Because they love it! Dancing is a passion for these girls and there's almost nothing they'd rather be doing.

I can certainly relate. As passionate as Julie, Alia, and Lucie are about dancing, I'm equally crazed about comics and graphic novels! For example, every Wednesday after spending the morning editing Papercutz graphic novels, where do you think I go during my lunch break? If you guessed the comicbook store, you're absolutely right! (I do pick up lunch too. I'm not that crazy!)

I'm sure I've mentioned this before, but I can't help mentioning it again. Over the years I've been lucky enough to take Ballroom dance classes myself, and it wasn't until many years later that I realized why it seemed to provide a wonderful sense of balance to my life. Comics, even DANCE CLASS, is an art form where there's no sound or movement, while dance, is all about moving to sound. By having both in your life, you've got the best of both worlds.

As this collection is being assembled, we're still in the midst of the Covid-19 global pandemic, but folks are starting to see a point in the not-too-distant future where things will be almost back to "normal." We can only imagine how difficult the pandemic must be for dancers. They not only have to deal with what everyone else had to deal with—tragic deaths, lockdowns, quarantines, mask-wearing, curfews, social distancing, countless hand-washings, and so much more—they had to find ways to continue dancing somehow. While I hope they all had spaces at home to continue practicing, I'm sure we're all looking forward to when they can dance in public again. So, until then, let's enjoy the wonderful shows Julie, Alia, Lucie, and all the rest perform on the pages of DANCE CLASS 3 IN 1.

Thanks,

Jim

STAY IN TOUCH!

EMAIL:	salicrup@papercutz.com
WEB:	www.papercutz.com
TWITTER:	@papercutzgn
INSTAGRAM:	@papercutzgn
FACEBOOK:	PAPERCUTZGRAPHICNOVELS
FANMAIL:	Papercutz, 160 Broadway, Suite 700, East Wing, New York, NY 10038

Go to papercutz.com and sign up for the free Papercutz e-newsletter!

MORE GREAT GRAPHIC NOVEL SERIES AVAILABLE FROM

PAPERCUTZ™

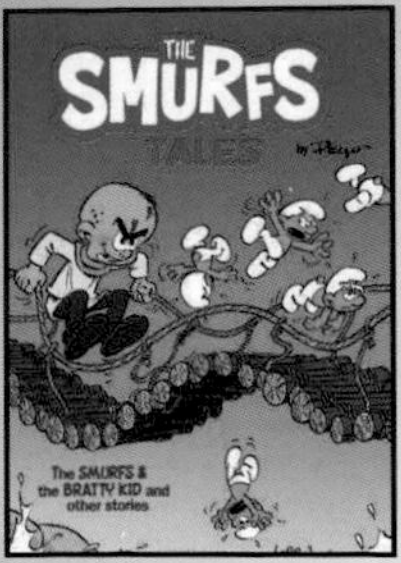
THE SMURFS
TALES
The SMURFS & the BRATTY KID and other stories
THE SMURFS TALES

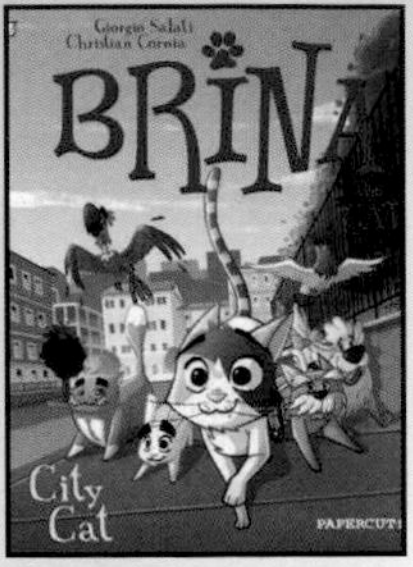
Giorgio Salati
Christian Cornia
BRINA
City Cat
PAPERCUTZ
BRINA THE CAT

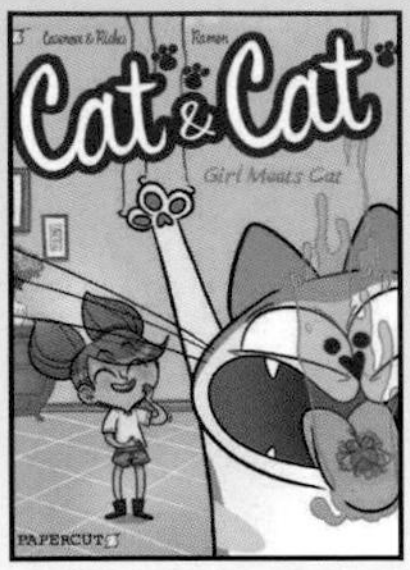
Cat & Cat
Girl Meets Cat
PAPERCUTZ
CAT & CAT

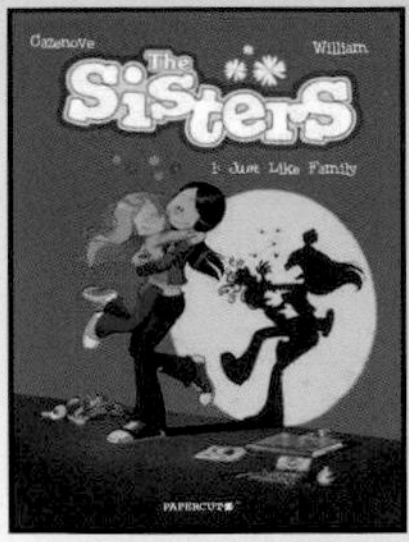
Cazenove
William
The Sisters
1. Just Like Family
PAPERCUTZ
THE SISTERS

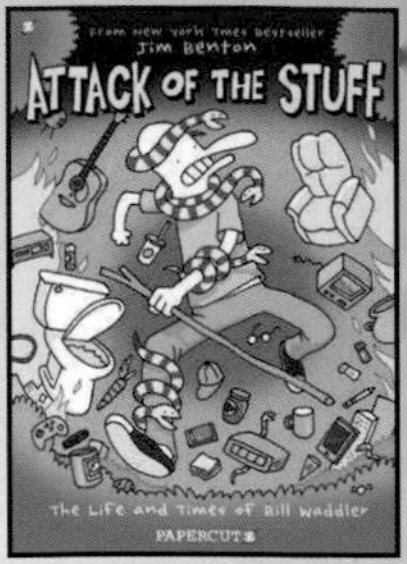
From New York Times bestseller Jim Benton
ATTACK OF THE STUFF
The Life and Times of Bill Waddler
PAPERCUTZ
ATTACK OF THE STUFF

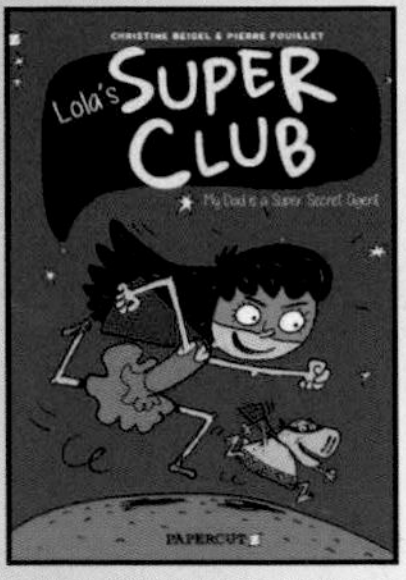
CHRISTINE BEIGEL & PIERRE FOUILLET
Lola's SUPER CLUB
My Dad is a Super Secret Agent
PAPERCUTZ
LOLA'S SUPER CLUB

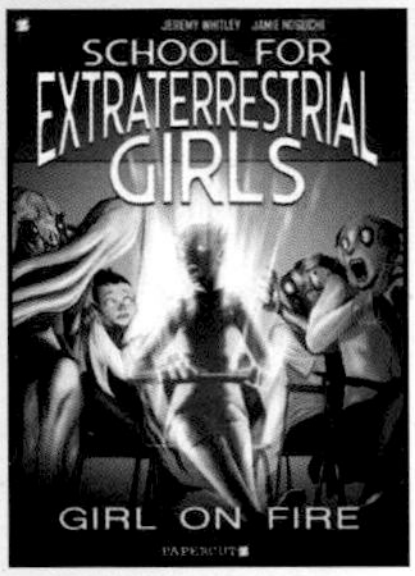
JEREMY WHITLEY JAMIE NOGUCHI
SCHOOL FOR EXTRATERRESTRIAL GIRLS
GIRL ON FIRE
PAPERCUTZ
SCHOOL FOR EXTRATERRESTRIAL GIRLS

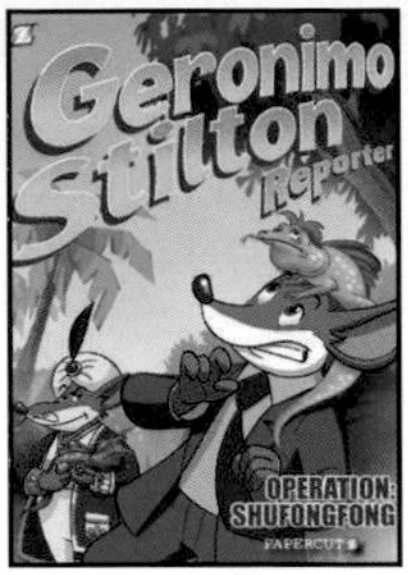
Geronimo Stilton
Reporter
OPERATION: SHUFONGFONG
PAPERCUTZ
GERONIMO STILTON REPORTER

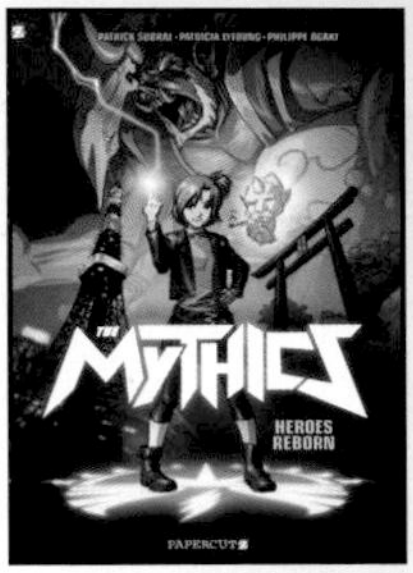
THE MYTHICS
HEROES REBORN
PAPERCUTZ
THE MYTHICS

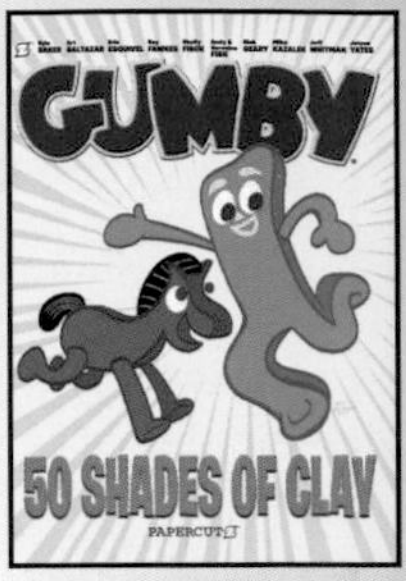
GUMBY
50 SHADES OF CLAY
PAPERCUTZ
GUMBY

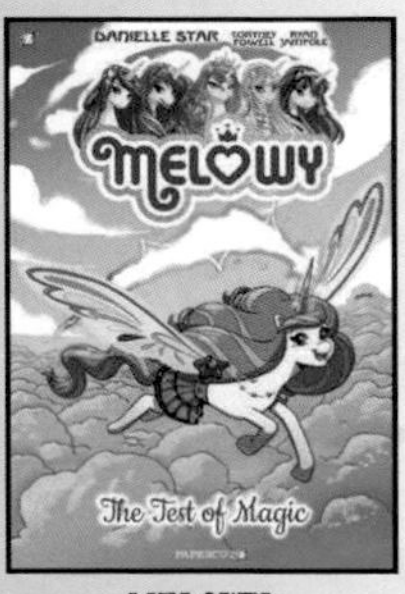
DANIELLE STAR
melowy
The Test of Magic
MELOWY

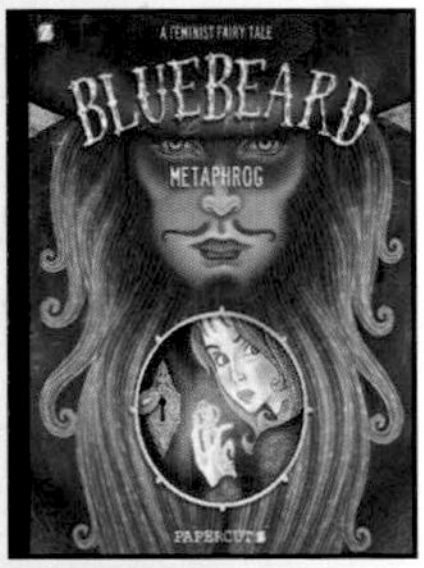
A FEMINIST FAIRY TALE
BLUEBEARD
METAPHROG
PAPERCUTZ
BLUEBEARD

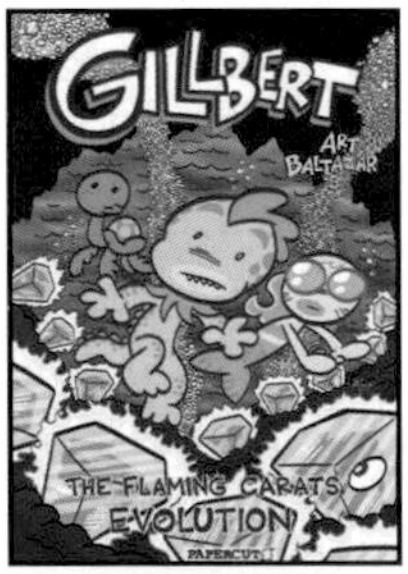
GILLBERT
ART BALTAZAR
THE FLAMING CARATS
EVOLUTION
PAPERCUTZ
GILLBERT

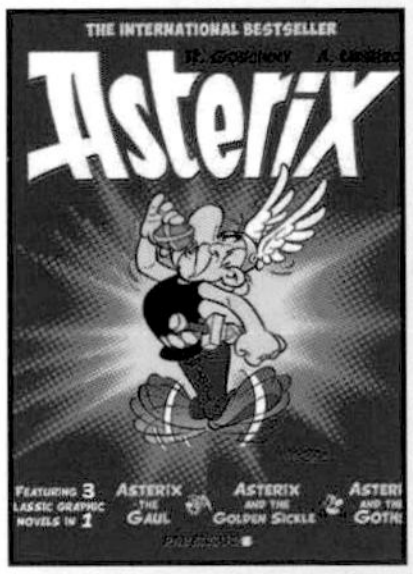
THE INTERNATIONAL BESTSELLER
Asterix
FEATURING 3 CLASSIC GRAPHIC NOVELS IN 1
ASTERIX THE GAUL
ASTERIX AND THE GOLDEN SICKLE
PAPERCUTZ
ASTERIX

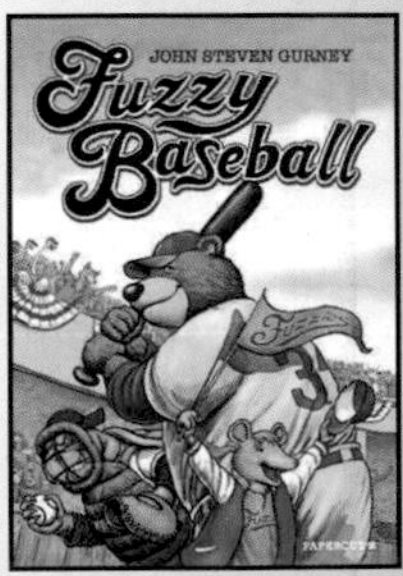
JOHN STEVEN GURNEY
Fuzzy Baseball
FUZZY BASEBALL

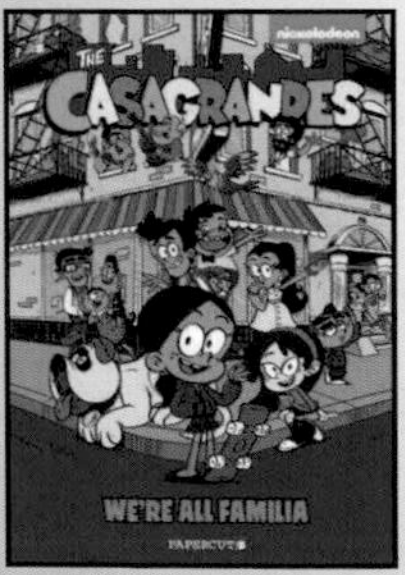
nickelodeon
THE CASAGRANDES
WE'RE ALL FAMILIA
PAPERCUTZ
THE CASAGRANDES

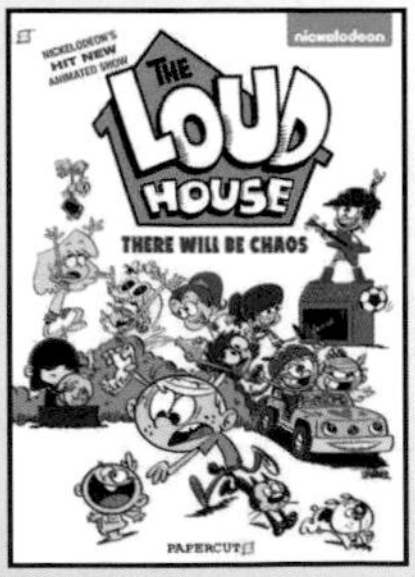
NICKELODEON'S HIT NEW ANIMATED SHOW
nickelodeon
THE LOUD HOUSE
THERE WILL BE CHAOS
THE LOUD HOUSE

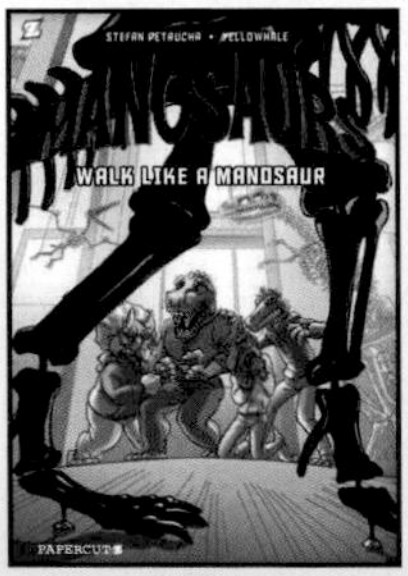
STEFAN PETRUCHA • MELLOWHALE
MANOSAURS
WALK LIKE A MANOSAUR
PAPERCUTZ
MANOSAURS

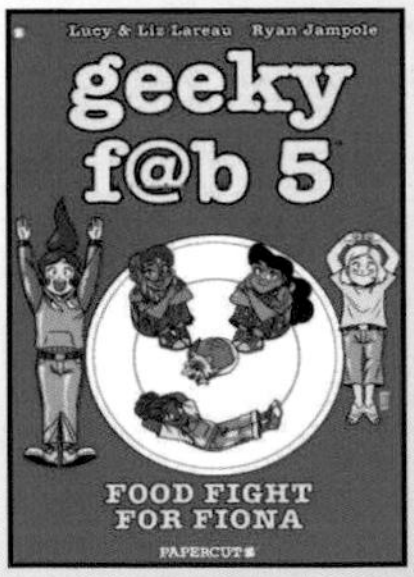
Lucy & Liz Lareau Ryan Jampole
geeky f@b 5
FOOD FIGHT FOR FIONA
PAPERCUTZ
GEEKY F@B 5

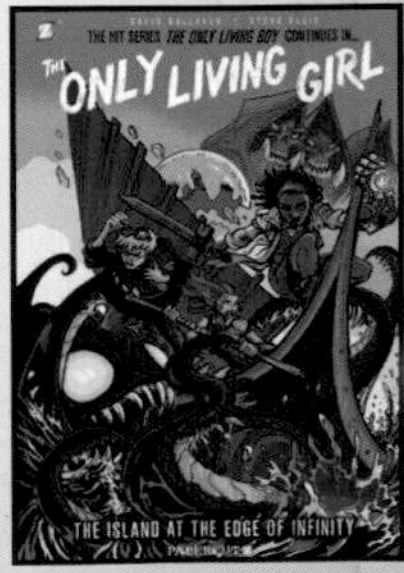
THE ONLY LIVING GIRL
THE ISLAND AT THE EDGE OF INFINITY
THE ONLY LIVING GIRL

papercutz.com

Also available where ebooks are sold.